Fated Souls
(The Fated Sa
by Sariah Sky

© 2016 Sariah Skye
Cover by Deranged Doctor Design
(www.derangeddoctordesign.com)

For Gramma Joan and Lizzie, and those who have left us way too soon.
You're loved, and missed daily.
You'll never be forgotten. Ever.

Chapter 1

I grumbled audibly, slamming my fist into the side panel of the espresso maker I was currently trying to "repair". I let loose a tirade of curse words under my breath as I fumbled with the nozzle and some random tool that I was trying to use to unclog the spout.

I heard laughter besides me and I jumped, startled to see my boss and friend Katrina Ryland—otherwise known as "Kit"—standing before me, covering her giggle with her palm. "What was that? German?"

"What was—oh." I grinned sheepishly; I hadn't realized I'd been swearing in my native tongue. It wasn't really German, but she didn't know that. "Sorry."

Kit shrugged. "No big deal, there's no one here besides—" she nodded off to her right to the two high school aged girls she had employed to work afternoons. We all work at Kit's small coffee house, Morningstar Coffee. I am a supervisor, and the two girls are baristas.

Currently, the two girls are oblivious to us as they pretend to clean the lobby. In actuality, they were gossiping.

Kit turned back towards the espresso machine I was trying to unsuccessfully fix. "Damn thing. I hoped by getting a brand new one it would eliminate the need for complicated repairs. Guess not, huh?" Kit was a quirky woman in her early to mid-thirties, with long wavy blonde hair that was streaked with whatever color she fancied today, piercing blue eyes, colorful makeup and a statuesque, tall body. She reminded me a bit of the hippie women I'd see pictured in the *Life* magazines I would borrow from my grandfather over the years. She was bright and breezy and always carried an air of peace about her; I admired her unconventional style and easy-going beauty.

Kit smoothed the apron that hung over her gauzy blue blouse and wide-legged, gaucho navy pants and sighed at me, defeated. She tugged a stray bright colored lock of her hair off her forehead and tucked it behind her ear; this week's fantasy color choice was a striking teal. "I should have known that thing would give us nothing but grief when it required *two* men to install it," she grumbled in dismay, eyeing it briefly. It was a monster; twice the size of its predecessor and three times as complicated. I missed the old one.

I snorted. "Well, it wouldn't be such a big deal but I couldn't fix a tire and make it round to save my life. I am no Tim Taylor."

Kit shook her head, with an amused chuckle. "Actually, you sort of are. He wasn't very handy, you know."

I scoffed. "Okay, yeah I guess so."

She paused to give me a strange look. "Isn't *Home Improvement* too old for you? You would have been like, what...two when it came out?"

"Nick at Nite," I said quickly, with an innocent smile.

"Ah, yes. *Right*. Well, it does help to read the manual." She reached underneath a counter nearby and pulled out a large paper book and handed it to me. "Try this. I'll go in back and fish the old one out of storage. Glad I didn't let the installers talk me out of keeping it, huh?"

I grunted a yes of approval and turned to look at the first page. It was a jumble of diagrams and words, written in five different languages; one of them with special characters that were totally unrecognizable to me. I groaned and dropped it on the counter with a loud *plop* and tried to make sense of the mumbo-jumbo before me. I didn't have any choice; if the old espresso machine wasn't working right, then we'd be in trouble. I mean...what's a coffee house without espresso? We wouldn't be able to serve anything but the pastries and regular, boring old coffee; which don't get me wrong—I loved and drank by the tankful but most customers came in for their snobby, complicated espresso mixed drinks that required more instruction to make then this damn manual before me. I wouldn't mind just serving plain old coffee but I don't think the customers would approve and thus, Kit wouldn't approve. And I probably wouldn't get paid and that was *no* damn good. No damn good at all.

I leaned over the counter, scanning the manual and flipping the pages in concentration, trying to find anything that would help me when I nearly jumped out of my black safety-soled clog shoes at a shriek from nearby.

It was my co-worker, Emily. "So did you get your dress?"

My other co-worker, Madison squealed. "I did! It's *so* awesome!"

Madison and Emily both squealed in unison. I tried *very* hard not to cringe. So much for quiet gossip. Their girly squealing was very hard on my sensitive hearing.

Thankfully I wasn't facing the two seventeen-year-old high school students, who were clearly excited for something called *Homecoming*. I didn't want to hurt their feelings or, even worse, be asked any opinions about it myself because of course I'd never been to one.

I tried to ignore their screams of delight as Madison described the dress in detail to her friend: pink sequined, spaghetti straps with cutouts on the bodice, and a long chiffon skirt. Whatever *that* meant.

"So did Landon do it? Did he rent the limo?" Emily asked.

This was met by a slight pause. "Yeah I guess. I was really hoping for the horse and carriage."

Horse and carriage? What is this, *Cinderella*? Who does that sort of thing? And where in the hell did someone even *find* that? Was this a normal occurrence; did people really rent out their horses and antique carriages for things like this?

I had to turn around and face them then. Madison was visibly miffed, her petite features downturned in a disappointed frown. "What's so bad about a limo?" I asked, looking expectantly at the two girls, both of them avoiding my eye sheepishly. I smirked to myself, as the realization dawned on them that I had overheard their banter. They both pretended to be really into dusting the same table they'd been pretending to clean for several minutes already. Not that I cared, considering how quiet things were.

When the two girls didn't answer about the limo, I continued, helping to ensure them I was mostly just interested and I wasn't mad or going to tattle on them to our *boss*. "I've seen them on TV; they look pretty cool. So what's so bad about it?"

"Well, nothing." Madison finally answered, then paused. "I was just really hoping for a fairy tale kinda day." Her lower lip puffed out.

"Aw," I tried to keep the sarcasm out of my tone, "I'm sure it will still be wonderful." I had to really fight the urge to roll my eyes into the back of my head. If I did, I'd surely give away that I thought they were absurd. My eyes would roll all the way back in their sockets and snap straight off my head and go rolling into the lobby. I didn't think that was a good idea. If they screamed like that over a dress—imagine how they'd scream to a pair of stray eyeballs rolling around the floor. I couldn't take that.

Madison grinned. "You bet it will!" I knew she was dying to say more and looked at me expectantly.

Clearly, I was supposed to go away and stop listening. I wasn't "cool" enough to be a part of their conversation. Fine with me. "I'll just be...over here. Not paying attention. Talk amongst yourselves. As long as you *actually* clean this time."

"Sorry," Emily replied with a chuckle. And she genuinely did start rubbing down the table tops with the rag she was carrying, after dunking it into the bucket of hot, soapy water that was on the chair in between them.

I smiled at them, shaking my head. I tried to imagine what it would have been like to dream only of fairy tale things back then when I was their age. Instead, I had fantasized about living in a place where no one knew who I was just so that I could escape the agony of constant ridicule from my family and their friends and—well, everyone really—about who I was, what I was, what I couldn't do compared to everyone else. Living under constant scrutiny was hard. I could do no right. I was an embarrassment. I was a freak. Here in Pineville, Minnesota I was still technically a freak too but, what people didn't know about me didn't hurt them. I appeared human. Although, I am not. At any moment if I truly desired, though, I could turn into my *real* self. My real *dragon* self.

Yes, that's right. Dragon. I am a dragon. We live in another realm, not unlike your own. Except the primary species in our realm are dragon-shifters.

Everything you've heard about dragons is probably true. We fly, breathe fire, are loud and a bit scaly. What you *don't* know is that we have magic both in our human and dragon forms. All dragons are capable of different kinds of magic; the type of magic you wield relates to the color of your dragon skin, and we exist in every color of the rainbow right down to silver and gold. My grandfather, an Elder in our home kingdom of Anarach because of his age, is silver. In his dragon form, his skin gleams like a pocketful of coins in a fountain, and he can use light magic which is beneficial in healing. Golden dragons also heal, but can harness the wind as well. My brother is a red dragon, and he is a fire user; my parents are black and yellow and wield powerful arcane magic and air magic respectively. A dragon for every color and a place for their magic in our society. Well, everyone except me.

All because I share my color with Cyril the Mad, a powerful dragon who was greatly respected until he lost his mind and was exiled by the King and Queen of the Court in that time. No one knows what drove him to madness, but he committed grievous crimes with his power against dragons in a nearby village. Deeds rumored to be so terrible that law forbade talk of Cyril and his kind. Over the centuries, stories of Cyril and his powers faded into myth and legend. Until another of his kind was born. Another pink dragon. Me.

Pink dragons? I know. I mean…really, it's ridiculous sounding. It's a color mutation, apparently. It doesn't exactly sound scary or intimidating as one expects a dragon should be. But Cyril was a pink dragon and the commonly held opinion is that something about the gene gifted him with immense power while cursing him with insanity. So it is assumed that any others of his kind will be the same: batshit crazy. And that's what they expect of me- the last remaining pink dragon, the only one of my kind. Rare, ridiculed and despised. But unlike Cyril, I have no magic, I cannot fly, and I don't even breathe fire. So how can I be a threat to anyone? Nobody seemed to care about that, though. There wasn't a day back home that I didn't face disdain and torment. Other drakes—our term for adolescent dragons—wanted nothing to do with me. My *parents* wanted nothing to do with me; I was a hindrance to their reputations. They were utterly convinced they'd be ruling Anarach and be King and Queen by now had it not been for the taint of shame my birth had left on their standing.

The only two souls that had shown me love and kindness were my brother, Braeden, and my grandfather. A few years ago, on my legal adult birthday back home in Anarach, I took the nearest portal I could find on the outskirts of our village, Green Knoll, and it took me here, to Pineville, Minnesota. With the help of a rogue orange dragon I obtained a last name, documentation and everything else that would be essential for me to live as a typical human in the United States. Coming to the realm of humans, I found it ironic that pink was stereotypically a color signifying weakness and girlish fantasy. You know, princesses, frilly dresses, that sort of thing. Perhaps it was a twist on the stigma that had carried over somehow from the dragon world. Of course, humans like Kit, and heroines in movies, proved to me time and time again that femininity wasn't weak and pink could equal strength. Pity the same didn't ring true for this pink dragon.

Back in my birth realm, I am known as *Leorah e'na Miradoste.* Loosely translated it means *"Leorah, daughter of Miradoste,"* although it would sound very different in the dragon tongue; rough and guttural to human ears. Amongst humans, I'm Leorah James. It's the name I prefer. Leorah James; an ordinary *human* girl with long, strawberry blonde hair, and green eyes. I am small as a dragon and whereas most dragons are tall and lithe in their human form; I am short and curvy with a larger than average chest, wide hips and a slightly soft stomach. No washboard abs for me—but I didn't desire them. I can shift at a moment's notice into my dragon form, but I can also live comfortably as a human. On the surface, I smelled, sounded and functioned the same as the people around me, set apart only by my mark.

Every dragon has a mark, resembling a tattoo, somewhere on their body. That mark is individual to them. Dragons in Anarach typically had Celtic symbols, dragon outlines with knotwork on them, in the color of their dragons. Mine was a round dragon, outlined in Celtic weaving with more intricate work in the middle and it was of course, pink. I knew the likelihood of anyone recognizing it as anything other than a tattoo or a birthmark even, was slim but just in case I wore my long hair down in a thick braid down my back. Paranoia wasn't a typical dragon trait but given my upbringing I had acquired it as a necessary skill along with sarcasm, bitterness and a penchant for all things geeky.

"Excuse me?"

I jumped again, shaking my head out of its haze. Crap, for a dragon with sensitive hearing everyone was sure having an easy time sneaking up on me today.

I had been ignoring the register for probably about ten minutes now, my back to the entrance pretending to look through some manual when someone stepped up to the line.

"I'm so sorry; I was spacing out and—" I set the unread manual under the counter and looked up to see a customer who'd visited us several times this week and a handful of times a couple of weeks before. He appeared to be in his mid-twenties. Average height, with broad shoulders underneath an array of hooded sweatshirts. Today, it was navy blue. So far since he had started coming to get coffee from us, this man had seen me space out, spill and swear several times already and never even flinched. I wasn't sure whether he had noticed my regularly embarrassing behavior but he made a good show of politely ignoring it if he did.

"Oh, hello again," I greeted pleasantly, trying to hide my surprise.

The man grinned, his smile bright and friendly was made more striking by the contrast from his dark stubble that lined his jaw and chin. He adjusted the black rimmed glasses on his face; a nervous habit perhaps. I'd seen him do this no less than a dozen times since he'd started frequenting Morningstar. Not sure why I noticed it, but I did. "Oh, a decaf mocha latte today, please."

I looked back at the defunct espresso machine behind me and gave him a half smile. "I'm afraid our machine is on the fritz. We're working on it but it might be a while before we get it working. I'm afraid I'm not very good at fixing things," I chuckled awkwardly.

"Really? Did you try smacking it around a bit?" He appeared serious except for an impish glint in his brown eyes.

I chuckled. "Yes and I believe it's planning to file a restraining order against me now; we'll see."

He threw his head back and let out a loud laugh. "I hate when that happens!"

I chuckled again. "I know, right? So can I get you a—" I raised a brow slightly, noticing he was intently staring at the machine. "You familiar with these?"

Appearing startled, he quickly looked away and grinned sheepishly. "Oh, a little. I was a barista for a short time at Starbucks a few years ago. I was just trying to see if it was a model I worked with at all."

I scowled back at it. "Doubt it. It's brand new and has given us—" I was interrupted by the unmistakable hissing of the machine as it began sputtering and out dripped a steady stream of espresso. "What the—" I began, dashing quickly to the machine. I grabbed for the nearest container I could find. Puzzled I spotted a single clean white coffee mug sitting conveniently on the counter that I was sure I had already cleared of all dishes. I shoved it under the nozzle to catch the black liquid. "Well then, what a moody piece of crap!" It hissed a bit more and sputtered violently, splashing my face and upper body with hot liquid. I let out a little yelp and stepped back, wiping the coffee off my cheek with the back of my hand. "Sorry!" the customer called out, and I swiveled around to shrug at him.

"Sorry? Not your fault this machine is cranky," I said.

"Oh I mean—" he stopped mid-sentence and just smiled. He reached for a stack of napkins that was on the counter and handed me a couple. "You got a little...um..."

I took them from him and used the napkins to wipe off the rest of my face and dab at my green t-shirt which was now stained. Thankfully, the black apron I was wearing caught most of it; I could just change that out. "Well, I guess it's working now. You still want that drink?"

He nodded with a cheerful smile. "Yes, please."

I gave him a nod and turned back to the machine, gathering cups and things nearby to help concoct his drink. I always felt like some sort of wizard concocting potions whenever I made these drinks. "Foam?" I asked and I heard him open his mouth and I finished for him, suddenly remembering his last two late night orders, "Extra."

He chuckled. "Yeah. I guess I've been coming here too much, huh?"

"Not at all, we like regulars here," I said. I pulled the lever on the machine, slowly as it let out a loud hissing sound again; this time on purpose. "Hot damn, it *does* work!" I said to myself under my breath. I poured the liquid into a metal cup for mixing and set it under the spout, and ducked down below to the small refrigerators near the ground that held the milk and creams we used to make the drinks.

"So ah...." he started to say but trailed off.

I pulled my head from the refrigerator to look at him expectantly. "Yeah?"

He laughed nervously, running his hand through his dark, nearly black hair that often seemed to hang in his eyes. At least, you know, that I've noticed from the handful of times I've seen him; not that I'd been paying attention or anything. "Do you know how to get from the highway from here?" he finally said.

I heard a snicker from the seating area. Madison and Emily huddled together yet again but apparently had paused in gossiping about their "Homecoming" plans to gawk at us. I turned to raise an eyebrow at them and they quickly looked away, giggling and talking in hushed tones. Next I turned to—him, the Extra Foam Guy—and gave him a bit of an odd look. Morningstar Coffee is located a grand total of two blocks from the highway. You could hear the hum of traffic from the front door.

"Yeah, it's two blocks down past Oak Street," I pointed in the direction Oak Street was, to the east. "Can't miss it." Perhaps he needed new glasses, and that's why he kept fiddling with them...

He smiled sheepishly. "Yeah? I should get a new GPS app...I'm pretty bad with directions."

"Yeah...from what I gather most guys are." I didn't know that firsthand, but I remembered seeing many sitcoms where the joke was the husband driving would be lost and refused to pull over for directions no matter how his wife nagged. Figured I'd be pretty safe with that response. I turned and added a quick wink at him to let him know I was joking.

He gave a slight smile, reaching back to rub his neck awkwardly. "Yeah..." he fidgeted with his glasses again and looked away, pretending to be very interested in a pamphlet on the counter asking for donations for the local high school choir.

I shrugged my shoulders and went back to concocting his drink. He was relatively silent as I worked. Being the supervisor, I decided I should make small talk and make him feel comfortable. Regular customers meant more money, which meant I might get more pay which means I could get a better car than the crappy Dodge I was currently driving. I wanted something loud, and fast so I could feel like I'm flying like *most* dragons get to do...

"So, you must not be from around here, huh?" I asked, pouring his drink ingredients into a to-go cup.

"No, I'm not," he spoke over the loud noise. "I'm just here...investigating."

Now my interest was piqued. "Investigating? Like what, *CSI*?" I really, really needed to get out more.

"Haha, no...just checking out the area and stuff."

"Oh, I see. Where are you from?"

"Up north." I paused to wait to hear if he was going to elaborate but as Minnesotans frequently assumed, "up north" was usually a good enough explanation to them. Seemingly anything outside the Twin Cities area of Minneapolis/St.Paul was "up north".

"Ah. Well there's not really much around Pineville except trees, some fields, some more trees and maybe a bed and breakfast. And here. Oh, and some trees," I spoke sarcastically as I fiddled around with a few more machines until I came up with the perfect drink concoction. Satisfied there was enough foam, I reached for a disposable lid on the countertop by the espresso maker and plopped it on top. "How's that?"

He took it from me, raised it in a sort of *cheers* gesture and took a sip. He smiled. "Perfect, as always. Thank you, Leorah."

I shot him a look. "How did you..." I snorted, looking down at my apron that covered my shirt. On it I had my name handwritten in silver Sharpie in an elaborate script like we were asked to do. Usually no one could read it; apparently dragons had funky handwriting. I was surprised he could. I laughed. "Right. The name tag thing."

He grinned. "It's hard to forget. It's pretty unusual."

I chortled. "Well I am pretty damn unusual."

"Oh, I highly doubt that." Oh if he had *any* idea. "Unique, I would say."

I started to raise my brow at him, when he spoke quickly. "So, you live around here, Leorah?"

"Why do you ask?"

"Huh? Oh well, I was just wondering if the football team was any good around here. I hear Homecoming is coming up."

I heard another squeal from the dining area. I turned to look at Emily severely. Sheepishly she had her mouth covered and quickly she dunked her mop in the bucket of water and started haphazardly dripping water everywhere.

"Careful there, Em!" She wasn't paying attention and was dripping dirty mop water all over the suede easy chair. She gasped and turned back to what she was doing and attempted to sop up the water with her apron.

I just shrugged at the customer. "I think they're a little excited for Homecoming as well."

"Yeah, I see." He laughed briefly and we exchanged a friendly look for a moment that felt almost.... awkward but I really didn't know why.

"So the team, is it any good?" he asked after an uncomfortable silence.

"Oh! Sorry!" Nervously, I started twirling the hair at the back of my neck. Oddly I had recently discovered myself doing this when this particular person came in. So strange. "Well I honestly wouldn't know. I'm not really from here myself."

"Oh really? Where are you from?"

"Uh, Norway," I answered, which was my general answer whenever someone asked me. I'd been to Norway once, for about five minutes when I discovered I went into the wrong portal the first time I ever tried to come over to the human side. Oops.

"Really? With that red hair? I would have guessed Ireland or Scotland."

I grabbed at it nervously and pulled the length of it forward, feeling defensive and nervous at once. Perhaps I was starting to look suspicious. Maybe Norway people never had red hair and I wouldn't fit in there. Maybe he was starting to see through my cover story and if *he* could it would only be a matter of time before—

"It's dyed," I said quickly. *Note to self: tell people from now on you're from Ireland, not Norway.* D'oh.

"Oh, I figured as much." He chuckled. I laughed nervously in response. "No biggie; I was just wondering. I used to play ball in high school and I kinda like to watch it, brings me back a little."

I smiled. Aw, he was a ball player...I guessed he meant football. I'd tried to watch a few minutes of that *football* thing...I didn't understand it. I think I fell asleep. But the players were pretty nice to look at—at least their backsides—even in their silly purple jerseys.

"Ah, well...you should. Ask those girls," I nodded towards my co-workers, "on your way out about it. They can tell you about it; they go to that school."

"Oh, okay," His smile was a ghost of his earlier grin. Another customer entered then; someone Emily knew and I was inexplicably grateful for the distraction.

"Well, hope you enjoy your coffee." I said, as Emily's friend came to the counter to place their order after a moment of chatting. I brushed my hair to the side, not meaning to leave my neck exposed as I turned with a sigh to make the new order.

While getting fresh beans from the fridge, I felt a shiver of paranoia as my hair brushed the counter. Quickly I tossed it back, covering my exposed mark. Extra Foam Guy had stopped to stare at me on his way at the door. I felt his stare on my braid, as though he was trying to cut through it with a laser. I turned my face towards him as I adjusted my hair with my fingers, making sure it was completely covered. He seemed to realize what he was doing then and disappeared out the exit, shooting me a quick smile before the door swung shut behind him. I exhaled, trying to shake off my discomfort. I never went out of my way to show my mark off the way most people did when they purposely got a tattoo, but most people that had spotted it crooned over it and asked where I got it, wanting something similar themselves. "Norway" was almost always my answer. My human Earth geography was poor, and that was all I could remember at first. I'm more knowledgeable on the subject now but, old habits die hard, apparently.

I finished Emily's friend's order and she was off to the seating area to talk with her friend as Madison took the opportunity to dash up to me and say "Oh my *god*!" she squealed.

"Um... what?" I asked dumbfounded, wincing slightly. There was that shriek again. Human teenage girls get *so* excited so easily.

Her mouth fell open. "What? *What* nothing! You didn't see that guy totally flirting with you?"

Is that what that was? I furrowed my brow in thought, replaying our conversation over in my mind and I couldn't pick out one thing that was flirtatious.

"Oh come on, Leo, you can't be *that* dense. He's cute! Don't you think so?"

I shrugged. I never really thought about dating a human, I wasn't even sure it was possible. I was just taking care of my customer. Although, the flush I felt prickling my cheeks might indicate that my body possibly had other ideas.

"Geez, Leo, you should lighten up. Do you do anything besides work?" she insisted. She was right I was here more often than the owner was, especially lately; my car had been acting up and was eager to purchase one of the newer ones down at the dealership at the end of town.

"Well, I need a new car. And I had to take my cat to the vet last week, and—" I said quickly, trying to come up with acceptable reasons why I worked my ten hour shifts when in reality, I didn't need to. I had plenty of dragon currency I could convert over if I wanted to even though it was a pain in the ass and I didn't prefer to. I didn't have to work quite so much but I guess I enjoyed it. I really didn't have anything else going on unless you counted the endless Netflix binges and various nerd marathons of *Harry Potter*, *Star Trek* and other things of various nerd ilk.

"—oh stop. You need to live a little! You should ask him out when he comes back!"

"Ha!" I exclaimed a little too loudly. Emily and her friend had stopped their excited chatter to pause and look at me. I just gave her a look that said "you are supposed to be cleaning the dining room" and she took the hint. She was still chatting with her friend but at least she was pretending to clean now. It didn't matter, I'd clean up again after her before I locked up for the night because I had nothing better to do. "I don't think that's a good idea. Besides...I don't think he was flirting with me."

"What? Are you kidding?" Madison's short blonde bobbed hair danced excitedly around her heart-shaped feminine face as she spoke animatedly. "Asking you for directions when anyone can clearly see the highway from here? Then making up that lie about football to ask you about the game?"

"What lie?"

"Oh he doesn't play. He's a nerd," she waved my question off with her hand.

"How can you tell?" I really had no idea. The glasses?

"Didn't you see his shirt? It has *HALO* written on it? And the glasses? And *all* the coffee?"

"What is *HALO*?"

"A video game. No one wears a shirt advertising a video game unless they are a gamer. And all gamers are nerds at least somewhat. Why else would he need the coffee?"

I raised my brow. I wasn't convinced of her logic—I played a video game myself, but I didn't consider myself a nerd. *Oh shit.* "I'm *not* a nerd!" I protested.

She snorted. "If you play, you're a nerd."

I scowled. Well that was just *crap*. She wasn't making *any* sense whatsoever. "He ordered decaf, though," I replied. I wasn't understanding her point or accusations and frankly felt a little perturbed about the *nerd* classification.

"Yeah because he's only coming in here to see *you*! He's probably got a whole fridge full of Redbull at his house," she insisted, like it was a commonly known fact. I didn't want to burst her bubble and tell her he wasn't even from here. "He's *never* in here when Emmy and I are here. *Never*! Just you."

"So?" She wasn't wrong, but I was here all the time; so much so I probably blended in with the furniture by now.

"So! He's trying to ask you out but too scared!" she insisted.

"But…I thought nerd was a bad thing?" Or at least, not *dateable*. Clearly there was something I missed in all my sitcom watching. Perhaps too many old Nick at Nite shows; I needed something newer.

She chuckled. "Oh no, only if they're ugly. He is cute—nerdy cute. I mean for an older guy anyways. For you!"

I rolled my eyes. Like I was ancient, I scoffed to myself. Well, I suppose to them I was. But I didn't *appear* it and that was all that mattered. I turned to the young girl and sighed. "I don't know Madison." I ran my fingers over my mark again, troubled by the uneasy feeling in my stomach. There was something about the way he had looked at me before he left... Perhaps I was just paranoid.

Madison opened her mouth to say something when Kit had emerged and interrupted her, "Hey, why don't you and Emily get out of here? It's pretty slow and I think Leo and I can handle things."

Madison didn't have to hear that twice. She jumped excitedly, my love life was forgotten, and shouted to Emily that they could leave. In less than a minute both girls had grabbed their purses and letterman jackets from the back and were darting out the door.

"Thank god." I didn't want to have to talk about him with her, or even attempt to ponder the notion of dating a human. And was he really "flirting" with me? And why was I even *thinking* about it? Of all the guys that had ever walked into this coffeehouse—why was I suddenly so intrigued with him?

Kit raised a brow at me. "What did I miss?" I noticed she was empty handed. "I heard the espresso machine—you got it working, how?"

I shrugged. "Magic I guess. It just started working again randomly."

"Huh," she said, with a laugh, going to inspect the machine.

I scoffed to myself as I mindlessly walked to the seating area to finish what they really hadn't started. "*Magic,*" I mumbled. If we were in the dragon realm, I might seriously consider magic being used to fix the machine. But since we were in the human world it was just a crazy coincidence.

I was grateful when no other customers arrived, affording me some time alone with my thoughts. I started mulling over tonight's meal plan and what shows I'd be watching with my cat.

I snorted to no one in particular when I realized that I was anticipating an evening with alone my cat. *Maybe Madison was right. Maybe I do need to lighten up. I guess I could ask him out, maybe?* But that could lead to so many other questions. I needed to talk to someone who knew; I hadn't ever thought about whether a human and a dragon could be together, romantically. I had never heard of another dragon and human coupling. Most dragons didn't want anything to do with humans. I was different in that respect. Occasionally I even spent time with humans when I wasn't required to; I had frequented bookstores with Kit and enjoyed that time away from the workplace in her company. I liked Kit. Respected her, even. I was more comfortable in human company than I was with my own people. Yet a*nother* way I was completely different than my dragon brethren.

I pushed all thoughts of Extra Foam Guy aside and reached for the calendar, bending over the counter to focus on scheduling next week's shifts. I stared at the page but instead I found myself imagining what it would be like to remove those black rimmed glasses and stare intently into Cute Coffee Guy's deep brown eyes. To run my fingers through those dark messy waves, over and over again. I covered my eyes with my hand—this was ridiculous. How had he suddenly become Cute Coffee Guy?

"Leo?"

Kit's voice shook me out of my haze. I hadn't noticed she'd been next to me.

I smiled sheepishly at her. "I'm sorry, I'm buggin' out, huh?"

"Buggin'? I haven't heard that one for a while," she said with a chuckle. I silently cursed myself. Until I'd come to Pineville, most of my human cultural exposure consisted of 1980s and 1990s movies, magazines and music. It took a while for the new stuff to drift over to the dragon realm; about twenty years actually. I had gotten some funny looks from everyone when I started working here with my *"As if"* and *"Totally bogus!"* outdated expressions.

"Whatever," I just said kiddingly, quoting Cher from one of my favorite 90s movies, *Clueless*.

She nudged me and pointed towards the calendar I'd been writing on. Inadvertently, I had been attempting to draw the logo of Cute Coffee Guy's sweatshirt under Monday's column instead of scheduling shifts.

I quickly covered it with my palm and smacked the book shut. "It's nothing."

Kit smiled playfully. "Right. Why don't you get out of here, since your mind is *clearly* not here tonight? I got some paperwork to do in back, anyway. You can do the schedule tomorrow and go get some rest."

I gave her an appreciative look. "Thanks. I'm sorry."

She just snorted. "Oh, Leorah, it's okay. If I had a dime for every time a hot man distracted me well…let's just say we wouldn't be here right now. I'd be…" she trailed off, eyes twinkling mischievously.

I slapped her forearm. "*Kit!*" But I took her advice and decided to go home and attempt to exorcise the images of Cute Coffee Guy's handsome face which were assaulting my brain. I liked to have tight control over my mind and that man was occupying more of my thoughts than any stranger should.

Chapter 2

I arrived at the parking lot of my apartment building—basically a three floor light-colored building with two apartments on each floor and shifted my purple Dodge sedan into park when I reached my spot. I was smiling to myself as I sauntered to my ground floor apartment. *Dammit, Leo!* I scolded myself in my head. *Stop thinking about the human!* I didn't even notice that the door was unlocked and I hadn't need to use the key when I opened the door.

"Leorah!"

I was so distracted I about jumped out of my skin when someone called my name. My handbag flew out of my hand in one direction and my keys flew in the other. The apartment was dark except for the TV. Quickly I slapped at the light switch illuminating the living area in my apartment.

I heaved a sigh of relief to see my brother sprawled out on my black sofa, looking uncomfortable in a pair of khakis and a button down blue and white striped shirt.

"Holy cow, Braeden! You scared the *shit* out of me!" I darted across the room and slapped him on the shoulder. "Asshole!"

Braeden laughed hysterically. "Oh Leo you should have seen the look on your face!"

I shoved him out of his lounged position on the couch so I could plop down next to him. "You suck."

"Ha ha, I know." he laughed, nudging me in the shoulder. "Wait—*holy cow?*"

I smirked and shook my head. "A human expression."

He stared blankly for a moment. "Why would a cow be holy? Is it blessed? Or did someone tear pieces out of it? I didn't know humans could *do* that…"

I rolled my eyes. "I don't think they can; I heard it on TV. In a movie or…show. One or the other."

He scoffed. "Humans are really weird."

I raised a brow expectantly. "To you, maybe."

He just shrugged his shoulders dismissively. "I don't know how you live with them like you do." I shot him daggers from my eyes, because he of all people should know.

He smiled sheepishly. "Yeah...I guess it's better than where you were. I'm sorry, Leo."

"Eh, whatever. I'm over it." It wasn't true, but I was trying. I heard of these things people used called *therapists* to help them get through tough times. I sometimes wondered if one would work for me. Hmm, probably not...it was probably my one-way ticket to the crazy house the second I said: *"Hi, my name is Leorah and I'm a non-magical dragon..."* Yeah, not so much. Don't think there is a twelve-step program for that one.

"So why are you here?" I asked. My brother didn't come visit very often, and never unannounced. Something had to be up. I cocked my brow suspiciously.

"What?" he asked, pressing a hand to his heart in mock offense. "I have to have a reason for visiting my favorite sister?"

I rolled my eyes. "I'm your *only* sister."

"Well, still makes you my favorite."

I pretended to slap my forehead with my palm. "Come on Brae, I know how you hate coming down here so there must be a reason you just decided to show up."

"Okay, okay... you are right," he relented with a laugh. He smiled. "I met someone."

My eyes widened. "*What*? What do you mean 'met someone'?" I asked, making quotation notes with my fingers.

His green eyes sparkled with happiness. "Like, *someone special*. Her name is Kiarra. She is a Baroness currently serving under Countess Nyzare, but there is talk that she might be nominated for the throne one day. She's very smart, and very progressive. Some say that's just what the Kingdom needs."

I fought a groan: dragon politics. I didn't want to think about it. Really, our government was arranged much like a human democracy, but with medieval titles just to make it interesting. Well not really, there was a point. The King and Queen ruled equally over everyone, with their own sets of advisors; usually referred to as Dukes or Duchesses. These advisors are either former monarchs no longer wishing to serve or someone serving the Court for many years, but still not quite an Elder. They don't make decisions themselves, but can influence the King and Queen.

Under them you have the two branches: the conservative House of Lords (and Ladies) and the more liberal Coterie of Earls (and

Countesses). Those who work for the Lords and Earls are Barons and Baronesses.

Then you have the Guard which is made up of another slew of titles and hierarchy and that's where I lost my interest completely. The sort of acted as the military, or police force. Anarach hadn't had a war in many years, so most of them relented to guarding portals and the palace, training newcomers, and standing around looking pretty. But if we were to enter a war, either with ourselves or a neighboring land, they'd be the first line of defense.

I sighed, daring to ask, further engaging in politics. "What in the world is she doing playing around then doing favors for Nyzare?" Nyzare was a gray dragon and, from my few meetings with her, she was entirely and utterly the most boring, dingbat twit of a dragon I'd ever encountered. And, not that smart either. How she held a place on the Court, I would never know. Generally, someone who had the potential for the throne wouldn't waste time serving under a dragon like that.

"I think she pities Nyzare. Everyone else appreciates Kiarra for working with Nyzare, because that means *they* don't have to," he said with a chuckle.

Braeden scratched at his short blonde hair. Aside from the blonde hair and height, we appeared very similar just as human siblings often did. We had the same bright green eyes as our father and impish grins. He was tall and trim with defined musculature from his shoulders down to his calves. Dragons in human form were never, ever small or qualify as demure. Guess I can't really imagine why…

I was baffled. Shocked. I sat in silence and just stared at him.

"Leo?" he waved his hand in my face.

I realized my mouth was still open in an *O* of stupefaction. "So you have a good friend, right?"

He chuckled. "Uh…it's a little more than that, Leo."

My mouth fell back open. "What? *What?*"

I was motionless. It couldn't be…could it? It hadn't been that long since I left.

Dragon relationships weren't generally discussed until they decided they wanted to be bonded—or as humans called it, married. Since we lived a long time—2,000 years if they are lucky—there was never any rush to hurry the relationship. But…no. It was too soon, wasn't it? I'd only been gone a couple of human Earth years.

Sometimes dragons put off the actual bonding for dozens of years; but never less than five for sure.

"We want to be bonded, Leorah."

I let out a shriek of surprise. "Oh my god." I rubbed at my forehead with the tips of my fingers, closing my eyes and trying to take in all that had happened. Dragons didn't have traditional marriage ceremonies like humans; it generally involved what humans call a *handfasting*. In fact, the Pagan ceremony of handfasting had deep roots in dragon tradition which usually included some sort of officiant reciting a poem or stanza, wrapping a cord in the color of both dragons around their hands, then tying them together. While he or she did this, the two becoming bonded openly stated their intent, or *vows*. Most of them just used generic ones as it were but, sometimes they chose to recite ones of their choosing. Very similar to human weddings but a lot simpler.

As if sensing my stress, my calico cat with bright green eyes took that moment to pat in the room and leaped into my lap. "Meow?"

I put my arms around her and clutched her close to my chest. She purred and nuzzled my face.

I felt my brother shudder next to me. "Ugh, why do you still *have* that thing?"

My cat—Sona—scratched at the air in front of her and let out a warning *hiss*.

"She's my baby!" I gave her a quick squeeze and released her to the floor. She darted quickly across the green and pink floral rug, slipped on the patch of hardwood floor that wasn't covered by and disappeared down the short hallway into my bedroom. Cats and dragons—well, let's say *most* animals and most dragons—didn't get along. Again, I was the exception to that rule.

Braeden wrinkled his nose in disgust. "Geez Leo, you're so weird."

I shot him a dirty look. "Where have *you* been my whole life? I am the epitome of *weird*. There isn't a thing about me that's normal, remember?"

Braeden held up his hands in surrender. "Okay, okay. You got me."

I shook my head and let out a low growl that was characteristically dragon. "So…why are you telling me this? You don't want me to act as a witness to you or anything, do you?" I swallowed nervously. It wasn't unusual for a sibling to ask another sibling to stand as witness to the bonding. It was the dragon equivalent of a best man or maid of honor.

"Well no. Not *yet* anyway," he replied. "She wants to meet you first."

"Me?" I squeaked in surprise. "*Me*? She knows who I am, right?" Surely everyone did, even dragons that lived nowhere near us knew of the crazy, pink dragon who couldn't breathe fire and couldn't fly and had seemingly no magic. And was pink. It needs mentioning twice because that in itself was bad enough.

He grinned. "Yes she knows who you are. I talk about you quite often; you know?"

That surprised me. Taken aback, I asked, "And she still wants to know you?"

He laughed. "*Yes* silly! Not everyone thinks you are a freak, you know."

"Really?" I asked with genuine surprise.

"Yes! Some people are quite intrigued by you, you know. First pink dragon born in years…pretty interesting to some you know."

I snorted. "Yeah, those who don't know me."

Now it was my brother's turn to punch me. "Seriously, Leo...not everyone is like mom and dad. And most the Court and—"

"—most our entire society." I finished for him, with a grumble. Feeling a bit on edge, I decided a glass of wine was in order. Or, a bottle. I went to the kitchen area and produced a bottle of cabernet from the fridge. It had already been opened but I had jammed the cork back in to help keep it from getting too much air in it—or whatever. I wasn't a wine connoisseur by any stretch. Coffee? Yes. Wine? Just give it to me, I don't care what kind it is.

I took a large swig from the bottle and brought it with me to the blue plush reclining chair I had across the room, looking across from the sofa.

"You gonna offer me some?" Braeden prompted.

In response I took another large gulp and narrowed my eyes at him. "Nope."

He frowned. "Is what I told you really so bad?"

I sighed. "Not bad, Brae just…very, *very* surprising. And also her wanting to meet me—a little unsettling." *No one* wants to know me.

He considered this. "I suppose. I guess it *is* a little shocking. I just figured you'd be happy for me."

I lowered the bottle mid swig. "Ack, I'm sorry, Brae. It's just... a huge surprise. And very unorthodox, you know? Usually this happens—*if* this happens—after like, ten years of 'dating'," I said, using the human term for it. "I didn't even know you were seeing anyone."

He just shrugged. "I know. I guess it just didn't make much sense you know. Waiting, waiting, waiting when...what's going to change? I love her so...not that."

Still feeling uneasy I tried to force a smile. "Well...I suppose that means I have to go home for a while, huh?" My attempt at smiling was quickly replaced by a disgusted groan. "Uggh...I don't want to."

"You don't have to. She said she has no problem coming here."

"Really?"

"Yeah...she thinks dragon customs are just too stuffy, and it's time to lighten up a bit."

"Can't argue with that reasoning." I groaned lightly. "Can I have some time to process this stuff first? I mean...I know what happens when you bond." I pouted. Usually when dragons became bonded, they spent a long time being apart from the rest of their families as they were attempting to build their own life together, without outside influence. I was afraid I wouldn't see him now until he had two baby drakes of his own in about twenty years.

"Aw, you'll miss me?" he joked.

"I *always* miss you!" I insisted.

His face softened. "Aw. I know it's gotta be hard for you, no matter how much you said you wanted to be by yourself."

I nodded reluctantly. "Yeah. I mean...I want to be here. It was too hard being there but here? I don't quite know how to act. I don't really even know what I'm feeling, sometimes."

"Oh, Leo..." My brother draped his arm around my shoulders and pulled me close so I rested my cheek on his strong chest. Despite how I felt, I found myself smiling contentedly. He often held me like this when we were little, after dragon school or another run in with our parents...or I shamed someone yet again by just being *me*. "Don't you have anyone here you like?"

I considered this. "Well...there's Kit."

"The owner of the coffee shop?"

I nodded. "Yeah. She's a bit older—well, older than my human self—but that's okay. We went to some bookstores once; she thought about expanding and adding a small bookstore with the coffee house. And we've been out for coffee a few times."

"Well, that's...something. Boring, but something. Anything...*romantic*?" He wiggled his eyebrows pointedly.

I snorted. "I really don't think so. I wouldn't even know how it would feel." I looked up at him expectantly. "What did it feel like when you started seeing Kiarra?"

My brother grinned from ear to ear. "Oh...the first time I saw her I started feeling nervous for no apparent reason. I didn't understand it at first. When I would talk to her I would get all tingly inside."

"Nervous? Tingly?" I thought back, thinking of Cute Coffee Guy. I recalled every time he came in and made small talk suddenly I found myself twirling my hair, watching his brown eyes light up as he spoke.

My brother gasped. "Oh! There *is* someone!"

I could feel my cheeks grow warm. "Well, no not really, but— "

"—you *wish* there was!"

I sighed and rolled my eyes. "See, I don't know. There is this guy coming into the shop—been doing so for a couple weeks now. The girls say he only comes in when I'm there and he tried drumming up a conversation today. Madison thinks he was trying to ask me out but I didn't hear what she heard, I guess."

"So? Ask him out."

"*What?*" I squeaked. "Are you kidding? I mean, he's human and I—"

"—you are posing as a human. It's natural to you to want to spend time with one," he insisted.

"Yeah but...what about...*that*." I raised my eyebrows pointedly.

"Sex?"

I gasped. I don't think I ever heard my brother utter that word before. Dragon society dictated it wasn't openly talked about. Yeah, we did it—a lot—but we didn't feel the need to talk about it. Then I shuddered in repulsion. Human or dragon you still didn't want to hear your brother mention that word, or even know they were thinking about it. *Bleccch*!

"Oh lighten up. I'm sure as long as you stay in your human form you're fine. I think," he said with a shrug and then a convulsion. "Ugh, I guess I'm not as liberal as I thought. I can't even think about you doing that."

I laughed and patted his hand. "It's okay. I guess I never really thought of it as a possibility. How can I possibly keep *this*—" I pointed to the back of my neck, "—a secret from someone I care about, you know?"

"I don't know, sister dear. I guess you'll have to find all that out for yourself."

"*Ugggh.* Maybe I just don't want to," I said dismissively, not convinced of that myself.

Braeden looked at my bottle of wine I paused in drinking, finally and nodded at it. "You gonna share now?"

I thrust the bottle toward my brother, not really even looking at him; I found myself once again dazed with the thoughts of the mysterious brunette nerd boy. "Something bothered me though when he was there. The guy in the shop."

"Oh?" He let out a loud burp after his third large swig. I just rolled my eyes. Nothing new there.

"He stared at my mark."

Braeden simply blinked, and wiped his mouth with his sleeve, leaving a red wine stain behind. "Aw damn," he muttered, handing the bottle back to me and rolling up the cuffs of his shirt. "Leo lots of people look at your mark, I'm sure."

"I know," I insisted. "But it was more than just a look. Almost like he…" I trailed off. I don't really know why it bugged me as much as it did. "Bah, I don't know."

"Just take it easy. If it happens, good if not well…you'll find another." Braeden continued rolling up his sleeve over his own mark—identical to mine but in red. "It's neat looking, something humans haven't seen before, I'm sure. So he probably just liked it."

"Yeah…yeah you're probably right," I agreed.

"You know, even if Kiarra and I become bonded and have twenty dragons, you'll always be a part of my family, okay?" Must be the wine talking, a rare moment of seriousness for my brother. Since we metabolized alcohol fast, it wouldn't last long. His eyes were earnest, though and he reached over and placed a comforting hand on my knee. "That won't change. You'll always be my sister and as long as I'm around, you'll always have a place to call home."

My face softened at his tenderness. I felt my lower lip tremble and my eyes started to sting with—tears? "Really?"

"Yes." He punched me in the same knee playfully and made a squished up, stupid face at me to lighten the mood. "Good. Now while I'm here can we watch some trashy human TV?"

I giggled and wiped my palm over my eyes to quickly wipe away any moisture that had accumulated, relieved for the respite from the schmaltz. I pointed at the end table next to the sofa to the remote. "Have at it, bro."

He beamed and proceeded to turn on the TV and flip through the channels. We had a silly evening watching cheesy reality shows and making fun of people…much like we used to do when we were little but without the trashy shows and the people part. There was enough about dragon life we could ridicule; we didn't need TV then.

Kit had me on dining room duty the next day, as she was manning the register and taking orders while we were slow in the afternoon. There wasn't actually much to do and Kit probably could have handled the shop herself, but I knew she liked the company. I always could find something that needed doing and that's probably why she liked to have me around.

She was a bit of a neat freak and had me armed with an upholstery cleaner to scour the chairs and tapestry that lay over the oak hardwood floor.

My heart nervously skipped a beat every time the bells over the door chimed, announcing the arrival of a customer. So far, Cute Coffee Guy hadn't graced us but, he had yet to come in in the early afternoon like this before. I was starting to get worried that he wouldn't show today when I was in the middle of sucking the upholstery shampoo off the microfiber sofa, I didn't hear the overhead bells and was startled when I turned around to see him standing there behind me. I let out a little shriek and ended up dropping the vacuum hose, which was in mid-suck and ended up splattering dirty couch shampoo on his red sweatshirt, face and glasses.

"Oh my *god*! I'm so sorry!" I darted off for some napkins behind the counter. When I produced them to him he just laughed.

"It's not a big deal," he said, taking a napkin and wiping of his face with a laugh.

"Ugh, I'm such a spaz, seriously!" I insisted, grabbing a napkin from him and dabbing at his sweatshirt with it.

He chuckled nervously as I did so. "Really...not a big deal. I do it to myself at least twice a day."

I smiled and reached up to dab at his glasses when I paused. This was the closest I had ever been to him and I had the urge to step closer. It felt...safe and warm and he smelled wonderful. Peaceful and relaxing like sandalwood and pine and... cinnamon. He forced a nervous smile and I pulled away. "Oh, sorry." I handed him the napkin and allowed him to clean off his own glasses.

"I said, don't be sorry," he insisted. "It's not often I get an excuse to stand next to a pretty girl." With his glasses off I could see his brown eyes sparkle. He smiled and wiped a lens on his shirt and put them back on.

I put my hand to my cheek to touch the heat that had formed and my knees began turning to jelly. I had to remind myself to stand up straight and not collapse into his form right now. I was dumbfounded. All I could do was stand there, smiling nervously. "Well...oh come on I'm sure it happens all the time." Why the hell was I so drawn to him?

He chuckled. "No...the closest I get is my brother and...the NPCs in a video game."

I gave him a look. "Your brother is pretty?"

"Uh...yeah kinda."

I let out a laugh. It helped break my nervousness so I could function; strength returning to my legs again. "So, you want coffee?"

"Um, actually, no." He paused, looked down at his shuffling feet before he looked up, pausing to find words. "I came to ask you about your tattoo."

My hand immediately went to the back of my neck, the smile fell from my face and was replaced with a look of discomfort. "My...my tattoo?" I swallowed, nervously. "Oh, ha, I got it in Norway, when I still lived there."

"Really? Because I swear I'd seen it before." The friendly, flirty look upon his face was gone. Instead his mouth was set in a straight line, his eyes boring through me suspiciously.

"This?" I squeaked. "Not this. The tattooist swore it was one of a kind."

"Yeah...yeah I'm sure it is. What does it mean?" He crossed his arms over his chest and waited for my answer.

"Who...who are you?" was all I could ask. Most of the time humans commented on my mark it was "Oh cool! Where'd you get it? So neat!" and that was it. No one ever asked me about it again.

"That depends. Who—or what—are you?" he asked.

Oh my God. He knows. Somehow, he knows.

Calm down, Leorah...he could just be another dragon from another city who's heard of the crazy pink dragon and wants to give you crap...nothing new. Nothing you can't handle. I took a breath and forced myself to smile. "What do you mean, what am I? What else could I be? An alien? A witch?" I scoffed, and waved him off with a laugh.

"What does it mean?" he persisted.

I backed away, towards the counter. "It's just a design. If you have to ask, you have no idea what it is, either."

"Leorah, can I borrow you a minute?" Kit called from behind the counter.

Relieved for the distraction, I didn't bother excusing myself and quickly joined her behind the counter. Kit's normally sunny, happy face was ridden with concern.

"Are you okay?" she whispered, pretending to show me something in our credit register. "You look pretty upset."

I looked up at her, panicked. "I...I don't know."

Cute (Now Creepy) Coffee Guy had come up to the counter and was staring at me, looking for answers.

"Pardon us," she let out a ditzy giggle. "I screwed up on some paperwork and I need Leorah here to help me out. Give us a few minutes and I'll make your order, okay?"

He nodded, not taking his eyes off me. "Sure, whatever you need. Is there a bathroom?"

"Of course; to the right, and down a slight hall," Kit said, with a point.

"Thanks." He paused to glance at me again, sending panicked shivers down my spine—not the nice ones when I was thinking about him earlier. But, terrified I'm-about-to-vomit shivers. Then he followed Kit's gesture and disappeared into the bathroom.

I let out a little yelp when he was gone. "Oh my god..." I muttered to myself.

"What? What's wrong, Leo? I almost thought you guys were hitting it off and then you started to panic. Did he say something nasty to you?" Kit questioned, putting a concerned hand on my shoulder.

"I—well...yes, I suppose he did." And I knew I had to get out of here and away from him. In the years that I've been in Minnesota, no one has ever said *they know what I am* before like that. It made me incredibly nervous to think I might have to run and start a new life somewhere, far away from this dude. Or had to go hide for a while.

Quickly I untied the apron strings behind my back and pulled it over my head, getting the neck string caught in my long brown hair in the panic. "Kit, I'm sorry but...I need to go. Call me if it gets busy but I really *really* need to get out of here." I never called in, never left work early (dragons rarely got sick—finally, an advantage!) but this was quite possibly life or death. I needed to leave. Normally I would have felt guilty about it but right now I could care less.

"Okay, hun...please call me and let me know what's going on, okay?" she insisted, as I shoved the apron under the counter in a cubby area that was supposed to house books.

I nodded and grabbed my jacket and purse from another cabinet beneath the register, I yanked my keys from out of my black jeans pocket and dashed as quickly as I could out the door, with Kit yelling, "Please call me!" as I left.

I ran across the parking lot, darting another customer driving in with his Jeep and jumped into my car, thankful that I never locked it. Waiting for the Jeep to get out of my way impatiently, I back out of my parking spot and peeled out to the driveway.

I took a glance at the rearview mirror; I saw Coffee Creepy Guy waving me down in the mirror. I didn't stop, just sped out the driveway onto the dirt road and I didn't look back until I was on the highway.

Relieved I seemed to be the only person on the highway; I calmed down a little but as I reached down the dash to switch on the radio I noticed that my hands were shaking. I could barely touch the button to turn it on.

Dragons rarely had anything to fear; except other dragons. Besides that, maybe a broken wing and a fall when flying, or a human with a flamethrower that would hurt like hell was about all that scared us. And in all actuality if I shifted I could eat him so there was little reason to be intimidated but the thought of having to start over in a new town, find a new job, and move my cat bothered me immensely. I had grown to like it here in this small Minnesota town.

It was the first time I'd felt content in my entire life and I hated to give that up.

I felt my eyes moisten and I blinked rapidly to keep the stinging tears out of my eyes. "Calm down. He probably has no idea what you are. You're overreacting. You just need to calm down."

I didn't know where I was headed until I decided I needed to relax. Suddenly my legs and arms felt restless and tight, like I was wearing a diving suit three sizes too small. I wouldn't shift out involuntarily but it became very, very uncomfortable. Probably some sort of instinctual need in times of stress; as our dragons were much tougher than our human forms.

Half your panic is probably just because you haven't shifted in a while. Yeah, that's it. I was overreacting because my human body was anxious because the dragon needed to come out. Just for a while.

I drove about four miles down the highway and turned off on a little dirt road that actually led to a farmhouse but the land was abandoned. Turn off before you hit the driveway and drive another mile or so into the woods. It was a path overgrown by shrubs and greenery and weeds and was rarely driven on. Word had it the old farmhouse was haunted so people rarely came out here.

I glanced up in the mirror to make sure I wasn't followed; when I was satisfied I wasn't I parked my car right before the little path gave way to the woods and proceeded to run as fast as I could into the thicket. The ground was covered in leaf litter but little else; the oaks, elms and willows in the woods were so large they blocked out all sun from hitting the ground and letting anything grow.

When I reached my spot in the middle of the woods I knelt down to the ground to catch my breath. I closed my eyes and inhaled the fresh scent of the woods, of the leaves and dirt and raised my arms over me. This distressed, I couldn't shift so I needed to calm myself first.

I sat and took several deep breaths and could feel the terror exiting my body into the ground, the earth absorbing my worries. It was a belief in human paganism that if you need a release, just ask the earth to take away your negative energy and if you believe, it will. While dragons weren't extremely religious any longer, we still had a few beliefs we stuck with and in this instance—at least the dragons in Anarach—agreed with human paganism here (after all, they are one and the same). This was something in common I had with Kit.

I felt the stillness of the ground, the coolness soothed my restless feet and legs…relieve the heavy pit in my stomach and relax my lungs. I exhaled with a sigh, and opened my eyes, standing slowly, feeling invigorated and renewed.

Now I could shift.

I glanced down at my clothes—my black jeans, flower-patterned doc marten boots and my silver lace tunic over a black camisole and groaned. I hadn't brought anything to change into and shifting would surely rip my clothes so I had to take them off first. I started to pull the silver shirt over my head when I heard a familiar voice call out:

"Wait!"

I gasped and quickly pulled it down back over my human form and swiveled around. There he was. He had followed me. How he'd gone unnoticed by me was unclear and disturbing—he was slick indeed.

I glowered at him. "Look, buddy…you do *not* want to mess with me. You have no idea what I am capable of so just turn and walk away."

"No! I'm sorry I freaked you out!" He slowly inched closer to me, his palms forward in the air in a sign of surrender. "I know what you're capable of. I know you can bite my head off—literally. I just…wanted to see for myself if you *really* are what I think you are?"

I crossed my arms over my chest. "And what do you think I am?"

A dreamy look spread across his face. "A powerful, magical, mythical, *amazing* being; and I've been looking for you all of my life."

Chapter 3

"*What?*" I sputtered in disbelief.

"You! I can't believe I've found you! You don't know how long we've been searching for one of you!" he was almost ready to burst with excitement. "For hundreds of years I and people like me have been searching for you or one of your kind and here, I'm the lucky one to actually *find* one of you!"

"Excuse me?" I cocked my brow at him and rolled my eyes.

"Oh," he laughed nervously. "I'm sorry. You might not be aware of what *I* am."

"A loopy human that just escaped the mental ward of the hospital?"

In a motion that totally surprised me, he knelt humbly down on the ground on one knee and started up at me. "I am a Knight. A knight of *Ord na Draconica Dianthus*." He bowed his head down. As if it explained *everything*.

I snorted. "What? What the hell are you talking about?"

He slowly looked up. "Loosely translated, Order of the Pink Dragon. But it sounds a lot cooler to say it like that." He looked up at me and winked.

I winced at the word *dragon*. So he did know what I was. But I was going to play stupid and pretend this guy was a whackjob. Which he obviously was but…

"A dragon?" I cackled wildly. "There is no such thing."

He looked up at me with a smirk. "I'm not stupid. That mark— you bear the mark of your dragon and it's in pink. You're a pink dragon. I have something similar."

"Coincidence. Clearly my tattooist was a liar."

"No…" he started to pull off his sweatshirt but stopped. "May I stand? So I can show you?"

I scoffed. "What the hell do I care?"

A smile crept across his face as he slowly stood and I watched as he pulled his sweatshirt over his head taking a heather gray t-shirt with it. His arms were completely covered in tattoos and Celtic symbols; I recognized most of them as symbols we used in our own dragon faiths. The tattoos covered his forearms and slightly defined biceps up to his shoulders and he had a few smaller ones on his chest. One was a triskele knot we used as a symbol for protection over his heart. I couldn't get a closer look at the ones on his stomach. He turned around and emblazoned across his shoulders was a dragon, pink in color, flying under the moon with a rose in her mouth. He turned back around and pointed at one smaller tattoo on his pectoral muscle. It was a simple, yet distinct mark of a simple dragon in a circle, nose touching its tail all in pink. Celtic knotwork wrapped around the dragon, swooping in and out of all the curves. Again, all in pink. Almost just like mine.

I gasped. It was in fact very similar to mine. The only difference was instead of my mark being totally round, it was stretched out lengthwise more...more appearing a birthmark than a tattoo sometimes. It probably was rounder at one time but with all the shifting and growing and whatnot it sort of lost some of its cohesiveness.

"But—how?"

He turned to face me, and gave me a fascinated look as if staring at god himself. "It appeared when I was ten years old and inducted into the Order."

"*Appeared*?"

"Probably just like yours does, when you're in your human form," he said knowingly.

I relented. "So you know I'm a dragon."

He smiled. "Yes, yes I know you're a dragon. A pretty awesome one too, I'll bet."

"Ha! No, not really."

He appeared disappointed. "No? You are selling yourself short. There's no way you are anything but amazing."

I laughed shortly. "Yeah okay. Sure. So what about this *Order* are you talking about?"

"Well the *Ord na*—Order—began years ago when dragons and humans roamed the earth together, before dragons sought refuge in your realm. There were many humans that worked in peace with the dragons and there were many that wanted to abuse the dragons' power, especially with the rising of some very powerful empires...the Roman, the Visigoth and later the Celtic and so on. I probably don't have those empires right," he said, pausing to laugh, "but the records are sort of sketchy. But, if the power of the dragon they worked with could be harnessed, they had a much better and easier chance taking over the empire, or the kingdom. The Order was created so that we could work alongside pink dragons and keep the peace amongst our two peoples'," he explained, fiddling with his sweatshirt in his hands.

"Wait…so there were more pink dragons?"

He nodded. "Oh yeah there were just as many pink as silver and gold ones back in those days. But, after a time, people started realizing exactly what pink dragons were capable of…and they began disappearing."

"No kidding."

He smiled sympathetically. "Back in the day, pink dragons were respected for their power; other dragons envied their power and their connection to the humans; sometimes to the point of getting quite annoying I would assume. At least, that's what I have heard," he said with a wink of his eye.

I let out a loud, unintelligible noise. "*Envy*? Respect? Are you kidding me? There has never been any respect for me. I was shamed. I am a disgrace to my entire family!"

He appeared shocked. "Are you serious? Wow…I can't believe that…" he trailed off. "*You* aren't even aware of what you are!" This reality seemed to stun and bother him. He covered his face with his palms. When he removed him after a moment, he asked, "How many of you are there now, about?"

"How many? *How many*? Well there's me. And…that's it. The last one we know of was hundreds of years ago."

His mouth fell open. "Oh my—wow. *Wow*. No wonder we haven't met up with you until now. Oh, that explains so much…" You could see in his eyes, the wheels turning in thought and realization in his head.

As he pondered, I stood there, glaring at him. "Are you going to clue me in here?"

He pulled himself from his thoughts. "I'm sorry. I will start from the beginning. I am Gabriel O'Donnell. I am tenth generation Order knight and however—whatever it takes—I will help you. It's what I was born for." He knelt to the ground on one knee again with a grand gesture of his arm. "If you will allow me, that is."

I snickered at his *chivalrous* behavior. "Oh stop, you look ridiculous."

He raised his eyes and gave me a wounded look. "Sorry but this is new to me. I don't know quite how to act."

I softened my rough expression but remained stubborn with my hands crossed over my chest. "I don't know. Act like you normally would, I guess. How do I know this is for real? And how come we have never *heard* of you."

He smirked. "Oh I guarantee there are plenty of your kind who have heard of us. If you could get one to admit it to you. And was old enough. Knowledge of us kind of…fell by the wayside as we separated realms."

I considered this. "Okay…so how many are you now?"

"Just myself."

I chuckled despite myself. "So we're both a dying breed?"

"I suppose so," he said with a laugh. "My uncle was a former member, but when I got my mark and came of age, I took his place. I always wondered why our numbers dwindled…I guess I have my answer, since there is only one of you."

"Guess so. But…why me? *Why* pink dragons?"

"Well of course you know that that color determines a dragon's abilities, sometimes personalities, what element they can harness and control and influences the strength of their dragon fire. You know that."

"Yeah but I don't breathe fire," I said with disdain, kicking my boot at a stray weed in the dirt like it was my non-ability and I could actually physically kick its ass.

"No you don't." He smiled knowingly. "What *do* you do?"

I snorted. "Sparkles. Misty foggy mist stuff. And…more sparkles. Some sparks, maybe if I'm lucky. Really?" I shook my head in disappointment. "They do nothing. Nothing at all. It looks kinda pretty though, I suppose."

"And, have you ever breathed your sparkly mist at any other dragons?"

"No well—" I suddenly remembered an incident in school, when I was a young dragon. Some older dragons were harassing me and one started breathing fire at me. He was black so it was a dirty, gritty fire. I hadn't attempted to breathe fire much except for when I was very small; before I knew better the sparkles amused me and made me and my brother giggle. Out of instinct, I breathed back at him and he instantly stopped. I was scolded by the professor and sent home for a week, until I promised never to breathe my misty stuff in school again—or ever in public—or else I would never be allowed back in school again. And I really haven't much, because there really never seemed to be much point. "I did. Once. I got in trouble."

"Really? And...what happened?" I retold the story for him and his eyes lit up.

"You don't realize what happened, do you?"

"Um...no..." I looked at him, stupefied.

"Leorah, he didn't *stop* breathing fire. You *made* him stop!" he explained excitedly.

"I—oh I did not. He stopped. The teacher or whatever was coming."

"Did you guys usually get in trouble for breathing fire?"

"No, just me," I said.

He smiled. "Why would you get in trouble, and they wouldn't?"

"I—because they hate me," I insisted.

"And why *do* they hate you?"

"Because I'm different."

"Because *you* have the power to stop them if you want to. Your fire—your sparkles—can stop their fire. And their magic. And *any* magic that is near you."

"I—what?" I was stunned. "I've never done it before!"

"Because you aren't allowed. Was it the adults that told you not to, or the kids?"

"Well, the adults obviously."

He laughed shortly. "Of course. Because they know *what* you are, and they don't want you to be able to stop them. So they left you in the dark. Probably over the centuries since Cyril was so powerful and he stopped many wars and many hostile takeovers since none of you ever were born, the eldest of dragons passed along false knowledge of your kind and what you are to stigmatize and seclude you...if you don't exist, you can't stop them from doing what they want to do, no matter how bad or good it is."

"I—are you kidding me?" It was more of a rhetorical whisper. "But...I can't believe it."

"Believe it. Once you are ready, I can show you."

"How?"

His eyes lit up. "Because, as one of the knights of the Order, I am also a powerful sorcerer. I have magic."

"Oh come on. You're human! You—"

Before my very eyes, Gabriel started concentrating, holding his palms together and after a few seconds, fireballs formed in his hands as he parted them. Small, but they were there. I stared at them, in complete awed silence, as he bobbed them in his hand like they were kids' toy balls. The glow of the fire shone in his eyes and lit up his face and I truly saw how gorgeous he was in this dim moonlight. My heart skipped a beat...or two.

The shirt being off helped a bit too. I couldn't help but smile despite my frustration, confusion and complete awe of the turn of events that were now laid out before me. And the fire in his hands.

"Holy...holy shit." I barely whispered in awe, watching as he closed the little balls of fire slowly, causing them to form one larger ball the size of a volleyball. "Now, watch this." He turned towards the nearest tree, and yelled out a loud "Hah!" as he pushed them towards the trunk, immediately singing the bark and sparking a small fire.

"Oh my—I can't believe you did that! You wanna burn down the entire forest?" I started to run to the fire to put it out, glaring at him in dismay when he put his hand out to stop me.

"Trust me." Was all he said. He pointed his palms to the ground and closed his eyes for a short moment. Then, as if pulling it out of the ground, a stream of water came out slowly as he turned his palms over and let the puddle float in the air for a bit. It sounded like it was raining, yet none fell out of the invisible containment field in his hands. He turned to me and wiggled his eyebrows excitedly.

"Okay, now you're just showing off," I said, and I watched his concentration nearly break, the water ball nearly falling from his hands. But he quickly composed himself and thrust the water at the tree trunk, dowsing the fire he started instantly.

"Are they—" It was hard to believe neither fire nor water touched his hands; hard to believe they weren't wet or burned. I hesitantly stepped closer to him to take a closer look at his palms. He held them out in front of him.

"See? Just fine." And he was right. Not a singe mark, not even a drop of water or red from the heat. Just...fine.

Not realizing what I was doing I grabbed them and pulled them closer to my line of vision, placing my fingertips along the lines of his palms, trying to feel the heat that was surely there.

And, there was that shiver again. And...heat, but not from the fire. I let out a small "*eek*" at the surprise and feeling of it, and the warm sensation that emanated off of him and tickled my skin, starting at my own palms, then up my arms and towards my cheeks which I surely knew had to be on fire themselves right about now. I dared to look up into his eyes and he smiled slowly. "Satisfied?"

"I think so," I whispered dreamily.

He chuckled, and let his hands fall to his sides. "You, Leorah are way more special than you could ever know."

I beamed. "Well...that's good to know." I was disappointed as he took a few steps back from me. Crestfallen, I frowned.

"Don't worry, it's not you. It's just...overwhelming." He insisted.

"What is? Surely not more than me...I just learned I actually serve a purpose!" I let out a fake gasp and pretended to hold my heart in shock.

"Ha!" He laughed. "No it's just...I can't believe this is happening to me. *Me*! One of the things I was told to prepare for was how to live my life just in case—and it was a huge probability—that you would never show up." He snorted shortly. "I trained for years and years, just like my uncle Christopher. For twenty years he practiced his magic, and his combat skills only to realize that, he needed to make a life for himself. And he had no idea what he wanted to do, he was so let down. So I—I trained, and did all the things I was supposed to do but I never really thought it would ever happen. I mean seriously like you said—it's been years. I went to college, let my magic lapse some and did normal people stuff. I graduated, got a degree and a job. I have a house—in *Canada*!"

"Oh," was all I could say, afraid now of what that meant. I turned away from him and started pacing as he continued talking. That would figure, the first person—human or dragon—that could relate to me and he was leaving. Or, if he chose to stay, I could make his life miserable.

"But!" he said quickly. "My brother—who is not a knight but a seer, told me I needed to come here. It would change things. I was reluctant but...I did it. Something dragged me into your coffeehouse. I don't know what it was. But the second I saw you I knew somehow, you were the reason I was supposed to be here." He chuckled. "I thought that he meant I was going to meet some amazing woman, not *the* dragon we've all been looking for, for—*years*! And now everything will change."

"Really? So the amazing pink dragon can't also be an amazing woman?" I countered sarcastically.

"Truthfully I was expecting some sort of troll. Or a dude." He chuckled. "Is that really how you look? I mean, can you change your appearance?"

I shook my head. "Nope. You have one human form, and you don't get to decide it. It grows and changes along the same lines as a normal human. Once I looked like a child, eventually I'll get silver and wrinkles." I frowned at the prospect. "Though, it will be a long time before that happens."

"Ah, I didn't know that."

"So, why does everything have to change?" I asked, somewhat fearing the answer.

"Because it is the sworn duty of a Knight of the Order to work alongside his dragon, above all other duties. And now I see I have a very large job to do, knowing now that you don't have hardly any clue of what your abilities are." He heaved a heavy sigh. "It will be a lot of work. Not sure I'm the right one for the job."

"So if you don't want to do it, don't. It's as simple as that. Just go back home, and live your life. I lived my entire life without you so far, I can live the rest without you. No worries." I bowed in a mock curtsy, "Good day to you, Gabriel, Knight of whatever Dragon Order. I relieve you of your duties." Could I do that? I didn't care. I turned to storm off towards my car, still parked in the clearing. Something inside me felt sick and unsure; like I wasn't really convinced of what I said. But, I was tough—sorta—I'd get through it somehow.

I felt a hand grasp my shoulder. "I didn't say I didn't want to," he said as he swiveled me around. "Just that I didn't know *how*."

"Oh. Well how long are you supposed to be here for?"

"Another couple of weeks before my sabbatical is up at work," he replied.

"Well, decide then. And I'll decide if I even want to deal with this. You know all I ever wanted to do was blend in, and be ignored. Live my life, go to work, have my little place in the world where I didn't have to worry about constant ridicule. Watch TV with my cat and go to sleep, tired from working or tired from stress but not tired from being upset at being teased or cut down or worried about not living up to my parents' expectations."

"I guess that's fair."

A gust of wind broke through the trees, howling as it wound over the branches, bringing it with it a wave of cold air. I could smell rain in the air, surely an early fall storm was looming in the sky. I shivered.

"Cold..." Gabriel shivered himself. "Listen can we debate this somewhere else? The coffeehouse still open? It's going to rain here soon, and it's pretty chilly."

"You can always put your shirt back on," I reminded him, pointing at the red hoodie on the ground.

He chuckled. "Right." He grabbed for it and pulled it over his head. "That's better." I had to struggle to hide the disappointment from my face when he covered his upper body. Dragon or not, I could still appreciate human attractiveness.

"We still should get out of here," I agreed. I pulled my cell phone out of my front jeans pocket to check the display. "Coffeehouse will be closing soon but if it's coffee you want; I have plenty at my place if you want."

"Are you sure?" he asked cautiously.

I laughed. "Oh trust me...you might be able to do magic but I could literally bite your head off if I wanted to. I'm not afraid of anyone except...well, another dragon."

He forced a smile through his nervous *gulp*. "Well that's...good to know."

Suddenly, a thought occurred to me out of the blue. I snapped my fingers and shouted, "*You*! You fixed the machine yesterday, didn't you?"

Gabriel smirked knowingly and just shrugged. "Maybe," he said, feigning innocence.

I clicked my tongue at him. "Damn you," I muttered, but motioned for him to follow me. Well, that explains it, at least. It *was* magic after all! I'll be damned...

Gabriel agreed to follow me once we reached the highway and as we turned off the dirt road he slowed down in his black Ford Ranger truck and allowed me to lead him the few blocks to my apartment.

We arrived at my apartment a few minutes later and he joined me in the doorway. "Wow so...you live here?" he asked rhetorically in disbelief.

"Why, doesn't it fit me?" I asked, unlocking the door and pushing the door open, hitting the light switch on the way in. I gestured for him to go in and he did.

"Honestly I pictured something less...humble and small," he replied, following me into the kitchenette area.

I laughed. "Oh so sorry your knightly-ness," I said, beginning the process of making coffee. "Perhaps maybe someday I'll afford something to your liking," I kidded, filling up the coffee pot with water from the sink and pouring it in the reservoir of my coffee maker.

"No! That's not what I mean," he said quickly, taking a seat over the bar area separating the kitchen from the living room. "I just mean, I always pictured dragons living in these huge, drafty castles with jeweled statues and..." he trailed off, smiling. "I've seen too many movies."

"Haha, well you're not entirely wrong. We have castles," I said, measuring the right amount of coffee into the basket and putting it in the maker,b hitting the brew button. "With fireplaces and stuff...you know we don't get much electricity up there."

"Yeah I imagine not."

"But what we do have we save for the internet," I said trying to sound as serious as possible producing a cheesy Harry Potter mug with the words "*Mischief Managed*" on it and placed it in front of him. He raised an eyebrow.

"Really?" he asked, raising it up.

"What?" I asked with a shrug. "You think that's bad, you should see my bedroom. *Harry Potter* stuff all over."

He laughed. "Well...I would love to see it sometime."

I paused, head in the cabinet, feeling that shiver up my spine again. I peeked my head out to say, "Really?"

"Well yeah for—wait! The *Harry Potter* stuff, not because I want to *see* your bedroom or anything." Gabriel turned fifty shades of crimson and pretended to be very interested in the map design on the other side of the mug.

I grabbed my own cup—this time a *Twilight* one that said "Team Jacob!" on it. "You mean you only want to see my nerd gear? That's it?" I asked, pretending to sound insulted, puffing out my lower lip.

"I mean, I—" His eyes widened. He facepalmed himself and groaned.

I laughed uproariously. "Oh I'm just kidding!" I wasn't sure if I was though, but I was enjoying giving him a hard time.

He peeked at me with a brown eye from in between his fingers. "Oh, you are...*evil* after all."

"Why whatever do you mean?" I asked, batting my eyelashes innocently.

He nodded towards my coffee cup. "Team Jacob? Really? Come on it's Edward all the way."

We laughed, as the coffee maker sputtered, announcing it was finished. I reached for the pot when I felt him next to me, nudging me out of the way. "Seriously, let me. You have done this for me now like, how many times? Allow me, for once."

I shivered again, feeling the pull between us at this close proximity. I didn't want to move away because I didn't want the feeling to end, not because I cared less if he poured my coffee, for once.

"May I?" he asked again, when I wouldn't move.

"Oh. Yeah." I stepped back, allowing him to reach for the coffee pot. While he poured two cups, I produced several bottles of creamer and a bowl of sugar from the refrigerator.

"Sugar in the fridge?"

"Yeah, my cat will eat it all otherwise. She has a sweet tooth," I explained.

"Ah." As if on cue knowing we were talking about her, my cat, Sona padded into the kitchen with a loud "*Meow!*" announcing her arrival.

"How is it that a dragon can live with a cat?" Gabriel asked, as she noticed him and cautiously tip-toed to him, smelling his shins daintily.

I shrugged. "I prefer salads," I replied.

"Uh-huh." Surprising to both of us, stranger-shy Sona jumped into his arms. Gabriel managed to catch her in a hug, and she nuzzled her fuzzy cheek against his unshaven chin.

I raised an eyebrow. "Well, that's a good sign."

"What is?" he scratched her in between her ears and she closed her eyes and purred.

"Sona doesn't like people."

"Just dragons?" he asked.

"Not even, every time she sees my brother she hisses and claws at his feet. She ignores my grandfather. Anytime someone comes to the door she yelps and hides," I watched with interest as she relaxed further in his arms and he rubbed her furry head. "All except my friend Kit."

Damn, I was jealous of that cat now.

"Huh...imagine that." With his free hand he poured some vanilla creamer into his coffee and a spoonful of sugar. He took a sip as I fixed my own and we sat down across from each other at the little metal card table and chairs in the kitchen/dining area.

"Tell me more about this magic stuff. So, I can stop dragons from breathing fire. That doesn't exactly sound like big deal," I said.

"Alone it's not," he agreed. "But the fact that you can stop *all* magic with your fire by all mythos that I know of...that is pretty impressive."

"You mean, there's more?" I asked, surprised.

"Oh yeah. Plenty of mythos."

"Mythos?" I repeated, confused.

"Mythological creatures. There's way more of us than you realize. Dragons. Sorcerers. Witches. Fairies."

I let out a low whistle. "Great. What's the difference between sorcerers and witches?"

"Sorcerers are born with their magic, usually hereditary. Witches learn their magic, usually conjured through spells and stuff," he explained.

"And you're a— "

"—sorcerer. Yes, I am."

"Your brother? Is he a sorcerer?" I asked, leaning on the counter top, sipping my coffee casually trying to fully fathom that I was having an actual conversation with someone about sorcerers and *not* talking about *Harry Potter*; it was serious and not fiction.

"He's an oracle. A Seer. He can predict future events, has visions...stuff like that."

"Does he use like, a crystal ball?" I asked, half joking and half serious.

"Well he uses crystals, but a lot of the time the visions just come to him. To ask him specific questions you need Tarot cards and crystals...herbs and stuff. It's pretty complicated. He doesn't do it often because the results are unpredictable at best."

I shook my head trying to comprehend the information. I was picturing in my head some turban wearing guy with a beard, speaking in a low, haunting voice. "So he saw you coming here?"

He nodded, interrupting his cat scratching to reach for the sugar bowl for another spoonful of sugar. Sona let out a disgruntled *mew* but was intrigued, watching him spoon the sugar into the cup, her tail twitching back and forth. "He pictured the entire town, me walking through it, walking into the coffee house."

"Did he see me?"

"No, his visions aren't usually that specific, but they can be if you ask specific questions," he replied.

"Can he tell me what the hell I'm supposed to do now?" I asked dryly.

Gabriel looked up from his coffee and smiled. I smiled myself, his smile, just his very presence was beginning to do odd things to me. I was honestly starting to understand why Emily and Madison were so excited they squealed and irritated everyone else. I felt warm inside, in the spot where my heartbeat starting quickening, and it wasn't due to the coffee. "He may be able to help out with that, but most of it's going to be up to you. Visions always change. No one's path is set. That's what he would tell you."

"Damn."

He laughed. "You wanna see something cool?" Gabriel set his mug down on the counter. "Um, a little help?" he motioned to the sleeping cat in his lap. "I don't want to startle her and have her claw me."

"Yeah." I gingerly reached for the contented cat on his lap, trying to ignore the proximity as I stood nearer to him again. She let out a little crabby noise but she allowed me to set her on a blanket on the reclining chair without too much fuss.

"By the window," he said, reaching for my upper arm and leading me to the tall plate glass window in my living room. I started a bit at the electricity his touch caused, and he pulled away.

"Sorry…"

"It's okay," I said, allowing him to guide me to an empty spot on the floor.

It was cold outside, but he slid open the window anyway, causing a draft that made me shiver. Dragons were rarely cold but it must have been the nerves; they were all on hyper mode.

"Okay, now you can feel…it's cold but not windy, right?" I nodded, and he continued. "Okay, now this might not work at all, but we can try. It depends on you."

"'Kay," was all I said, as he shut his eyes and began to channel…something. Concentrating, he moved his palms across from each other in a circular motion, as if turning a ball that was in his hands, but nothing was there for a few moments.

"Close your eyes," he instructed, and I did.

"Okay, now when you feel it's right, lean forward and blow gently towards my hands. If it works, you'll know." I nodded, didn't dare speak and break his concentration.

I wasn't sure what I was supposed to feel, but I felt the energy level in the room gradually increase, not sure how but I could feel it there like a certain...heaviness. It was lighter than air and yet, it touched every fiber of my being. I could hear a small breeze whistling from outside, felt a slight tickle of cold on my nose.

I leaned closer to him and slowly pursed my lips together and exhaled, gently as he said. I didn't feel it at first but suddenly I felt a gust of wind zipping around me, so cold the hair on my arms stood on end. Or maybe that was the energy.

"Open your eyes," he said softly.

I did, and I could see the white gauze curtains over the window blowing as if from a strong storm outside. It rustled the pages of a magazine on the couch and the papers across the room on my fridge were threatening to fall from the wind. Amazed I looked back towards Gabriel, his wavy hair blowing in the frigid cold, but he was smiling widely.

"You conjured the wind?" I questioned, not sure what I had done.

"I did but you made it stronger," he said, his palms were upright and outstretched, he pulled them in then, willing the air to come with him. It followed his request and was once again contained in the little imaginary ball in his hands. "Do you see it? In the air in here?"

I leaned closer and closer still, squinting my eyes until I saw the tiniest of sparkled specks, twirling around and around like the storms on Jupiter's atmosphere. "The sparkles?"

He nodded. "*That* is you. You breathed on the air, even in your human form and you amplified my magic to nearly three times the strength of what it was. You did that, not me. All I did was grab the air from outside. Eventually when you get more control, you won't even need to use your dragon fire; it'll just happen."

I moved my fingertips to my lips, feeling awed and a new sense of elation. "Can I do it again?" I had to watch this time.

"Of course," he said, and I blew a little harder this time. The wind gusted then throughout the apartment, small speckles of glittery dust danced on the wind around me, blowing through my hair, across my shoulders. It was charged, almost like you could feel lightning impending before a storm. I watched, enchanted as the wind blew photos of my fridge, blew the curtains around like a tornado. Gabriel moved his hands apart and the wind grew stronger still, nearly blowing me over, startling Sona from a sound sleep where she let out a yelp and dashed for cover in the bedroom down the small hall.

Quickly Gabriel pulled his hands together with a clap, and the wind was gone but the charged energized dust fell to the ground slowly, becoming less visible as they fell until they were eventually gone.

I grinned. "Crap, that was *awesome!*"

Gabriel blinked, like he had something in his eye. "Yes, it was. I can't believe, you…" he trailed off, turning away. "You trust me?"

I was taken aback by his question. "What do you mean? I trust you? I mean, I…." I wasn't sure until he asked the question, but something inside told me I did but I couldn't vocalize it just yet.

"You see me as an ally, at least… or else you wouldn't have been able to amplify my magic," he said, befuddled with amazement. "I was figuring you would just extinguish it."

I shrugged, pretending to be nonchalant. "Well, you know…I am a freak, I do freakish things." It was odd though, that I seemed to trust him already as I never trusted anyone but, there was just something about him.

"Don't! Don't *ever* say that again!" With a serious, stern look upon his face, intensity in his eyes he grabbed me firmly by the shoulders. "You are *not* a freak, not by a long shot. You have to stop saying that. Your days of thinking like that are over, do you hear me? If I'm going to be around at all, you have to start seeing yourself as I see you: as a miracle. Not a freak. You are going to do some unique things, but they aren't freakish. You are only made to feel that way by an ignorant society. Do you understand me, Leorah? Do you?"

Feeling stunned, wide eyed I slowly nodded. "Y-yes, I'm sorry, I guess, old habits—" Suddenly my breath was taken away from me as he pulled me closer and pressed his lips against mine, cutting off my words.

My neck and arms went slack, and I used his warm body to support me as I melted into him, his lips entwined with mine and every particle in my body was awake, on fire, charged as he kissed me. My first kiss…*ever*.

He surprised me when he pulled away, looking at everything but me like he was ashamed. "I'm sorry, I didn't mean to do that."

I put a fingertip on his chin to force him to look back at me. "Don't be sorry. Not for that." I smiled.

He smiled back in reply, but there was something conflicting in his eyes.

"Well," he said, standing. "I suppose it's late, I should let you get some sleep."

Refusing to get up, I just sat there stubbornly. "I'm a dragon, I don't need that much sleep. If you leave I'm just going to be up watching TV." I didn't want him to go. For the first time ever, I felt the need to be near someone that wasn't my brother, or grandfather. It felt good when he was around, talking to him made me happy; probably happier than I ever felt. *Ever*.

He sighed. "I have something I need to do, okay?"

I winced. "Oh well, I—" I put a finger to my lips, where he kissed me. I could still feel the pressure, the heat of his lips there. I didn't want the sensation to go away.

"It's not you. I'm just afraid..." he trailed off, heading towards the door.

Quickly, I dashed up to him, reaching for his forearm. "I don't work tomorrow. I have the day off." I wanted to ask if I could see him again, but the way he was acting, something hesitated inside me.

"I will see you later," he said. He opened the door, and paused.

Feeling slighted, I crossed my arms in front of me, fixing my face in an expression of neutrality. I didn't want to show him how I felt. "Well, then. See you." *Pretend we didn't just kiss. Pretend it wasn't amazing!*

He gave me a small smile. Reluctantly, he reached for my hand and put it to his lips. His brown eyes lit up briefly as he said, "Farewell, milady." He let my hand fall to my side then and was gone out the door, the sound of it shutting felt like a weight on my heart.

I stood there blankly, feeling a million things I'd never felt in that very moment that I had never felt before, completely dazed and confused.

"*Meow*?" Sona had emerged from the bedroom. I slid down the wall until I was sitting, pressing my palm against my cheek, nuzzling the spot where he kissed. Sona brought me out of my daze with a lick of her sandpapery feeling tongue on my arm.

I hugged her near me, appreciating the tangibility of her presence. She was here and suddenly, he was not.

"What the hell was *that*?" I whispered to her. She said nothing, as I expected but I had no idea myself.

Chapter 4

Much as I anticipated, I did not sleep well last night. My mind kept playing movies of Gabriel over and over: the electricity I felt when I was near him, the magic we (literally!) made and of course…that kiss. It was *amazing*. Then I began debating; was the kiss amazing because it was my first and only one? Was it actually quite bad and I had nothing to compare it to? Did I kiss him or did he kiss me? I was pretty sure it was he who kissed me so…why all the strange behavior, and tearing out of my apartment like he couldn't get away from me fast enough?

Then there was the realization that, *Holy shit! I was powerful!* If they only knew; all those dragons that taunted me in school, poking fun at me because I didn't have any magic, or specialize in any element like everyone else, and how ridiculous was it that I breathed sparkly mist like Tinkerbell's fairy dust. But what was the point of it all?

So…I could stop and amplify magic, at my very whim. So what? What good was it going to do me now? Perhaps I could go around schools and anytime dragons get too rowdy on the play fields I just exhale and put an end to the incident.

Then there was Gabriel. Was I really going to allow some guy whom I barely knew change his whole life around just because someone decided his destiny a long time ago? And why now? And was he even being truthful? So he had the dragon tattoo. Or, mark, whatever. He had the magic. He could just be a super-hot human who just knows how to do magic. None of that had anything to do with me.

I won't even start about…the kiss.

I lay in bed and stretched my arms over my head, smiling as I thought about it. Why did he freak out like that? Maybe it was just too soon for him. Or…

…maybe he wasn't who he said he was.

I groaned, thinking of the words my grandfather often said to me: "*Leorah, there are good people out there, and bad. Sometimes it's hard to tell who the good ones are from the bad. Sometimes people are going to take advantage of you. Someday someone is going to come along you are going to have to decide if they are worth trusting, and only you can make that decision because you are* more *than you realize. You are special. You'll show them all, one day."*

I pulled the blanket over my head, hoping it would drown out his words as they echoed over and over in my mind. I never thought much of it, just a loving grandfather giving advice to his favorite (okay, *only*) granddaughter. But now I wondered…did he know something? Something I didn't?

I sat up and tossed the covers off of me. It was time to go have a talk with my grandfather. Even if he was just being wise, perhaps he could tell me if he had ever heard anything about this Order…he was old enough, he might remember it and could tell me if what Gabriel said held any truth.

With new resolve I showered, got dressed in a super low cut tank top under a tattered red plaid flannel shirt and blue jeans with holes in them. My parents hated anything but the traditional dragon robes and other such attire—especially human clothes that were anything less than perfect or revealing. I tossed my strawberry hair up in a ponytail and with a quick pat on Sona's head, I grabbed my keys and handbag and sped out in my car down the highway. The closest portal to Anarach was about fifteen miles away, east; about two small towns over.

Along the way I called Kit at her shop to tell her I was going to be gone for a day or so, I wasn't sure. Time moved by more slowly in the dragon realm and just in case I was there longer than expected I wanted to make sure she came in and fed Sona. Thankfully she already had a key from the many times I went home and needed her assistance to care for the cat. Kit was of course panicked but she understood.

"What ever happened with that guy that was in the shop the other day? The cute one with the glasses that freaked you out so much?" she asked, before I could hang up the phone.

"Oh, uh…nothing really. He thought he knew me but turns out he didn't," I lied. Well, it was kind of true, I suppose.

"Oh. Is everything else okay, Leo?" she asked concerned. Out of everyone on Earth (well, the *human* version of Earth), Kit probably knew me the best and could sense something was obviously wrong.

"Yeah…just…well my brother is getting engaged. Some family shit going on…it's a bit…unexpected," I said, settling on an explanation. Wasn't entirely a lie, I was pretty sure when my parents found out they'd go crazy but, that's for my brother to deal with, not me.

"Ah, okay. Well don't worry, take as long as you need. I'll just make Maddy and Em work some more; I'm sure they'll love that," she said with sarcasm. "I'll make sure Sona is taken care of. Oh and I'll light a candle for you at my altar tonight, I hope everything goes well," she said, speaking of her Wiccan altar. Kit was a witch—the non-magical kind, or so I assumed.

"Thanks, Kit," I said, and we said our good-byes and hung up.

It was a colorful, bright autumn day here in Minnesota, and normally I would relish in the scenic drive but today I was too distracted to even care. The road was fairly empty, thankfully, so I could speed without worrying too much about injuring another driver. I was on a damn mission.

The drive seemed like forever although it was only about fifteen minutes, it felt like hours. Finally, I reached the turn-off road—marked with only a wooden stake with an "X" carved on it—and it was another five miles down a bumpy, dirty gravel road which led me through the middle of a corn field and eventually to a handful of trees which gave way to a full blown pine forest.

I couldn't drive any further, so I parked my car underneath a small area that I had dug before during my many times out here, out of brush and bushes and hoped that locking it and keeping it hidden underneath some branches would keep it safe. Thankfully this portal was rarely used; I was pretty sure that I was the only one who had used it in the past year.

Slinging my backpack over my shoulder containing my dragon robes and other essentials you couldn't find in the dragon realm. I shoved my keys in my jeans pocket and made my way to the portal, located about 200 feet away, cloaked by a willow sapling. It was out of place and shouldn't exist in the middle of such a large forest but the average human wouldn't think anything of it. To anyone that would, it would look and feel just like a regular tree. Ah, the wonders of dragon magic!

Before I even reached it, I could feel the energy emanating off the concealed portal. There was a fresh set of heavy boot prints around the portal, whose edges hadn't yet faded with the wind or been trampled by animals or covered by pine needles.

"Huh...wonder who's been through here," I wondered aloud, not giving it much thought. I made a mental note to question the portal guard on the other side. Typically, that information was private but…being the granddaughter of Elder Aleron even though I was a pink dragon freak did have its advantages if it was one of the nicer guards that stood watch on the other side.

I closed my eyes and reached my hands out to the portal, feeling the air around them crackle and hum like static electricity. I felt the electricity around me as the portal opened. It was only mere seconds of a slight blur and something of a breathless, sucking feeling as my world changed from human Earth to the dragon kingdom of Anarach; most specifically the village of Green Knoll where my family currently resided.

I opened my eyes as the rolling green hills spread out before me, as far as the eye could see. As much as I hated the society, the land was breathtaking. Green hills looking like something out of Ireland rolled and met the piercing blue, cloudless sky. Patches of wildflowers in every color and size broke up the landscape. I smiled, and took a deep breath while taking it all in.

"Leorah, good to see you!" a rather bored looking portal guardian spoke. A green dragon named Baron Maxxus looked up from a book he was reading to grin his wide smile at me.

I jumped at the sound of his voice. "Oh, Maxxus…you startled me. I don't know why; I know you're always here. Gets me every time!"

Maxxus chuckled. Sometimes he'd been in his green dragon form when I crossed over but not today; today he opted for his rather attractive human form that resembled a handsome old-world Hollywood actor complete with dignified glamour. He had an electric smile and piercing blue eyes underneath a mass of slightly wavy, rusty-hued dark blonde hair. I'd actually known Maxxus before his position as a guard; he was the dragon my grandfather had sponsored for him to get his Court position so we were previously acquainted. My grandfather thought very highly of him and so, I did too.

"You surprised me, too! It's been weeks since anyone came through on my shift. Nicodemus and I were just complaining about why we were even here…*no one's* come through in ages!" Maxxus spoke with a light, British-sounding accent; very proper but not at all stuffy. A lot of dragons in Anarach had some sort of mild accent depending upon where they grew up (and how angry they were). I had lost most of mine living in Minnesota but it came out now and then.

I let out a chuckle before I remembered the fresh footsteps and the warm portal on the other side. "No one at all? Are you sure?" I asked, raising my eye brow, attempting to read his face for dishonesty. "The portal was charged like it had been used recently."

"Not at all. Believe me, Milady Leorah, I would know if they did. Nic and I have a bet going on the first person to come through on our shift, the other owes a beer. Been *months* since we made that bet, but it makes it interesting," he chuckled, grinning. "I guess he owes me a drink!"

"Huh, that's weird," I mused. "Must have been a magic surge," I said, knowing fully well that a magic surge was a line of bull. Nothing but someone using the portal could cause it to charge like that.

"I really don't know," he said. "I'll ask Nicodemus when I see him again if he noticed anything weird going on. Maybe someone was messing around with it on the other side. I don't know. It'll be awhile though before I can; I took over for him." He shrugged in confusion, but his face was honest so I just let it slide.

I smiled. "That's good, have a beer for me, too." I tossed my backpack on the ground and rummaged through it, pulling out the heavy, bright pink robes and flipping them around my shoulders to block out some of the autumn chill, fastening the emerald and silver clasp at the neck.

"What, no dragon form today?" Maxxus asked, knowing fully well I never shifted. Usually it pissed off my parents that I refused and I liked that but also there wasn't any purpose to it; it wasn't like I could fly.

"Do I ever?" I questioned rhetorically, and he just laughed.

"No, I guess not," he replied. "What brings you here? Usually you avoid this place like the plague."

I shot him a look. "Now now...is it nice to question a Lady on her business?" I admonished kiddingly. Even though it wasn't required—and, certainly not of me—the children of dragons serving on the court were generally given the unofficial, generic title of Milady and Milord...just a formality more than anything to show respect. No one but Maxxus ever referred to me with a special title and I so loved to give him shit for it every damn time.

Maxxus appeared worried for a second, his blue eyes wide before his face fell into a smile. "Ah you almost had me there!"

I grinned widely and winked at him, as I pulled out my cell phone from my front jeans pocket and dialed my brother's number.

"Those things work out here?" Maxxus asked in surprise.

I nodded, as my brother answered. "Hey," I said, when I heard his voice. "Come get me. I'm at the South-side Green Knoll portal as usual. 'Kay?"

"What? Why?" was Braeden's first response.

"Later!" I insisted. "I need to see Grandfather. *Now*. It's an emergency!"

"Are you okay?" My brother was suddenly worried. "I didn't expect to see you here for...months."

"I am not sure. Yes. No! I don't know...it's just...*weird*. Please come get me!" I demanded.

"Okay! It's gonna be awhile...I'm in training right now but I can leave shortly. Are you alone?"

"No, not really...guard Baron Maxxus is here. I can wait with him," I said, looking to Maxxus who nodded eagerly. Probably the most excitement he's had in months. That's sad because besides being pink I'm the most boring dragon ever.

"Okay. Be there soon." He ended the call.

I chuckled as I shoved the phone back in my pocket. "They really need a light rail system or buses here," I kidded.

"What's that?"

"Public transportation," I explained.

"Why? When we can—" he almost said *fly* and then remembered that I couldn't. His cheeks flushed. "Sorry."

I shrugged. "It's okay." I sat down cross-legged in a patch of soft grass near him. I caught his eye and offered a smile.

"So...what's new on Earth lately?" he questioned, trying to make small talk.

"Eh...nothing really." Everything, actually—a new season of shows, some blockbuster movies, a few dozen scandals and even a presidential election but, it wouldn't be anything he would understand or anyone he'd know. "Do you ever get over there?"

He shook his head. "Naw, I have no reason to go over there, really."

"You should visit, sometime. There are a lot of interesting things...like art and museums and plays and— "

"—TV?" he asked hopefully.

I grinned. I pulled out my smartphone and opened up the Netflix app and handed it to him. "There. Pick a show—anything that looks interesting." The service was sketchy out here at times but I knew we were nearby the tower my grandfather—who *loved* electronic gadgets and technology—insisted we had installed. And, not that hardly anyone used it, but it was infused with some sort of silver dragon magic that boosted the signal.

His eyes widened as he awkwardly tried to navigate the small touch screen with his rather large fingertips. "I...had no idea there were this many!"

"Oh that? That's only a handful of them, too," I said with a smirk.

"Wow...." He said, amazed and I laughed. I helped him select the first episode of *Star Trek: The Next Generation* (thankfully, I splurged on the really good data plan!) and we set the phone in between us in the grass. I smiled widely as he picked one of my very favorite shows and we sat basically silent as we watched.

"This is pretty amazing," Maxxus said, in the last few minutes of the episode, his eyes never leaving the little screen. "TV in the palm of your hand. Frickin' awesome."

I snorted. "This coming from a dragon who can fly somersaults in the air and can bend dirt at his will. I think most humans would gladly give up their TV in order to have that."

"Really?"

I laughed. "Well come on, you have a computer and stuff, right? They sell those here now. Even Grandfather has the internet."

"Yeah but...well we greens aren't exactly the most technological dragons...that stuff usually confuses me," he said with a frown. "My sister attempted to teach me how to use her little computer. I ended up snapping it in half." He laughed shortly, a hint of bitterness in his tone. "Well, that was a long time ago, when we actually spoke."

I lifted a brow at his tone and paused, waiting for him to elaborate. When he didn't, I just let it slide. "Well, just find my grandfather. He's patient, he can help you," I said, as the episode ended and we waited for the next one to begin.

"You think he would?"

"Definitely. I know he'd love to see you again."

He smiled. "Thanks. Then maybe I can come to Minnesota and you can show me how to use this...TV net thing?"

I nodded. "Sure."

We continued watching the episode and were about thirty minutes into it when my brother appeared in front of us in his formidable red dragon form, steam exuding from his nose as he snorted with laughter.

"Oh how I wish I had a camera. You two look ridiculous! Two big ol' dragons snuggling together over a little, teensy phone!" Braeden laughed, but in his dragon form it sounded like a mixture of roaring and thunder. A little scary it would be if I wasn't already used to it.

"You're a douche! We're not even in dragon form!" I grabbed a handful of dirt from the ground and tossed it into his face. It was barely a dusting but he inhaled and Maxxus had to quickly throw himself over me to protect me chivalrously from the hot, red flame that my brother sneezed out.

"It's all right, we're just joking!" I insisted as Maxxus released me and blushed as my brother gave him a (pretend) dirty look.

Maxxus chuckled sheepishly. "Sorry; it's been awhile since I dealt with the sibling rivalry."

"Can I ask what you were doing?" Braeden questioned, nodding his massive head at my phone.

I lifted it up to his view. "Um...*Star Trek*...d'uh."

My brother rolled his large, bright green dragon eyes. "You and your human fetishes."

I stuck my tongue out at him playfully. "Bite me, Brae."

Braeden mashed his large jaws at me. "Sure thing, sis. Your human form is nothing more than a swallow for me."

I narrowed my eyes at his challenge. Normally since I felt completely comfortable around my brother, I would have shifted right then and clawed at his snout but—I didn't want to strip down in front of Maxxus. Although most dragons had no shame in their naked, human forms I had lived on Earth long enough to attain some of their modesty. Besides I had to remain in human form to ride my brother's back.

"Leo can we go now? Please? I need to meet up with Kiarra soon."

I took my cue and shoved my phone in the front pocket of my backpack and slung it over my shoulders. "Thanks, Maxxus for hanging out."

"No, thank you...I've been so bored here lately you gave me some entertainment," he replied. "Stay safe, Milady Leorah."

I nodded, and my brother squatted on his haunches to allow me to climb on his back. I grasped the base of his large, thick wing and he raised it to give me some height and I managed to toss my leg over him. I pulled out a satin rope from my bag and he allowed me to place it around his neck for me to hang on to. Normally, a human riding a dragon—especially with a harness—was demeaning but neither of us cared, and I wasn't a real human anyways. It was a common sight to see Braeden and me soaring over the fields of Anarach, so most dragons didn't give it much thought—other than to bear me scorn since I was such an embarrassment of a dragon.

"Thanks for watching out for her," Braeden said, with a respectful nod at Maxxus. He gave a slight bow in response, and my brother started flapping his wings in order to put some air under him to gain flight.

"Oh and Leo, I'll ask my partner about that thing when we change shifts and I'll let you know when you come back through," he yelled after us as we were airborne.

I waved to him in response. "Thank you!" I smiled at him and Maxxus grinned warmly in reply. He bowed his head slightly as Braeden beat his wings and slowly began to take off.

"What is he talking about? What thing?" Braeden called over his shoulder when we were about two stories above the ground. I was a little nervous about being so high up so he normally kept his flying as close to the ground as he could and still have some decent speed.

How ridiculous is that? A dragon—afraid of heights? If it wasn't me I'd facepalm myself in disgust. Sigh.

"Oh," I tried to be dismissive. "I thought someone had gone through before me, the portal was charged already but he assured me no one had come through on his shift anyways."

"Huh. That's weird. Probably someone just messing around with it on the other side. Or maybe some black dragon was performing some kind of magic maintenance on Earth with it," Braeden offered.

I doubted it but I pretended to agree with him anyways. "Yeah, you're probably right. I just wanted to check it out…. just in case."

"Never hurts to check," he said. We spent the rest of the ride to my family's home in silence as I watched the land spread out and change as we rode gracefully over it.

Rolling green hills and pristine blue streams and waterfalls patterned the landscape, occasionally adorned by a random stone or brick house or castle and a handful of large farmlands broke up the bright green. As much as I hated being here—it sure was beautiful.

We came across a large hill that abruptly broke into a chasm below, giving way to a rushing river whose tributaries fed the farms for the next one hundred miles. On the hill sat a rather formidable, white stone castle that had grayed with age and wear. The sparkled flecks in the stone occasionally caught the bright sun and was nearly blinding as we got closer. Our family home was a semi-large stone structure, resembling castles humans would view in photos of medieval Scotland or Britain. The stone was worn, but strong, in hues of light gray. Slight turrets rose out of the walls, indicating chambers that belonged to my parents, or my brother. I was home.

Chapter 5

Braeden gracefully landed just outside of the large wooden door that hung on heavy iron hinges and lowered himself in order to allow me to slide off his back.

"Home sweet home," Braeden quipped sarcastically, knowing fully well how I felt about being there. It was stunning but…it was a home of much ridicule with the exceptions of course being my brother and grandfather. I didn't enjoy being there at all anymore. But I was excited about seeing my grandfather, even despite the stress and confusing of the knowledge I had just gained in the past day. Seeing him always made me feel like a carefree dragon, as he never held my color against me. I was just his granddaughter and he was as proud as any grandpa could be—maybe more so, knowing how much I faced on a daily basis he probably felt like he had to overcompensate.

"Thanks," I said.

He paused as I reached for the circular iron pull to open the door. "You…are going in like that?"

"Like what?" I motioned down towards my grungy shirt and ripped jeans. "Do you think Mother would hate it?"

"Yes," he said simply, trying to stifle a grin.

"Oh. Good." I pulled open the heavy door and entered. I was met by a large great room with two huge stone staircases each leading up to different wings of the fortress. Where the two met on the wall hung a large tapestry of our family's official crest in black, with our individual signatures on the outside of it; even mine—though they refused to allow me to write it in pink, so I settled for red like Braeden. Close enough.

"Leo!" a husky voice called from atop one of the stairs. I beamed as my grandfather stood at the balcony above and opened his arms. "Come here!"

I quickly dashed up the enormous stairs and threw myself into my grandfather's human form. He was just as silver as a human as he was in dragon from; with long, silver hair and beard and gray eyes. All of which just blended in with his traditional silver dragon robes he always wore; with the symbol of Anarach on the back of them in black embroidery.

"What brings you here?" he said, in his husky, friendly tone. "Is everything okay?"

I tossed a pointed look at my brother who still waited downstairs. "I gotta go meet up with Kiarra anyways. See you soon," he said, and had turned out the door, it shut with a loud *thud* behind him.

"I don't know. Maybe?" Seeing my grandfather's concern left me feeling befuddled as I struggled to find the words. "Is...is mother here?"

He shook his head. "No, dearest...they are both at Court for the day. Planning the Harvest/ Mabon Festival for the town, you know. But your mother should return later at some point. My son is spending a couple days there; he is helping the Court try to pass a declaration to deny the Brownies access to our homes." He rolled his eyes at that one. Brownies were tiny little elf like beings that lived in forests and pond areas that liked to play tricks on people. Or dragons. Much like Leprechauns (yes, they existed in certain kingdoms in the dragon realm; just not in Anarach) but smaller, and hard to understand with their simple speech. They didn't have the knack for seeking out treasure like Leprechauns did. Leprechauns caused mayhem because they were always on the hunt for something shiny; Brownies just enjoyed it. They also enjoyed treasures themselves; but sought nothing of value. They enjoyed trash and garbage. I liked them; there is a group of them that live in the gardens behind our home. I'd bring them old socks and empty wrappers and they'd play pranks on my parents for me. The best thing was my parents had *no* idea and it was hilarity to watch them nearly go insane trying to figure out why the tapestry kept falling down or why the door wouldn't stop randomly shutting.

My grandfather scoffed. "Like they'd listen, anyway."

"Right?" I said with a laugh. "Good; glad they'll be gone awhile at least."

My grandfather gestured down a great hallway adorned with antique paintings and some newer photos much to my mother's chagrin that my grandfather insisted upon to his large series of rooms that all belonged to him. We each had our own chambers, even me although mine was now being used for entertaining guests like I hadn't even existed. At least they left up all my cheesy human teenager décor. Though, that was probably more Braeden's insistence then anything. Upon entering my grandfather's chambers, we were met by a large entryway entered into a library and sitting room, with a roaring stone fireplace and several plush chaises and chairs and bookshelves along every wall.

My grandfather carefully rested himself on a red plush chaise and kicked his feet out in front of him. He patiently set his hands in his lap and watched me pace in front of the bookshelf mindlessly.

I was always amazed at my grandfather's book collection; it would put most local libraries to shame. He had everyone from history to human history—all about the crusades, ancient Rome, Celtic Warriors—classic literature like all volumes of Shakespeare, the Christian Bible, Charles Dickens and current stuff like *Twilight* and even *50 Shades of Grey* which made me chuckle insanely. Hard to imagine a centuries-old Elder dragon getting into something like that.

Actually I didn't want to imagine that at all.

"Are you looking for something, dear?" he asked expectantly as I continued to pace, running my fingers along every volume within my reach, tracing my footsteps back towards the earliest parts of his collection which contained ancient texts on dragon history. But I was pretty sure the knowledge wouldn't be found in a book.

I heaved a heavy sigh. "Not sure. Do you have anything on some old Order of Knights that used to like, help out dragons? Maybe even…dragons like me?"

I expected to swivel around and see him there, mouth and eyes agape, surprised that I'd come up with such an off-the-wall topic but instead he just sat there calmly, a finger on his right hand raised to casually scratch his nose, a smug smile slowly spread underneath the wiry silver hair around his mouth.

I crossed my arms stubbornly. "I take that look to mean you know something."

He laughed softly. "Yes, dear. I'm relieved to finally be able to freely talk about this with you."

Now my mouth fell open. "Finally? What do you mean?"

He waved me off dismissively. "First things first. Did you meet someone?"

I nodded. "Yes he called himself a Knight of some pink Order or something like that."

"*Ord na Draconica Dianthus.*" He offered, and I nodded. He smiled even more widely. "Ah, good. What was his name?"

"Gabriel O'Donnell."

At the name he appeared somewhat surprised. "You're sure that was the name? O'Donnell?"

I nodded slowly, suspicious of his reaction. "Yes, I'm sure. Why?"

A moment of silence before he spoke. "Oh, no real reason, just that I'm familiar with the O'Donnells from long ago. Powerful sorcerers. Noble knights for sure," he said, turning to me and forcing a smile to save face.

"So you know about them? And the Order?" I felt my forehead crease involuntarily at his acknowledgment of Gabriel's family.

He cut me off with a wave of his hand. "Soon, m'dear. Soon. I promise I will give you all the answers I can. First I need to ask you a couple things to make absolutely sure of something—it's for your safety. Please, be patient, child."

I started to protest and quickly chided myself. My grandfather always knew best, I knew that. Instead I just kept my mouth closed and then nodded.

"Good, good. So…what was he?" my grandfather questioned carefully.

"What do you mean? He was just a guy," I said, trying to prevent my mind from wandering to that electrifying kiss. I tried to keep my face as stoic as possible, fighting a pleased smile as I tried unsuccessfully not to think about it.

"Sure, sure. But could he do anything….out of the ordinary? Did he show you anything that you found interesting?" my grandfather probed.

"Um…you mean other than the fireballs and the waterballs and the fact that he could summon the wind? And I'm *not* talking about the *farting* kind of wind," I retorted, with a snorting laugh, amused by my own joke. My grandfather didn't seem to catch it and I stopped laughing because of his stoicism. "No, nothing out of the ordinary," I said feeling rather perturbed he didn't find my quip funny.

My grandfather forced a smile. "What did he call himself? Besides this *Knight* title?"

"He called himself a sorcerer."

My grandfather took his turn, narrowing his eyes at me suspiciously. "You're sure?"

I nodded slowly. "Yes. I saw the balls—well the magic ones—and he is definitely a sorcerer."

He turned away from me and, appeared distant and thoughtful; like he was calculating his next words he said to me. I allowed him his silence for a moment and he finally spoke, thankfully because I thought I was going out of my mind, wondering what he was going to say.

"Okay, Leorah what I am about to tell you is dangerous information. I should be killed just knowing it, but since I hold a fairly high authority in the Court—and since there aren't too many other dragons that rival my age or even remember—I am probably one of very few privileged to know this. But first things first. Yes, Leorah, your 'Pink Order' is real. *Ord na Draconica Dianthus* has existed for many years. Gabriel is very much a part of it, in fact I was honored to know his ancestor, Niall ó Domhnaill. Niall was a highly revered knight of the Order; in fact, he was the direct knight of the last known pink dragon."

"Cyril?" I asked with surprise, and he nodded.

"There were other families of course when dragons of your kind were more prevalent but as pink dragons became less common, so did the knights. But the purpose of the Knights was to aid pink dragons in the maintenance of magic, so as it wouldn't be abused by the wrong people or at certain times, to be amplified if need be. It was a tricky task, though…the pink dragon had to be completely clear minded, open to all possibilities and at the very most, fair. Pink dragons were *almost* always neutral. They helped keep the balance between our worlds—human and dragon alike as there are many power-hungry souls out there who seek magic for their own benefit.

"When pink dragons were abundant, their tasks were pretty mundane. Amplifying rain over the land so crops wouldn't die off in a drought. Easing fights. Simple stuff like that. But as time wore on, corruption started spreading out the land. At first it was greedy feudal Lords trying to squeeze out every last bit of wealth from his' people, then it was the people fighting back…then it was…. more…"

"…more?" I prompted him to continue.

My grandfather's brow furrowed, his one hand stroked his long beard thoughtfully. "How do I put it? People started wanting more than just their own land…they wanted *everything*. Land. All the riches of a kingdom… entire civilizations would seek to destroy others…well, you know your history. Rulers would kidnap pink dragons from their neutral service and force them to work for them."

I nodded knowingly. "Gabriel mentioned something about that."

He nodded. "Yes indeed. The downfall of many prosperous civilizations would be thanks to the—albeit forced—aid of dragons. He who captured a pink dragon would almost always be victorious."

"Almost?"

"Well, many knights of the Order sacrificed themselves trying to save their dragons…once captured the pink dragons would try to escape, if they could not, they would kill themselves to prevent further disaster. It was a terrible time to be a dragon. This is eventually why we created our own realm in the sky and we usually stick to it. Humans are passionate beings. When inspired by good, the outcome is generally beautiful. But bad…." My grandfather trailed off and shook his head. "Well, you've seen the outcome I'm sure; watching their news and reading their media.

"The need for pink dragons, once we separated began to wane…eventually to avoid situations like had grown on Earth it seemed evolution took over, and less were being born. But the ones that were…. well most dragons uphold a strict code of conduct and honor. Occasionally an unscrupulous dragon is appointed and to further one's agenda…would seek the help of a pink dragon. This was the case of Cyril." My grandfather heaved a heavy, burdened sigh. "He was once a very, very close friend of mine. We trained for Court together, battled and learned fighting skills."

"Cyril? You mean, Cyril the Crazed? The Mad?" Of course that wasn't his official name, but that's what everyone unofficially called him. Like, most dragons knew me as Leorah the Pathetic; Leorah the Waste…

Good times.

My grandfather smiled slowly. "Yes that was what he was to become but he wasn't that when I knew him…it was rumored that, after time he married and had a drake—a violet drake. She was stillborn and his mate also died, so Cyril was heartbroken. After that he…changed. I didn't know him after he married, but after his daughter and mate passed he wasn't quite the same. Rumor has it he left for one of the Eurasian realms. He met a group of corrupt humans and well…they committed many acts of treason, taking over kingdom after kingdom until finally, he was executed. Supposedly. Unfortunately, the stigma remained, and pink dragons were known to be highly susceptible to mind control and were dangerous. Rarely, a pink dragon like you was born. They were to be immediately surrendered and murdered at the hands of the King or Queen, in case they became like them."

"Murdered? Newborn drakes?" I felt a lump swell in my throat, at the idea of murdering innocent dragons.

"That was what was said although, I never heard of any being born until you. That's what makes you so special," my grandfather said with a smile.

"Special? But...why me? Why now?"

"Clearly, you are here for a reason. I don't know why; I don't know how. But you serve a purpose." He patted at the empty space at the end of his chaise, indicating he wanted me to sit. I did so, dangling my legs over the side and looking at my grandfather earnestly. "I don't know what's about to happen, but I can assume that you were spared, somehow, to help us."

"Help? *How*? And why?" I squeaked out the words as if being choked. "How am I supposed to help? I can't even *fly*!"

There was a glimmer in Grandfather's eyes. "I'm sure that you will figure that out. Somehow. But you will have help."

"Help? Gabriel?" I asked hopefully.

Grandfather shrugged. "I don't know anything for sure, but, I know you're here for a reason. And, you'll not be alone. But, you never were, you know." He beamed, remembering a faraway memory. "Your Grandmother was quite taken with you; I could barely fight you away from her. You know, she left the Court to take care of you full time; she was so afraid something would happen to you. She never left your side."

A smile slowly spread across my face as tears began to sting my eyes. "I miss her. Still. Even though it's been a long time."

"As do I, child. As do I...." He said, with a faraway look in his eyes, his gaze wandering to a portrait of her that had hung in his (well, theirs at one time) chambers near the bed of when she was young. She was a graceful, green dragon the color of springtime flower buds...who had a knack for flowers and plants. This portrait showed her in her elaborate rose garden as she stared off into the land. "But..." my grandfather shook himself out of his daze and turned to me and forced the despair off his face. The years gone by clearly did nothing to rid himself of the pain her sudden death caused. It didn't me, either...but I was fairly young when she passed—only around eight or so—I still remembered her though not clearly as he did. I didn't even know the full details of her passing; I was only told it was due to a magic accident. It sounded odd, but I didn't question it. My grandfather did not like speaking about it and neither did my father (to be fair, he hated discussing anything with me at all).

"She knew you were meant for greatness, too." He said, reaching out and stroking my cheek. "You look like her, you know…in your human form. A lot like her. So very lovely."

I blushed, and grasped my grandfather's hand. "Really?"

"Yes…she was a wonderful dragon, and did many great things. She fought *so* hard for you, called in a great many favors to help you when so many others had been ready to just write you off as hopeless. She saw the great in you, as I do," Grandfather said, giving my hand a squeeze before resting it in his lap. "There is no doubt in my mind you are phenomenal because you and she are very much alike. You know she saved entire villages from ruin? She tended their crops, pulled water out of the depths of the Earth during heavy dry spells to save lives? This was even after we separated and most dragons had just written humanity off and were bitter. Not her. She saw the value in every life and somehow managed to bring it out in everyone. I believe you have that in you, too. That's why I know whatever this task is, you'll be successful. She's watching over us, now, from the Heavens…and she'll be aiding you whenever she can."

I grinned. "I'm glad. Because I'll need her."

He chuckled. "Yes…but just remember I'm here for you too. No matter what, you can always come to me. Okay?"

I nodded. "Okay."

"Good," he said. "So…I'm sure you have questions. Go ahead, ask. I'll try to answer them."

I opened my mouth to speak but quickly stopped, realizing that I had so many but couldn't properly express them. "I don't…know where to begin."

He offered a light smile.

"Why the hell can't I fly?" I blurted. In the human realm it didn't bother me so much but before that, it was probably the bane of my existence—well, that and being *pink* of course.

My grandfather burst out in uproarious laughter.

"And…well all dragons have special little added talents. Red dragons can harness fire. Blue ones can manipulate water…what can *pink* do?" I asked, wrinkling my nose at the word pink.

He smiled. "I'm not for sure—years ago it took a Knight of the Order to fully encompass pink magic but...you know each dragon has a ruling element, yes? To help tie us to the planet? Some say we were given the abilities for us to help protect it, though in recent years it certainly doesn't seem that way anymore. Silver can heal, of course. And harness air, like yellow. White dragons can heal wounds, but they take their power from the air or water as well; like me."

"So why don't pink dragons have a ruling magic?" I questioned.

"Well, I think they do. Earth. Fire. Air. Water. Arcane. And recently, we've started acknowledging another magic; that which exists in every living force. Spirit."

"*Spirit?*" I repeated in disbelief.

"Yes. See, many faiths believe that there is a form of energy in all things. The trees, the water, rocks...even in crafted works by people. Their thoughts, feelings, experiences all go into the making of an object whether it be a book or a metal sword or—well the possibilities are endless. Some say they leave a tiny bit of their soul or life essence in whatever they create, love and cherish...this is called spirit. It's everywhere, in all things. This is why when we die, we are never truly dead—both dragon and human and all other life— because memories, thoughts, experiences—they reside in the brain and become energy. And energy never dies."

I gave him a skeptic glance. "So what does spirit have to do with me? And why am I the only kind of dragon to use it? "

"Ah...well that's how you can amplify the magic of your allies. It's all in your intent. You trust the magic user; you can will the magic to be stronger. You don't, squash it. But I think eventually you will be able to hone in on other abilities as well. We think that dragons like me—silver—and white dragons may also tap into those powers to heal as well; but we're not proficient in it like a pink dragon would be. You should have many skills we do not. But, it explains why no one has spoken of it for years; because everyone's afraid of what you could do to them if we acknowledged its existence."

My fingers drummed on my leg, tingling with excited anticipation. "Like what? Mind control?"

"Maybe. It was said that Cyril could influence decisions of others, sometimes hear their thoughts."

I gasped at the idea. "Really? I was so just joking!"

Grandfather chuckled. "Yes, well, we won't know for sure until you start working but...I think you'll find the answers to a lot of your questions soon, upon working with Gabriel. Who knows, you may even learn how to fly," he said with a wink.

I smiled. It would be nice not to have to depend on "Brother Transportation" while I was here. "I hope so. If Gabriel even chooses to stay."

It was my grandfather's turn to appear skeptic. "Why do you say that? Isn't that his duty?"

"Well, yes I guess so but he has his own life in Canada. A job. A home. His family. How can he just leave that behind?" I didn't mention that I had a moment of bitterness and told him he could go back not really meaning it of course.

"His family? He's married?" Grandfather asked, sounding somewhat surprised.

"No, I mean his dad and his brother and... well whatever else he has. He's not married," I replied. *I don't think so, anyway*, I thought to myself. I really didn't know much about him at all. I felt uneasy with the thought.

"Oh," my grandfather simply said. He seemed to ponder something in silence before he forced a smile and continued to question me. "Is he unhappy about being a knight?"

"I think he's...surprised."

"Yes, I'm sure. Well if he isn't up to the task I suppose we can figure out something else."

I shrugged, feeling slightly depressed at the thought. "I guess..."

"Well..." he rose, and crossed the room, walking slowly and gingerly to a spot on the brick wall where he touched a corner of a brick lightly and a small section of the wall popped open, exposing another bookshelf. Well, that was new.

"You're kidding me..." I said in awe, as he fingered each of the extremely old appearing, worn, tattered books until he landed on the one he sought. He pulled it out, carefully, and handed it to me.

The red leather cover was worn, but still holding on to its contents inside. I carefully opened it and on the first page was a symbol— hand drawn and similar to the one that was on Gabriel's chest. Underneath were words I didn't recognize.

"What is this mean?" I asked my grandfather.

He handed me a second book entitled *Gaelic to English Translation*. "This will help you," he said. "That book you have there is a handwritten, underground document written years ago. I can't tell by who," he gestured towards the book, intending that I should flip through the pages. Carefully. The book was very worn and definitely fragile. "I assumed it was written by the *Ord na* years ago since it was Niall who gave it to me and it was Cyril that gave it to *him*...but I can't be certain about that. But if you look...there are several pages that seem to talk about dragons. Maybe even a pink one like he. Or you."

I didn't notice anything that stood out. A few symbols here, a few pictograms there but admittedly I was too afraid to really touch the book; afraid it would promptly fall apart due to age. When I reached a little more than halfway through the book, though, it became blank. I shrugged. "Well not sure how this will help but, I might show this to him later and see if he recognizes anything about it," I said, "him" meaning Gabriel, of course.

"Please do. I can only assume that Cyril gave it to Niall in hopes that one day it might reach the hands of a pink dragon again," Grandfather said. "Niall was a great man: I'm sure that Gabriel is as well."

I felt my cheeks warm at the thought. Memories of that kiss kept trying to penetrate my thoughts but I quickly shooed them away. Clearly it freaked him out—rightly so. I suppose it would be a daunting thing to be romantically linked to a *dragon*.

"Uh...I have a strange question, actually. Not necessarily about this—" I said, holding up the book he gave me, "—but about...other things."

My grandfather swiveled around and raised his eyebrow. "Oh?"

"Are...is it possible for humans and dragons to be...well..."

He chuckled. "Romantically involved?" he offered.

"Yes." I said quickly, feeling embarrassed asking my grandfather the question.

My grandfather lifted a brow at me and scratched at his chin. "You are having romantic thoughts about Gabriel? You haven't known him very long, have you?"

I bit my lip sheepishly. "No, I haven't. It's probably too early to be thinking that, but..." I groaned at myself at the question I was about to ask, "is it even possible for a human and dragon to...um..."

"Hook up?" Grandfather offered, his tone innocent.

I choked down a surprised laugh and smacked my forehead with my hand. "Oh lord, you did *not* just say that..."

He laughed. "Well, is that what you mean?"

"More or less," I said, with a grimace.

"Yes, Leo…humans and dragons can be romantically involved, and it's perfectly fine," he replied, with a chuckle.

"Oh." That was all I could say. "Well…how does anyone know?"

My grandfather laughed. "Oh, dragons and humans have been knocking boots for years." I snorted at his use of common slang. He smirked, and continued, "It just doesn't happen much now because dragons and humans don't spend much time together anymore. But it's possible, and happens all the time. Well, happened." He gave me a knowing look. "Just…whatever you do be careful."

He raised a brow at me, as he stroked his long, gray beard. "So, do you have…feelings for this sorcerer?"

I felt my face flush with heat. "Oh um, well…I'm not sure. For some reason I just feel drawn to him, you know?"

My grandfather raised his brow. "Is that so?" He sighed, and turned away from me for a moment, clearly in some sort of deep thought.

"Grandfather?" I prompted.

He swiveled back around in his seat and offered a nervous chuckle. "Sorry, it is sort of fretful to imagine my youngest grandchild thinking about a romantic relationship with someone."

"Romantic? Oh, I am not sure—" but I cut myself off, because I honestly *wasn't* sure what I felt. A thought suddenly occurred to me where he was heading with his thought. "Wait—so what if…? What if a human and a dragon got pregnant…? Would that person be a dragon or a human or…?" My head ached at the possibilities. "A monster?"

My grandfather laughed. "Well not a monster any more than a regular dragon. But that person—or dragon—would be born in the form in which it was conceived. So if you were…*mating*," he *ahemed* pointedly, "as human, you would be pregnant as human. It would be human when it was born, but could shift into dragon form at any time and might not be able to shift back. It's very unpredictable, but it has happened before."

My mouth fell open. "Really? Do you know anyone?"

"Not myself personally but I do remember hearing about it happening in a village *eons* ago…the mother didn't survive the childbirth but that was a normal occurrence then. The baby was born human in human form but soon changed shortly after. Dragon DNA always takes control."

"So the person—the mother—was human? And the father a dragon?"

He nodded. "I am not sure what would happen in your case, but I know you'd be strong enough to handle it. But...with what may await you I *highly* urge you not to let that happen, okay?"

I nodded quickly. "Yes, Grandfather...definitely. I don't even know how I feel I mean...he left in a hurry the last time I saw him. I wasn't even sure if he was telling the truth, honestly. It sounded so unbelievable! Me? Something special? Please!"

My grandfather smiled. "Oh I always knew you were special. Somehow, you were saved in a world where your kind is discarded. The fates chose to save you. I have no doubt that whatever lies ahead you will succeed. But you will need help."

I sighed slowly, feeling weighted by the burden.

"Oh, come now...I believe in you, and I believe that whatever it is, you'll be just fine. Just...trust in your allies." My grandfather reached over to pat me comfortingly on the shoulder. "You'll be fine."

I forced a smile. "If you say so..." I trailed off, unconvinced. I glanced down at the book one more time and traced the embossed design on the cover...a part of my mind wandered, and I was sort of imagining tracing the tattoos on Gabriel's chest instead of this book, when my reverie was interrupted by the sound of the large door to the entryway of our home opening and shutting, rather loudly (couldn't be helped—it was large and heavy).

The smiles fell off our faces and my grandfather nodded towards the ancient book. "Keep that safe. Don't let anyone but Gabriel see it; or whomever you learn you can trust, later. But no one in this house and *certainly* not your mother or father. Possession of this book is punishable by torture to whoever has it, and death to whoever owns it. If you value my life, please—" he pointed towards my backpack that I had tossed carelessly on the floor near the opening to his chambers. Quickly I scampered across the floor for it and quickly sealed it with a zip into the main pocket, covering it with the sweatshirt and other minute possessions I bothered to bring with me.

"Oh, and Leo," he said. "Please, just be careful with relationships and what not. Sometimes they just pull you in and before you know it, you're lost. Don't let that happen to you."

I squished my eyes, giving him a grimace. "I don't think we're at that point."

He nodded quickly. "Good, good." Another noise from downstairs and we paused a minute listening for voices.

"Think it's Mother and Father?" Usually when they came back from Court, my father, Saladin, came to Grandfather's chambers to regale the day's topics. When no one came after a few beats, I figured it was safe.

"What are you going to do now?" Grandfather asked. "You going back now?" He sounded a little disappointed and saddened.

I had planned on it—time did move slower here than on Earth but seeing the lonely look on my grandfather's face, I softened my resolve and decided to stay. "Well, no, I can stay for a while. Anything special you want to do?"

He beamed. "Well…I am confused by this new Book-Face thing."

I stifled a laugh. "You mean *Facebook*? You want to join Facebook? Do dragons even do that?"

He shrugged. "This dragon wants to. I hear they have some ridiculously great time wasting games on there. You can grow your own crops and farm them!"

"Don't you do that for real?" I said in between giggles.

"Well yes, but this way I don't have to sit in the hot sun. Help me get on?"

"Oh Grandfather, you never cease to amaze me," I said, leaning over and giving him a kiss on the cheek. "I suppose I better go show myself to Mother and get the ridicule over with."

He agreed. "You'd better or else it'll be ten times worse when she sees you in your chambers wearing your 'tattered garments' and catch her by surprise."

"Oh, I'd hate to do that," I said dryly, but I grumbled, slowly rising and perching the backpack next to Grandfather's chaise for safekeeping. "I'll be right back," I said reluctantly.

Sullenly, I tried not to stomp my feet unhappily at the thought of meeting up with my parents; either one would be equally painful. I did *not* feel like listening to their crap tonight.

"Mother?" I called when I reached the foyer area. "Father?" My voice echoed and bounced across the room, off the brick walls. Silence.

"Hmm…" I said under my breath, stomping down the hard stairs. "Braeden?"

The next sound I heard was most unexpected: a piercing shriek.
I jumped about three feet in the air and stepped back from the stranger in our doorway.

Chapter 6

"Oh my gods, I am so sorry!" A pretty young woman stood in the foyer who was listening to something on a pair of earbuds and tapping into her fancy phone. She reached out and steadied me as I attempted to regain my footing after being startled.

"Who the hell are you?" I demanded, finally composing myself, narrowing my eyes at her.

She held out her hand. "I'm Kiarra. You must be Leorah. Oh I'm so glad I caught you before you left!"

I took her hand and shook it firmly. "Really now?"

She nodded. "Brae has told me so much about you, I'm glad to finally meet you!"

"He told you about me...and you're glad to meet me." I crossed my arms over my chest and narrowed my eyes at her. "Really? And why's that? You eager to meet the freak dragon he has for a sister?"

Kiarra seemed momentarily taken aback by my comment, but she brushed it off and smiled widely. "Oh that must be that sarcasm he told me so much about. He said you were absolutely hysterical!" She laughed, her musical voice seemed to dance off the walls.

"Uh-huh..." I said, rolling my eyes. I didn't know why I was so surly with this girl. I mean, I had just met her. But she caught me off guard and I hadn't had enough time to work up enough patience to deal with the notion of someone taking away my brother (still worried me no matter what he said) and what chippie had possibly caught his eye this time. In the past, he didn't exactly have the greatest taste when it came to females. At least, those we knew about. They were either dumb, dumber or just plain stupid. Like people, some dragons weren't all that smart.

"Oh, I'm sorry...I bet this is all really weird to you, huh? Your brother and me?" she said, sympathetically, a look of pity on her pretty face.

Reluctantly, I had to admit it: Kiarra was quite beautiful in her human form at least. Long straight black hair, light cocoa skin and deep brown eyes. Her face was heart-shaped and friendly; her full lips seemed to be in a permanent smile from the little I'd seen her so far.

"That's the understatement of the century," I retorted dryly.

"Aw, yeah that's what I thought. But I assure you, I do love your brother and I'm not taking him away. That's why I agreed to meet you in the human realm but I just talked to your brother and he mentioned you were here for a visit, well, forgive me but I couldn't help it—I just had to come see you." She said that last part like she was actually excited.

"Why so eager to meet me?" I asked skeptically.

"Well because I've met the rest of your family, silly. Braeden talks about you non-stop, more than anyone else and you were the only one I had yet to meet. Of course I'm excited to meet you!"

I fixed my sour face into an even more skeptic, sour expression. "Excited? Excited to meet the freak dragon in town?"

She laughed. "Freak? What makes you say that?"

I raised my eyebrows. I couldn't decide if she was just being nice or if she truly didn't know. "Um, hello? Freaky *pink* dragon here! Can't fly! Always ridiculed, never liked! Hello?" I pointed at myself.

"Oh that," she waved me off with a gesture and a big grin. "I don't listen to what people say, I hear a lot of things and meet a lot of interesting people working where I do. Nothing phases me."

I stared at her blankly. Interesting people...in the Court? Court was anything but interesting....

Surely she had to be lying. "A pink dragon doesn't faze you? You never heard of Cyril the Mad?"

If I didn't know better, I would have thought she winced at my remark. But I couldn't tell because she was smiling brightly and laughing. "Oh seriously...you can't be any worse than some red dragons I deal with. Really? Those guys are weird." She gave a scoff, both of us knowing fully well that my brother was a red dragon and they were prone to having "fiery" tempers.

My crabby resolve softened. "Yes, yes they are. One very much in particular."

She giggled. "Yes. And if you can put up with him growing up, you have to be okay because honestly, he's a handful."

I chortled. "You have no idea."

I caught a glimmer in her eye. "Oh I'm beginning to really. I hoped you'd help me handle him when he gets out of control."

Against my better judgment and resolve that I wanted to remain eternally surly towards her, I found myself softening to her. Perhaps I could like her.

Give her a chance, you don't know her, quit being a bitch, I thought to myself.

"Well, maybe. But that would require too much time and I have a job back home. And a cat."

"Oh a cat!" She squealed. "I've always wanted to see one of those! Is he cute?"

"She. And yes she's adorable. You like cats?" I asked surprised. Most dragons just viewed them and other house pets as a waste of time. Anything that couldn't be eaten was just a burden.

She nodded. "Well, from what I see in books and stuff. Never actually seen one."

"Well you'll have to come Earthside with Braeden sometime. Although, Sona hates him."

"Smart cat."

I snorted. "Yeah, probably." There was an awkward pause then, and I started shuffling my feet and examining my nails; I'd just noticed they were getting a little long.

She spoke first. She heaved a sigh and said, "So...this must be kind of weird for you, huh?"

"What's that?" I asked, pretending to be in the dark. Which part was weird? The part where my only brother was getting engaged after just a few months? The part where someone wasn't instantly offended by my presence?

"Well...your brother and I. He told me how close you guys were, and how responsible he feels for you because of all the...ridicule you've faced." Kiarra gave me a sympathetic gaze.

I smiled slowly, a skeptic smile. "He told you about some of that?"

She nodded. Reaching out her hand, she tenderly squeezed my upper arm in a gesture of compassion. "Like that day at school when all those dragons were breathing fire at you," she shook her head. "A dragon breathing fire at another unprovoked? That's just messed up."

I started to nod when I suddenly recalled the incident, and the new information I came across upon talking about it with Gabriel. "What did Braeden tell you about that, exactly?"

She shrugged. "Oh I don't know, just one of the many times dragons have come after you for who you are. They were calling you Stinker or—"

"—Tinkerbell," I corrected.

She chuckled. "Tinkerbell. Whatever that means. Then Lorusto started breathing fire and you got freaked out and did your sparkly thing."

"Sparkly thing...you know about that?" Most dragons knew I couldn't breathe fire, but most did *not* know about my fairy dust.... *thing* because they frankly didn't pay close enough attention.

"Well...yeah. Should he not have? Oh no, I probably shouldn't have said anything, I don't want to get him in trouble for— " I waved her off with a hand gesture.

"Forget about it," I said, dismissing her. "It's not a big deal. I won't tell him you told me." I forced a smile. "After all, we're going to be family right?" I was trying to hide the dryness from my tone, something about this conversation was sending up red flags and warning lights in my brain, but I didn't want to appear suspicious and make my brother mad.

I must have been hiding it pretty well, because Kiarra got all teary-eyed and weepy. Her lower lip trembled and she threw her arms around me in a one-sided hug. Human or dragon, I was not a hugger at all so I just stood there, ramrod straight, eyes bugged out as she gushed.

"Oh, Leorah...what a sweet thing to say! I'm so sorry everyone has been so mean to you, I know it must have been hard but I just have a great feeling we're going to be great friends! Your brother has so many great things to say about you and the fact that you want to consider me family, well..." she trailed off into a cacophony of loud sniffling and sobbing, crying into my shoulder. I would care more if I was wearing one of my favorite plaid flannel shirts but this was one I wore just to piss off my parents. The grubbier it got, the better.

I reached up and gave her a tentative pat on the back. "There, there...I'm sure it will be just...*great*." I knew some of the sand in my dry tone squeezed through on that last word, but if she noticed I'll never know as we were interrupted just then.

"Do I have to separate you two?" Braeden asked suspiciously.

Oh, I hope so, I thought, but actually said nothing.

Still blubbering, Kiarra (*thankfully!*) pulled away, wiping her nose on the sleeve of her buttoned up, blue silk blouse. "Oh, I just had the best conversation with your sister! She's just as lovely as you said!" She threw her arms around my brother and kissed his cheek.

I winced, shocked at the open display of affection. Dragons were not known for *affection* and such acts were usually frowned upon. Kiarra apparently was different and didn't care.

Braeden allowed it and put his hands on her shoulders and pushed her to arm's length as he eyed her simpering. He cocked an eyebrow over her shoulder at me. "My sister? Lovely? Are we talking about the same dragon?"

I stuck my tongue out at him and made a bitter face. Kiarra let out a high-pitched giggle and gave him a playful shove. "Oh Brae, stop it!"

He chuckled and gave her a small hug. "Well, I'm glad no one's killing anyone, that's a good sign. Leo, you need a lift back to the portal or are you sticking around awhile?"

"I—umm, promised Grandfather I would help set up his Facebook. He's waiting on me so…I better go." Awkwardly, I forced a cheesy smile and gave Kiarra and my brother a little wave and I turned to walk up the large staircase to my grandfather.

Before I could take a step Kiarra wrapped her arms around me. "It's so good to meet you Leo, really!" she squealed.

"Leorah." I corrected. Only family and friends called me Leo…I didn't know her yet and frankly was a little weirded out by her cheerful disposition towards me.

I pulled away, offered her another forced smile and turned to go up the stairs.

I heard my brother mumble something to her and the large door opened and closed again. I assumed they left but I felt a hand on my shoulder as I reached the top of the stairs.

"So?" he prompted, like he was waiting for some kind of reaction from me.

"So, what? You *told* her about Lorusto trying to *barbecue* me at school?" I asked, outraged.

Braeden paused in his tracks and frowned sheepishly. "Well yes, I'm sorry. Was I not supposed to? I mean a lot already know about it so it was just natural that she would ask about it, don't you think?"

"She *asked* about it?" I asked incredulously. "What did you say?"

"Just the truth; what happened. You were getting taunted and this big black bully dragon started to breathe fire at you, you panicked

80

and did your sparkly thing, and it must have freaked him out and he stopped and that was it."

I looked at him with wide eyes. "That's it?" I shook my head. Normally, I wouldn't have thought too much of it. Certainly lots of dragons spread nasty rumors about me; about that day. There were only about twenty-five dragons there, counting Professors and since I was a mockery of the dragon community I was used to hearing about my shortcomings nearly every day.

But the fact that according to my grandfather there was something big coming (because otherwise why would I be here, apparently), something I was supposed to be careful of *and* the fact that according to Gabriel that was the *first* time I performed my magic in public, I was on high alert now.

Coupled with the fact that she and my brother's union was a bit unorthodox and sudden...well, there was just something that didn't sit right with me. Add in the fact that she was overly friendly-- perhaps she was just that way normally, but even friendly dragons had a tendency to be stand-offish with me, usually preferring to ignore me. Hardly anyone was ever eager to meet me. Even Maxxus and a handful of other dragons were *not* keen on dealing with me at first but apparently some of them grew to like or tolerate me. I'd been going through that portal now for a couple years, regularly over the past year or so and Nicodemus still barely uttered more than a polite word to me, recognizing only that I was an Elder silver dragon's granddaughter and I earned some respect for that reason alone.

So either she was hiding something, was really stupid (blue dragons were not known for their stupidity) or foolishness or had some odd interest in me.

"Leo, what's the big deal? She just wants to get to know you. What's the problem?" my brother asked, hushed with a shrug.

I narrowed my eyes. "Because *no one* wants to know me—at least not anyone with wings." I retorted. I spun on my heels and stormed up the steps. "Don't spill anymore secrets, okay? I'm going to go help my grandfather waste time on Facebook. Later."

"Leo—" he called after but I had already walked away.

I found my grandfather in his chambers, in his electronics room. For an old dragon, he sure loved new gadgets; he had an entire room devoted to them located just off his library. It always made me chuckle walking through the old-fashioned brick and mortar castle that could have been standing in medieval times on earth and enter a room that looked like something out of NASA's mission control. Walls of speakers, a couple big flat screened TVs, a desk with a computer sprawl and printers and—well, you name it.

Currently my grandfather was sitting before his computer, the internet turned on the *World of Warcraft* homepage and he was mumbling something crabbily under his breath. Just because he liked computers and had gadgets and technology didn't mean he could use it well.

"Really? You want to play *WoW*?" I asked, referring to it as the acronym it was known for and stifling a laugh.

He pulled a pair of headphones off his ears and swiveled in his large leather chair to face me. He laughed. "Oh well, I heard you talk about it enough. Figured I should try it right? There are dragons you said?"

"Yes, Grandfather there are…. but you don't play dragons, you ride on them," I explained.

He frowned and looked disgusted. "Oh…well perhaps not for me then."

"You can be a gnome or an elf or a werewolf type thing. And you don't have to ride the dragons," I offered, knowing the werewolf bit would get him.

"Werewolf you say? No vampires?"

I shook my head. "Undead is the closest but it's more like a zombie."

"Oh! That sounds like fun!"

"You get to eat corpses, it's a good time," I said sarcastically.

"Hmm…well perhaps later," he said, with a chuckle, taking his mouse and awkwardly managing to close the window by clicking shakily on the 'x' in the corner. "Now what's troubling you?"

I smiled sheepishly. "What do you mean?"

He just gave me a look that saw right through me and I held up my hands in defeat.

"Okay…okay. What do you think of Kiarra?"

"Ah…so that was your brother's betrothed downstairs, not your parents?"

I nodded. "She is…interesting."

He chortled shortly. "That's an understatement. Probably one of the strangest dragons I have ever met, and I'm an Elder for Pete's sake. I've met some strange dragons."

"Really?" Perhaps I was right to be suspicious.

"Yes. But strange doesn't necessarily mean *bad*. She's passionate and very kind. Your parents like her very much, despite her unorthodox ways which is saying something."

"Really." Great, so their future daughter in law is more likable than their actual daughter. Fabulous. Something to be proud of.

"Why do you ask? Is something bothering you?"

"Well, I was just thinking of what you said. About feeling that there are difficulties ahead for me but not knowing what they are. There's something off-putting about her, I just can't put my fingers on what."

"Now that's a hypocritical attitude coming from you, Leorah dear," he said with a scolding tone.

"No—not like that. I mean…knowing what I know about myself. Why was she so eager to meet me? She was friendly—no one is friendly with me. At least not at first and hell most never are. She knows about the incident in the yard long ago with the fire-breathing…she almost seemed like she was asking about my magic."

My grandfather raised his brow. "How can you tell?"

I shrugged. "I think she's been drilling Braeden for information; he said she was asking him questions about me, and she was so interested in meeting me. That's a bit…bizarre even for a bizarre dragon. The engagement is rather sudden; wouldn't you say?"

My grandfather tried not to cringe. "That's the *unorthodox* part, yes?"

I nodded in agreement.

"So what do you think she could want from you?"

"I don't know…I mean of course no one but Gabriel and perhaps you know my magic—hell I don't really even know my magic! She was asking about the sparkle-thing. What it felt like, how the other dragon responded…that to me just seems a little odd. Most dragons go ahead making fun of me and calling me Tinkerbell when they hear about my fairy dust breath. No one asks anything about it because no one bothers to care."

"Hmmm…yes given the new light of ways you've been shown I can see why that would be disconcerting. But perhaps you're just being a little overcautious and jumpy now? Maybe?"

"Maybe but that's why I was asking you. I can't trust my judgment now but as always; I can trust yours."

My grandfather heaved a sigh. "Yes, a dilemma indeed. Faced with so much unknown. Truthfully, Leo...she hasn't given me any reason to believe she is up to anything out of the ordinary. In fact, I've only spoken to her personally a handful of times, she was interested in hearing about my time spent with Cyril long ago. I was so young then, I can barely remember but I managed to tell her a few things. I really only met him as he was in his last days of sanity, and then he was quarantined until his execution. Or whatever."

"Hmm...." I tapped my fingers on my chin in thought. "So I am not the only pink dragon she's interested in hearing about, huh?"

"There's really nothing unusual about that. I get asked about Cyril all the time. Everyone is interested in hearing about him; there are very few dragons out there who have any memory of him at all, the rest is hearsay. It's like telling ghost stories or discussing urban myths: everyone hears things and everyone is interested to hear if it's true."

"Yeah, but does anyone ever ask you about me?" I challenged.

My grandfather thought back. "No, very rarely. Only if your name comes up for some other reason, the politest of dragons will address you as *Granddaughter* and ask if you are well. That's the extent."

I shook my head. "I don't know. There's just a lot about it that is strange."

He chuckled. "Yes, my dear child it is strange. There is little about it that is normal. I think her interest is just pure curiosity and wanting to fit in with the family. Her parents aren't the warmest of dragons and perhaps she's just reaching out."

"To me, of all people?" I was incredulous at the notion.

"I don't know what to tell you, Leo. I think she seems like a wise, intelligent dragon but yes she's a little strange. Personally I think she reads too many books and watches too much TV because she enjoys conducting life as humans do—you know, getting excited about dresses and weddings, formal engagements and parties—I think it's just a silly innocent fun. Lots of dragons are very into learning about humanity, even if they don't want to be a part of it." My grandfather patted at another chair next to him, urging me to sit down. "If I think there is something dangerous about her, I will tell you. For now, just keep your guard up, always. I don't think anything is wrong with her, but well...you're the spirit dragon, you may have better instincts about this than I. I will keep my eyes peeled for you, if that will make you feel better. Okay?"

I sighed and reluctantly gave him a grin. He patted the chair again when I hadn't budged and this time I laughed and sat down.

He leaned over to put a worn palm on each side of my face and looked deep into my eyes with his gray ones, sharp and bright for such an ancient soul. "You, my dear Leorah, I will always watch out for you and I will do everything I can to keep you from harm. Okay?"

I melted under his words. My frown softened into a grin, and I reached up to place my hands over his and gave them a light squeeze. "Okay, Grandfather." His words relieved me for now. I clapped my hands together, determined to get the taste of suspicion out of my mouth and pointed towards his computer screen.

"Facebook huh? Still wanna do it?"

My grandfather smiled wide like a child being handed a plateful of cake to eat. "Oh good, I'm excited!" He turned to his screen and his expression went blank. "Where do I go now?"

I laughed and leaned over him to type the correct address and move the mouse around for him. He clapped excitedly. He really was one of a kind.

Awhile later my grandfather was content with his 'profile' and was now giggling along with his 'farming' on whatever stupid game he was playing now and even though I kept trying to inch out the door he insisted that I stay for a while in case he needed my help. So far, he hadn't but I think he just wanted the company. Things at the Court were pretty slow right now, he had told me, and there was little need for Elder expertise. Supposedly that's what he'd been told. He assumed, though, that everyone just thought he was getting too old and needed a 'rest'. He'd had to mediate a weather issue. One blue dragon was using her magic to over water her potato crops, and it was blocking another yellow dragon from the sun. The combined magic ended up in a massive thunderstorm that damaged several others' fields and there was…chaos. Dragons, not surprisingly have nasty tempers. Including my grandfather who used his light magic to level both their fields—the yellow and blue dragons' respectively—calling them "Impudent children that need to be taught a lesson." He assumed the King and Queen were having him take it easier from his Court duties for a bit until the whole debacle could be forgotten.

So I remained for a while to help alleviate my grandfather's boredom; I had told Kit that I'd more than likely be gone a couple of days, anyway. I sat now, cross-legged "Indian" style atop my grandfather's red velvet plush bed, leaning over one of the vintage *TV Guide* magazines he hoarded by the truck load. He, like me, had a certain interest in human culture and TV of course was a good representation on that. This issue was from the 1960s and it was discussing the new sci-fi show that was all the rage: *Star Trek*. Of course. In the middle of my page flipping I grabbed my phone from beside me on the bed to check the time: nearly midnight in Minnesota on Earth. I wrinkled my nose and tossed it back down, hoping it was accurate. Since time moved differently somehow in Anarach I had no way to be sure if it was. For a while it would be then all of a sudden jump ahead a day or two. Cell towers obviously had a hard time reaching here, even with the towers my grandfather had put in.

"*Aleron*?" came a voice from on the other side of the door, followed by a series of three firm, loud knocks.

I tried to—rather unsuccessfully—to stifle an irritated groan as my mother pushed open the door and entered the bedchambers.

Normally in her dragon form she was a rather plain, unassuming yellow color but as a human she was severe and harsh in appearance. But, maybe she wasn't really that bad. Perhaps I was biased by my disgust for her, though. It was entirely mutual.

Her blue eyes fell on me and she didn't even bother to hide her scorn. "Oh, you *are* here. I didn't think you would be; it's been too soon between visits. I think we last saw you...six months ago?" My mother, Miradoste, didn't hide her displeasure with me in her surly expression. She was unassumingly beautiful with long, straight, straw-colored hair and light blue eyes that upturned slightly at the corners in an almond-like shape. Her eyebrows were formed in a permanent sneer, starting at the bridge of her nose and raising so slightly as they grew outward. They almost looked manicured that way but, Miradoste believed that vanity was for humans so, they most certainly were not. Her mouth was angular with a severe Cupid's bow on her top lip making her appear to scowl constantly. If you looked up Resting Bitch Face in the dictionary, there should be a picture of my mother in her human form in the entry. But, she had a classic Scarlett O'Hara type glamour that was enduring—to everyone else. To me, she was just a royal bitch.

"Wonderful to see you too, Mother *dear*," I sneered, offering her a sickly sweet smile.

"Miradoste, we had no idea you were home," My grandfather added.

She scoffed. "Oh come off it. Normally I wouldn't care, but you have a friend here that's bothering our nightly meal. He assured me you were here and... I guess you are."

"Friend?" I raised a brow. I didn't have any friends here.

"Yes, I know. Shocking, isn't it? It's that...invalid green fellow...Maxer or Max," she said, with a large roll of her eyes.

"*Maxxus*," I corrected. "And he's not just my friend but Grandfather's protégé, remember?" I glanced at Grandfather whose expression was overall blank, watching my mother speak. He forced a smile then before he spoke.

"Yes, Maxxus. And I'll ask you kindly to not refer to him as an invalid. He's just as capable of making magic as any other dragon, you know. It just took a bit more effort," he explained.

My mother let out a groan of disdain. "Yes yes yes, I know. Good thing the Guard doesn't require magic proficiency; he's lucky you vouched for him so he could attain that position."

My grandfather, who had endless patience, did not enjoy anyone speaking ill of anyone who couldn't help who they were. He stroked his beard and spoke, very calmly and with purpose. "Maxxus earned that position because he is good at what he does. My helping him or not does not matter; every dragon that tries for a position in the court must be sponsored by another, and you know that, before they can be accepted. But he wouldn't have gotten that position, regardless, if he couldn't do the job."

My mother heaved an irritated sigh. "Whatever. Leorah, please tend to him rather quickly, so the rest of your family can get to their dinner in peace, shall we? He's in the foyer." She turned on her heels so quickly, her draped blue robes *thwacked* lightly against the door frame as she left.

My grandfather snorted at her departure. "Thank you, my dear for calling us for dinner!" He called after her and we exchanged a laugh and a snort. "Why would Maxxus be here for you?"

I shrugged. "Not sure. I had asked him a question but it's nothing that couldn't have waited until tomorrow." I slid off the side of the bed and my bare feet hit the cold, stone floor with a slight smack. "Yeouch, you need a rug Gramps!"

He chuckled. "I'll put that on the agenda. Right after the dinner we weren't invited to."

We chatted on the way to the foyer and met Maxxus as he stood at the bottom of the stairs, awaiting our arrival. "Elder," he said, offering a slight bow of his head upon seeing my grandfather.

My grandfather clapped him on the shoulder and offered him a wide smile. "Maxxus, so good to see you. Guard treating you well, I gather?"

He nodded. "Oh yes. It's a very good job. Just a little slow right now," he added with a slight laugh, turning to me. "That's why I'm here; I hope you can help me."

I shrugged. "I'll see what I can do, I think."

My grandfather smiled and patted us both on the back before taking his leave. "I hope you'll join us for dinner, Baron Maxxus!" he called back, as he made his way to the dining area off the hallway to the west. He said this loudly enough, knowing his voice would echo down the corridor and irritate my family. I snickered, faintly hearing a groan in reply from the dining area.

I suppressed a laugh and turned to Maxxus. "What can I help you with?"

He half-smiled, rather sheepishly. "Um, your phone. I was hoping you could help me get one."

I raised a brow at him. "Really? You want a phone?" As I said earlier, most dragons had no use for technology so this was surprising.

"Yes. One like yours that plays the...plays the shows," he said.

I chuckled. "Ah yes. Well, I think I can help you with that." I motioned for him to follow me up the stairs. He had to be careful in his step to not surpass me up the stairs with his long legs and once again I felt inadequate in my unusual form.

Maxxus miss-stepped and actually bumped into my back while I reached the top stair; he had to take a step back to avoid clobbering me. "Oh, I'm sorry!" he exclaimed, grabbing my waist with his large hands and righting me again before I could stumble backwards.

I turned to look over my shoulder at him and suddenly felt dizzy as my vision blurred. I saw nothing but white, and a hazy pair of ocean blue eyes. Just as soon as I spaced out, I came back to reality, shaking myself slightly.

"Are you okay?" he questioned, with concern in his eyes. My gaze lingered on them momentarily, suddenly and strangely dazed again. But my mouth turned up slightly upon seeing his eyes clearly. "You have...very nice eyes."

Maxxus appeared affronted, a slight flush washing over his high cheekbones. "Thanks," he just said, biting his lip. "You sure you are okay?" He held his hands on my sides for a bit longer than was permissible, probably assuming I'd fall again so I said, pointedly, "I'm good now."

He quickly pulled his hands away, blushing. "Oh sorry. I just...was afraid you were going to fall."

I waved him off. "It's okay. It's just...stress I suppose." We exchanged a knowing glance; we'd exchanged stories of familial strife before many times at the portal.

"I totally understand."

I nodded down the hallway. "This way."

"To your chambers?" he asked hesitantly.

"Yeah. Why, is that weird?" I asked, eyeing him oddly.

"No not really. I mean, it's always weird being in a girl's room," he said with an embarrassed chuckle.

I laughed. "Surely you've been in plenty of girls' rooms." I scanned his broad shouldered, tall form as he ran his hands through his wavy ginger hair, trying to get the front to stick behind his ears. "Strapping thing like you? Surely been in *a lot* of girls' rooms."

He laughed shortly. "Not even close."

"Really? I guess these dragons over here are more stupid than I thought." I left it at that and led him down the tapestry-covered hallway to my room.

You could tell it was my room because I had painted the door in all rainbow colors. My mother had tried to paint over it but, I had used spelled paint, given to me by the Brownies in the forest. Where they acquired it—I had no idea, and I didn't ask. All I know is it drove my mother nuts that she could not properly cover the door. The Brownies and I appreciated a good, spiteful prank.

"You'll have to excuse the décor. I have it this way to really piss off my parents," I said with a mischievous look.

Maxxus chuckled as I pushed open the door, seeing my array of multi-colored walls, 1990s teen celebrity, movie and band posters. Of course, I had the smallest room of anyone in the home but I didn't mind. Less to clean. I motioned for him to take a sit on the ratty, orange and lime green 1970s patterned chair next to my bed which had a handmade quilt in red, white and blue; Americana style complete with stars and stripes. My entire bedroom clashed like a set of cymbals right in your ear and ten times as annoying.

Across the room was an armoire where I hid my electronic gadgets. It was black, that I'd graffiti-d popular, irritating 90s slang all over it like *"whatever"* and *"as if!"*. Two purple dyed ropes were shoved into holes where there had once been doorknob hardware and I yanked on them to open the over-stuffed piece of furniture.

I could just about hear Maxxus' inquisition as to the contents of the armoire as I rummaged through it; my treasured belongings covered with more remnants of the 90s—JNCO elephant leg pants, flared jeans, hoards of flannel shirts, square-necked spaghetti-strap tank tops and platform sandals. I shoved my head in and pulled and pushed the contents around before finally coming across a small, fire-proof safe. I lifted it out, shoving everything back in and quickly pushing the doors shut before everything could collapse back out.

"What?" I questioned Maxxus' intrigued raise of one eyebrow.

He roared with laughter, reaching over to finger the worn, tattered quilt on my bed. I playfully slapped his hand and gave him a mock scolding glare. He stifled his laugh. "I'm sorry...it's just so unexpected."

Now it was my turn to raise a brow at him. "Really? Is it *really* that unexpected? I'm weird, this room is weird."

He considered this with a nod of his head. "Okay, you got me there. But where did you find all this stuff!?! I have never seen anything like most of it here."

I looked at him knowingly and we both answered, "Grandfather," in unison. He laughed again.

I didn't have a key for the safe but if they didn't open it the correct way, a balloon I'd rigged on some yarn would rip and explode in a puff of glitter—and we all know glitter is a bitch to get out of anything—so I'd surely be alerted eventually to the culprit. I carefully lifted the lid and slid my hand inside to unhook the jury-rigged booby trap and looked through my papers.

"What are you looking for?" Maxxus inquired, peering over the boxes' lid.

"Aha!" I said, pulling out small notebook which didn't contain much but some doodles, song lyrics and the name of the rogue orange dragon who helped me get my ID and paperwork when I had come to Earth. I had little use for it now since I was established and besides, I knew where he was if I needed to find him. I thrust the half sheet of folded paper at him. "Here. You'll need to get in touch with Imansi. Rogue orange dragon. He can set you up with the needed paperwork and things you'll need in order to sign up for a phone, as well as help you transfer some of your silver into human money."

I produced another stack of paper from the safe and shut the lid. "Here. Follow the purple marker....it will help you find his cabin in the woods. Or cave, whatever."

"This seems complicated," he said, eyeing the oddly marked map in confusion. But, he carefully folded the two documents and slide them in the front pocket of his emerald green robes. "But, thank you."

"Oh!" I snapped my fingers, remembering something else in the safe he might be interested in. I shoved my hand inside and felt around for something taped to the side, toward the bottom and carefully ripped it off. "Here."

Maxxus held out his hand and I put the small, inch-long micro SD card with the reader in it. "What's this?"

"When you get your phone you can put this inside of it, and it will have a ton of music of mine already programmed into it. Some of it is older, some is a bit newer but it's all my favorite stuff. It's a place to start anyway."

He nodded, with a smile and put it in his pocket as well. He rose to his feet. "Well, Leorah...thank you. I appreciate it."

I shrugged. "No biggie. I don't need any of it anymore; I have it all saved on a computer at home. Err...on Earth. Whatever."

I led him out of my room and down the hallway. My grandfather was just coming up the stairs. "Oh, there you are. Maxxus, I was earnest in my dinner invite. There's an extra place since my son is still away at Court and, I know it would really tick off the Countess," he added, giving me a playful wink.

Maxxus hesitated, glancing at me briefly and forcing a smile. He looked back away and shoved his hands into his pockets. "I better not." He offered us each a friendly smile before spinning on his heels. "I should go, but thank you, Leorah for your help."

"Sure," I said, exchanging an odd look at him as he quickly strode down the stairs with his long legs and out the front door without so much as a wave as he left.

I crossed my arms over my chest and narrowed my eyes. "Well, that was odd."

"Indeed. What did he want?"

"He wanted to know how to get a cell phone like mine," I said. My grandfather just shook his head, and I followed him through the cold stone hallways to the dining area for dinner.

I paused just outside the room, hearing a clamor of high-pitched giggles erupt from the room before me. I stopped, dead in my tracks. "Oh fuck no," and turned to run in horror in the opposite direction, but my grandfather stopped me by grabbing my forearm. He gently pulled me so I stood directly in front of him and he offered a stern, fatherly glance.

"Leo, this is your home too and you have every right to be here. I'm not going to allow you to wallow in your room while we eat down here, no matter how annoyed you are," he said, with a sigh. "This girl is important to your brother, just try to make an effort, will you?"

I let out a low grumble from the back of my throat, rolling my eyes. "Ugh."

He patted my shoulder. "That's a girl." I started to follow him down the slight corridor when I paused briefly and looked down at myself. My tank was slightly yellowed, my red flannel shirt was frayed at the ends of the sleeves and my black jeans were faded and holy at the knees. "*Harrumph*, still too nice." I knew my mother's appearance would be immaculate at the dinner table. I smirked, and yanked at the low scooped neckline of my tank and pulled it outwards and down, while shoving my larger-than-average-for-a-dragon boobs up so that I showed twice the cleavage. Mother *hated* that.

She looked at me scornfully as I entered the room. "Honestly, Leorah. Flaunting those *human* traits is just really, really childish."

I just smiled innocently at her and, just to be a bitch, grabbed my own boobs and made a honking sound. "No, *that* was childish."

From across the long, wooden table I heard a clatter of silverware on a ceramic plate as my brother apparently was laughing, choking on his food. Kiarra patted his back with motherly concern as he finally cleared his throat and roared with laughter.

My mother shot him a warning look and he promptly stopped. But, when she turned to take her place at the head of the table, he covered his mouth in silent laughter and shook his head at me.

"You're such a bad influence," Mother admonished. "I should make you change before eating here—look how nicely Kiarra here is dressed," she said, motioning to Kiarra's perfectly coiffed ebony hair and clean, fresh blue robes. Kiarra tossed a lock of her hair over her shoulder, giving me an apologetic look. "But I know if I don't just allow you to eat, you'll argue and rave and I'd just rather have a peaceful meal. Can you at *least* button the—" my mother cringed in disgust, "—*shirt*, if that's what you want to call it."

I opened my mouth to protest but my grandfather let out a dull cough. He shot me a look that clearly said "*Just button the damn shirt*" so, with a large sigh I did. But I was missing the top three buttons so, I still had ample amounts of cleavage on display. I guess I still won after all.

I took my place next to my grandfather, directly across from Kiarra (much to my dismay) who gave me a wide grin. I begrudged an insincere smile at her as my grandfather passed me a plate of some sort of roast, potatoes (a dragon staple here in Anarach) and a thick slice of buttered bread. I joked when I said I was a salad person to Gabriel—unless that salad consisted of Russets and butter, that is. He passed me a large, metal tankard of buttermilk and I took a long, loud, sloppy swig, earning yet another glare from my mother.

I ate in silence, but my mother, brother and Kiarra proceeded to ignore me, talking about gossip and regular happenings at the Court. You know, the usual...who was trying to pass what laws, who was humping who—the *usual*.

Or, rather I asked that question about the humping but it fell on deaf ears. Defeated, after a while I just stared at the torch on the stark gray wall before me and let my mind wander to thoughts of that kiss.

I was so lost in thought I didn't hear Kiarra speaking to me until my mother scolded me, once again.

"*Leorah*, honestly. She's a guest and for some reason she's being friendly to you; the *least* you could do is respond to her!" My mother shook her head in dismay.

I forced an apologetic smile at Kiarra. "Sorry. What did you say?"

"I asked what you did for fun in—what's it called—Mini-florida?" she questioned, daintily cutting up her food with a knife and fork. I fought the urge to scowl at her prim behavior. No *wonder* Mother simply loved her.

I snorted. *Mini-florida*? Good gods what a tool. "*Minnesota*," I corrected haughtily.

She let out a high-pitched, embarrassed giggle, covering her mouth with her fingertips to avoid showing the food in her mouth. "Oh dear, what a silly I am!"

"Ha ha," I said, grabbing for a hunk of bread on my plate and shoving it awkwardly in my mouth. "Well, for *fun* I watch a lot of movies, read, listen to music, play with my cat." I exaggerated my words, chewing loudly as I spoke.

Kiarra didn't seem to notice, though, I could nearly feel my mother glowering at me from the end of the table. "Oh! A cat! What is that?"

I gave her an odd look; we'd just discussed my cat not more than an hour ago. Even cracked a joke about how much the cat hated my brother. Was she really that stupid, that she couldn't recall a conversation from an hour ago, or, was there another reason for her idiotic behavior? But, to save face I decided to ignore it, or question her later. So, I just shrugged, swallowing loudly. "Oh, it's a little four-legged mammal with hair. Really cute."

My brother chortled. "Cute? That thing? She tries to scratch my eyes out every time I see her!"

I grinned widely. "I taught her everything she knows."

He grumbled and Kiarra nudged him playfully in his side.

"Is that all you do? Do you have a job...or something important?" Kiarra questioned.

"I'm a barista," I said plainly.

"A what?"

"*Barista*. I make coffee drinks for customers. I work at my friend's coffee house. Actually, I'm a manager," I said, proudly.

I heard a groan of dismay from my mother. "My daughter slings coffee for humans all day. *So* important."

I glared at her. "Without caffeine, some of these humans would become murderous. I'm helping save their civilization, one cup at a time. It's serious business!"

"A marvelous job you do too, I'm sure!" my grandfather praised, lifting up his tankard and taking a drink.

I granted him a grateful smile.

"Do you have a lot of friends over there?" Kiarra asked.

I hesitated. Of course, I didn't. Kit was it but, I didn't want to appear pathetic—anymore than I already did—in front of her, and my mother. I smiled sweetly, taking another large bite of bread before speaking. "A few, but I don't need many." I sat up straighter in my seat, feigning an air of pride and defiance. I tossed the rest of the bread on my plate, suddenly losing my appetite.

Kiarra gave a piteous look. "Oh, that's too bad."

"Sure. Well, you know it's hard to make friends when most of everyone you knew tormented you to the point of tears every day; socialization isn't a priority. It's self-preservation you must master, you know," I snapped bitterly.

My mother scoffed. "Oh come now. It wasn't as bad as all that."

Braeden let out a low whistle. "Mother...you have to be kidding me," he said, through gritted teeth.

I clamped down hard on my bottom lip to keep the angry tirade that desperately wanted to escape my mouth; instead I silently stared down at the table, choking down the fury that was boiling inside me.

Slowly, I got to my feet, and stood there, silently for a moment. As much as I wanted to scream and holler, I wouldn't give my mother the satisfaction of seeing me lose it; or Kiarra. I wasn't a fan but, at least I didn't want to prove that the rumors were true after all: pink dragons were unstable.

I took a few deep, calming breaths and looked directly at Kiarra who was still smiling cheerfully even though everyone else was wearing looks of fearful doom upon their faces. "Well, thank you for bringing it up, Kiarra. But I have to say the worst thing of all is knowing that your parents—" I shot my mother a scalding look, "—just diminish your struggles and write you off all the time. She could have spoken up, or told them to lay off on me but no. *No!*" I exclaimed as I slammed my fists on the table top, causing everyone's plates and silverware to shake; my grandfather's empty tankard fell over. "*Excuse* me." I shoved my chair back forcefully as Kiarra winced, the smile finally wiped off her face. *Good*, I thought, smugly. I stalked out of the dining area, my angry heart beating rapidly.

I was only to the stairs when the tears started to sting my eyes. I let out a slight sob, pausing on the bottom stair a moment to compose myself.

"Leo..." my brother said behind me; apparently he had followed me. "I'm sorry, she didn't know..."

I sniffed, wiping away a tear on my cheek before turning and shooting him a daring glare. "Didn't know? Didn't *know*? What, did she just think that the most feared dragon of *all* time was just given parades every day? Boxes of chocolates and flowers? Good gods, Braeden! How could she *not* know?"

Braeden appeared sympathetic as he reached out to me. I swatted his hand away forcefully and took a couple steps backwards, up the stairs. "Don't. Just don't. Just...just keep her away from me, for now. Okay? Bad enough I have to deal with everything from our parents. I don't need Little Miss Perfect rubbing her *perfect* self in my face too, okay?" I spat, mockingly. Through my tear-blinded haze I left him in the foyer silent as I stormed to my chamber, slammed the door and threw myself on the bed. "Be sure to fill her in all about my torment, just like you have everything else!" I yelled through the door at him, not sure and not caring if he heard me.

I probably wasn't being fair, but I didn't really care. I couldn't wait until morning when I could leave.

Chapter 7

My brother was mostly silent on the flight back to the portal, he was surely sore at me for questioning Kiarra's motives and snapping at her but, caution is and always was my friend. And, I just didn't like her. Something about her didn't add up whether she was just odd (far be it for me to judge someone else for being *odd*) or up to something no good. In all fairness I was wary of any dragon or any human really. It took me quite a while and a great many night shifts to open up to Kit and she still didn't know a great deal about me. Of course no one could know my real secret. He did chuckle a bit about my display at dinner the previous night, but it was short lived.

I was hoping Maxxus was guarding the portal again; but as Braeden touched down and kneeled to the ground to allow me to slide down his back. Nicodemus stood there looking intimidating as ever in a set of long black robes that trailed down to the tops of his clunky, black boots. His human form was large, and broad shouldered with severe brown eyes, a shaggy black beard over his leathery tanned skin; as if he'd been in the sun way too long. It was surprising he wasn't in his dragon form as he usually was but, it wasn't required of being a Guard so I didn't think anything of it. Black dragons were frequently very serious, made great soldiers and warriors and had a great deal of size and strength as well in addition to their magical abilities.

He spoke my name in Dragon, bowing his head at me dutifully. I gave him a slight bow as dragon custom dictated and turned to my brother who was already flapping his wings to touch off in flight, leaving without saying good-bye.

"So, you're pissed," I said loudly over his wing-beats, speaking in fact; not assumption.

My brother sighed, and stilled his wide red wings. "No, I'm not really pissed just…disappointed, I guess."

I resisted the urge to roll my eyes and instead opted too for a heavy sigh. "Okay, shoot. Just let me have it. Straight between the eyes," I said, pointing my finger at my forehead.

"I just…I don't know how to explain it, really. Kiarra was really looking forward to meeting you and I really wanted you guys to hit it off but...I guess I realized that is pretty difficult for you, given all you have been through," Braeden explained, his voice low and booming. Dragon voices always sounded like small or large rumbles of thunder, like echoes in a cave, a bit unsettling if you aren't expecting it.

I sighed. "Brae, look...I can't divulge a lot right now but just trust me when I say I need to be careful, okay?" I took a quick glance at Nicodemus as he, remembering he was there before nodding my head further away from the portal motioning for us to move away from him. "No, I'm not in her Fan Club but it's more than that."

"What do you mean? Is something going on?" Braeden asked with concern.

"I can't really tell you right now, but I will. I don't really have much to tell but once I do I will fill you in more," I explained in a hushed manner.

"Something to do with why you suddenly came here?"

I nodded. "Talk to grandfather, he will tell you that I am for real. But in the meantime...please do not talk to people about me anything other than I am fine and leave it at that. Don't talk about my dragon dust, where I am, anything. Okay?"

Braeden exhaled, a vapor of dry smoke escaping through his nose. "Are you in trouble?"

I shook my head. I wasn't...well, not yet. "No but I still need to operate with caution. Okay? Until I know more about what is going on."

He nodded with a sigh that in his dragon form, sounded a bit more like a growl. "Okay. I will do what you say. But please—I know Kiarra seems a little eager but she is a very kind dragon. I really think you will like her if you give her a chance so perhaps you can meet with her again, sometime on your terms and not feel so—blindsided?"

I cringed, but forced a smile. "I will try," I spoke through gritted teeth.

"All right," he said, satisfied. "Well, stay safe, sister...and let me know if you need anything."

I nodded. "I will."

"Okay." He craned his neck down to give my side a nuzzle with his nose, and I wrapped my arms around his large snout and planted a kiss right between the nostrils. He snorted at the gesture, causing a puff of smoke to come out and I giggled.

"Silly fairy dragon," he retorted, sticking his long dragon tongue out at me. I laughed and flicked him off.

He began flapping his wings and he was airborne. "Stay safe!" he called after me as he went higher into the sky.

I nodded and gave a wave. "Bye brother!"

He hovered in the air, probably waiting for me to make safe passage through the portal.

"Nicodemus, you are well, I hope?" I asked, trying to be formal with the stern dragon.

"Of course, and you as well?"

"Yes."

I reached out towards the portal, palm first trying to feel it's energy. It was cold, calm...no one had passed through since I'd came through. That also meant that I had been in Anarach for a couple days as well, but that wasn't surprising. I spent the rest of the night after dinner in my 'family' home, sitting up with Grandfather for a few hours setting up his page and teaching him how to navigate it, even setting up a *World of Warcraft* account for him to putz around on even though the internet connection understandably wasn't the greatest but he was still excited. He was playing well into the morning, as I crashed out on his large bed. Thankfully I managed to avoid seeing my mother again who had entered his chambers in the morning to inquire what he wanted for breakfast but I pretended to be asleep. She didn't even question my presence or acknowledge I was there, and I was glad for that.

"Oh, per Maxxus' request, I can assure you that no one but you have crossed during my watch in weeks," Nicodemus said. "It has been very quiet."

I nodded. I wasn't surprised this is what I would hear but I thanked him for his information anyways.

"Safe passage, Leorah," he said, as I stepped through the portal feeling myself get whisked away from my old home and to my new.

After a few moments disorientation, I stepped out of the portal in the woods in Minnesota, taking a quick scan of the area for anything suspicious.

It was early evening or late afternoon (though it was still morning in the dragon realm) but it was hard to tell by the sun's position as it was hidden behind a thick covering of clouds overhead, gray and looming with a low rumble of thunder in the distance. A storm seemed imminent and it was a good idea to get on the highway before it hit, not wanting to get stuck in the woods during a downpour.

My purple Dodge sat untouched in the spot I left it. I fished my car keys out of my backpack and unlocked the door and slipped inside. I was relieved when the engine turned over and I spun out of the clearing onto the makeshift dirt, brush-covered path that would lead me eventually to the dirt road that would lead me to the highway.

I was on the highway barely a minute when it started raining. It wasn't hard yet but I knew it probably would be—I could feel the energy charge in the air and it would probably be wise to pull over and wait it out or else risk turning the twenty-minute trek into an hour.

I pulled off at a gas station about a mile and a half down the road—a truckstop that was well-lit with a diner and a coffee bar. I grabbed a blue hoodie sweatshirt out of the backseat and pulled it over my heather gray t-shirt and pulled the hood over my hair. I shoved my long, red braid down my back and made a mad dash into the truckstop for some coffee and a snack.

"Crazy weather, we're having eh?" the cashier, a middle-aged man wearing a fishing hat and a plaid shirt asked from behind the counter, setting down the fishing magazine he was reading.

I nodded, shaking myself off like a dog. "Yeah, really!" Although it was just a storm, not all that unusual for Minnesota in September. But I just humored him.

I shot him a pleasant smile and went to the coffee bar and grabbed a couple of sugary donuts and brought them to the counter along with a tall cup of dark coffee with French vanilla creamer. "Been raining long? I've been out of…eh…*town* for a while."

He gave me a dumbfounded look. "Long? Try three days straight! Not a ray of sunshine. Sirens have been going off for nearly twenty-four hours; nearly every two hours. Straight line-winds. Tornado came awfully close, just outside of that little town Pineville."

My mouth fell open. "Oh my *god*! That's where I'm from!"

He gave me a sympathetic smile as the warning sirens started going off outside.

"Oh my…." That was one thing I had only experienced once, a tornado warning. Thankfully it was only a wind event but cramming an entire four-plex into the small cellar of the complex with my cat screeching and the neighbor's dog howling was not a pleasant experience. "My cat!" I scrambled for my phone in the front pocket of my backpack, slung over my shoulder and pulled it out. "Shit. Dead." I rummaged for the charger in the large pocket. I quickly covered my mouth, realizing I'd just sworn out loud in front of a stranger—sometimes I noticed humans had these weird hang ups about words. The truckstop guy didn't even flinch though.

"Need this?" the cashier asked, producing a couple of chargers from under the desk.

I sighed in relief. "Oh thank you!"

"Normally I charge the truckers five dollars a charge but for you, it's on the house. You look like you've had a rough go of it," he said. We compared chargers to my phone, found one that fit and he handed it to me.

"Thank you so much," I said.

"So where were you? Must have been pretty far off the grid if you didn't know about the storms in Pineville?"

I raised a suspicious brow. *Calm yourself,* I said in my head. *He's just a nice guy working a truckstop...Minnesota nice, remember?* Not everyone was going to be after me. At least, not out here.

"Yeah I was...*up north*. No cell towers or nothing. Pretty rustic," I explained. Yeah I was up north. *Wayyyyy* north.

"Sounds heavenly," he said with a laugh. "Now grab your coffee, and donuts, you're going to need 'em. We don't have a cellar but the bathrooms are surrounded by plumbing and reinforced walls. I'll keep up with the radio and let you know when we need to go. In the meantime, I hope you're not planning on heading out in that?"

I sighed. "No.... I guess not. Though I would like to get to my cat. She's probably scared shitless."

"Can a neighbor grab her?"

"Well my friend was looking out for her. I just hope she's still there or she took her or...something," I handed the man a five-dollar bill and some change and he placed it in the register.

"Well I sure hope she's okay," he said. His back pocket started playing a Country song and he mouthed *"Excuse me"* and grabbed it.

I left him to his phone call and I took the phone and my goodies to a table across the room away from any windows. The sirens had already stopped so I was hoping whatever it was was gone. I plugged the charger into the outlet over the table and shoved it into my phone. It took a minute to start up but when it did, it started chiming like crazy. I had twenty or so missed text messages.

Just wanted to let you know I checked on Sona. Everything is okay.

Checked on Sona again. She seems a little spooked, must be the weather. Call me when you can so I know everything's okay.

That guy stopped in today, asking about you. I didn't know what to say. I just said you were out of town for a few days and left it at that. He left shortly after.

Leo? Everything okay?

There were about five of those, asking if I was okay before *Leo, given the weather I took Sona with me to my place. I didn't want to leave her just in case there is a tornado or other bad weather. Let me know what's up, I haven't heard from you and we're worried!*

Leo! Did you hear about the tornado? Went right by the shop! So glad I closed early, someone could have been leaving and gotten stuck in it! Call me NOW! I need to know you're okay! OKAY!?!!

That was the latest one from Kit. I breathed a sigh of relief, at least I knew my cat was safe.

Leorah.... I'm sorry for the abrupt way I left. Things are just...a bit overwhelming. I know I've said that already. I don't know what else to say. You didn't have to leave town. I'm guessing you went home. I hope you found what you needed. I'll come by and check on you in a couple of days.

Did you hear about this weather? It's really crazy. I don't think it's entirely natural. I will explain later. Please call me. –Gabriel

I let out a low-whistle. Not natural? What else could it be?

As if on cue, I felt a rattling. Quiet at first and then progressively got louder. The building started shaking, causing the racing memorabilia, and truck and beer advertisements that were hanging on the walls to shake and fall.

"Oh my god!" The man behind the counter dropped his cell phone and pointed out the glass window and door.

I shifted in my seat to see what he was talking about. My mouth fell open in horror, seeing the dark clouds over head dropping lower and lower, churning and shifting into a full-fledged twister. It didn't seem very large but I know it didn't have to be to do a lot of damage.

The man behind the counter had apparently found his dropped cell phone and was yelling into it. "Daisy! Get the kids, there's a tornado outside the store! No I'm *not* kidding, just go to the basement! I know the sirens stopped going off, just *do it*! I can see it heading right for us! I gotta go—I gotta yell outside to the truckers!"

I didn't have to be asked. There was a side door that led to the truck area of the stop, with long parking spots for truckers to sleep off the day, diesel gas pumps that accommodated the large cabs and loads. I took one more glance at the tornado, it was struggling a bit, touching down and lifting back up, thinning out. I was hoping it would dissipate before long. Still, didn't want to risk it.

I shoved open the door, feeling the heavy air and wind try to push back. I managed to get it open and started yelling at the top of my lungs. "*Tornado! Tornado! Get inside! Tornado!*"

There were about six trucks either parked or getting fuel. The one getting the fuel stopped and stared at me and I pointed towards the west. He let out a yell, ungrasped the gas pump and quickly shoved it back in the slot. I saw his mouth moving but the wind was roaring so loud it was all I could hear.

The trucker—a tall man with a cowboy hat, jeans, red flannel shirt and cowboy boots started running through the stop pounding on trucks and yelling. I assume he was yelling "*Tornado!*" too but I couldn't know for sure. Even with my sensitive dragon hearing I couldn't hear anything over the wind howling outside.

Random truckers started rousing from their cabs or their dinners in the front seat and were starting to dart across the lot into the building. One trucker—a middle-aged woman wearing a Harley t-shirt and with tattoos up her arms—carried a small toy breed dog that was shaking and yipping. The barking of the tiny dog was all I could make out; voices I couldn't distinguish so much.

"In here!" I struggled to hold the door open for the shocked truckers against the gusting wind. The sky was beginning to turn a particularly menacing shade of yellow and I knew that was not a good sign.

I took another glance at the twister. It was beginning to be more organized, staying on the ground longer and thickening its funnel. I could see from far away the debris getting kicked up. Thankfully there wasn't much out there—the truckstop, the highway and large corn fields as far as the eye could see. I knew there were some farm houses tucked away aside those fields but I couldn't see them.

"In here, in here!" The man behind the counter herded the truckers like sheep into one of the bathrooms; which were more centrally located in the building. I stayed outside to watch as it spun closer, we didn't have tornadoes typically in Anarach so it was actually rather fascinating to watch.

"Miss! You should really get in here!" The man behind the counter insisted.

I nodded and said "Coming!" though over the roar of the wind I'm sure he couldn't hear me. I waved him off and he shrugged and shut the door, with himself and the truckers inside.

"Did you hear about this weather? It's crazy. I don't think it's entirely natural." The text message from Gabriel rattled on in my head, in his voice as I watched the thing spin, inching ever so closely to us.

The sound was deafening. Imagine the sound of your washing machine spinning rapidly on the fast cycle with a heavy load inside, times a hundred. It banged in rhythm but still was mind-numbingly loud especially on my sensitive hearing. It seemed to be avoiding everything—not that there was much to be avoiding but it wasn't hitting any utility poles or signage.

It wasn't a thick funnel at all but despite the black clouds—and I do mean *black* with the alarming yellow hue below the funnel was stark white like a bleached white sheet. Now it was perfectly formed up and down. It had no tail, and didn't change shape as it spun closer and closer.

Not natural. Gabriel's voice echoed again in my head.

I don't know how I wasn't panicking. My heart was palpitating, my fingers were feeling a bit nervous and twitching. At what, I didn't know.

Wait, I did know. They felt the same way now as they did when Gabriel was performing his summon the wind trick.

Perhaps it wasn't natural, perhaps this tornado was summoned by *magic*.

"So I should be able to disable it, right?" I said to myself. The only problem was I didn't know how.

Concentrate.

Despite wanting to watch desperately, I reluctantly shut my eyes. I tried to feel the energy surrounding me. It was raw, powerful and charged. A bit like how it felt when I crossed the portal and it felt warm, like someone had just gone through it. You could feel the particles of energy buzzing around, alive.

I envisioned the funnel in my mind. Strong and powerful. I knew it was getting close—real close as I could feel the spinning more intensely, hear the deafening roar. It didn't let up; it was constant.

Reaching out my hands I said quietly, "Go away, go away, go away...do not harm us..." I pictured my hands around each side of the funnel, holding the charged particles in my grasp. I pushed my palms together and just kept imagining getting smaller and smaller.

And smaller.

And smaller.

As it spun closer and closer, I could feel the hair raise on my arms and the back of my neck. Thunder rolled and rumbled the walls, shaking them like an earthquake. The lightning was so bright it was blinding and nearly constant; I could see it through the lids of my eyes.

I dared to open an eye when the thunder started lessening. It was dark for a few moments, no lightning and I heard no wind. Everything was still.

I began to breathe a sigh of relief when the loudest, most bone-rattling crack of thunder I have *ever* heard shook the building, knocking just about everything off the walls, bringing them crashing to the ground and blew the glass walls and windows from out of their frame, causing shards to rain down.

I screamed and tried to duck, pulling the hood of my hoodie over my head. Thunder roared again, this time with a brilliant flash of light and I saw the funnel, larger this time, very thick and strong barreling towards me and the truckstop at top speed.

"*Shit..*" Was all I could say, to no one in particular. Perhaps it was naturally caused if my magic wasn't affecting it. Or perhaps I just didn't know what I was doing, and the magic was too strong for me. After all, I had only performed magic maybe three times in all my life, now. The magic could easily surpass my skill. Even dragons who could channel lightning and weather had their limits, this far surpassed them.

I wish I had had a chance to speak to Gabriel about this storm before it rolled in. Surely he must be convinced of its magic origin to bring it up to me, even given how we parted. He was a Knight and his job was to assist me. Surely he couldn't be wrong.

Hell I didn't know sorcerers existed until a few days ago.

"Come on pink power...do your thing," I mumbled to myself, trying to steady my stance against the counter, leaning on it for balance through the roaring winds trying to knock me down.

I closed my eyes again. Even if this wasn't magic-created, perhaps I could at least lessen the severity of it. I did it before without knowing it, I could at least try to do it again.

A few yards away, from behind the bathroom door, I could hear shrieks and panicked barking. Fear had taken over the patrons of the truckstop, and even through the cacophony of the storm I could hear them screaming, yelling comforting words to each other, praying. The sole animal of the group was barking and whining ferociously. I could hear its owner trying to console it through her own tears.

I summoned up all my gumption and resolve. I didn't know how to do it, but I had to try to save these people. If this was magic caused, they didn't deserve to go out like this. If it wasn't I would never be able to live with myself years later if I didn't at least give it a good attempt to subside this insane weather.

I closed my eyes again, picturing the twisted white funnel. I held my hands out, willing myself to feel that *tingle* I felt when I had increased Gabriel's wind magic in my apartment.

My hands started to quiver. I could feel the energy of the storm. It felt violent and angry. Determined and strong. It was out to destroy. I could almost hear it saying "I'm coming for you...."

"The hell you are," I uttered aloud. I inhaled deeply and concentrated on the energy. I thought of it dispersing, spinning up and away, the clouds parting and leaving behind the sunshine.

My entire body was shaking now. I inhaled deeply, as if taking all the negative storm's energy inside me. It was so strong and so frightening I wanted to cry. But instead I exhaled deeply, blowing into the wind like the Big Bad Wolf blowing down the brick house. Only I would be successful. I would knock this tornado down.

I did this for as long as I could until I nearly collapsed from exhaustion; the expelled magic draining all my energy reserves.

The thunder went quiet. The wind stopped. There was no more shaking, no more rattling. I opened my eyes. It was not sunny but it was no longer green with the hue of danger. The last remnants of the funnel struggled to hold together, to put itself back together. I exhaled again, releasing my sparkly mist into the air. The twisting wind sucked up my energy, twisting it around and finally it burst, causing the sparkly mist to rain down on the ground like snow.

It was gone.

Feeling weak and listless, I slid down the counter, still smiling to myself. Either it was a miracle or, I did it.

"Whoa, there," the man from behind the counter said, just in time to grab my shoulders and slowly assist me to the ground. "Be careful. You're losing a lot of blood now; I don't know what you were thinking staying out here like that."

"Look!" The female trucker with the dog pointed out the glass-blown window. The black sky was parting, the sun's rays struggling to stab through them and warm the storm-weary land below. A sliver of a rainbow descended from the clouds over the field where the tornado stopped short of blowing this building to bits.

The other truckers stood in awe at the sight. We all heard how strong it had been, we saw the straight strip of land it had cut through the field just hundreds of yards before us. Besides the broken glass and the wall hangings now laying on the ground, the truckstop had been totally spared.

"It just…stopped," said another trucker, taking off his blue fishing hat and scratching his bald scalp and shaking his head. "Crazy!"

"It's like, magic," I said woozily.

The man behind the counter barked at someone to grab something behind the desk—I didn't understand what. Another trucker, a young heavy set man but handsome in the face darted off behind the counter and produced a large box and handed it to the man.

He rummaged through it but I could barely tell what he was doing, my skin tingled from energy loss, my eyes were feeling heavy.

"Whoa now, stay with me now. My name is Ben Needles, what is yours?" He produced a clean towel from inside the box and started dabbing at my cheek. I winced, and hissed through my teeth at the pain.

"I know I know. Just be thankful a few inches higher and that glass would have gotten you in your eye," he said.

"Glass?" I reached up to touch the area he was dabbing at but he pushed my hand aside. "No, don't. Don't want to push that glass in any further. We should get you to the hospital, have them remove that. And get you stitched up. I know head wounds bleed fast but you should get that checked out."

I shook my head. Through the daze of energy loss, I could remember that as a dragon showing up at a hospital would be a bad idea. On the surface I looked human but my blood would come across as somewhat of a freakshow cocktail; complete with two full DNA sequences and genetic forms that scientists hadn't even begun to think up. What I wouldn't do for grandfather's healing silver magic right about now…but I knew even in my human form I would heal quickly. It would be very uncomfortable though if I began healing around the shard of glass lodged into my cheek.

"Honey, this needs to get checked out, it looks pretty deep."

I shook my head again. "No, no. It's okay, it doesn't hurt. Just take it out. I'll be okay."

He raised an eyebrow. "Are you sure about that?"

I nodded. "Yes. Please it'll feel much better once it's out. I hate hospitals, and I don't have insurance. Please just take it out…if it keeps bleeding after you bandage it up, I'll go, I promise. But just get the glass out."

"Okay," he said reluctantly. He rummaged through the box and produced a large pair of tweezers. "I'm sorry, this will probably hurt a bit."

I shrugged and just shut my eyes. I could feel the blood now, the charge of energy that was making me feel woozy was starting to fade and the injury was starting to throb. I knew that wasn't the only one either but I could feel the skin starting to close up around the glass, it would hurt worse if it didn't come out and I had to get a piece of glass ripped out from a healed area. Not to mention if Ben Needles saw me heal quickly he'd probably get freaked out. Once bandaged I could pretend that I was feeling off because of the blood loss and not because of the energy I expelled in attempting to disperse the storm.

I felt a tug on my cheek and a sharp, shooting pain shoot down my face; up my forehead. I tried to control a scream and gritted my teeth, biting down on my bottom lip as Ben Needles slowly and carefully pulled the shard of glass out that was lodged in my flesh.

I did yelp as I felt the last tug and my skin was free of the foreign object, followed by a hot sensation surrounding it. I knew I was going to heal fast, even though it was still bleeding pretty hard. I felt the blood gush out, and down my neck pooling on my chest permanently staining my favorite hoodie. I tried not to swear out loud at the thought of the stain removing I was going to have to do over the next couple days to salvage it. I smelled an acrid-scent as Ben leaned over me and swabbed at the area with an alcohol pad to clean it. I winced, more at the smell than the sting of the antiseptic, and Ben assumed I was hurting and, attempted to comfort me with a soothing voice.

"You never did tell me your name. Are you feeling okay?" Ben asked with a concerned look on his earnest face, as he taped some butterfly bandages over the wound area. He worked fast and for that I was thankful.

"Leo," I replied, trying to force a groggy smile.

"Leo. Well it's nice to meet you, Leo," he said, with a polite nod. "What on Earth were you doing out here?"

"I ah—" just *trying to save the world from the evil magic tornado, no big deal*. "I thought I heard someone outside screaming. By the time I noticed I was hearing things it was already right on top of us. The glass shattered then and I guess I went into a bit of shock." I hoped that sounded believable.

He nodded. "Yeah, crazy weather been messing with all of us lately. Noble thing to do, trying to rescue someone in need. You're lucky though this was all that hit you," he said.

I felt a burning sensation as the blood started to cauterize, I was healing faster now that it was sealed up. "Um, do you have a big band aid in there? I kind of can't stand the sight of blood," I said with a chuckle.

He smiled. "Sure thing, Leo," he said, producing a medium sized gauze pad and some paper tape. "This do?"

I nodded, and he taped the gauze carefully over the wound.

"Thanks," I said, trying slowly to compose myself. I slowly started to stand, felt my legs turn to gelatin and quickly fell to my feet again. Ben caught me before I landed, softening the blow.

"Whoa slow down there. You need to get some sugar in you. Blood loss will make you woozy. Want some pop? Another doughnut? On the house," he said.

I nodded.

"What's your favorite?"

"Mountain Dew."

"All right. Hey, one of you—can you get Leo here a big cup of pop? Some Dew? And grab a doughnut from the case there? All of you can help yourselves too."

The younger gentleman scurried to the pop machine next to the pastry case—surprisingly untouched—moved a large framed poster to the side that had fallen off in front of the counter and returned with a glazed raised doughnut and a large pop with a straw. The other truckers chatting up a storm, joined him in grabbing their own snacks.

I gave him a thankful smile as I took the pop from him and took a large sip. I sighed as the cool liquid quelled my nerves.

109

"Better?" he asked.

I nodded. "Thank you. And thank *you*," I said nodding towards Ben.

He waved me off. "Ah no worries. That's what we do here, this is Minnesota."

I grinned. Yes, yes it was.

It was a couple of hours before Ben would allow me to drive home. He still insisted I go to the hospital but if I wouldn't, he insisted on pumping me full of sugar and hot dogs and pastries until I felt right as rain and could walk solidly without stumbling. In the meantime, I texted both Kit and Gabriel to let them know I was back in town and I would see them soon. Kit was going to meet me at my apartment with Sona, saying she was missing me like crazy and ready to go home. Gabriel didn't get back to me, even after I told him about the storm.

The weather had completely cleared, not a cloud in the sky as I drove home that early evening. The land alongside the highway was beaten and battered—limbs from trees torn and tossed to the ground, fields of crops bent all in one direction….it had been a nasty couple of days' weather wise, and I felt kind of guilty that I hadn't been here to even notice.

It was nearly 8pm as I pulled into my parking spot. The complex looked to of escaped excessive damage, the only thing out of place was a couple of siding panels had been ripped off the walls and some planters of mine and my neighbor's plants had been turned over.

I scooped up my hibiscus plant from its side and grabbed handfuls of dirt that had fallen out and tucked it back around the plant, setting it by the door where it had been.

I twisted the knob and opened the door and was met with a loud "*MEOW*!" as my cat jumped into my arms, nuzzling my face.

From the couch Kit laughed. "I told you she missed you," she said with a laugh.

"I see," I said with a laugh, scratching her head and setting her down at her food dish in the kitchen which Kit must have already filled. Sona let out a little *mew* and started eating heartily.

"There's something for you on the counter," Kit said with a wink, motioning her head towards the center island that served as a bar table as well.

"Oh?" On the counter sat a single pink rose and a folded in half sheet of yellow tablet paper with my name printed on the front. *How did that get in here?*

I tried to hide my smile as I lifted the rose to my nose and inhaled its fragrance. I opened the paper and read the contents.

Leorah,

I'm sorry I freaked out a bit. It's not an excuse, I just kind of crumbled under the pressure. But that's not your fault, it's mine and mine alone. Please forgive me and I hope you'll give me the time to adjust to our new relationship whatever it turns out to be.

You are an amazing 'person', both your sides...regardless of what happens, don't forget that. I spoke to my brother today. He saw you—described you perfectly—and said you did some great things. He couldn't tell me specifics but he is looking forward to meeting you someday. He made me promise to at the least be your friend and 'protector' though I know you don't need protecting but you certainly could use a friend. I'm ready to do my 'duty', and I'm ready to start as friends.

As for the kiss, I'm sorry if that offended you. The magic, the situation.... everything fogged my brain and I was caught in the moment. It was very nice if you don't mind me saying so but I will understand if you don't know what you feel yet. I don't know what I feel yet. Regardless I will always be here for you, as a Knight and as a friend. Whatever else happens is entirely up to you.

I hope you come back soon and you get things sorted out.
With love,
Gabriel

"What's that?" Kit questioned in a sing-song voice, wiggling her eyebrows hintingly. "Is that from that cute nerdy guy who keeps coming into the shop?"

Despite myself I felt my cheeks flushing. "Maybe."

She grinned. "I knew that when you took off you were freaking out. I know how hard it is for you to get close to people, Leo. I hope you dealt with your...stuff at home."

I waved her off. "Oh, just some family drama. My brother is getting married, it's kind of sudden and just very...weird."

"How so?"

I shrugged. "She was...odd. Not really his type. And where we come from tradition is big and they're kind of...not traditional."

Kit laughed. "Not traditional? Where are you from? 1930?"

I forced a laugh. Little did she know how right on she was. Well, more like 1830 actually but.... hey. What's 100 or so years?

"Nah it's just our family. They're just kind of stuck in their ways," I explained.

"Well, that's what the young people do, shake stuff up a bit. I hope everything is okay though?"

I nodded. "Yeah. Most of the time I just sat around with my grandfather signing him up for Facebook and teaching him to play *World of Warcraft*."

Kit's mouth fell open. "You're kidding me?"

I shook my head. "Nope, I'm not. It's hilarious. He's terrible but...he was having fun when I left."

Kit exploded in uproarious laughter. "Oh my Goddess that's hysterical! How old is he again?"

"Umm...old. Really old. Like...eighty-eight or so," I said trying to quickly equivocate the dragon years to human ones.

She laughed even harder. "Oh gosh that's good!"

I nodded, glancing at the digital clock behind me on the oven. Almost 6pm. As much as I wanted to visit with Kit I was tired and kind of wanted to go to sleep. Okay...play an hour or so of *World of Warcraft* with my grandfather and *then* go to sleep. Or watch some TVLand. "So, crazy weather?"

"Goodness yes!" She proceeded to tell me about the handful of tornadoes that struck the area, the days of rain, her flooded basement and the off and on hail that kept pouring down and damaged her car.

I shook my head. "Wow, that's crazy!"

"Yeah it was even on the national news. Even the big internet headlines!"

"Really?" I grabbed my phone and pushed the internet browser icon and went straight to Yahoo. Sure enough one of the first headlines was *Severe Weather and Tornadoes Slam Minnesota For Days*. "Huh. How did I miss that?"

"You were busy," Kit said with a shrug. "It's fine, I don't even think anyone was killed. Lots of injuries but...thank the Goddess the weather service in this state is so good."

"Yeah..." I went on to read the article. Everything from EF4 tornadoes, straight line winds, baseball sized hail.... all around our neck of the woods.

"Severe weather plagues the small Minnesota town of Pineville for nearly 4 days, starting shortly after noon on Monday," I read aloud from the article.

"Wow...that was shortly after I left, huh?" I mused.

Kit nodded, with a sigh. "Yeah, it was crazy. The local storm chasers said they had never seen anything like it—just out of the blue, like it was conjured!"

I looked at her expectantly. "Conjured? Could that be your doing?" I said sarcastically. "Doing any spells to the Goddess of Weather lately?"

Kit chuckled. "Ha, I wish I had that kind of power. No I even missed Circle this week because of all the storms. The only thing I cast was a 'Stop the Weather' spell!" she said with a scoffed laugh. "Didn't work, of course."

I raised a brow slightly. "Of course not."

Kit ran her fingers through her long, tangled hair. I just now noticed how tired she looked. Dark circles under her brown eyes, her cheeks shallow, skin pale and her bright teal lock of hair had faded dramatically; could hardly tell it was there. She looked bedraggled and sullen; a far cry from her generally cheery demeanor. She crossed her legs under her long knit yellow skirt and leaned back into the couch with a sigh.

"Geez, Kit. You look tired. You wanna go grab a shower? Crash on the couch? Least I can do for having you take care of Sona for me, especially in all that chaos," I said.

Kit looked at me and smiled. "Oh, no.... I gotta get up early in the morning and meet with the insurance adjuster to have them look at the shop. You know how I am sleeping in places other than my own bed."

I nodded. "Are you thirsty?"

Kit thought a moment. "Do you have any pop? *Anything*? I could really use the sugar rush until I get home. That whole five-minute drive you know..."

"Do I have pop..." It was rhetorical. I went to the fridge and produced a can of orange pop from the fridge from amongst the five different kinds I usually carried in there. Thankfully even though I was built a bit thicker than most dragon's in their human form— about a size 10/12 or so—dragons had a hard time gaining weight. Good metabolism. It was a good thing because damn I just *loved* human junk food.

"This okay? I have more if you don't like this," I said, crossing the room and handing it to her.

She grabbed it from me, popped the top and took a long swig. "Nope, this is fine." She let out a small burp and giggled. "Oops."

"You sure you're feeling okay?" I asked. Kit rarely drank pop or ate anything junky or sugary...mostly vegetables from her garden or produce from the Farmers Market.

"Oh sure," she said. "I actually had a craving for a steak today— "

I let out a gasp. Kit was a strict vegetarian; I'd never seen her even touch a piece of meat before. "Did you have one?"

She shook her head. "No! No way but I wanted to for some reason. Then I saw that pop in the fridge as I was looking for Sona's leftover food from the other day to give her—I wasn't sure how long you'd be getting home—and it just sounded good for some reason. I figured at least *that* craving would be okay." She let out a small laugh, and took another long drink from the can, letting out a much louder and longer burp this time. She laughed. "I see why people like this so much—been so long since I had some."

"What's with the sudden cravings?" I put on a mock face of horror. "Oh no! Are you pregnant?"

Kit howled. "No, definitely not. I can't even tell you the last time I..." she made a suggestive gesture and I chuckled. "Well.... you know. Must be that damn peri- menopause or whatever."

I shrugged. "Stress?"

"Probably," she said. She stood slowly, almost labored. She gave me a smile. "With the damage to the shop we probably won't be opening tomorrow, but would you mind coming in later in the day for some cleanup work? I already called Madison and Emily and told them I didn't need them until at least this weekend but...I could use an extra pair of hands."

I nodded. "Of course. How damaged is it?"

"Not too bad, but the front window shattered—and there's leaves and mud all over the floor. After the insurance guy leaves I can start to clean and board up. Remember that pine out on the corner of the lot?"

I nodded.

"Well that came down too—thankfully it fell into the highway so the town had it hauled away already, but I still have to get rid of the branches and stuff. Plus, there's some debris from the apartment complex down the road in the parking lot."

"Wow, I had no idea the shop got hit that hard," I said.

She shrugged. "Yeah well….it happens. We haven't had any big storms for a while so, I guess we were due. But it could have been worse."

"Well I'll definitely be there."

"Great. I'll call you," she said. She gave me a limp, one armed hug and started for the door, pausing to give Sona a quick scratch between the ears before leaving. Sona let out a meow and continued her nap.

"Thanks—for everything," I said to her earnestly.

She nodded. "Of course, of course. That's what friends are for right? You've bailed me out of a busy day or a jam many times at the shop so it's the least I could do."

I smiled. "Get some rest."

"I will. It's been crazy." With a little wave she smiled and left.

Chapter 8

I had fallen asleep on the couch watching—of all things—the movie *Twister* on one of the cable channels but it was still dark when I heard a banging on the door.

I practically leaped from my spot, causing Sona who had apparently fallen asleep on my stomach to jump in terror and let out a startled meow.

"Leorah? Are you there?" asked a muffled voice from outside. "It's Gabriel!"

"Coming!" I started for the door, kicking aside my backpack, some pop cans I had tossed on the floor and a plaid shirt. I had been too tired and lazy to pick up last night's mess. I stopped short, glancing at all my sloppiness on the ground. "Oh shit!" I muttered to myself, quickly grabbing at the garbage and tossing it into the can in the kitchen; all except the plaid shirt which got flung onto the sofa.

I caught a glimpse of myself in the decorative mirror I had in the entryway and grimaced with an audible "Ew!"

"What?" said Gabriel from the other side.

"Never mind!" I shouted, pulling my hair out of its messy ponytail and redoing it into a messy bun quickly. My eyes were puffy and rimmed with purple and the neckline of my tank top was dotted with cola spills from me lazily sipping Coke while laying down, mindlessly shuffling through the channels on TV. "Um…" I opened the door and ducked behind it. "Close your eyes, and come in."

"Huh?" he asked, confused.

"Just do it!" I insisted.

He heaved a sigh loud enough to hear from the opposite side of the door and chuckled. "Okay. They're closed."

"Okay. You can come in." Smiling he took a few steps forward and stopped while I shut the door behind me. I snuck behind him down the little hallway to my bedroom. "Make yourself at home! I'll be right there!"

"What are you doing?" he called after me.

"Changing. Just…hang on." I shut my bedroom door and rummaged through my closet. I found a pair of black yoga pants and a gray hooded sweatshirt. It matched my disorderly appearance and I didn't feel like wearing jeans. Even after a couple hours of sleep and all that sugar, I was still feeling groggy. I took them into the bathroom and splashed my face with water and rubbed my sleepy eyes with a towel. Glancing at my reflection in the mirror the bags and circles were still there but my face was slightly flushed. I cringed, noticing my hair was still rather messy—and not the good, on-purpose messy but was kinky and greasy. I exhaled with a groan, wetting a brush from the counter and running it through my hair a few times taming the kinks a bit and hopefully washing out the greasies. I put it into another more purposeful ponytail and with a frown decided that was about the best I was going to get without a full shower, a twelve-hour nap and a Hollywood makeover.

"Sorry," I said, emerging from my bedroom. Gabriel was sitting cross-legged on the floor in front of the couch with Sona purring in his lap.

"Are you okay? I've been trying to get a hold of you for a while now," he asked, lifting my cat from his lap and carefully placing her on the ground. He rose and reached out his hand, stroking my cheek lightly. "What happened?"

"What do you mean?"

"It looks like...a scar. I didn't notice that before."

"What?" I didn't see any scar when I had looked in the mirror. I dashed back to the mirror in the entry to get a second look. Under the bandage Ben had put on me it had long healed over by the time I had arrived home; I had taken it off in the car to avoid getting drilled by Kit about the tornado. She didn't even know I had been caught in it. "There's nothing there!"

"It's faint but I can see it...right...there," he pointed to the spot on my upper cheek and traced the exact path I had been cut by the glass from the tornado.

"But—there's nothing— "

"You can't see it, but I can," he said. "If the injury was caused by magic, it leaves an imprint behind. Those who wield magic can see it. Your skin may have healed, but the magic that caused it is still there."

"You can really see that?" I gingerly touched the spot as if it were burning acid.

He nodded. "What happened? Did something get crazy back home?"

"No...this was after I got home. I was like a quarter of the way home and it started raining really hard. So I pulled off at a truck stop and the sirens started going off," I explained.

Gabriel's eyes widened in surprise. "Was it outside of Tillsdale?"

I nodded. "Yeah, I think."

Gabriel produced his phone out of his front jeans pocket. It beeped and clicked as he touched it and he produced a picture. "Pineville *receives close call—tornado almost takes out truck stop,*" read the caption below a photo of the truckstop I had been at, with Ben Needles and a couple other people I didn't recognize trying to board up the front of the window that had been blown out.

"That's Ben! That's the guy who helped me out when the window broke and cut my cheek!"

"Well I'm glad you weren't alone, at least. Leo, these storms were *not* natural," he said. "That's why that glass that cut you left a magic imprint: because it was caused by magic."

"But—how? Can you conjure a tornado?" I knew he could make a breeze but this I guessed was out of his realm of expertise.

"No, I can't. Maybe one about two feet high; that's it. And I'm not sure who can either, but...whoever it was, they were looking for you, I think."

I snorted. "Me? Why do you say that?"

"Because, Leo—all of these tornadoes happened in places you frequented. But since you weren't here, they didn't end up being very strong—just small ones. The big one happened when you were here! Did you see what they rated that storm? An EF-3! That's a pretty big tornado! All the rest were barely even substantial enough to qualify as a tornado, the largest one besides that was an EF-1 that just touched down briefly just outside your apartment."

"But—why me?"

He shrugged. "I don't know. Perhaps it wasn't you particularly but *any* magical being. You're probably the most magical being in this state—quite possibly even the country right now. Maybe it just honed in on you." He didn't sound entirely convinced, though.

"Oh god..." I groaned. He patted me on the shoulder and I pushed past him for my refrigerator and grabbed a pop. "I need sugar...." I flung myself on the couch and took a long drink, resisting the urge to let out a huge belch.

"So…" he began hesitantly, sitting on the recliner next to the couch and rocking slowly. "Did you figure out what you wanted to figure out? I assume you went home, right?"

I nodded. "Yeah…it was time to see Grandfather. Apparently he knew one of your ancestors, although I can't recall the name right now…. Neal or Niles or something…."

"Niall?" he offered.

"Yes!" I said, snapping my fingers. "That was it."

"Your grandfather must be very old. That was like…my great-great-great-great grandfather."

"Oh yes. He's an Elder. You have to be at least 1,700 to achieve Elder status."

"An *Elder*? Wow…" Gabriel said in awe.

"Do you know a lot about dragon society?" I questioned him, finishing off the pop and setting the can down on the cluttered table in front of me with a metal *clink*.

Gabriel folded himself into the couch opposite side of me, shrugging his shoulders. "Well, a little but not really. Just what was handed down for years and years and who's to know how much of that is accurate? I know the basic structure but things have changed so much I'm sure."

I nodded in agreement. "I'm sure." My stomach took that precise moment to start rumbling audibly, and my cheeks reddened in embarrassment.

Gabriel chuckled. "A little hungry, huh?"

"I guess so," I said with a laugh. "Last thing I ate really was…whatever I had at that truck stop like, twelve hours ago."

"Twelve? Try like, twenty," he said.

"Huh?" I asked in alarm, reaching for my cell phone in all the clutter on my coffee table. "8:15! What?" I shook my head in confusion.

Gabriel took it upon himself to draw the curtains to show the twilight outside.

"It's *nighttime*?" I asked rhetorically in shock. "Oh shit, I was supposed to help Kit today with the shop!" I started flipping through my phone looking for all the frantic messages today from Kit that I must have missed.

"I wouldn't worry about it; I drove by there looking for you earlier when you wouldn't answer your phone. It was closed, hadn't been opened up all day," he explained.

"It hasn't?" I clicked through all my messages, seeing the ones from Gabriel and one on Facebook from my grandfather (which caused me to chuckle as he was asking for help on how to get to a capital city on his *World of Warcraft* character) but none from Kit.

"No, it still looks just like it did yesterday with all the damage, and there was a piece of paper taped to the door," he said.

"That's not good, that was probably from the inspector. That's not like Kit," I said, frantically hitting Kit's number on my speed dial. I was pacing now, as the phone rang and went straight to voicemail. "Kit—it's Leo. I'm sorry I missed you today. Give me a call. Now. Heard the shop has been shut down all day. Call me!" I pushed the *end* icon and started texting her. "*Dammit*!" I cursed. "How could I have been asleep *all day*!?!?!"

"Maybe the tornado caused some kind of magic drain on you," Gabriel speculated. "You still do look kind of tired."

I groaned, tossing my phone on the couch and falling back into the couch with a pout. "I know; I still feel like crap." Besides being hungry I just felt weak and spacey.

"That is odd. That must be a strong draining spell that was there, most magic users are only out of it for a couple of hours before they feel better, unless they were actually *using* magic—then it could take days to recover."

I bit my lip sheepishly and looked down at my hands in my lap.

Gabriel gave me an expectant look. "You couldn't have done magic, could you? I mean how could you have known it was not naturally occurring? I didn't talk to you at all."

"Your text message? I checked them while I was at the truckstop waiting out the rain, before it worsened," I said. "It was so weird, Gabriel. There was this *huge* tornado and there was like no damage around it, just directly in front and in back. There were people hiding in the bathrooms and I remembered your wind spell…I figured, it couldn't be that hard, right? If I can make it stronger, I can make it stop, right?" I avoided his glare.

"You didn't?"

I nodded. "I did. I wasn't even sure what I was doing or if it would work…. I just stood there watching it come towards me. I knew it wouldn't kill me but all those people…I couldn't just let them die if I could do something about it. I had to at least try. I just closed my eyes and imagined it getting smaller and smaller and I exhaled. My sparkles went everywhere and after a couple of minutes

I opened my eyes and it was going away. I didn't even notice my cheek was cut until Ben came out with all the people. He fixed it up and tried to take me to the hospital but I refused. I was pretty groggy and he gave me all this sugar and stuff to eat and I felt better enough after a while to drive...then I came home, and Kit was here with Sona and we talked for a bit and she said she was tired and went home. I sat down on the couch and I guess I fell asleep until now."

Gabriel's mouth was open wide in awe. "You've never done magic before and yet, you diffused a huge tornado? Just like that?" He let out a low whistle. "Wow, I wish I could have seen that. I wish I had been there. I *should* have been there." He started cursing under his breath. "Some knight I am, you needed me and I failed. If I had been there, you wouldn't have been drained at all...we could have stopped it before it came anywhere near that shop. Shit!"

"How could you have known?" I shrugged. "This is...this is new to both of us. I wasn't even sure if you were telling me the truth until I talked to my grandfather. I couldn't have brought you to the Anarach even if I wanted to...you would have been eaten alive. Literally," I said with a laugh.

Gabriel gave a small smile. "Yeah I suppose. Still I—"

"No." I said, reaching over and giving him a playful shove. "It was worth it. I saved those people. I ended the magic. I will be okay. I just need more of these." I said, grabbing for the empty pop can on the table. My stomach rumbled again, on cue. "And some dinner, I guess. Although, breakfast sounds much better."

Gabriel grinned. "Well...we can do breakfast then." He was up and rummaging through my cabinets for food. "What do you have?"

"Umm...not much," he said, as he looked through my refrigerator full of pop and a mostly-empty gallon of milk.

"Don't you eat?" he asked incredulously, producing an expired box of pancake batter from the pantry and shaking it at me.

"Yes, yes I do. That's why there's nothing there," I said. "I didn't do any shopping before I left, I just kind of took off..."

He rolled his eyes.

"Okay. Give me fifteen minutes, I'll get provisions." I started to stand and he pointed to the couch.

"No. I will go. You need your rest. I am not the greatest cook but I picked up a few things from my brother. I think I can manage some pancakes or waffles or...something. Okay? You need some real food not just pop. This isn't a raid or anything." I chuckled at the *WoW* reference. "You need sustenance, not crap."

"Fine," I said with a laugh, relenting. He produced his keys from his pocket.

"I'll be back. Are you going to let me in?" he kidded, with a hint of hesitance in his voice.

"Maybe," I kidded back.

He wiggled his fingers at me. "Doesn't matter. I know a spell for that." He winked at me before closing the door behind him.

I chuckled after him and leaned back into the couch, closed my eyes and exhaled slowly. I wrinkled my nose. "Yuck! I really need to bathe!" Despite my promise to rest I dragged my feet to the bathroom and doused myself off in the shower. After soaping up and shampooing off I just stood there for a few minutes, letting the hot water relax my tired shoulders. I stayed in a bit longer than I wanted to; at least thirty minutes had gone by since Gabriel left.

I dried off and wrapped the towel around myself and examined my appearance in the mirror. It was fogged over so I wiped it with my palm, with the humidity in the room it just re-fogged.

"Hmmm," I mused thoughtfully. Feeling sheepish, I inhaled and blew out slowly on the mirror. The sparkly mist stuck to the glass and warmed it, thereby dispersing the fog on the mirror. "Neat," I said, but my amusement was short-lived.

"Ugggh!" I said at my appearance in the mirror. Purple still pooled under my eyes and my face just looked dull and…tired. I rummaged through my drawer frantically looking for something to make my face just look a little better.

"Foundation…no…concealer…maybe," I took it out and set it on the counter. "Ah-ha!" I produced a bottle of tinted moisturizer and started slathering it over my face, quickly. My shower had taken at least twenty minutes; Gabriel would be back anytime now. I felt guilty because I said I would be resting, not showering although it was necessary. I dabbed at some red areas with concealer and rubbed it in, concentrating on the area under my eyes. They were still purple but now they looked like they obviously were trying to be covered up. I swore under my breath and tried to rub it off with a makeup remover wipe. It just made the area appear more irritated.

I sighed heavily, dabbing more moisturizer on them and calling it good. I applied a tinted lip balm and ran some black mascara over my lashes. I wouldn't say I looked better but, at least I didn't want to hurl looking at my appearance. Maybe just dry-heave.

I unwrapped the towel from my hair and the long strawberry strands fell in tangles around my shoulders. I shook my head with a frown and ran a brush through it, starting at the ends and working my way up. I didn't have hours to spare to blow-dry it so my secret would be out of the bag. I shrugged. "Oh well."

I left the bathroom then and rummaged through my dresser for a clean pair of sweats, a t-shirt that held up the "Live Long and Prosper" hand gesture on it with the saying underneath, my favorite ratty gray sweatshirt that said "Minnesota" emblazoned across the front in red and tossed them on the bed. I dropped the towel and switched into a clean pair of 'granny' briefs—no thongs for this dragon—and a black cotton bra. I was pulling my sweatshirt over my head when I smelled something.

I sniffed the air. "Bacon?" I left the bedroom and followed the smell into the kitchen, where Gabriel was already at work in the kitchen. Dragons—like people—cannot resist bacon. It's a weakness. A chewy, salty weakness...

"But..." I began, confused, trying not to drool. I wasn't a werewolf, dragons didn't drool. Unless there was a bacon.

"You didn't lock it behind you. Shame, shame," Gabriel chided kiddingly, clicking his tongue at me.

"I'm sorry, if I had known you came back so soon I wouldn't have taken so long in the bathroom," I said.

He waved me off. "No worries. Shower make you feel better?"

"A little, thanks," I said, setting myself down on the counter across from him in the kitchen. He was poking at a panful of bacon frying on the stove with his left hand and attempting to flip a pancake with a spatula in his right hand.

"Ooh look at you Gordon Ramsey," said, admiring his kitchen-skills. It was the ultimate compliment; with Gordon Ramsey's adoration of food and his strong temper I was *convinced* he was really a dragon. I loved him—so grumpy and snarly—it was a compliment indeed for the sorcerer.

He grinned. "Don't be too impressed. My first batch is a little...charred." He nodded back towards two plates of bacon and pancakes that were blackened on the edges.

I shrugged. "I'm a dragon. We like things well-done. Usually we're the ones doing the cooking, though."

He glanced at me worriedly. "Remind me not to get on your bad side."

I laughed. "Well…that doesn't really apply to me, you know. I can't really char your food but I can make it shiny!"

Gabriel laughed too. "I'd rather have that then dragon-charred. Ooh you can turn me into a sparkly vampire like from the book!"

I rolled my eyes. "Can I turn you into a werewolf instead?"

"Only if you bite me," he said.

I cocked a brow. "So…wait here. Tell me now…if there are sorcerers like you what else is there? And why haven't I heard of them, yet?"

"I'm sure dragons have reasons to hide this knowledge from you, though I can't speak for them. Here on Earth some humans started exploiting them— "

"—who's *'them'*?"

"Sorcerers. Witches. Warlocks. Fairies. Umm…what else?"

"Vampires?"

Gabriel snorted. "Not in the Hollywood sense but, yeah." I let out a whistle.

"Werewolves?"

"No werewolves, as far as I know."

I snapped my fingers. "Damn," I said. "But—witches and warlocks? What's the difference?"

"Well, as you know a sorcerer is someone whose magic is passed down through the bloodline. It's inherited. Witches learn their magic. Most of them aren't very powerful but every now and then you can get one that actually can attain a decent amount of power. Some of them can use telekinesis, some elemental magic but it's pretty rare. Most of them just practice rituals and spells like your friend Kit."

"What about warlocks?"

"Well, a warlock is a sorcerer or maybe even a witch that practices magic for evil purposes, or to harm someone."

"Like, black magic?"

He considered this. "Well, magic is really not black or white. It all serves a purpose, at times. It's the intent behind it. Like your magic."

I nodded. "I see. Interesting…" The coffee maker sputtered, announcing a fresh pot of coffee was finished brewing. I rose to get some but Gabriel promptly waved me down. "Sit. *Sit!*" he insisted, producing a couple of mugs and pouring us both some. I cocked a brow at the picture of Tinkerbell on the mug he gave me. "Fairies? Really?"

Gabriel nodded, taking a sip of his black coffee. "Believe it or not. Gnomes too but not in Minnesota."

I considered this. We had Brownies—the playful, prank-loving little guys that lived in mushrooms—so it wasn't all that surprising, I suppose. We had normal animals in Anarach like squirrels and birds and whatnot, just a lot less of them.

"Hobbits? Ewoks? Elves?"

"Elves, maybe. But no one's seen one in years."

"Wow...that's insane." I laughed. "I was just kidding about elves."

"Well they're there...just another breed of human really."

"Are they magical?"

Gabriel shrugged. "I don't know been a long time since anyone has seen one."

"So since you're magical maybe you're part elf?" I said, in between bites of pancake.

He chuckled. "It's possible though, I don't think so."

"Where does your magic come from, then? Is your whole family that way? Are there others?"

"No my whole family isn't this way but there *are* others," he said. "In most families it's random who gets it, we think it's like a gene that comes out in certain people. In our line though, it seems that at least one child receives it, usually the oldest but not always. My brother's talent though seems to be an anomaly."

"His foresight?"

He nodded. "Yeah, according to history a Seer is only born when something big is about to happen."

I gulped down my pancake, it suddenly feeling a lot heavier than it was previously. "Big? Big *bad* or big *good*?"

"Could be either. But think about it...would we need a warning if something good was about to happen?"

I sighed. "I was afraid of that. And you think this "something big" has to do with me, huh?"

"Daniel thinks so," he agreed reluctantly. "He won't tell me much more, he can't actually. He's physically unable to. He can be vague and try to guide but...things are going to happen the way they are meant to be and he can't interfere."

"What a terrible burden that must be," I mused, shaking my head. "Your poor brother."

He nodded in agreement. "Though it's not all bad. He's the better looking, stronger one."

"So he doesn't have any other magical ability other than just Seeing?"

Gabriel shook his head. "No, I got all the magic this time around. My uncle and my father—both brothers—received sorcery, though my uncle was certainly better at it. Neither of his kids got it, that's why it was a bit of a blow when I received it. I'm not the strongest, or the smartest but I am pretty powerful. I'm the most skeptical, and I figured all of this was just crap. I fulfilled my obligations, learned how to harness my magic but I didn't really think I'd use it for this. Which is why against my family's wishes I went to college, got a degree…"

"You think they'd be proud, that's a great accomplishment. Daniel didn't go to college?"

"No he did, but there was never any chance he'd be an actual knight. I really, really didn't think it would be me either, though."

"What did he go for?"

Gabriel snorted. "Physical fitness. He's a black belt in tae kwon do, and a personal trainer."

I raised a brow. "Wow."

"Yes, it's always fun being introduced by my parents, 'These are our sons, Gabriel and Daniel,' and they are always shocked to learn I am not the gay one."

"Daniel is gay?"

He nodded. "Yeah. I mean I don't care; I have nothing against it. It was a struggle for him, for sure. But it's not fun being mistaken for something you aren't, you know?"

I muttered under my breath, "Yeah that's for sure."

Gabriel paused, mid-sip in his coffee as if thinking deeply. After a moment he shook himself out of his daze and forced a smile. "But it is what it is."

"Hey you can play with fire, that's pretty cool," I said, trying to be reassuring. "That fireball trick in the woods—not too shabby!"

"Well, I'm glad you're impressed. According to my father I was never good enough," he said, I hint of bitterness to his tone.

I frowned. "I'm sorry." I reached across the counter to touch his arm supportively. "I know how it feels to disappoint your parents."

"Not my mom…just my dad. I don't know how my mom feels, really. She took off with my sister years ago, she didn't want any part of this magic business."

My eyes widened. "She just…left?"

He nodded. "Yup. Just left. I haven't seen her since I was about…five or six. My sister was just a baby. I don't even know if she has any powers or not."

"Wow…I am very sorry," I said, feeling sad for him.

He shrugged. "What can you do?"

"Why would she leave though? Is it…dangerous?"

"No I mean, not any more than anything else, really. But my father claimed it was some sort of *religious* ideals that drove her away."

"And your father just let her take your sister?"

"Yup."

"Wow…" Suddenly my family didn't seem quite so horrible.

After about six more pancakes, two cups of coffee and a bunch more bacon, I was finally starting to feel more energized. I checked my cell phone to check not only the time but to see if Kit had called me back and for some reason I missed it.

"Something wrong?"

"Kit," I said, setting my phone down. "I can't believe both of us didn't make it to the shop. I can't believe she hasn't called me back!"

"Worried?"

"To say the least; she was so tired yesterday. She must have been coming down with something. She actually drank a pop of mine!"

"She doesn't drink pop?"

"No," I shook my head. "Kit is a vegan. Well, most of the time. Coffee is her vice but mostly she eats all-organic gerbil food. Nothing processed. She even drinks the coffee black at the shop with fresh butter."

"Butter?" Gabriel grimaced.

I nodded. "Yeah, she makes it herself."

"Wow…. that's so, odd."

"Apparently it's quite the thing to do in like Europe or whatever; butter in your coffee." I grimaced. "I've never heard that before; sometimes I think she's yankin' my chain."

"I've never heard of that either." Gabriel made a sour face. "Well, should we go check on her? Do you feel up to that?"

"I won't be able to relax anymore until I do, honestly," I said, pushing my plate away and reaching for my purse on the couch.

"Well, let's go," he said. "We can clean this up later."

"Yeah," I pulled my keys out of my front purse pocket but he shook his head. "No, let me drive."

I didn't argue and followed him out to his truck, locking the door to my apartment behind me, calling a quick "*Bye, be back soon!*" to my cat. Not like she could understand me, but, you never know.

Sona uttered a small, disinterested *mew*, barely audible before the door shut.

Chapter 9

Driving the short distance from my apartment to the shop in Gabriel's Ford Ranger pickup, the traces of storm damage were evident alongside the road, and in the yards we passed. Tree branches in the road we had to dodge; roof damage in the form of shingles blown off, gutters falling off, hanging by screws or a few metal shards to their awnings. A few cars parked in driveways had their windows or windshields smashed in by what I assumed was hail.

"Wow..." I said as we pulled into the parking lot of Morningstar Coffee. There was portable lawn furniture in the parking lot—I wasn't sure who it belonged to—branches and leaves all over the ground and mud caked to the walls, as if whatever winds were blowing it was blowing *directly* at the shop. The other buildings and homes around us did not have that particular damage.

"I know," Gabriel said, pulling into the lot and finding an area large enough for his truck to park. "This is definitely the most damaged building in the area, that's for sure."

I shook my head. The front window was blown in, glass was shattered, sprayed all over the parking lot and inside the lobby. The chairs were toppled over, the knick-knacks, art and photos that had been on the walls were now shattered on the floor.

I crossed the parking lot, kicking twigs and leaves out of my way to the front door—remarkably the glass pane of that had remained intact. I ripped off the card left behind by the insurance adjuster and pulled out my phone to dial her number.

"What'cha doing?" Gabriel asked.

"Kit missed her, I'm going to help get the ball rolling again so we can start cleaning up," I explained, just in time for Marta Andersen to pick up on her end.

While I spoke to her, Gabriel slowly walked around the building and around the damaged areas, holding out his hands and closing his eyes in concentration. When he looked up momentarily at me, when I was on hold with Marta I mouthed "*What are you doing?*"

"Trying to sense for magic. I can see traces of it left behind but, I'm trying to see if I can get a feel for what kind it was...maybe I can figure out where it came from?" he said, sounding unconvinced.

"You can do that?" I asked.

He shrugged. "Well, yes. Mostly. It's not an exact science. If someone doesn't want to be found, they won't be."

"Do you feel...anything?" I asked, before Marta came back on the line, telling me she'd already began drawing up the claim. On my word she said she'd have a cleaning crew out in the next twenty-four hours to begin cleaning, which sounded a lot better than doing it ourselves so I gave the okay, but she would just need Kit to sign some forms or for Kit to call her and give the verbal go ahead that I could come out and sign the forms when I described that Kit seemed to be ill and that's why she missed her, earlier.

Gabriel slowly shook his head but kept concentrating. He paused at a spot just before where the window broke and stood for a while. I raised a brow.

Right then, a newer-model yellow Volkswagen Beetle entered the parking lot and a frantic, bedraggled looking Kit stepped out frantically. "Oh my I'm so sorry, I can't believe that—"

I waved her off. "Marta? I actually have Kit here, she just arrived. Can I give you to her? Great, thanks." I handed Kit the phone who looked at me with heavily-lidded eyes, and reluctantly took it.

"Insurance agent," I whispered.

"Oh!" She immediately started speaking into the phone but not before whispering a "Thank you!" to me. I paused, watching her momentarily. Her movements seemed sluggish and labored and her voice was hoarse and she kept slurring. She was apologizing profusely into the phone.

I slowly stepped up to Gabriel who was still deep in concentration.

"Anything?" I asked.

He jumped slightly. "Oh! Sorry," he said with a laugh. He held his hands out once more. "There is.... a concentration of something around here. Right around where the glass broke. If I go closer to the inside, it gets a bit stronger."

"What is 'it'?" I asked.

He shook his head slowly. "I'm not sure. I think I feel arcane magic."

"Arcane? That's not good, huh?"

"No, not necessarily. Just very, very powerful," he explained, looking somewhat intimidated.

"That's bad?" It was more rhetorical then a question.

"Well, it's not good."

I heaved a heavy sigh. "Any idea what— "

"—Leo!" she thrust my phone back in my empty hand and gave me a weak squeeze on the shoulder.

I leapt slightly as a small electric shock went through my shoulder blades.

"Oh! I'm sorry!" she said, pulling away. "Damn, I need better fabric softener I think. Been doing that all day."

"Au naturale isn't working anymore?" I said, half kidding, trying to nonchalantly rub my shoulder where she static-shocked me.

"Guess not. Or perhaps it's this damn cold. Oh Leo, I'm so sorry I'm just getting here now!" Kit looked positively panicked, even disheveled looking in out-of-character ratty gray sweatpants and a baggy t-shirt instead her usual Bohemian flair. Normally her hair was intricately braided around her head or fishtailed and but today it hung long down her back, looking matted and stringy. "I over-slept; I don't know how! Finally, I heard my phone beeping at me and it was you!"

I waved her off. "No worries, I actually just got here myself," I said. "I saw the note on the door and figured I'd call her and get the ball rolling."

"Glad you did. Actually it should be fairly easy, we don't have to do much. She'll send a cleaning crew out here tomorrow to clean up the water and mud, and a contractor will come fix the window but she did say we should board it up in the meantime. So besides that, we don't have to do anything unless I want to open, then I should— "

I gave her an uncertain look. "Kit, you are in no condition to be working. You look sicker than a dog!"

She groaned, scrubbing a palm across her face. "I *know*. I need to get into to doctor. I'm not going to worry about opening; Marta said I'm covered financially for a few weeks and it won't take that long. But I should see about getting this boarded up, though— "

Gabriel stepped closer at that moment and interrupted. He wore a look of seriousness on his face, more so then usual. "Well, we can take care of that. I have my truck. Leo, know of a good lumber yard around here?"

I nodded. "Yeah there's one a couple miles down."

"Yeah. So...don't worry about it. You can go rest." His face was stern but he forced a friendly smile. The energy emanating off him was one of *caution*. "Leo here was really worried about you."

Kit smiled slowly. "I know, she's a good friend." She reached out to grab my hand but Gabriel pretended to lose his balance and knock into me, my hand out of her reach.

"Oh! Sorry! God I'm a klutz!" he said, with a laugh.

I gave him a strange look I hoped Kit didn't notice. "It's okay."

Gabriel smiled at Kit and held out his hand. "I'm sorry, we haven't officially been introduced. I'm Gabriel O'Donnell, Leo and I have become friends over the past couple of days. So any friend of hers is a friend of mind. Hope you don't mind me here."

Kit took his hand and shook it loosely, weakly. She smiled. "Good to meet you officially, Gabriel. I'm Katrina Ryland but everyone calls me Kit."

"Kit. Yes." He hesitated to let go of her hand but Kit's grip had gone non-existent so he was basically hanging on her hand. "Good to meet you." He let go, her hand fell limply to her side.

"Well, I mean it shouldn't be too hard to board up a window right?" she said, trying to stifle a yawn unsuccessfully. "I should be able to handle that."

"Oh it's really okay," I insisted.

"Well..." she paused. "I have hammers and nails at my house, I can go get them. So we don't have to re-buy stuff we already have."

"Sure," I said. "Meet back in about...an hour?"

Gabriel nodded up towards the sky, the sun was hanging down awfully low on the horizon, indicating sunset was impending. "Really, you can just go home. We got this, it'll take about thirty minutes, tops. Leo is worried about you, and even I can tell you don't feel well. You should be in bed resting until that cold or whatever goes away."

I shot Gabriel a confused look. Sure, she looked ill but if she felt like helping, who were we to stop her? It was her place of business.

Kit hesitated. "Well...you know I think I'll just run through the shop for a few minutes. Make sure there isn't anything important left behind." She gave a weak smile and gingerly stepped around the glass. She paused at the door and laughed, deciding to go through the broken window instead. I chucked at Kit's dippy display. Normally she was always with it and put together. This cold was *really* taking its toll on her.

"Good idea," I said. "Gabriel?" I motioned my head towards the truck. "Let's let her rest then."

He paused and started to open his mouth but I shot him daggers with my eyes. He relented and quickly followed me to the truck like a dog who'd just got caught eating out of the garbage.

"What was that?" I asked, as we got in and shut our doors to the truck behind us in unison, glaring at him.

Gabriel gave me a serious stare. "You know that magic? On the shop?"

"Yeah?"

"Your friend has the same magic signature on her," he said.

I gasped. "What?"

He nodded, while turning the ignition over and pulling carefully out of the parking lot. "Yeah. She's full of arcane energy."

"Does that mean...she's...*possessed*?" I stammered, feeling mortified at the idea.

"No, no. Just that whatever magic was used here, she caught a big brunt of it," he explained. "I don't know how, but she did. I think that's what happened when she touched you. It wasn't a static charge. It was a magic charge. That magic clearly doesn't like yours."

I rubbed my shoulder, recalling a few moments ago the shock. Now that he mentioned it, it really didn't *feel* like static electricity. Static usually didn't hurt like *that*.

"Rest assured that's *no* cold she has," Gabriel said, a stern expression on his face as he traversed the highway. "By the way, tell me where we are heading?"

I gave him directions to continue a few miles down the highway, there'd be a frontage road to the right. "Is she going to be okay?"

He nodded. "Oh yeah, sure. It's like you, you expended a lot of energy using that magic to fight whatever *that* was. Even though she isn't magical, the human body can still repel magic on the rare instance they are exposed to it but it takes a *lot* out of her."

I breathed a sigh of relief. "That's good. She is a pagan, you know. She calls herself a 'witch' sometimes."

"Really? Well perhaps that could be a bit of it. A pagan's spellcasting is all about intent. Perhaps she drew the energy to her, if it was nearby. Perhaps she's learning to hone magic a bit."

"Dark magic?" I was alarmed.

"Magic isn't dark or light, necessarily. It's all about intent, remember."

"So trying to raise someone from the dead isn't a bad thing?" I challenged, partially kidding. I wasn't even sure if that was possible. If sorcerers and oracles were well, I guessed there was a possibility.

Gabriel chuckled. "Necromancy is a tricky thing. You don't really raise the dead but…channel their spirit."

"What?" My mouth fell open. "Zombies?"

He roared. "Once a body is dead, it's dead. No coming back. But a necromancer is a good example of someone who works with perceived 'black' magic usually to help rid a home of specters, or help a soul on its right path."

"Wow," I said. "As if dragons weren't strange enough, huh?"

"Yeah, as if." He sat in silent thought for a moment. "But anyway, that's why I was trying to get her to go home. If that magic jumped from her to you just from that brief touch, then being around her for very long might not be the wisest thing."

"You're saying you think Kit would attack me?"

"No, but the magic obviously was triggered when it was near you. If it's draining her, it would certainly drain you if you aren't careful. She really just needs to sleep it off for a few days. Since she isn't *actually* magical there's nothing to keep it there for long, it will fade away," he said. "But I still want to perform some kind of a cleansing protection spell on her, if she's still there. It should help expel the signature faster and she should feel better by morning, especially if you help me channel it."

"Sure," I said. "Whatever I have to do."

"Good." He said. We pulled into the local lumberyard and selected a sheet of plywood and a box of nails and a hammer, paid and were on our way.

We arrived back at the coffee shop, unloaded the plywood and were carrying it over to the window when I saw Kit slumped over the counter inside the shop, not moving.

I shrieked, and started to drop the wood when I remembered I was carrying one side. "Oh no, Kit!"

"Drop it," Gabriel said, and we both let the wood fall to the ground with a slight thud and dashed through the broken glass wall into the shop.

"Kit! Kit?" I screamed frantically, shaking her shoulder.

Kit stood upright again with a gasp. "Oh! Oh, Leo! I'm sorry!" She peeled some hair stuck to her face off and wiped some spittle off the corner of her mouth. "I don't know what's gotten into me, seriously!"

"God, Kit! Seriously...you really need to get home. This is nuts! I can handle the shop, the cleaning crew will be here tomorrow, I'll let them in...you just go home and *get better*, okay?"

Kit heaved a heavy sigh. "Oh, Leo, you're right. I just...whatever this is it's awful. I feel like I've been run over by a truck. My head is fuzzy and I'm like so hungry all the time for the most disgusting food!"

I shot Gabriel a helpless look, while I wrapped my arms around my friend and gave her a big hug.

He nodded.

"It'll be okay, Kit. You just need some rest. The storms just rattled you; you got sick, that's all," I tried to be soothing as I patted her back.

Kit let out a pitiful whimper. "I know but, I never get sick. This is awful!"

"I know, I know. Just let it out. Tell me all about it," I said soothingly, trying to sound like someone's comforting mother (even though I have no idea what that would sound like, of course).

Kit began to explode into sobs. Uncontrollable, gasping sobs. I just held her and let her cry. Kit was *not* a crier—unless we were watching *Titanic* or something equally as depressing.

Gabriel inhaled deeply and shut his eyes. He held out his palms. I couldn't tell what he was doing, exactly but when he'd been like that for a few moments, I inhaled and exhaled myself, letting out a shower of sparkles into the air. I watched as they flew about a moment and finally settled into Kit's messy hair and unkempt clothes.

Gabriel nodded in approval when I looked to him and seemed more relaxed.

Kit's sobs subsided to sniffles and she pulled away after a few moments. "Oh, sorry Leo...it really is surprising to feel this bad. I have *never* felt this bad before, seriously."

"I know," I said, wishing I could tell her exactly *why* she was feeling this badly but it was better to let her think it was a bad cold.

"And just *look* at this place!" she gestured around the lobby. About the only thing left standing were the heavy machines. Most of the mugs, cups and saucers lay shattered on the floor, papers were blown about everywhere, all the knick-knacks (carved wooden

Minnesota animals, signage and etc.) were tossed about on the floor or knocked over. It didn't look like too many of them were broken beyond repair—which was good because I knew how Kit loved her tchotchkes (as she liked to call them).

"Kit, why don't you just go in the car, Leo here will drive you home and I'll get this boarded up. It'll only take a minute or two to get that board up and then I'll be behind you and I can bring Leo back," Gabriel offered.

She nodded. "Yeah, I'm sure that's best," she said, wiping her nose on her sleeve with a sniffle. She chuckled. "Wow, I must have really needed that cry, I'm actually feeling a bit better now."

I tried to hide a smirk and Gabriel winked at me. "That's good. I'm glad to hear that." I patted her on the back and tried to wipe some of the sparkles out of her hair, hoping she wouldn't notice but she did anyway.

"Oh! Glitter!" she groaned, trying to shake out her hair and pointed at a snowglobe that had fallen to the ground. "Must have gotten glitter on me from that. Geez, how'd that happen?" she asked rhetorically with a chuckle. "That sucks, I liked that one," she said regrettably. It was a snowman with a sign in front saying "Welcome to Minnesota" and when you shook it, it looked like a white-out blizzard.

"We'll find another, the internet is a great thing," I said, with a laugh. I began to lead her out of the shop.

"Oh, are you sure you are okay here? It's awfully nice of you to do this and you barely even know me," she said, as we passed Gabriel in the lobby she reached out and grasped his forearm. He tried not to wince and instead forced a smile.

"Well, any friend of Leo's is a friend of mine, like I said," he said cheerfully.

"You haven't known Leo long though, right?" she asked.

Gabriel smiled warmly. "Not personally I suppose, but I've known *of* her for a long time."

I grinned. "On Facebook, that's why I freaked out. At first I thought he was just some nut then I remembered we've talked on Facebook a few times."

"Oh, that's nice! Where'd you find each other?"

"On a page about loving dragons," Gabriel said, his face totally serious.

I tried not to snort, but it came out as an incredulous barking sound. "Yeah, that was it."

"That's cute," she said with a giggle. "Okay well...I suppose we should get going. Gabriel, seriously, thank you so much."

He waved her off. "Not at all. It's the Minnesota nice thing to do right?"

She nodded and smiled. "Absolutely."

I gave Gabriel a smile and told him to call me so I could direct him to Kit's, and I led Kit out the shop via the door instead of having her step over the broken window frame and piled her into her car.

"So, you said you're feeling better, a little?" I questioned.

"Oh! Oh yes. Leo, I can't thank you enough for stepping in and—"

"God, Kit. Don't thank me. All the stuff you do for me? You watched Sona countless times for me, picked up my slack at the shop when I ran off? It's the *least* I could do."

"Still." She sat in silence for a moment, I glanced over at her, she was deep in thought. "You *saved* my ass, Leorah? You know that? More than once. It's time I— "

"—Kit, come on! I was just doing what anyone would do who needed a job. And a friend. You don't have to do that, you really don't," I insisted, feeling a bit overwhelmed.

Kit placed her palm on my forearm earnestly. I felt a small shock, but not painful like before. A zap of sleepy electricity. I didn't pull away, this time. "Seriously I do. I would not have made it without you, you are like a super woman. Or maybe a super hero. Or not even human, I don't know."

I tried to stifle a laugh. Oh if she only knew. But that really didn't have much to do with it. Dragons, like humans could be totally lazy if they wanted to be.

"Kit I'm nothing of the sort. I just really needed a job, you were there, I helped. That's it."

"Well," she began, a hint of stubbornness in her tone. "When I'm feeling better and the shop is fully rehabilitated, you'll allow me to take you to dinner? Drinks?"

I grinned. "Now *that* I will allow," I said, pulling into the entrance of her long driveway and up to her tiny farmhouse on the outskirts of town.

When we arrived I insisted Kit change into some comfortable sweats. I made her a relaxing blend of chamomile tea and made sure all her cats were fed before making her camp out on her cozy couch. It wasn't long before she drifted off to sleep; one of her cats sidled up beside her. The white kitty purred away in time with Kit's slight snore. It wasn't much longer until Gabriel arrived to pick me up. I was reluctant to leave but some of the blush in her cheeks had returned, her under-eye bags were not as pronounced and she appeared less haggard. I felt she'd be okay after a good night's sleep. Whatever Gabriel did, it definitely seemed to help. I asked him what exactly it was, when I climbed into the cab of his truck and shut the door behind me.

"Oh well...hard to explain, really. Whatever energy it was inhabiting Kit, it was negative."

"Dark?"

He made a hesitant noise. "Eh, no not dark. Dark energy isn't necessarily bad, remember?"

I nodded. "Right, right... I guess I read too many paranormal fantasy books," I said, with a chuckle.

"Why does that not surprise me?" he laughed. "For Kit, I tried to channel the positive energy coming from you and channel it into her in hopes that it would help expel the negative force in her," he continued. "She seemed like she was feeling a bit better. Do you think it worked?"

"Oh, yes, definitely. She was beginning to perk up. She was smiling and laughing again. She didn't look quite so tired. She did fall asleep before I left but that's probably a good thing, right?"

He nodded. "Definitely," he said. "Since she's not magical really it won't have anything to *grab* onto, I guess you could say. Sleep is the body's way of regenerating itself, of course. She would have slept it off anyways, but hopefully we gave her a good boost to help heal faster."

"How did she get like that, anyways?" I asked.

He sighed, thoughtfully. "Well, you know how we were in the shop and I stopped suddenly? I couldn't go any further. It was there."

"It?"

"Whatever that energy is. Probably part of that conjured storm. The damage at the shop was the worst I've seen, besides the truckstop like I said before."

I was baffled by his words. Some random energy? Like a poltergeist or evil spirit or something from *Harry Potter* or some other horror-type flick? "But...what *is* it?"

Gabriel exhaled slowly. "I don't know, really. Someone somewhere with some really bad intentions."

I groaned. "Wonderful. Could it be like a bad ghost or evil spirit?"

"No..." he trailed off in the middle of his thought. "No," he continued, "ghosts aren't good or evil. They are manifestations of our very souls, but without a physical body they cannot do any harm."

My mouth fell, open, agape. "So could Kit have been *possessed?*"

Gabriel said nothing, I could see his mouth purse out of the peripheral vision of my eye, his knuckles tensing, turning white on the steering wheel.

"Shit," was all I said. "*Shit!*"

"I wouldn't worry about that," Gabriel finally said, as we pulled into the lot outside my apartment. "Like I said, she's not magical. Whatever this is, it's magical in nature, more than likely she wasn't possessed by anything," he said. "But that doesn't mean something bad wasn't around, trying."

I let out a low whistle.

"Since we don't know what that was that was around the shop, causing the storm—my guess is some jackass warlock with some sort of personal vendetta—I can't rule it out completely. She isn't actually possessed but something nasty was around."

"Why would a warlock want to do that?"

"I don't know, really." He sighed, pulling into the empty spot beside my Neon and turning the truck off. "But, I'm sure we'll find out, sooner or later."

"Ugh," I grimaced, climbing down from the truck and rummaging through my purse for the keys to the apartment. "I was afraid you'd say that." I glanced around the complex briefly, shadows had fallen on the walls from the sun setting in the horizon, hiding some of the damage.

I entered my little home and tossed my keys and purse on the coffee table. It didn't even rattle Sona who was dozing off in the middle of the sofa. I sighed in dismay, seeing the disarray and unkempt state of my apartment. "Ugh, well, I guess I better get to it," I said, wrinkling my nose, grabbing a handful of empty pop cans for the recycling.

"I think you should rest," Gabriel insisted, trying to snatch the cans away from me.

"No!" I protested, with a pout. "I am feeling better, now, really! Whatever you did to Kit, after you did it I felt a bit energized too," I said, pulling the cans out of his grasp. I pranced the ten steps to the recycling bin in the kitchen with a little kick to my heels and tossed the cans in. I turned around and stuck my tongue out at him. "See? I'm just fine."

He rolled his eyes, but smiled too. "Okay, okay. Far be it for me to argue with someone who could literally chew me out."

I wiggled my eyebrows at him. "You have no idea."

He chuckled. "Can I at least help?"

"Eh, sure. You can help by getting that lazy damn cat off my couch and getting her some dinner," I said, motioning towards her bowls and a plastic bin full of dry cat food in the corner of the kitchen. "I'll take care of these plates," I said, grabbing an armful of dishes and tossing them into the sink, as they made *plink*ing sounds.

I listened to food pour into Sona's food bowl and the pitter-patter of little paws across the linoleum. The calico cat mewed and started nibbling.

I paused in my dish-tossing to turn to Gabriel. "You know, you don't have to stick around. If you've got something to do...go ahead. I'll be fine, now. Kit's okay. I'm just going to pick up and maybe play some *World of Warcraft* and take a long bath and relax. Nothing interesting here."

Gabriel crossed his arms over his chest. "Are you trying to get rid of me?" he said, puffing out his lower lip in a mock pout.

"No!" I said, with a grin. I wiped my wet hands off on my shirt and stomped over to him. I poked at his pouty lip with my index finger and pretending to glare. "Don't you go trying to guilt me, Mr. Knight *sir*," I said, with a half-hearted curtsy.

"I would never," he said, with a laugh as he grabbed my hand and held it up to his lips. "At least not for about ten years or so."

I shivered slightly at the sensation of his lips gently touching the top of my hand.

The corners of his lips upturned in a smile, a smile that went all the way up to his twinkling brown eyes. I couldn't help but return the smile.

He let my hand lower slightly and loosened his grip, but I didn't move my hand. I *so* didn't want to. My eyes looked to his for a moment, then I felt a flush of uncomfortable heat as I looked away. He let my hand drop then, and let out an awkward cough.

I took a step back slowly, while looking at the floor. I stumbled a bit over my feet but I caught my balance by grasping the fridge handle next to me.

He stifled a laugh. "I'm sorry. I guess…I got carried away."

"Oh, no. Don't be sorry," I insisted. "I just don't do people well. Or dragons or anything else. Kit is really the only person I've ever gotten along with."

He frowned slightly. "I *am* sorry about that. I wish you had lived your life knowing how wonderful you were supposed to be instead of ridiculed by everyone."

I shrugged. "Eh, well…what are you going to do?"

"But I guess that makes you more, human," he said. "That happens all too often over here." He said this with an undertone of shame in his tone.

"Something you know about, huh?" I said, as I started to empty the dishes from the dishwasher and put them away.

"Maybe," he said. "I never got along very well with people much either. Growing up the only person I really was friends with was my brother. It was hard to explain to people that instead of football or soccer I had to be at home learning magic spells and conjuring in the woods. Someone saw me while they were on a camping trip, doing magic but not seeing any like, fireballs or anything. But, I was chanting. Rumors started going around school that I was a freaky wizard and…well, you can imagine the rest…" he trailed off, shrugging his shoulders, picking at some leftover bacon on a plate.

I turned to him and frowned. "I'm sorry, I know that feeling well."

He chuckled. "Thing is; they were right basically. I'm a sorcerer, not that I could ever admit to it. Perhaps if I could actually throw some fireballs at them, they'd shut up. But obviously I can't do that, so…I got bullied quite a bit. My brother who actually *was* smaller than me for a while decided he needed to be my protector. That was humiliating in its own right but, I don't blame him for that. He started running and weight training and he had a huge growth spurt. He beat up quite a few kids in our school days for calling me names. Finally, in high school, it stopped but no one was really nice to me. I was just ignored. I didn't get to go to Homecoming or Prom or anything normal kids did."

"Well we didn't have anything like that back home," I said. "No dances or anything. Dragons aren't big on *fun*."

"What did you guys even do, then?"

I shrugged. "Well, we do dinners, and dinner parties though usually they consist of talking and sometimes drinking. Though dragons don't really get drunk, but it might make a few of us laugh a little. Well...they can if the liquor is spelled by a witch but, we don't generally have a lot of those lying around. Ha. The younger dragons would do stuff together. Flower picking, swimming in the rivers, flying and setting things on fire, you know...pretty typical stuff."

Gabriel snorted. "Yeah, setting things on fire, so *typical*."

I shot him a pretend dirty look, but grinned anyways. "But of course, since I didn't have any friends or anyone that even liked me I just sat in my room just reading books and listening to music. Sometimes if I were lucky we'd get movies. Everything was about ten years old or so by the time it migrated to us so, my taste is a little behind the times. I didn't even get to finish the series until I came here. All I could get a hold of there was the first and second books. I watched all the movies over a span of like, two days when I came over here for good," I said with a chuckle.

"Well, you're ahead of me, then. I haven't even seen the last one."

My mouth fell open in an "O" of shock. "You *haven't*? How could you see part one and not see the second one? I mean that's like..." I trailed off, and just made a weird sound and gasped.

Gabriel laughed.

"You don't have anything else to do tonight, right?" I grabbed him by the sleeve of his sweatshirt and dragged him over to the sofa. I pushed him down and said forcibly, "*Sit*. You must finish *Deathly Hallows*. Right now."

He raised his eyebrows playfully. "Wow. Pushy."

I glared at him, as I reached for my stack of Blu-rays on a shelf next to my TV. I pulled out *Harry Potter and the Deathly Hallows, Part Two* and put it in the player.

"Am I being held hostage?" he asked with a joking tone.

"At least until you finish the movie," I said, sitting down opposite him on the sofa with the remote.

"Yes, ma'am," he said with a mock salute.

We were about ten minutes into the movie, when I heard someone pounding on the door.

"Who could that be? Kit?" I mused, hitting the pause button on the remote and standing up. The pounding came again, a bit louder and much more forceful then Kit would do (actually, Kit would ring the doorbell). "That's not Kit..." I said, heading to the door.

Gabriel rose, and motioned for me to sit. "No, let me. If there is some screwed up warlock out there searching for magic, I don't really want them to find you. I don't know what they are capable of."

"I'm a dragon, I'll just eat him," I said, with a shrug.

Gabriel gave me a stern look. "Okay, I know I'm new to this Knight thing but I'm pretty sure allowing some nasty warlock to get a hold of your magic would be a bad idea. You *may* or may not be able to be possessed, I don't know. You haven't honed your magic fully yet; you may be vulnerable. Besides, you can't shift in here anyways I would imagine without you tearing up the entire room so if you will..." he motioned to the sofa for me to sit.

Gabriel opened the door, and I heard a familiar voice, "Who the *hell* are you?"

I rolled my eyes, and pushed past Gabriel, who was having a visual stand-off with my brother, Braeden.

"Gabriel, this is my brother, Braeden," I said, to him, and Gabriel softened his glare.

"Ah, yes," he held out his hand with a genuine smile, "I have heard about you. I'm Gabriel O'Donnell."

Braeden snorted, you could almost see smoke puff out his nostrils. "Gabriel? Funny, I haven't heard crap about you," he said, shoving past Gabriel and making his way inside, glaring at Gabriel the entire time, his eyes never leaving his.

"Oh lord," I said to myself, under my breath.

A high-pitched, girly giggle broke the silence. Kiarra appeared from around the corner. "Oh! Leo! It's so good to see you again!"

Now it was my *turn to glare*. I forced a cheerful smile instead. "Kiarra. How lovely to see you again," I said, my voice dripping with sarcasm.

She shoved past my brother and Gabriel and wrapped her arms around me for a big hug.

"Kiarra," Braeden said, in a warning tone.

"Oh!" Kiarra pulled away, putting her fingertips to her lips and smiling sheepishly. "Oops! I'm sorry, Brae here tells me you're not much of a hugger. He said if you're ever going to like me, I should...hold off on the hugging."

I cocked a brow. "I would appreciate that." I gestured for them to come in, and I shut the door behind them.

"What the Hell are you doing here?" I asked, as my brother and Kiarra sat next to each other on the sofa. And when I say next to each other I mean not an inch of space between them, Kiarra's legs draped over his lap. Very unusual behavior for dragons who are not known for public displays of affection. I sat on the recliner and Gabriel leaned against it casually.

Braeden gave Gabriel one crabby gaze, and then allowed his face to soften. "I caught word that Earth—specifically here—had some really, really bad weather. I needed to see for myself that you were okay," he explained.

"Um...cell phone?" I said, pulling my phone out of my pocket and wiggling it at him. "Or e-mail or whatever. Would have been quicker."

Kiarra piped up. "That's my fault, really. Braeden and I were talking about you, and I was afraid I came off too strong and said some bonehead things," she explained, "I wanted to come apologize to you in person. I know how much you mean to Braeden here, it's really important that you feel comfortable with me—with us," she said quickly, with a laugh. "I know you are worried that I might '*take him away*' from you but I'm here to tell you I would never do that."

"Well, that's good to know," I said, not even bothering to smile this time.

"Um, why would she think that you would take him away?" Gabriel asked, confused.

"Remember, I told you about our *ways* earlier?" I explained, with an eye roll. "We don't normally...*court* like this."

"Wait—what? Who is this? What have you told him?" Braeden stood up, pushing aside Kiarra (she kind of fell back on the couch from the force of him, and I couldn't help but snicker a bit at the scene).

"What have *you* told *her?*" I stood up myself, crossing my arms across my chest, staring him down.

Braeden backed down some. "Look, she just wants to get to know you, I don't think there is anything wrong with that. Not like telling this perfect stranger about...well, you know."

I rolled my eyes. "First of all, he's not a perfect stranger. I've known him for a few weeks now, we talk when he would come into the shop a little. Then I learned that he...well, he's a friend." I added that last part, feeling lame. I didn't want to divulge his whole purpose.

"Friend?" Braeden guffawed.

Gabriel rose. "She is right. I'm a part of an ancient organization that has worked with your kind for thousands of years. Most specifically, we would assist dragons like your sister with their magic and helping both our races."

"You worked with *us?* Oh come on!" Braeden laughed uproariously. "Leo, he's feeding you a line of bullshit!"

"Oh? Is that so?" I reached for my backpack that was next to the chair and rummaged for the book Grandfather gave me. I handed it to him. "Open it."

Braeden took it, reluctantly. "What the hell is this?"

"It's this crazy little thing called a *book*, genius," I retorted snidely.

I heard Gabriel stifle a laugh, I shoved my elbow into his ribs as a warning to knock it off.

Braeden snorted, and gingerly leafed through it. "Well it's old and...a bunch of nonsense," he said, stopping to look at one page. "Except...this is interesting. This sort of looks like your mark," he said, pointing at the tribal symbol on one of the first pages. "Where did you get this?"

"Our grandfather," I replied smugly.

"What?"

"Also..." I nudged Gabriel, "*Show* him."

"Show him—oh." He frowned. "Um, Leo, I don't know— "

"See? He's a liar," Braeden challenged.

"Ha!" Gabriel lifted up his shirt and exposed the tattoo on his chest. "This is the symbol of our Order. I got it when I was officially a member when I was eighteen. It just appeared on my birthday unlike the rest of this ink I had to actually pay for. If that book belonged to your grandfather—how the hell would I have known about it unless I'm telling the truth?"

Braeden snorted. "Oh, there could be a million reasons for that. Humans are quite sneaky."

"Really? You don't believe me?" Gabriel opened his palms and closed his eyes a moment. A fireball sparked in his hands and floated there.

"Whoa—what the—" Braeden's mouth opened in shock.

Kiarra let out a little yelp. "Oh my..." Her eyes widened.

145

"How did you do that?" Braeden demanded, bewildered.

"All the Knights are sorcerers," Gabriel explained. "A pink dragon and a Knight of the Order would work together to amplify magic to help out."

"Help with what?"

"According to Grandfather, years ago humans and dragons lived together as we all already know—happily. We would work together to build houses, take care of farms, ward off famines, stuff like that," I explained.

"Wow...I had no idea," Braeden said, relenting in his fight and sitting back down.

"Not something they teach in Dragon school is it?" Kiarra said, in a near mumble under her breath. It was so grumbly and uncharacteristic to her normal cheeriness (at least based on the one time I met her) it barely registered in my brain that it was her.

Gabriel closed his palms together and the fireball dispersed in a puff of smoke, looking smug.

"That's pretty cool, actually," Braeden was impressed. "I didn't know that humans had any sort of magic."

"Apparently, there is a lot of things we do not know," I replied dryly.

"No, you don't," Gabriel said. "Pink dragons have the ability to amplify—or disperse—magic. It's actually quite a valuable ability to have. There are records of humans trying to abuse that magic—or even other dragons."

"And that seems to be about the time dragons separated to their own realm," I explained.

"So, why now?" Braeden questioned. "Why you?"

Gabriel just shrugged. "No one really knows," he said. "But as far as we know Leorah is the first pink dragon born in—"

"Nine hundred and ninety-eight years," Kiarra muttered.

I raised my brow. "That long, huh?"

Kiarra quickly switched her surly frown into her normal cheery smile. "Well, you know I'm kind of a dragon history buff. I mean, you know the best way to keep bad things from happening is to learn about them, right?"

"And we don't want me going insane like Cyril, right?" I crabbed, narrowing my eyes.

I swear I almost saw Kiarra wince at that, but she just giggled. "Oh stop, Leo—"

"—*Leorah*!" I insisted. I heard Gabriel cough under his breath, stifling a laugh. I elbowed him again.

"No it's not that of course. I have a certain fascination with humanity too," Kiarra said, with a smile. "That's something we have in common, you know?"

"I don't have so much a *fascination* with them as much as I enjoy just blending in and not getting tortured, you know?" I quipped.

Braeden coughed then, pointedly in an attempt to make me stop glaring at his fiancée. "That's actually part of the reason she wanted to come here. We don't have weather like tornadoes and stuff, she wanted to see it for herself."

"And of course, make sure you made it home okay," Kiarra said, reaching over and tapping my knee.

I couldn't help but let out a guttural growl of anger in annoyance at the blue dragon sitting here in my living room.

"Well, I'd take you on the tour of misery but most of the damage has been cleaned up by now," I said.

"I'm just glad no one was really hurt," she said. "So I could really enjoy the scenery. There was a little damage in the woods by the portal but otherwise you're right, not much left. Like it never really happened, almost."

"Yeah, almost," Gabriel said, his arms crossed over his chest. He offered a friendly smile. "We humans are pretty hardy, you know. And the tornadoes ended up being kind of small, coupled with a great weather service and we managed to keep safe. Thankfully, right?"

"Right!" Kiarra let out a peal of cheery laughter. "Well I suppose we're intruding; we should get going. They look like they're about to watch a movie," she said, pointing to the paused picture on the TV. "Looks like *Twilight*, right?"

I felt the heat rise in my face. "*Harry Potter*." Was all I said.

Braeden rose to his feet, pulling Kiarra with him. "Well we can go now. Leo here takes her movies really, really seriously. You want to get on her good side…don't ever mistake *Twilight* for anything but *Twilight*," he said with a short laugh.

I crossed my arms across my chest and narrowed my eyes at them.

"Oh! We can try that little coffee house we drove by on the way in!" Kiarra said giddily.

"On the way in?" Gabriel questioned. "*Your* coffeehouse isn't on the road in from the portal, is it?"

I shook my head. "No, it's not. How did you know about that?" I challenged her.

"Oh well—we saw it, you know. Maybe it wasn't on the way in but I swear—"

"—and was open?" I asked, knowing fully well obviously that it wasn't.

"Well, yeah, why wouldn't it be?" Kiarra said, with a confused shrug.

"Huh. Interesting, because I'm the manager at that coffeehouse. My best friend, Kit, owns it. It's been shut down for about two days now due to storm damage. You can see the blown-out windows from the street," I said, rather snidely.

Braeden appeared confused. "Yeah, I don't recall passing any coffeehouse, you must have been seeing another building," he said patting her on the shoulders as he was trying to coax her towards the door.

"Oh, yeah maybe. Too bad, coffee sounded good," she said, with a whine in her tone.

Gabriel and I exchanged looks. I mouthed "*Told you*" to him and he nodded.

I rose and went to my brother's side. "Give Grandfather a hug for me, okay?" I said, grasping his elbow.

Braeden released his fiancée momentarily and nodded. He gave me an earnest smile and said, "I'm glad you're okay. Really, I was worried."

"You could have called?" But I knew even that sometimes wouldn't work, connections from Earth to Anarach were unreliable at best. "Well, email? Facebook?"

He chuckled. "I know, but Kiarra was really eager to come Earth side, she hasn't had much of an opportunity to do so. We were going to come see you and then just wander around. Maybe go out to Minneapolis or the big mall."

I nodded. "Have fun with that," I said with a cringe at the idea.

He laughed, gave me a brief hug and ushered Kiarra out the door, as she giggled and talked the entire time. I think she was trying to say good-bye but, I wasn't really listening. Nor did I care.

"*Ugggggggggggggh!*" I screamed in frustration, shutting the door behind them. I put my hands in my hair and started yanking it out of its ponytail.

"Whoa there!" Gabriel was there, pulling my arms down and down to my sides. "Breathe, Leo. Just breathe," he said, demonstrating by taking a long, deep breath and exhaling.

I attempted it, but I ended up exhaling in a growl.

"Wow, Leo—chill!" He said, shaking out his hands. "You almost sparked a fire in my hands!"

"Huh? How is that possible unless you were making fireballs?" I asked, puzzled.

"Well sometimes when I'm angry, they have been known to…happen," he said, with an innocent laugh.

"Angry?" We sat back down on the sofa, I was trying not to growl the whole time. "Am I right though? There is…*something* about her!"

"Well, when she started talking about the coffee house, that's when red flags started going up for me," he explained. "There is something off about her, I can't place it."

"Evil?"

"No," he said with a sigh. "I know you want her to be the devil incarnate but, I think she's just a dippy, dingy weirdo."

"You don't think she conjured that evil magic at the shop? How did she even know about the shop? Like I said—you do *not* drive by the shop on the road back from the portal," I said.

"Did they fly here?" he questioned, going off-subject.

"No, they probably called the rogue dragon who lives on the edge of town, Ismani. He's an orange dragon. He hooked me up with my first fake ID and all that. He probably arranged a cab for them," I rubbed my fingers together, "for a price, of course. But lots of dragons live here like him. The rogues live near portals a lot of times in order to be of service to any dragons who might need their expertise. They do lots of off-the-grid illegal things, but they are really good at it so they don't get caught."

"Still doesn't explain how she knew about the coffeehouse unless she's been here before. Has she?"

I shrugged. "I don't know. This is the first time I've seen her here. I suppose she could have come to human Earth before. Most dragons do at one time or another, but this particular portal is very slow, not many dragons use it. They prefer a colder climate."

"Colder than Minnesota?" Gabriel said with a guffaw.

"Yeah who would ever think Minnesota wouldn't be cold enough?" I said with a laugh. "But yeah, there are many more portals in Montana, I think one in Maine, a handful in Alaska, upstate New York and lots in Canada."

"Really?"

I nodded. "Yeah. Way more in Europe. Dragons generally prefer it over there, I don't know why. I just wanted to be away from any dragons. There is only a handful that I know of living in Minnesota so that's why I picked here."

"Anyway, it still doesn't explain what Kiarra's problem is." I said, grumbling.

Gabriel shrugged. "I don't know. You are right, something is off about her. I don't think she's evil but— "

"—could she be possessed maybe?" I asked, with a gasp at the idea.

He shook his head. "No, I sensed no possession. But she *is* hiding something."

"I knew it!" I exclaimed.

"Most people are hiding something so, don't get your hopes up on that; it doesn't necessarily mean anything," Gabriel chided me. "*But* pink dragons are supposed to have good instincts. If you think something's up with her, there probably is."

"Maybe she's just hosing my brother over," I said, frowning. "Better not be it."

Gabriel chuckled, reaching over and patting my knee. "I know, you'll eat her."

I beamed proudly. "Yeah. I haven't eaten anyone in a while, it might be fun!"

Gabriel blinked and slowly moved away. "I sure hope you're joking."

I cackled evilly, grabbing the remote and switching the movie back on. "Fuck her, let's finish the movie before I decide to eat the couch or the chair."

"You are scary," he said with a laugh.

I smacked him playfully in the chest and pointed at the movie. "*Harry Potter* is on. No talking." I put a finger to my lips and whispered *"Shhhhh!"*

He chuckled, but didn't respect my "no talking" rule. He kept making snarky comments as it went on, first during the first scene after the "funeral" he had to ask "Who died again?" I didn't eat him, but I did give him a good smack for that one.

About halfway through, Gabriel became more relaxed and he had propped his legs up on the middle cushion, dangling his feet and ankles off the front. His calves were remarkably close to me—just centimeters away—and I found myself very uncomfortable with the notion. First I felt just socially awkward. Did he need to stretch out? Should I let him stretch out his legs over my lap? Do I just ask him? Or do I just grab his legs and put them there? But would he think I was coming on to him?

Now I found myself consumed with thoughts of touching Gabriel. First it started with his legs and if I should ignore them or not. Was I being a bad friend not letting him stretch out? But my eyes trailed up towards his wide chest and broad shoulders. No, he wasn't extremely buff or anything but his body had muscular definition. In the short times I'd seen him with his shirt off, it was a nice chest. I thought about—*gulp*! —resting my head on his stomach, and then wrapping my arms around him, listening to his heart beat and relaxing at the sound, the feeling of being close to someone while tracing my fingertips over the outlines of all his ink…I trembled slightly at the notion.

For a dragon, these were odd thoughts to have. As dragons of course were not big on showing affection. Perhaps I'd seen too many rom-com movies but, I couldn't help but be intrigued by the notion.

I've seen plenty of human men though; even dragons in their human forms and I never had that urge before. Well I kind of did when I watched *The Notebook* once before but I wasn't picturing anyone in particular. Until I met Gabriel.

Perhaps something was changing in young dragons, or perhaps we were just told (like so many other things, apparently) that touching was just something dragons didn't do but the thought of being close to someone was nice. *Comforting*.

But the thoughts were kind of blown out of my head by another sarcastic comment from Gabriel, when the movie was winding down:

"So, who was fighting again?" He had a mischievous glint in his brown eyes.

I slowly turned to him, with a glare that would scald his eyebrows. "Oh, now you're asking for it! Ever get punched by a dragon?" I balled up my fist and attempted to lean over and punch him playfully in the chest, but he caught my arms and pinned them against my chest. I tried to break free, I ended up falling over backwards on the sofa, pulling Gabriel with me who landed on top of me and was now looking me square in the eye.

I felt the heat instantly scald my cheeks. "Oops, I'm sorry," I said, struggling under him to get up.

"No, I'm sorry," he said, blushing himself, scrambling to move.

We managed to pull ourselves into a sitting position, but somehow he was still kind of perched over me.

"Um," I said, uncomfortably. "I'm kind of stuck. I think you're sitting on my leg."

"Oh, I'm sorry," he said, trying to shift his weight off of me, when my cat took that opportune time to jump from the floor onto his lap. Startled, he fell into my chest.

"Oh shit!" he exclaimed, his words muffled by—well my boobs in his face.

I felt my face turn ablaze. "It's okay," I managed to squeak, afraid to move and give him an even larger face full of chest.

Sona was digging her paws into his lap, like she was scratching. Since she was declawed by whoever her previous owner was (she was a rescued kitty) it didn't hurt him, but apparently, it tickled because he began laughing hysterically.

"What?" I asked, confused and bashful.

He peeked up at me, over my boobs in between laughs. "I don't know; I can't stop laughing!"

I feigned offense. "Uh! So you're telling me there is something funny about my…" I trailed off, looking down at my chest.

His eyes widened, as he scrambled to get up. "No! No I swear, I'm sure they're very nice, it's just that—"

I cut him off with a raucous laugh. "Ha! The look on your face!"

He frowned, and narrowed his eyes at me. "You are an evil, evil person."

"Dragon," I corrected, giving him an angelic smile.

"Whatever," he said, rolling his eyes with a sigh. "God, I suck at this."

"Suck? At what?" I asked.

"Uggh," he said, scrubbing his face with his palms, leaning his elbows on his lap.

"*What*!?!"

"Women! I'm just awful with them," he said in frustration.

I raised my brow at him. "What do you mean? You're fine with me."

Gabriel gave me a pointed look. "Fine? I just fell over on your chest and laughed at it."

I giggled. "Oh come on, I was just joking around."

"I know, I know," he exhaled. "I just… I don't know…"

"Don't know what?"

"I don't know how to bring up that kiss!" he blurted out. "I mean, I'm sorry it's all I've been thinking about since I saw you the other day. When you ran off I figured that you were weirded out by it, especially when you wouldn't answer my texts or anything."

I winced. I forced myself to awkwardly put my hand on his forearm. "Aw, Gabriel. You know why I left now."

He nodded. "I know now, but over the past few days I was just freaking out, thinking that I came on too strong—I *never* act that way, ever! I figured I freaked you out, or—"

"Gabriel," I cut him off. "If you must know, the entire time Harry was fighting Voldemort and you had your legs next to me, all I could think about was how confused I was about how I was supposed to touch you now. As you know, PDA is not really something we do as dragons so it's all weird to me but all I could think of was how nice it'd be to relax—*really* relax—and lean next to you and cuddle," I admitted, looking at everything but him; the empty pop cans on the coffee table, my cell phone, the credits on the TV screen announcing the movie was over. *Anything* but him.

"Really?" he asked with uncertainty.

I nodded, forcing myself to look at him when all I wanted to do was hide my blushing face. I stared intently into his brown eyes although they were hard to see fully, covered up by his black-rimmed glasses. I dared to reach over—slowly—and pull them off his face. Smile-lines crinkled around his twinkling brown eyes as I did so. "Really," I insisted. "All I thought about was how confused you made me the entire time I was speaking with Grandfather."

"Confused?"

"Yeah. Dragons don't often bond for love. Generally, it's for position, or lust. Or convenience. Rarely love. Feelings like this aren't something I've ever had to deal with before."

"Feelings? Like what?" he asked expectantly.

"Like the fact that I really enjoyed that kiss but I didn't know what to think about it when you darted off afterwards," I said, with a hint of disapproval in my voice.

He sighed heavily. "Shit, Leorah, I'm really sorry about that," he said. "But I wanted to make sure I wasn't violating any Order rules that would end up with me being smote with lightning or something equally as painful."

I snorted. "Smote?"

He didn't speak, but smiled. "Also, after I met you, it sent my entire world into a tail spin. Regardless of what happens—" he motioned at the air between us with his hand pointedly, "—I have a duty to you, and the dragon realm essentially. I have to change my entire life around."

I frowned. "Shit, I'm sorry about— "

He cut me off. "—you're not understanding. I *want* to. I always figured that if on the rare chance I ever *did* meet you or another you or whatever that we'd come together for some missions or events or whatever, spit out some magic and go home. Even though it is not supposed to be that way I was determined to keep this separate from my own life and everything I worked hard for."

I opened my mouth to protest but he waved me off again. "But I also worked hard for this, and not giving it my all would be a disgrace to my uncle and all the people who came before me that trained for years just to be disappointed. And to boot you're a pretty awesome person to be around, dragon *or* human. It could be *so* much worse!"

I grinned. "Yeah. I could be a Trekkie instead of a Potterhead."

He pretended to be disappointed. "You don't like *Star Trek*?"

I looked away and whistled nonchalantly, casually motioning to a DVD tower full of DVDs.

He looked over and laughed. "Ah, I see," he said, with a laugh, reading off the titles of my DVDs. "*Star Trek: The Next Generation* seasons one through seven and—"

"—all the other ones that ever existed including the original pilot episode that was recast, it was never shown on TV," I said.

"Wow, I guess it is bad," he said with a laugh. "I love *Star Trek* but I'm probably more fanatical about...*other* things."

I snorted. "Well what is *your* thing?"

"Games," he said. "Lots and lots of video games. In fact, that's my job. I'm a game manager for an up and coming MMO that's releasing, so far I just manage the beta testers because that's all we have but..." he shrugged, "there you go."

"Wow, really? That's pretty cool," I said earnestly. "So now what are you going to do?"

"Well, not sure yet. I know that especially after that tornado incident, I can't leave you again," he began, as I opened my mouth to protest but he finished for me, "*I know* you can take care of yourself but this magic—whatever it is—was actually able to hurt you. Even just a little. That means it's big. You are at the very least going to need help. Or advice."

I considered this, pushing aside my stubbornness. Although I've witnessed many dragons and their magic, for myself it was new. Even I had to admit I needed some guidance.

And a friend would be nice too.

"I may be able to do some game stuff online from wherever I am, it doesn't actually require me to be in any one place, most of the time but, I can always find something else," he said. "I am not going to leave you alone again. Even if you hate me and I have to follow behind you twenty feet so you can have your space."

I smiled. "Well, you don't have to do that. It'll be nice not to be alone *all* the time."

"Since the game hasn't exactly taken off yet, I still have a lot of time to decide so, it's all up in the air anyways. It could flop and I'd be unemployed anyways."

"So what do you do then?"

"Build websites, design graphic artwork for people. Freelance."

"Wow, nice! Better than working in a coffee house," I said dryly.

"Hey, that's okay too, Kit relies on you. It's a big deal," he said, as I looked away to pout.

"Thing is I don't really need the money. Dragons live so long; my grandfather will give me anything I need. I just wanted to try to make it on my own, you know?"

"I do know," he said. "Just how I wanted to live out of my brother's shadow."

I forced a smile. "Yeah I know how that feels."

The credits stopped rolling on the DVD and the menu came on, the loud theme of *Harry Potter* startling me a bit. I reached over Gabriel on the sofa to reach for the remote to turn it off, but he pulled my arm away instead and pulled me down on his chest.

I sat there rigidly and said, "What the—"

He shushed me. "You said you wanted to. I'm telling you it's okay, you don't ever have to wonder if I want to. I *want* to. It's just a cuddle."

"What does it mean?" I said, trying to relax the side of my face into his chest as he smoothed my hair down my back.

I could almost hear him smile, as I sunk into the warmth of his chest and listening to the relaxing sound of his heartbeat.

"Well, Leo, it means we like to cuddle," he said, with a contented sigh.

Chapter 10

I don't know how I managed it, but I actually relaxed and fell asleep while laying on Gabriel's chest, his arms wrapped around me. After the first like, fifteen minutes it stopped feeling totally weird being *that* close to someone—*anyone* but most of all, *him*!

It was a combination of his steady heartbeat and his scent. He wasn't wearing any cologne or anything scented; I can always pick out artificial scents from natural ones. I can actually smell the chemical additives and fillers they put in—*blecch*! Somehow though he smelled of a mix of sandalwood, cinnamon and a hint of vanilla. I actually was trying to pinpoint the scents as I inhaled deeply, and relaxed…and drifted off.

I woke up at about ten after eleven at night, it was dark in the apartment except for the overhead light over the sink I kept on all the time since I wasn't the most graceful of dragons and I tripped over things in the dark often. One of Gabriel's arms had fallen off me and was dangling over the side of the sofa; his head nodded off onto the sofa arm and he was still breathing steadily.

"Shit, I gotta pee," I muttered to myself. I sighed, not wanting to leave the comfort of the cuddle but even a dragon's got to relieve herself now and then. Carefully, I untangled Gabriel's arm from my waist and sat up, slowly, setting his arm gently on his stomach. I looked back down at him, sleeping peacefully and smiled to myself.

But the urge to run to the bathroom took over (damn those two cans of pop!) and I made a mad dash. Afterward, even though I had slept most of the day and for another forty-five minutes or so just now, I realized I was still extremely drained. I couldn't stifle the large yawn or the urge to stretch out my sore bones. I groaned. Thankfully in the human world we had Advil and it was time for some now.

I grabbed my backpack that was tossed haphazardly on the floor next to the recliner and rummaged for the medicine. I popped two pills and swallowed some flat pop from the coffee table and grimaced as it went down. "Yuck!" I said out loud, as Gabriel rustled on the couch.

I struggled to choke down a yawn and felt my bed calling my name. I didn't want to wake him so I took the blanket from the recliner and carefully draped it over him as he slept. I sighed regrettably, wanting to join him again but a night on the couch wasn't exactly my idea of a restful sleep. Great for a cuddle or a nap but more than that? I'd tried it before; I woke up haggard. A cranky dragon is *not* a good dragon. Besides I'd probably trip and knee him in the crotch; wasn't exactly a good way to wake someone up.

"Mrow," Sona said, leaping up on the couch and circling on Gabriel's lap. She rested her head on her paws and let out a huffy noise that said "*Ha ha, I get to sleep here, you don't!*"

I scoffed. "Damn cat," I said. She ignored me and drifted off to sleep herself.

I glanced once more at Gabriel's cute, peaceful self and sighed. Well it was nice while it lasted.

I checked to make sure the door was locked, pulled off my sweatshirt on the way to my bedroom and tossed it in the hallway somewhere. I climbed into bed under the covers (a maroon and gold crocheted afghan and maroon flannel sheets—*Harry Potter* house colors, you know) and it felt like heaven finally resting my head on the pillow. Not more than a few seconds went by and I was out like a light.

It was...dark. Not just the normal dark you see when you walk outside your house on a moonlight night. It was like standing in the middle of a tall forest; trees so dense not even the strongest beam of sunlight could peek through. So dark, you couldn't see your hand in front of your face. So dark in fact that you could feel it seep into your soul and chill you to the bone.

I didn't know where I was or why I was there, all I could recall was that it was so insanely black as far as I could tell...miles and miles and miles of just pure black, soul-numbing darkness.

"Hello?" I called into the nothingness, not really expecting to hear anything, but maybe the sound of my own voice echoing back at me. Except there was no echo. It was as if my voice just disappeared. "Hello?" I asked again, with even more uncertainty. I spun around on my heels, looking for something—anything—to give me some kind of idea of where the Hell I was. Maybe it was *in fact Hell. I couldn't imagine anything scarier than pure, ample darkness and*

nothingness. No matter where I turned, where I looked, I saw nothing. Heard nothing. Felt nothing but absolute emptiness.

I tried to recall something—anything at all. Something to make me feel real, feel whole, feel something *but I couldn't think of a damn thing. All I felt was empty. Hollow.*

"Is anyone there?" I called into the void again. "Anything? Where am I?"

No one or nothing replied but I could swear I heard the faintest low growl in the distance.

"Hello?" Now I was starting to feel something: fear. Absolute terror that encapsulated every nerve, every pore of my body. I started to scream, even though there wasn't technically anything to scream at.

The growl sounded again, a bit lower, a bit fiercer and a bit louder.

I whimpered to myself, wrapping my arms around my body to try to control the shiver that was shaking throughout my body. "Where am I..." I trailed off, asking no one in particular, just wanting to hear the sound of my own voice to remind myself that I was in fact, real and here. Wherever here *was, I had no idea.*

I heard the growl again. And again getting closer, closer, closer.

My heart was pounding in my chest, harder and faster the closer it got.

The growl was so loud now it was almost deafening. I pressed my palms over my ears to somehow drown it out but nothing I did helped; it kept getting louder and louder, the vibrations of each growl reverberating through my body like I was a metal object being struck with a tuning fork.

Finally, it was here. The growl. I could see nothing but blackness on top of blackness but I knew it was here. The terror I felt was greater than any fear I had experienced ever in my life; it took my breath away. I was screaming, gasping at the sensation, of the sheer nothingness.

It said something. I don't know how it did because whatever it was, it was not corporeal. It wasn't real but yet, it was. I couldn't reach out and touch it, but whatever it was, it was there.

"Death..." Growled the menacing voice.

All of a sudden, I felt something grasp around my throat. It was cold and hard and everything about it just felt wrong. Very wrong. It felt poisonous and destructive and unforgiving.

It started squeezing my throat. Instinctively my hands went to whatever it was to try to pry them away; to stop them from choking me but I could grasp nothing because there was nothing actually there.

I just stood there, motionless for a moment due to shock before falling to my feet helplessly choking and gasping for breath. Tighter and tighter the grasp felt, and the area in front of me started going gray, then white then blinding light.

Somehow, before the blinding light I managed to squeak out a raspy whisper of "Help!" *before the final squeeze around my throat, my chest. All the air was choked out of me. My eyes grew heavy as I felt the life leave my body. Just as I was about to give in, I saw a blinding light scald my vision. And then...*

Nothing.

"Leo!"

My eyes flew open and I inhaled as if I was just taking my first breath of air after being underwater for too long.

"Oh my god, Leo!"

I couldn't see anything, but I could recognize the voice. It was deep, soothing and incredibly panicked.

I blinked rapidly, trying to wash the darkness away. My body felt listless as I tried to move my limbs to no avail.

The voice wrapped something around me and seemed to pull my body closer to a firm surface. It was warm and familiar and soothing. I let the feeling wash over me, as if being outside on a sunny day after a year of ice and snow, the warm brightness tingled my senses starting in my fingertips and emanating through my arms and eventually my shoulders.

I heard a steady *thump. Thump. Thump.*

When the warmth touched my core—my heart or my center or whatever, I couldn't help let out a contented sigh.

"Oh my god, Leo! Are you okay?"

I blinked a few more times. A face started coming into view: brown eyes, black hair, porcelain skin with a shadowed jaw. I gasped, realizing who it was.

"Gabriel!" I cried, clumsily wrapping my arms around him but not quite grasping correctly, as they just fell back to my side again. "Gabriel, what—where—"

"I'm here, I'm here," he just said, trying to sound calm but the panic in his tone betrayed him. He pulled me tighter against him, sniffling. "Oh my God what the Hell happened? What was that?"

"Wha..." my mouth tried to form words, but nothing intelligible was coming out.

I felt another surge of warmth radiate through my body, it was enough to melt the frost out of my fingers and arms and I was able to grasp my arms around him. I pulled myself tight, close—closer than I had ever been to another being ever in my life. "Gabriel! Wha—"

"What happened? I don't know, Leo. I heard you scream and when I came in here, there was this...*thing* surrounding you."

"Thing?" I questioned.

"I don't know what it was, I cannot explain it. But it felt evil and wrong and— "

"—dark?" I suggested to him.

He nodded. "Yes, dark. It was like little dark hands were around your throat and there was this emptiness around you. Like these evil, dark little tendrils were surrounding you. Almost like...a shadow?" he said the word to himself unconvinced. "I don't know what it was but I do know it was trying to kill you."

"*Kill* me?" I squeaked.

"Yes. I barely got in time. If you hadn't managed to scream, I don't know if I would have been here until it was too late. I managed to summon some moonlight from outside and shoot it at you and that seemed to chase whatever it was away; it disappeared instantly."

I whimpered, feeling tears swell in my eyes. Although I was with Gabriel now, the terror I felt—or couldn't feel—in that void was getting to me. The reality of what happened—whatever it was—was sinking in. I started to shake violently.

"Whoa, whoa there...calm down," he said, trying to sound soothing but again, panic was betraying him. He pried my arms off of him and gently set me back down on the bed as I was crying, sobbing uncontrollably.

"I don't know what it was!" I said, reaching my hand out for him, as if touching him was the anchor to reality away from the emptiness I felt. "It was horrible! It was dark and— "

He shushed me, putting a gentle fingertip to my lips. "Leo, it's okay now. I can tell how drained you are, again. You need rest. Whatever it was will not come back to you as long as I'm here, okay? I won't leave you, but you need to rest."

Through sobs I managed to whimper out an "Okay." I managed to catch a blurry glimpse of his expression, he was trying to smile but he was worried, I could see the trepidation wrinkling his eyes, his forehead. He reached out and smoothed my hair away from my face, with two fingers he smeared the tears off my cheeks.

Still crying, he managed to pull my covers over me as I shuddered violently. They were warm but no number of blankets right now would help banish the fear that grasped me.

"Leorah, I'm going to try to put a cleansing spell on you—kind of like I did for Kit earlier, remember?"

I managed a small nod, barely recalling anything before five seconds ago. Somehow deep in my mind I knew what he was talking about.

"Okay. Now the reason that spell worked so well was because I was channeling positive energy from you, but you don't have any more to give right now, I can feel that you are drained. Now do you have any herbs? Sea salt? *Anything?*"

"I-I think so. Kit would— "

He cut me off, hearing me struggle to speak. "I don't need much but if I cannot find anything, I'll call her. I just need some salt or some lavender. I am going to go really quickly to search your kitchen," he reached his other hand out and squeezed my shoulder as the other one continued to smooth my hair down my back. "Okay? You'll be okay, I'll be back in a flash."

I tried to nod bravely but I couldn't.

"Just two seconds," he said pulling away from me, and slowly stepping backwards until he was in the doorway.

Whatever relaxation I had been feeling—and it wasn't much—escaped the second he left the room. I felt the fear grasp me again, the darkness starting to shroud my eyes. I reached out for him and tried to call out his name but it merely came out as a weak noise.

"I'm here!" he said, and I felt him again, solid yet gentle. He grasped my outstretched hand. "Now, I found this sea salt shaker, okay? It should help, since I can't draw from your energy. I'm going to sprinkle it around the room but while I do that, I need you to somehow think happy thoughts. Can you do that? Anything happy. Anything joyous at all," he said, shaking a handful of salt into his palm and tossing it on my lower body. "Close your eyes and concentrate on it, feel it as if you were there. Positive energy is everything, and I need something positive from you right now. Anything. I mean it," he instructed.

"Okay," I said, in a small voice. I clenched my eyes shut and recalled just a few seconds ago, how wonderful it felt, how warm it was being close to him. A memory flooded through me then—it was a recent memory but I was having a hard time recalling it. I struggled to pull it out of my mind, finally smiling as I recalled it fully:

It was just about a couple hours ago, in my apartment, cuddling on the couch in Gabriel's arms. I recalled the way he felt, how warm it was, how he smelled.

I smiled despite myself, and felt my insides warm like spring sun penetrating the ice of a lake.

"Good," he said, some of the panic leaving his voice. "Good. Really good. Keep it up."

There wasn't much to think about but I remembered the sound of his heartbeat in my ear, strong and steady over and over again as I nuzzled my cheek deeper into his chest. I didn't mean to but involuntarily I let out a relaxed, "*Mmmmm.*"

Gabriel didn't say anything, but I heard him rustling about the room, saying something softly under his breath. The more he said, the more terror I felt escaping my body, being replaced with feelings of warmth...like the first rays of sunshine in the springtime after a hard, freezing winter.

"Good," he said again, and I felt his weight on my bed. He grasped my hand again, and pulled it into his lap. "Now, Leo," he said, pulling my palm up to his cheek and squeezing it. I could feel the roughness of his cheek, like sandpaper but it wasn't unpleasant; it just reminded me that he was here. That I wasn't alone, and the total darkness that I felt was either not real or was totally gone.

"Now, rest, Leo. You need rest. You don't need to worry; I will be here. I'll keep you safe," he said softly.

I nodded, opening my eyes briefly to get another look at him. "Just promise me you won't go."

He smiled earnestly. "I won't go anywhere. I won't even pee, okay? I'll be right here," he said, pulling his legs into the bed and sliding next to me. He laid down and rested his head on his hand, propped up by his elbow. His other hand was still grasping mine.

I sighed, feeling the solidity of his body next to mine. "Okay," was all I said. My hand went limp in his and I struggled to stay awake although this time, I didn't feel like I was afraid. I was safe and warm, in my bed next to him. I wasn't alone. I'd be okay from…whatever it was.

I wasn't quite sure what time it was when I woke up but the sun was streaming in brightly from the window, at some point the curtains and blinds were drawn open. Before I even opened my eyes I could feel the light beating on my face.

I tried to sit up but I felt weighted down. I turned my head to see the source of the weight, Gabriel's left arm was draped over my back. He was sound asleep, cuddled up in the blanket from the sofa, his jeans draped over the end of my bed.

"We didn't—huh?" I asked myself, reaching down to see if my own sweatpants were still on. I breathed a sigh of relief: they were.

At least if I'm going to *do* that I'd like to remember it!

"Hmm," was all I could say. I tried to pry his arm off me but the second I lifted up my head I felt hammers pounding and stars in my eyes. "Oh god…" I mumbled, giving into the urge to lay back down. I felt as if I had a hangover—at least the way I heard humans describe it. Heavy head, tired and groggy, massive headache. "Hopefully I have enough Tylenol," I mumbled, knowing fully well I didn't have many left.

I tried to ignore the stabbing sensation behind my eyes and laid my head down on my pillow again and turned to look at Gabriel's sleeping face. I couldn't hold back a smile, both the fact that he looked so damned cute asleep, and because I realized that I actually had a *man* in my bed. The thought was preposterous yet, here he was…with his strong, unshaven jaw and messy dark brown hair (this time messy *not* on purpose) and a pouty mouth. Really, he actually appeared to be pouting in his sleep. I had to stifle a laugh to avoid howling and waking him up.

He stirred and slowly opened his eyes, blinking a handful of times and smiling at me. "Well, hello Gorgeous," he said in a weird voice.

"Huh?" I questioned, blushing. "Gorgeous?"

He chuckled. "A quote from a really old movie. So, how are you feeling?" He asked, quickly changing the subject.

I groaned, trying to prop myself up on my elbows but instead was met with resistance and stabbing pains in my head. "Ugh…well I'm alive but man my damned head hurts."

"But you're not feeling like, weird or anything? Empty? Depressed?" he asked with concern.

I gave him a blank look. "What do you mean? Why would I feel that? And why we're on the subject of why, didn't I leave you on the couch?"

Gabriel immediately shot up. "Whoa, whoa. You mean, you don't remember anything?"

I blinked. "Remember what?"

He let out a low-whistle. "Damn, Leo. You almost died last night and you don't even remember? This is probably way worse than I thought—way, way worse..." He reached over and grabbed his jeans on the end of the bed, strategically keeping the blanket positioned over his waist and legs. He patted the pockets for something, and finally pulled his cell phone out of a side pocket. It began ticking as he started typing on it.

"*What?*" was all I could ask.

"I was asleep on the couch and I heard a scream. It was you! You screamed and I came running in to your bedroom. The entire room was pitch black like—indescribably dark. You were sitting in bed, asleep, acting like you were choking to death, but there was nothing there. I panicked and tried to grab for you, something shoved me away, all I saw was something like a dark flash but there was no light. At all." He began to explain, looking up between beeps on his phone.

My mouth fell open. "What the hell? Shit, I don't remember a thing!"

"I did the only thing I could think of; I threw a fireball at—well I just threw it. There was nothing to throw it at so..." he trailed off, looking sheepish. "Well I'm sorry I kinda obliterated your nightstand. I hope there wasn't anything too important on it."

I gasped, sitting up despite the nagging pain and seeing the scorched nightstand on the side of my bed, along with the burn mark on the wall—right through the paint and drywall. "Oh no..."

"I'm sorry! You were—" He sighed. "Well to try to make a stronger fireball I summoned down some moonlight. Light up the entire room and then—*poof*! —it was gone!"

I shook my head. "Wow, really? What was it?"

He shrugged. "I don't know," he said, holding up his phone. "I've been trying to get a hold of my brother all night to see if he knew anything but, so far I got an *'I'll look into it'* message about fifteen minutes after you feel asleep last night and I haven't heard from him since."

165

I frowned at the damage in my bedroom. "Well, that's one damage deposit I am not getting back," I murmured under my breath.

"Leo, I swear. You were dying. When the—*whatever*—was gone, you were shaking. *Terrified.* You were so pale you actually were *gray;* like you were dead. You were freezing cold; like ice." Gabriel, his lower lip trembling a little reached out and grabbed my hand and held it in both his palms, resting them in his lap. "I'm so sorry, I almost didn't make it in time. The energy left over in the room was unlike anything I've ever felt before. Like, nothing."

"Like nothing was there?" I offered.

"No I mean really, like *nothing*. Usually any place at all has some sort of energy, some sort of being. But this? There was nothing. No energy. Like a big, black hole. A void," he said, rubbing his thumbs along the top of my hand. "I cast a positive energy spell on you, hoping to disperse any residual...*whatever* the fuck it was in here last night and help you feel better. You were really freaking out. Like. Really."

"Shit." That was all I could say.

"I was scared to leave you alone so I pulled the blanket in here and wrapped myself up in it and finally fell asleep about two hours after you did. I kept watching you; to make sure whatever happened did *not* happen again. Or to catch whatever the Hell it was if it did," he shuddered. "Seriously whatever it was...was not good."

"I'm sorry." I didn't know what to say. I didn't remember a damn thing, but he was obviously very bothered and shaken by it.

"Sorry?" he asked incredulously. "I'm the one that should be sorry! This sort of thing shouldn't have happened to you; I should never have— "

I cut him off with a wave of my hand. "Gabriel. I appreciate that but you can't be with me everywhere, every time. What are you going to do? Follow me to work? Watch me piss?"

He snorted. "How ladylike."

I rolled my eyes.

He heaved a big sigh. "I don't know; I just feel like I'm failing you. It's my job to keep you safe."

"Gabriel, I'm a dragon. There isn't much out there that can harm me," I said with a chuckle.

"Yes that's true, but this was killing you, and you were helpless to stop it," he said sternly, looking straight into my eyes. "That should give you an idea of how dire this is, yes?"

I winced, feeling sobered. "Yeah, I..."

Gabriel scooted closer to me on the bed. "Leo, when I thought you were dying, I—" He dropped my hand and put a warm palm to my cheek. I felt the electricity current flowing through me, down to my core and a smile escaped my lips even though I tried to fight it. I nuzzled my cheek in his hand, I couldn't help myself, it felt warm and comforting.

"You scared the crap out of me. Like, seriously I'm still shaking," he said, lifting up his other hand to show his trembling.

I frowned. "I'm sorry."

"It's not your fault!" he exclaimed, dropping his hand away suddenly and shifting around. "It's mine. When I felt this awful presence I should have done more to stop it. Learn about it. Find out what the hell it was!"

I grasped his shoulder and spun him back around to face me forcefully. "Dammit, Gabriel! What could you have done? You did all you could for me! You came in and saved me, somehow, and you still barely even know me! Your life is going to turn upside down because of me, someone you barely know!"

Gabriel softened his pout, he opened his mouth to say something when his phone started ringing—or at least I think it was a ring, it started playing some loud song about "radioactivity" or something that caused me to jump. "Sorry," he mouthed and started talking into the phone. "Daniel, it's about fucking time!" he yelled angrily into the phone. He sat back down next to me and I lay down, listening to Gabriel's end of the conversation.

Gabriel began to sound alarmed. "Are you serious? Really?" He let out a huge sigh, and put his palm over the mouthpiece and turned to me. "This is bad."

"Yeah it is. You realize you have a mute button, right?" I pointed out sarcastically.

Gabriel blinked once and scowled. "Anyways."

I snorted and couldn't hold back a laugh. I could hear laughter coming from the phone too.

"This isn't the time!" he yelled back into the phone, poking at a button and setting it down.

"I'm sorry," I said, seeing the severe expression on his face. "Really."

He sighed again. "Once again. I called Daniel last night to see if he had seen anything, if he had *any* idea what could be going on and he had a…bad vision."

"Bad? What do you mean?" I questioned, getting serious.

"A death vision," he said.

"A *what*? Like, the death card in tarot!?"

A voice hollered from the earpiece on the phone. "The death card doesn't necessarily mean death, oh pink one!"

"Then what does it mean?" I yelled back at him, loud enough so he could hear me from a couple feet away over the phone. "A trip to the Bahamas?"

A peal of laughter sounded from the phone. "Oh, she's funny too!" Daniel tittered. I was surprised by how similar they sounded—I guess it's reasonable, they *were* twins. The only difference was Daniel seemed to have a lilt in his tone as he spoke. At least, from what I could hear on the phone.

Gabriel groaned. He put the microphone part of his cell right by his mouth and shouted. "Don't instigate, *bro*!" I heard Daniel yelp on the other line and this time Gabriel did hit the mute button after demanding *"Hang on,"* before turning to me solemnly.

"It's bad, Leo. Really, really bad," he said sternly. "A death vision happens in a seer when something monumentally bad is going to happen. He had one two days before the World Trade Center attack on September 11th happened."

I winced. I wasn't here for that event but, I'd seen the footage. Positively horrifying. News of it even traveled quickly to the dragon realm. It was…nasty business. Quite scary what humans are capable of; I sometimes could see why our dragon ancestors chose to separate from them.

"What happens during the vision?" I asked.

"It's not good, but it depends on each one. Last time all he heard was people screaming, he felt like he was falling and he ended up having a huge seizure," he explained. "That's why I couldn't get a hold of him last night, because he was at the hospital getting checked out after the seizure."

I gasped, covering my open mouth with my fingertips. "Oh no! Is he going to be okay?"

He nodded. "Yeah, our uncle just took him out of precaution but he's fine. They couldn't even tell he had a seizure really because it's nothing physical, it's *magical*."

"Wow. So this isn't good right? What did he see then?"

"Not much, really. Just a lot of panic and a lot of…darkness."

"Like me?" I squealed.

"We think so, with how we are tied to you…" he trailed off. "But that also means we think that it could mean *your* death."

"Well according to you, I almost died last night," I said. "Doesn't mean it's going to happen again, right?"

"I wish I could be sure," he said, audibly frustrated. He scrubbed his palm over his face and let out what sounded like a low growl. My dragon was proud of it, actually. "I have no idea what that was last night. But it was *bad*. Really bad."

"Maybe you killed it?" I offered, glancing over at my burned end table and singed wall. "Certainly killed my table."

"Maybe. I wish I could be sure, but I really don't know," he said. "Until we know what we're up against, I can't really say."

I frowned. "Daniel didn't see *anything* else in his vision?"

"Unfortunately not," Gabriel said with a sigh.

"Do you think it'll come back?" I asked in a small voice.

"Well, without knowing exactly what it is…" He gave me a reassuring smile instead of finishing his sentence, leaning over to squeeze my arm. "We'll figure it out. I'll be here, no matter what, even if I have to crash on your couch for the rest of my life or, whatever."

I forced a smile. "Thanks. But that's no way for either of us to live: in fear."

He shrugged. "No, but the best I can gather is whatever it was has something to do somehow with the force or entity or whatever that was causing all those storms: we know for sure it was coming after you now, and it found you."

"You think it could have been a warlock spell?" I asked.

"Not sure but, that would be good news," he said. "If it was, that means I could probably counter it somehow."

"And if not?"

Gabriel remained silent.

"I wonder…" I trailed off, searching around my bed for my phone even though I was pretty sure it wasn't there, I left it on the coffee table last night.

Gabriel produced it from his jeans pocket. "Looking for this?"

I narrowed my eyes at him. "Why do you have this?"

"I panicked!" he exclaimed in exasperation. "I went through your contacts looking for your grandfather or your brother or *someone*! Anyone who might know anything about this thing that nearly killed you!"

"Ah, well...good thinking. Did you get anyone?"

"Your brother...I sent him a message telling him to have your grandfather get in touch with me. Or you. Or whoever," he explained.

I nodded. "Okay, good." I slowly stood up, feeling the pins and needles stab at my eyes. "Oh God..." I said woozily, stumbling back over on the bed. Gabriel caught me as I fell back and helped ease me back against the pillows, as a black curtain began to fall over my line of vision.

"Shit, Leo, you okay?" Gabriel asked, extremely concerned.

I felt it again...the darkness. The void. The nothing. The invisible hands that weren't there wrapping around my throat, choking the life out of me. There was no light, there was no sound. There was nothing except for me and the thing that was draining me.

I gasped. "I remember!" I started shaking violently, recalling the terror I felt. Gabriel was immediately attentive, wrapping his arms around me and letting me hyperventilate into his chest.

I didn't hear my phone chime, but Gabriel did and he checked it for me. Sniffling, I managed to pull myself away from him for a few moments to inquire.

"It's from your brother," he said, "he said he's with your grandfather right now, and to explain to him the problem. Should we call him?"

I shook my head. "Texts are easier to get through, phone calls not so much," I said, composing myself momentarily.

Gabriel gave me a sympathetic look. He patted the pillow and motioned for me to lie back down. "I got this," he said, already tapping on my phone.

I couldn't believe this was happening to me. I buried my face in the pillow—the one Gabriel had slept on—and inhaled his lingering scent. It was relaxing and a bit stressful at the same time.

Just a few days ago, I was just a girl in a coffee shop, working to attempt to buy herself a newer car and support her silly fandom obsessions.

Okay so I was a *dragon* girl in a coffee shop but...hey. I'd been living as a human now for a couple of years and it was becoming quite comfortable. I'd even made a friend and had a purpose, even if that purpose was only to deliver beverage sustenance to cranky morning people on their way to work, or evening gamers looking for that extra kick, *or* stressed out Moms needing a pick me up on their way to their umpteenth kids' sporting event that week. It wasn't much but, it was better than living under constant scorn and scrutiny back home.

I watched movies, I watched shows, I went to the movie theater and saw movies alone, I listened to my co-workers talk about life, school and romance and I learned a little about humanity along the way. All I wanted to do was blend in.

I never really thought about romance or relationships, friendships were hard enough for me. But in the past week those thoughts were tested. *Now* I was in the presence of an incredibly handsome and talented human male and I was beside myself. Since he came around I found my brain all a-jumble, my heart all a-flutter and I was now the target of evil unknown forces.

That sort of puts my blending in/anonymity ideas on the backburner for a while.

Hmmm...that is a rather interesting coincidence. Everything was fine until he came around and figured out who I was. Perhaps, somehow, he is a catalyst.

That would be my luck. The first guy to come along that displayed an interest in me *would* turn out to be evil.

But if that were the case, why would he still be here? What happened to me was...the scariest thing that had ever happened. He banished it, and had been by my side ever since. Right?

After this short time, I feel pulled to him...why him? Like, whenever he's gone, I just feel incomplete and empty. I didn't like that feeling but, perhaps it was just how infatuation or—*yikes*—love felt?

I snickered to myself. *Don't be stupid, Leorah,* I admonished myself in my head. *Grandfather verified his story, he said he was fine. Grandfather would know. You're being overly suspicious.*

Not everyone *is as nasty as all those dragons you encountered growing up. There are some decent souls out there. There has to be.*

"Okay, according to Braeden, your grandfather thinks you would be safer up there, not here. He says you should come back immediately," Gabriel said interrupting my self-loathing.

I lifted my head up momentarily. "Does he know what that was?"

Gabriel shook his head. "No, not really. But he was really alarmed by it. Good news is he thinks that the chances of it being able to travel through the portal to another realm are pretty slim to nil. Even if it could, you'll have a house full of dragons there to protect you, and a sorcerer too. It's not getting by *all* of us."

I tilted a brow. "You? You can't go there. You'll get…eaten. Or killed. I don't even know what portal travel will do to you, and—"

He cut me off. "Wherever you go, I go, period. You won't let me get eaten. As for the portal," he shrugged nonchalantly, "I'll be fine. It's just a form of magic, and I'm not fully human anyways so…I'll be okay."

"You're not?" I mean when I think about it, no he wasn't, really. I mean he was but…*oh I'm confused.*

"Well I am but…not. I'm a sorcerer. I can wield magic. Humans can't do that," he said, in a moment of boastful pride.

"What about witches?" I quipped.

He rolled his eyes. "I'll be fine."

"But…as far as I know, a human has never been over there. I can't promise that you'll not be thrown in a jail or some scary dungeons. Or— "

He waved me off. "I'll be fine. After all I've got my balls, you've got your…teeth?"

I snickered. "Right."

I managed—with assistance—to pull myself off the bed and shower and barely get dressed. It was slow going through the knives stabbing at me behind the eyes but somehow I managed. At one point I freaked out Gabriel by emptying my bottle of Tylenol and swallowing them all with a couple swigs of Mountain Dew. I assured him that much was nothing for a dragon and our rapid metabolisms. He said he believed me but as I disappeared back into the bathroom to pretty myself up I swear I heard him putting some sort of spell on me.

"I can't believe I have to go back there again already," I muttered under my breath, stumbling around my room grabbing for things I might need.

I felt something nudge against my calves. "Aww, Sona! Shit, what am I going to do with you?" I sighed.

"What's that?" Gabriel called from the sofa.

I leaned over and picked up the cat who nuzzled my cheek and purred. She was sucking up to me, she probably sensed something was up and she didn't want to get left again. I was just going to have to bring her along.

I chortled. "Wonderful: two things not typically allowed in the dragon realm, a cat and a human. Everyone's *really* going to love me now!"

"*What?*"

"Just grumbling. I don't want to go home." I quickly applied some BB cream, concealer and a quick swipe of mascara and lip gloss and braided my wet hair to the side. It wouldn't matter much anyways because once I shifted, my hair would get messed up as would my makeup.

I grabbed some belongings I had gathered on my bed and shoved them in my backpack I had brought with me from living room. "I'm going to need you to carry Sona. She's not going to be a happy kitty either. She hates the carrier."

"You're bringing her?" He sounded surprised.

I shrugged. "What else can I do? I don't know how long we'll be gone. Even if I could find someone to take her, it's too much to ask them to take her indefinitely."

He considered this. "Yeah I suppose…will she be okay there?"

I nodded. "I'll leave her in my room, it's big enough to where she won't really care. There *are* animals over there though, rarely domestic. Most dragons don't keep pets. As long as she stays put she shouldn't get eaten or anything."

Gabriel's eyes widened in horror. "Someone would really *eat* her?"

I gave him a "look". "You should be more concerned with yourself; they really will not be happy to have a human over there."

"Who's 'they'?"

"They. Everyone. Name it," I said.

He grumbled. "Well, they'll just have to deal. And if not, we'll be dragon food," he said, only half kidding to the cat as I plopped her in his lap. "Wait…why do I have to have her?"

"I can't really hold her when I've got no hands and four feet and shitty wings now, can I?"

Gabriel appeared giddy. "You mean I really get to see you shift?"

"Almost. You get to see me *after* I shift. I don't want to ruin my clothes, you know," I said.

"So you go all Hulk like when you shift? That's pretty..." he didn't finish his sentence, instead he smirked.

I rolled my eyes. "Whatever," I said. "But I kind of don't have a choice. Bringing you around, it's going to rattle some cages, I better be my bad ass dragon self just in case I need to claw someone in the face. Well...as bad ass as a pink dragon can be, anyways," I finished under my breath with a wry tone. *Maybe I'll just burp on them, or something equally as gross.*

"You really think it'll come to that?" he asked uncertainly.

"Don't know. Hope not. But they might not be happy to learn about some secret human society devoted to me so...anything is possible, really," I said, with a laugh.

Gabriel forced a chuckle. "Oh, goody."

I drove us out to the portal in the woods, leaving behind Gabriel's truck parked in my spot and my spare key in the mailbox for Kit. I couldn't get a hold of her but I asked her if she could come check on my apartment once in a while. I know she was going to be baffled but, I couldn't really divulge more than that. When I couldn't get a hold of her I actually called Madison and asked her to check in on Kit and get back to me if she hadn't heard from her in about a day, that she was sick last time I saw her. Thankfully, Madison being a slightly self-centered teenager didn't ask questions, she just agreed quickly and tried to go into talking about a big football game that had occurred while I was gone. She didn't even ask about when she could come back to work; she was just regaling in all the things she was up to since the shop had been closed.

Must be nice to have that carefree life.

We did drive by Gabriel's hotel really quick where he checked out and moved the small amount of things he had there to my apartment; it was little more than a laptop, some clothes and a video game system with controllers.

"That's *all* you have?" I questioned uncertainly, eyeing the items he shoved into the small compartment in between the seat and the window.

He flung a backpack off his shoulder and tossed it on top of them. "There's this too."

It didn't even make a *thud* as it hit the seat. I chuckled. "What's in there? Like a pair of underwear and a t-shirt?"

He made a face at me. "Something like that."

I groaned. "You have *no* clothes?"

He shrugged. "I have a few. I've been washing them over and over again. There's a washing and drying unit in the room and unfortunately when I left, they were in the washer. So, I don't have much left."

"Well, I guess we'll just have to take some stuff from Braeden, but it might not be much more than court robes and things. Maybe a couple pairs of pants. He dresses a bit preppy with polos and khakis." Gabriel gagged mockingly at the idea; I couldn't picture him in anything but t-shirts and sweatshirts anyhow. Well, actually I pictured him *without* the shirts on currently, but he didn't have to know that. "*Please* tell me you at least have a *couple* pairs of underwear?" I asked.

He chuckled, and nodded. "That's one thing I'm anal about, I wash them separately on the delicate cycle."

I burst out in uproarious laughter. "What do you wear? Silk g-strings?" I asked, immediately blushing at the incoming thought of him in his skivvies...although I couldn't make the image of him in a g-string come to mind; my brain forced him into some manly boxers instead. My heart made a wild leap in my chest and I had to shake myself quickly to push the distracting image out of my mind.

He blushed; red like lava. "Haha, no. No g-strings. I just like it when they're soft and comfortable, I hate re-buying new ones. They're all stiff and stuff."

"Stiff?" I howled again, immaturely.

"Okay, *okay*," he said, holding up his hands in surrender. "Yes, okay. I'm a big, big dork." He shook his head, grinning bashfully.

By this point we were at the portal in the woods. I grabbed my own backpack, and Sona's cat carrier—she was audibly upset at this point, she hated car rides to boot—while Gabriel started to shove his few Earthly belongings in a black rolled duffle bag he produced from the cab of the truck. I set the backpack and Sona in front of him. "Sorry...dragons don't have great arms for this."

He shrugged. "It's okay. I'll manage."

I hesitated, glancing around the empty clearing. I pulled off my oversized sweatshirt and tossed it at him. He cocked an eyebrow. "I get a show?" he asked.

"No!" I insisted. "Just…put that away. And…the rest of the stuff. Once I'm done. Please?"

He nodded, with a smirk on his face.

"Now…turn around. Stand behind the truck or…something. Please. I've never done this in front of anyone before," I said nervous, but anxious to finally get the chance to shift and stretch out.

Gabriel reluctantly ducked behind the truck. I started to unbutton my jeans when I saw the top of his head through the window

"*No peeking*!" I growled.

"Sorry!"

I shook my head with a laugh. I stripped down to nothing and suddenly I was quite aware of the cute guy hunched behind the pickup truck a few feet away from me so I was a little apprehensive.

I closed my eyes and willed the shift. Now to an outsider, it could probably look pretty painful but it wasn't really. It felt tingly, mostly from toe to head and happened rather fast—fingertips and toes and all the way inward.

When I'd fully shifted, I let out an uncontrollable growl, which was just the voice's way of readjusting to its larger form.

"What the—" Gabriel slowly re-emerged from his hiding spot, and his mouth fell open. "Leorah?"

"Yeah, what were you expecting? " I asked, with my same voice but only slightly lower.

He blinked, as if surprised. "Wow, it still sounds like you."

"You were expecting Morgan Freeman?" I moved my now larger head from side to side. It felt heavy for a second but as I got adjusted and stretched my limbs it felt good.

"Well?" I asked, shrugging my dragon shoulders.

Gabriel stared in awe, taking in my bright pink skin, four legs, long tail and flimsy little iridescent wings. I was about the size of a female horse, slightly taller on all fours. Most people assumed dragons were scaly, like lizards but in actuality it was mostly smooth and only slightly rough; like toughened human skin.

"Your…your eyes," he said, stammering. "They're still green."

I blinked. "Yeah, I guess," I said with a nervous laugh.

Gabriel just remained there, open-mouthed.

"What?" I asked, feeling exposed, suddenly wishing I could hide behind a tree. Well, I could…but it'd be like an ostrich sticking his head in the sand; pretty pointless.

He slowly fell to the ground, on his knees. He took off his glasses and tossed them to the ground.

"*What*!?!" I demanded with irritation. "So, now you see the big freaky dragon. Was it everything you imagined?"

Gabriel shook his head. "You're way more amazing then we ever could have pictured. Those wings they are...*exquisite*."

I squinted an eye at him and snorted. "These? My *My Little Pony* wings?" I looked back and opened and closed them slightly.

He nodded. "I never pictured wings would look like that. They're like...stained glass, kind of. Like artwork."

I snorted. "Well that's about all they're good for, they don't *do* anything," I said.

"They're beautiful...I can't imagine they don't serve a purpose..."

I scoffed. "Well, they don't."

"And you're just...well not what we pictured, but so, *so* much better," he said. "We figured you'd be...scary looking and scaly. You're like..."

"Like what?"

"Magical. Beautiful!" Gabriel said.

I rolled my eyes. "Great...well can you get up? Are you done worshiping me yet or can we get this over with?"

He shook himself. "Yeah, I'm sorry it's just...well until I saw your dragon-form, you were just this amazing, awesome girl who worked at the coffee shop I was becoming rather...*enamored* with. Now you're the dragon that my family has been searching for—well, years. It's real, everything we've been working for—it's *real*! And for once instead of being a skeptic and cranky about the whole thing, I can see it. And accept it. And...I'm looking forward to the challenge of being a knight. *Your* knight."

If I wasn't already pink well, my cheeks would have turned it after that one. For the first time ever, I was thankful for being pink.

"Leo this is like...you meeting the author of *Harry Potter* or Patrick Stewart or something like that. It's pretty damn epic," he said.

I considered this. "Yeah, okay...but that would be so much cooler though than me, seriously."

He reached out slowly. "Can I? "

I lowered my head nearer to him, and he slowly reached his hand out and gingerly brushed his fingertips across my nose. Even in dragon-form, his touch was warm, soothing and almost...electric. It sent shivers down my dragon-spine which made Gabriel jump back a little.

"Sorry," I said. "Not used to being touched as a dragon, either."

He gave me a sad smile. "That's really too bad." He reached out again, this time with more confidence. "Is it like, taboo for someone to touch dragons? Like another dragon even?"

"Not really. Just, my pink is like some kind of deformity or contagious disease. *No one* touches me.," I explained, thinking back dryly.

"I'm sorry," he said, placing his palm on the side of my face. "Wow! It's not rough at all! Smooth. Cold like…like water almost." He rubbed my cheek a little, with a goofy smile on his face. He giggled giddily, almost like a young school girl.

"What?" I asked, with a deep chuckle.

"This is just…cool!" he said.

I rolled my eyes. "Yeah…okay can we get going now before I lose my nerve, here?"

Gabriel grinned. "Yeah, I'm sorry. It's just—you're a dragon!"

I gave him a stone-faced "*D'uh!*" look. "Get used to it, knight-boy!"

"I know, I know." He chuckled and turned back to the truck. He grabbed the backpacks and slung them over his shoulders, grabbed the wheeled duffel with one hand and Sona's carrier with the other.

"Is she scared of you?" he asked.

I knelt down on all fours and looked into her carrier. "Sona, baby?"

She eyed me momentarily, and let out an uninterested *mew* before turning away to lick her behind. "She seems unaffected."

Gabriel snorted. "I see that. I thought cats didn't like dragons?"

"Well, we're animals inasmuch as they are in this form. Besides, she can smell it's me," I said. "Shall we?" I waited for him to cumbersomely catch up to me before I crossed the clearing.

"So where is this portal?"

I motioned my head towards an unassuming shrub. "Behind here. There really isn't much to see, it looks like kind of how on a hot day, you see those shimmers on the road in front of you? That's all it is."

He nodded.

"Well…whatever you do, stick close. Hopefully it's Maxxus on the other side, he's good dragon folk. The other guard is a bit of an ass. If we timed this right, Braeden or Grandfather should be waiting on the other side; you'll need protection. Even with your fiery balls," I said with a snort.

I reached out my front leg to test the energy of the portal. It felt warm and buzzed of electricity, and it got more intense as the moment went on.

"Gabriel! Get back!" I yelled, my voice booming through the clearing. I could hear Sona yelp, and Gabriel tripped backwards on the luggage. I stepped back, putting a little bit of distance in between the portal and I so I could react to whoever was coming out.

"Maxxus?" I asked questionably, as a large, green dragon stepped through the portal.

"Leorah! Thank Goddesses I caught you!" he said. Maxxus' dragon form was about twice the size of me—most dragons were larger than me, but Maxxus was *huge*. He was the color of emeralds with the same ocean blue eyes as in his human form. "You can't come over, it's too dangerous."

"Dangerous?" I quipped skeptically.

Maxxus scanned our surroundings, his gaze landing on Gabriel and he lowered his head nearer to the ground and bared his teeth, letting out a low, guttural growl.

"This is the *nice* one?" Gabriel asked uncertainly, stepping backwards a bit, looking extremely intimidated. He set the luggage and Sona down slowly, and started rubbing his palms together, I could feel the energy between his palms start to swell.

"Who's *that*?" Maxxus demanded. "You know him?"

"Settle down, everyone. Gabriel's a friend," I told Maxxus.

Maxxus stared Gabriel down, but Gabriel puffed out his chest and I could hear some low chanting. "But he's human."

"Not totally," Gabriel said, a plasma ball erupting in his hands.

Maxxus raised a brow—or where his brow would have been had we had them. "Nice parlor trick, human."

"Stop!" I demanded. I shot Gabriel a dirty look that said: *put that fireball away*. He scowled, and dispersed it in his hands. Then I shot Maxxus a dirty stare. "Gabriel is a friend, and a sorcerer. He's coming with me over there, you can't stop us."

"But I have to, you can't go over there. They're looking for you," he explained, finally pulling his glare away from Gabriel to give me a small frown.

"They? Who's *they*?" I gulped, thinking of the worst.

"The Court. They're summoning you back over; saying you're over here illegally," Maxxus explained.

"Illegal? They knew I was heading over here! Hell they practically *pushed* me over!" I exclaimed, astonished.

Maxxus shook his head. "I know, I know, I don't understand it myself. All I know is that I have orders to bring you directly to the King if you should come through."

I turned around and looked at Gabriel, alarmed. "Could it be— "

Gabriel shrugged. "I don't know. Your grandfather said it would be safer so I can't understand..." he trailed off, looking pensive. "I don't know."

I let out a little whimper. "Why the Hell do they want me?" I asked Maxxus. "You have no idea?"

"No, I really don't," he said, his eyes darting back and forth to the portal to me. "Look, Nicodemus is on the other side, but I managed to distract him with something for a few moments when I felt the portal starting to open but he'll be coming back soon. You better get out of here, he isn't a fan of yours like I am," he said. He gasped, seeing the portal shimmer. "Go! Now!"

I nodded and stormed off to the trees behind Gabriel's truck. Gabriel followed suit, more slowly, dragging the luggage and Sona. He placed them in the cab of his truck and jumped in. "How fast can you shift?"

"Just—close your eyes!"

"Leo! This is no time to be modest, you need to hurry!" Maxxus called.

I leaped behind the truck and ducked down as low as I could, willing the shift back to human to come over me.

"What's going on? Did you see her?" Nicodemus' booming voice growled in Dragon, emerging through the portal in his human form.

"No. I thought it was becoming active. Turns out it's just someone camping. He," Maxxus nodded towards Gabriel, who was just climbing into the cab of the truck, "was setting a fire near the portal, and I must have felt that."

Nicodemus didn't appear convinced. "No one ever comes camping around here."

Even from behind the truck in my human form, I could hear Gabriel swallow nervously. "I'm sorry, I didn't know it was bothering anyone. I just needed an empty spot for some experiments."

"Experiments?" Nicodemus asked, growling in poor English so Gabriel could understand him.

"Yes," Gabriel reached for the game console behind the seat and pulled it out. "Weather experiments. I'm a storm chaser. I need an empty spot where this stuff would remain undisturbed. After all that crazy weather we had, we decided we needed more monitoring."

I grinned to myself, kneeling down behind the tire and hugging my legs into my chest so that my ass didn't fall into the dirt. He was an expert liar, apparently.

Hmm...perhaps that wasn't the *best* thing, I thought to myself.

Nicodemus snorted. "Well, fine." He didn't sound entirely convinced but after looking around, he didn't appear to see anything. "Maxxus make sure you do something to alter his mind so he doesn't remember this conversation. Knock him out, something. Kill him for all I care. Just make sure he doesn't remember. You shouldn't be in your dragon form over here anyways, what were you thinking?"

Maxxus looked sheepish. "Apologies; I just didn't want her to get away. I'll take care of it."

"See that you do, or I will," Nicodemus stepped back through the portal not before glaring at Gabriel and snorting. I let out a breath I didn't realize I was holding.

"Wow, that was close," Gabriel said.

I started to stand and remembered I was naked in human form. "Umm...some help here?"

Gabriel chuckled and tossed me the sweatshirt he was wearing. I pulled it over my head and stood up. "Thanks, Maxxus."

He nodded. "I better get back before he realizes something is up. Whatever you do, don't come over here. I don't know what's up, but it doesn't sound good. Okay?"

"Okay. Just...if you see my brother or grandfather— "

"—after my shift I'll go to them and let them know what's going on, okay?" Maxxus said. He snorted towards Gabriel's direction. "You better keep quiet about what you saw here. Don't go blabbing about us. I don't know what's going on here, but if Leo chooses to keep company with you, you must be okay. So...be careful. Got it?"

Gabriel nodded. "Okay."

Maxxus ducked through the portal and disappeared, the portal shimmering and fading as he did.

"What the hell was that?" I asked just as he said, "Oh, this is not good."

No, it wasn't indeed.

Chapter 11

We entered my apartment again that evening feeling defeated. I set Sona's carrier down in the entryway as she was meowing and clawing to get out and unlatched the door. She scurried out and down the small hallway into my room where her cat bed was, hissing the entire way.

"Told you she hates this thing," I said, opening up a small coat closet and shoving it in there.

Gabriel dumped the luggage in the middle of the floor and slumped back into the recliner. He scrubbed his palms over his face and let out a frustrated noise.

"Well. This sucks." I said. "I'm going to find some new pants..." I trailed off as I walked to my own bedroom. My jeans had inadvertently gotten tossed into some mud, so I wasn't able to put them back on (thankfully, my underwear remained untouched!). All I was wearing was Gabriel's oversized hoodie and my underwear. I spent most of the entire ride home trying to pull the end of the sweatshirt over my knees to prevent him from seeing anything (I was just relieved I had remembered to shave...not that it lasted too long but, better than nothing) too private.

I shut the door and paused behind it, with a heavy sigh. All of a sudden, there was mysterious evil coming at me from all sides. Why on Earth would the Court want me back? Why now, all of a sudden? I've been on Earth now for...almost three years. Something had to happen to alert them. Were they somehow watching me? Did they know I was able to use magic now?

Maybe it wasn't bad...maybe they just want me to help?

I scoffed at the idea. There was no way that was possible.

But, there had to be some kind of connection between everything. The storms around here; the void last night and me almost dying...Kiarra's suspicious presence...now court wanting me to come back.

It all started when Gabriel arrived, when we started messing with magic. Did I somehow trigger some alarms on some mystical system somewhere? No one wants the crazy, pink dragon to do magic...

I wondered if this is what Cyril—the last known pink dragon—had to deal with: paranoia. Perhaps that's what drove him crazy.

I heard a chime from my computer. I guess in all the chaos I forgot to turn it off. I rummaged through my dresser quick for some pants—a pair of black leggings—and pulled them on before sitting down at the computer.

An instant message on Facebook (from someone named Draco Silverface with a profile picture of a pixelated gray dragon) was staring at me, from—

"—Grandfather?" I asked, clicking the box and reading the message.

"Leorah? Are you there? Are you okay?"

"I'm okay. What's going on? I can't go back!"

"I know, Leo. Just hang tight, Brae and I are trying to figure it out."

"Hang tight!?! How am I supposed to do that? There's something evil after me, and now the Court is after me! Could the two be related somehow?"

"I don't know. Perhaps someone caught wind that one of the Knights caught up with you, and they're worried you're going to go nuts like Cyril did or take over the kingdom or something equally as ridiculous."

"But...who? The only ones that know about Gabriel besides you and Braeden is— "

Kiarra.

I felt the fury burn my cheeks at the revelation. "Gabriel!" I called to him, insistently.

"What?" Footsteps bounded as he came running into the bedroom in a panic. "What's wrong?" He appeared worried until he saw my angry face.

"What? Long raid queue?" he kidded, motioning to my computer screen.

"Ha. No, it's Grandfather...he thinks someone may have alerted the Court that I've met you. The only ones that know about you are him, my brother and— "

"—Kiarra!" he finished.

I nodded, my eyes narrowing at the thought.

"You don't think she—" he couldn't even finish his thought. "I don't know. It makes sense, though."

I turned back to the computer and started typing again, Gabriel peering over my shoulder as I did.

"Kiarra is the only one besides Brae and yourself that knows about Gabriel's being here. She just thinks he's a—" I gulped nervously, blushing at the thought as I typed, *"boyfriend but I'm sure Brae might have said something, or she figured it out somehow. I knew there wasn't something right about her!"*

There was a pause before Grandfather typed back: *"How would she know about the knights? The Order is top-secret, hardly anyone knows of their existence."*

"Perhaps more than he realizes," Gabriel offered dryly.

"Obviously," I said aloud. *"Gabriel and I still think there's something up with her."*

I could almost hear him sighing at the screen, in his chambers. *"I will talk to Braeden."*

"Guess that's all I can expect for now, huh?" I let out a low breath, shaking my head.

"I guess." He chuckled. "God you can just feel the tension pouring off of you."

"A sorcerer thing?"

"No, just a hunch." Gabriel grasped my shoulders and squeezed gently. "Yup. Tense."

"Oh jeez…that's…" I trailed off as my neck and shoulders went slack as Gabriel massaged my shoulders.

"Is this normal for a dragon? I swear your muscles feel like…tires," he mused.

"I don't think so…it's been a rough day," I said, closing my eyes and taking a deep breath. My computer kept making chiming noises but I ignored them for the time being.

"Yeah…hmm, I wonder if teaching you how to meditate would help?"

My eyes flew open. "Meditate? Sorcerers meditate?" I tittered, an image of Gabriel in long robes sitting silently atop a mountain, cross legged and palms folded together in front of him. The image made me chuckle to myself.

"Well, no not typically. It's something Daniel does to help him when visions are particularly disturbing or disruptive. He taught me a little. Perhaps it would help?" Gabriel stopped rubbing my shoulders and I groaned.

"No...maybe a spell? Like protection?" Gabriel fumbled for his phone out of his jeans pocket and started tapping at it.

"You know who's good at that stuff..." I began.

"Kit," he finished for me. "Perhaps it's worth giving her a call, if she's around. Practical magic is not my forte. I can summon fireballs, create small earthquakes but when it comes down to mixing potions and stuff...well that's beyond me."

"Can't you summon like some protective wind?" I suggested. "A soothing rain?"

"Well, yes but...to sustain it? I'd get awfully tired after about an hour. Now if you conjure the elements and channel their energies into a potion; well...that would be much more realistic. I'll see what I can find..."

I sighed. Grandfather had messaged again, insisting that he didn't think Kiarra was up to anything sinister. He was no help there. Of course I didn't have any proof—just a hunch—so I let the subject drop. Since I had no plans to go back to the dragon realm anytime soon (at least until the search for me had been forgotten—which more than likely would never happen) I could avoid her anyway and she shouldn't be any kind of threat. Braeden didn't know much about Gabriel in any event, so there wasn't much she could get out of him.

My phone chimed then, and I pulled it out of Gabriel's kangaroo pocket of his shirt I was still wearing (and refused to take off!).

Leo? It's Maxxus? You get home all right?

I did, thank you. Wait...he had a phone now? He must have followed my advice. *New phone?*

Pause. *Yes. With the info you gave me it was pretty painless.* Again, another pause between messages.

You're not alone, are you?

I smiled to myself. He was a nice one; one of the very few who wasn't related to me to actually be nice. *No, I'm not.*

A pause. *That fireball guy with you?*

Yes. His name is Gabriel.

Ah. Okay. I wasn't aware you were seeing anyone.

I snickered, and blushed. *We're just*—I stopped. I was about to say we were just friends, but, I wasn't entirely sure. So I deleted it and said instead: *I'll be okay. Just watch out for Grandfather for me, please.*

I will. Take care of yourself.
You too. Thanks, Maxxus.

"Who's that?" Gabriel chimed in. He was sitting Indian-style on my bed, fervently tapping and flipping the screen on his phone.

"Oh, just Maxxus, making sure I got home okay," I said, nonchalantly.

This caught his attention. Gabriel looked up, brow raised.

"What?" I asked innocently.

"Sounds like a lot of trouble to go through for someone who's just a guard," Gabriel said.

I waved him off. "Oh, it's nothing. Since I can't fly I have to wait for someone to come get me when I go over there, and it usually takes about thirty minutes or so to wait for my brother to fly over. To kill time, we just talk or whatever. Really, he wants lessons on how to use the internet, no big deal."

"Right..." Gabriel sounded unconvinced.

"Aww, you're jealous?" I giggled. "You think the big, bad green dragon likes little ol' me?"

Gabriel's face flushed immediately. "No! I mean it's—" he cut himself off, swallowing nervously. "Not that I have the right to get upset, even if you guys were like...whatever..."

I giggled again. I got up from the computer and sat down next to him on my bed, patting his leg for reassurance. "We may have just met, but I've known Maxxus for a long time. He's only a friend. It'd be social suicide for anyone to have much to do with me, especially romantically, over there. He'd probably lose his position as a guard and get demoted to like...sewer management, or something else nasty. Even if for some unknown reason he *did* like me like that, nothing would ever happen."

Gabriel forced a thin smile. "It's really not my business I guess but like you said we did just meet so, I don't have any reason to feel anything like jealousy."

"You don't? You don't feel anything at all?" I fluttered my eyelashes innocently, letting my lower lip puff out.

He smirked, but remained silent.

"Fine." I turned back to my phone, mindlessly flipping through my old text messages.

I felt a gaze on me and I glanced up momentarily. "What?"

Gabriel smiled. "You're still wearing my shirt."

I looked down at his red, worn sweatshirt and wrapped my arms around myself. "It's comfortable." And plus, it smelled absolutely fabulous...

"No, it's okay. It's cute on you." I blushed, yet again and he chuckled. "This might sound stupid, but I've never had a girl wear something of mine. It's kind of one of those guy things, you know? Like in high school, you give your girlfriend your football jersey to wear the day of the big game for good luck? The girls would always look so proud wearing them." He exhaled. "No one was lining up to wear my messy stage crew t-shirt." He frowned, looking down at his palms in his lap. He grunted. "Pretty stupid, huh?"

"No, not stupid at all," I said, sympathetically. I looked him over. With his strong jawline and dreamy eyes, I had a difficult time believing *no one* ever had any interest in him. I mean, perhaps he wasn't traditionally man-pretty enough to grace the cover of *GQ* (although, with the right suit…I shivered at the thought). I think it was that non-traditional, not-overtly so in your face gorgeousness that struck me. No, he wasn't perfect but I think that was part of his charm. That and his shyness created a certain mystery about him. I didn't know much about human women but if they chose over and over again to pass him up, I didn't have much of a positive opinion on them for sure.

"No one?" I said, unconvinced.

He shrugged half-heartedly. "Not for a long time, anyway. Well, I went out with a couple of girls but, the rumors always surfaced, even after high school. After I graduated from high school I couldn't wait to move away and start somewhere else, but I was too chicken shit to ever say anything to anyone, afraid that somehow they'd know my secret or that I would have to keep hiding it from everyone." He grinned and placed his palms together. He opened them again between them floated a small ball of water. "I don't have to hide it from you."

I nudged him slightly. "No you don't. And you realize you're the only human ever to see my dragon form?"

He beamed brightly. "Nice to just be yourself for once, huh?"

I nodded in agreement. "Can't deny that. Although it's way more embarrassing to have you see— "I motioned around my room at all my cheesy fangirl loot.

He laughed. "Oh it's not that bad. One of the guys in my classes turned his entire bedroom to look like the bridge of the starship *Enterprise*."

"Really?" I asked, amazed. "Wait, when you say 'one of the guys,' you really mean yourself, right?"

He smiled nonchalantly and shrugged.

I just chuckled. "That's not so bad."

"Ha, no really it was. I did a bad job. Tried to turn my bed into a captain's chair," he shook his head, making a sour face. "Yeah. Bad." We giggled a moment, and I tried picturing him in a *Star Trek* uniform, sitting on a bed with Spock sheets. I had to stifle a huge laugh at that thought.

"What?" he questioned, as I tried to avoid his gaze. I just shook my head, and tried to choke back the laugh.

"*What*!?!" This time he was more insistent. He took his index finger and hooked it on the side of my chin, moving my face gently towards him. "You tell me. Now."

Still trying not to laugh, I did the most distracting thing I could think of; I grasped each side of his face and kissed him right on the lips. Instantly, he stopped protesting and kissed me back. Hard.

And just as suddenly as I began, I pulled away and stopped.

Eyes still closed, he just sat there, motionless. I giggled.

"What...what was that?" he stammered, slowly opening his eyes, an expression of surprise still on his face.

I shrugged. "Well, you did it to me, once. Now we are even. Are you mad?"

He blinked a few times, and finally opened his eyes. "No," he replied with a nervous chuckle. "No, not at all, just...surprised."

"Good." I said smugly. I pulled the sleeves of his sweatshirt over my hands so they were tucked inside and hugged the sleeves across my chest.

"Why?" he asked, still puzzled.

"Well, there's a couple reasons. One, because *I've* never really kissed a human before myself, and I was curious. Two, because I wanted to kiss *you* again. Three, because I wanted to stop laughing at the fact that I was picturing you with Spock sheets."

He laughed heartily. "Ah great. So I'm an experiment and a distraction!"

"A fun one, though!" I insisted.

Shaking his head, he laughed.

"I'm sorry," I said, "it's just despite the bad things going on...it's nice to have some company. You know?"

"Yeah...I *do* know," he sympathized.

"And...because I don't want to give you back your sweatshirt," I kidded, pulling the blanket up to my chin.

"Well then...if you're not giving that back, I need to go get more. If you're feeling up to it, can we go back to my hotel and get the rest of my clothes I left in the washer? You saw all that I have with me...and I don't dare leave you by yourself so I need you to come with? If that's okay?"

"So...basically you're telling me that at least for the time being, you're going to use my stuff, crash in my apartment and basically cohabitate with me? And we've only known each other a couple of weeks? Is that normal for humans?" I asked. In the movies it happened all the time but I had learned in my time here that movies and TV weren't always a realistic depiction of human life.

"Hmm...not unheard of but no, not normal," he replied. "Look, it's weird I know. But until we figure out the—"

I waved him off. "I know, I know. That's why you're here, right? Just to make sure I don't die?"

Gabriel reached over and pulled down my blanket, and grabbed my arm and gave it a squeeze. "No, that's not the *only* reason I'm here. Sure, okay, so my *calling* obligates me to be here. But it *doesn't* obligate me to like you, care about you or be attracted to you, does it?" He pushed the sleeve down, exposing my hand and pulled it to his lips. "And, even though it hasn't been long, I really have started to care about you, a lot. And I enjoy being around you. Okay?"

I smiled. "Okay."

He stood up, and pulled me along with him. There I stood, looking up at him, him looking down at me with his big eyes and handsome face for a moment.

Even though I'd just kissed him, the affection in his words and the tenderness in his stare made me feel slightly weird. Dragons—or people—didn't look at me that way. I almost was starting to believe he *did* have feelings for me. I felt the shivers again up my spine, and the fluttering in my tummy, so hard this time it shocked me.

My shiver seemed to bring him out of his daze. He forced a nervous grin at me, and chuckled uncomfortably. "Well then. Hey if I'm going to crash at your place, the least I can do is supply you with food," he said.

I chuckled. "I don't think you have that kind of money."

He smirked. "Well, we can try at least. You up for some shopping before we stop by the hotel?"

I began to wrinkle my nose but my stomach betrayed me and offered an obnoxious growl indicating that I was probably hungry.

"Well, I'm not, but my stomach apparently is. Let's go, I guess," I said, with a laugh. "You know where to go?"

He nodded, pulling a set of keys out of his pocket. "Yes. I have been here a couple months, remember?"

"Right, right..." I grabbed my purse, locked up behind us and climbed into his truck.

Pineville only had a small convenience store, so we opted for the larger one in the town of Waseca just south of us. It was a nearly silent fifteen minute or so drive, except for the music mix he played in his truck from his iPod. I recognized none of it but didn't protest; after all, it wasn't my vehicle. It wasn't bad, but I did decide if we were going to be driving together anymore I *was* putting a copy of my 90s mix in here, stat.

We parked and entered the sliding glass doors to a spread of marked aisles filled with food and other supplies. I grabbed a cart and headed for the frozen aisles.

"Leorah?" a familiar voice from behind me chimed.

I spun around from scanning the cooler for my favorite frozen pizza, while Gabriel frowned, claiming frozen pizza was gross because his brother spoiled him with homemade, healthier options. Madison's small, blonde self was behind me carrying a basket full of things.

"Oh, hi!" I greeted.

"I thought you were going somewhere for a couple of days?" she questioned, the highlighted brown hair tied in a knot on top of her head bobbing with each word. She was dressed in her school danceline sweatpants and sweatshirt and had an embroidered bag draped across her chest and along her side. Her brown eyes looked tired and her skin slightly flushed, I assumed she just came from danceline practice—which I just recently learned is a little like cheerleading but...not. At least that's how she described it to me.

"Yeah I was but things changed," I replied.

Madison eyed Gabriel hintingly, as he stood silent, shyly looking down as he shuffled his feet. He looked up momentarily and blushed. "Um...I need to grab something on the other side of the store. Meet you in about ten minutes?"

I nodded and he nearly tore off down the aisle like a racecar. I had to choke back a laugh.

"So...he finally asked you out huh?" Madison raised her eyebrows. "It's about time!"

I just smiled uncomfortably, because I couldn't tell her the real reason...and I was a little embarrassed because he technically *hadn't* asked me out at this point. But, he was crashing at my apartment and we were buying food together like an old married couple.

"Uh-huh..." she grinned. "Things must be okay, then if you're here together at the store in the *middle* of the day no less. Did you...you know...?" she asked, giving me a coy expression.

"Did we...?" I started, confused. Then I realized what she was talking about. "Oh! No! *No!*"

Madison appeared disappointed. "Why? I mean I know you're shy but...come on! You can totally tell he wants to! Hell, he's a man, they *all* want to," she said dryly, with a roll of the eye.

I shrugged. "I'm just not sure how I feel about stuff yet. Things are just kind of...weird." I wished I could explain the real reason to someone—*anyone*—even young Madison. Kit was nowhere to be found and I really had no one else.

"Hmm. Well I know you have to feel something, after all the guys that have come into the shop fawning over you, this is the first time you've ever seen one outside of work," she said knowingly.

"What guys?" I asked, taken aback. I certainly had never noticed this, but then she's right, I didn't really pay attention. Dating a human, it never occurred to me. Until now.

She chuckled. "Oh you're so modest. Lots of guys, but none of them have been as obvious as *that* one," she said, pointing vaguely in the direction that Gabriel had walked off in. "So, what is his name, anyways?"

"Gabriel," I replied, feeling a slight flush in my cheeks

Madison grinned. "You do like him. I never see you blush!"

I shrugged. "I think I do, but..."

"Well, do you feel nervous around him sometimes, like your stomach is flopping around like a fish?" She set her basket down, filled with junk food (a girl after my own heart!) like chips, candy and pop and crossed her arms over her chest, the index finger of one of her hands tapping at her chin thoughtfully.

"Well..." I hesitated. Just thinking about it sent my stomach into spasms.

"Do you find excuses to touch him? Are you smiling more than you usually do?" She grinned, giving me a nudge. "Yes, you do." She pointed at the nervous smile I was wearing on my face.

"I smile!" I insisted.

"Yes, you do. But not like *that*!"

"That?"

"Like it's going to fall right off your face!" Madison said, with a laugh.

I rolled my eyes. "What's your point?"

"That's love, Leo!"

"*Love*?" Just saying it out loud made my voice squeak.

"Yes! I should know, I've been in love now about three times just this year. I can totally see the signs," she said, a hint of bragging in her tone.

I knitted my brow at her—surely, you can't be an expert of love if you are doing it all the time—more like, lust?

"But how can that be, I mean I've only known him a few days?" And in that few days he's introduced me to magic, saved my life, cuddled with me in my bed, we've kissed twice and now we're practically living together.

"Oh, Leo! It just happens, there's no reason to it! It's not like, practical or anything," she explained. "It's sweet, like a fairy tale!"

I wrinkled my face, she was obsessed with that idea of *fairy tales*. I really didn't relate to young humans at *all*.

"The good thing is, I'm pretty sure he feels the same way," she said. "I've caught the way he looks at you."

"When? That short time you just saw him now?"

She shook her head. "No, silly, all the times at the shop. And then now."

"How can you tell?" I asked.

"I just can," she said, sounding confident. There was a chirp from her bag and she rummaged around in it for a moment and pulled out her phone. She rolled her eyes upon seeing the screen. "Emily. She wants Twizzlers."

I chuckled. "Having a party?"

"Sort of, these are for tomorrow, we're going to get ready for the dance together!" she said, clapping her hands together giddily.

"Ah, sounds like fun!" I offered, but I really wouldn't know.

"It should be, I'm excited! My dress is so awesome!" she began telling me all about her hot little coral-colored dress with the slits cut out on the sides and the rhinestones on the straps. Before she could continue describing the underwear she was planning to wear I cut her off.

"You hear from Kit?" I asked.

She gave me a strange look, like I just asked her if she had seen the unicorn down the aisle. "No, why would I?" It's true, normally she wouldn't. Madison just came in, worked her shift and was done. She was a good worker but a friend outside the shop, well, she was too young to really travel in the same social circles as us (which my circle consisted only of Kit, so…).

"Just wondering, because I asked you to look in on her because—"

She waved me off, "Oh yeah, I remember. No I haven't. Any idea when the shop is opening again?"

"Not sure, really. It'll be a few days before it gets cleaned up. It's a mess right now," I explained.

She didn't appear distressed at the news. "Just as well. We have a competition coming up soon anyways, I don't need any more distractions. Well, I'll see ya later…your man is coming back. I think I make him nervous," she said with a laugh, and she walked off.

"See ya," I called after her, as Gabriel joined up carrying an armful of man toiletries.

"What's all that?" I asked, as he tossed it in the cart

"Um, a new razor, some shaving cream, deodorant and shampoo. I saw the stuff you have in your shower," he grimaced, and wrinkled his nose.

"What? You don't like vanilla?" I pretended to be offended.

He snorted. "On you it's fabulous. On me? Well, I get called *Cupcake* enough, I don't want to smell like one."

I shook my head. "Right…"

"So, all this time, you still haven't picked out a pizza?" he asked, nodding towards the nearly empty cart (besides the stuff he just put in it)

"Oh, Madison was just talking about her dress for the dance and whatever," I said. "I couldn't really start diving into the coolers without looking rude."

"Just as well. That stuff is gross anyways compared to Daniel's pizza," he insisted.

"So…" I said, "…grocery shopping and stuff. Together. That's kind of weird, huh?

He shrugged. "I guess?" he retorted, sounding confused.

"You know, Maddie thought we were here like *together* together," I said, as we sauntered down the coffee aisle, not really looking at much of anything, although suddenly Gabriel was extremely interested in some green tea on the shelf.

"She did?" Gabriel asked, not looking up from the box.

I smirked, but he couldn't see me. "Yeah, she thought that since we were here in the middle of the day that we must of...well..." I trailed off to allow his imagination to finish off.

"Well what? Oh. *Oh!*" He quickly set the box back on the shelf in the wrong spot and gave me an alarmed expression on his face. "She thought we...did...?"

"Yeah. I told her that was silly, we haven't known each other that long," I said, with a chuckle.

"Silly, right," Gabriel said with an uneasy chuckle. He eyed the shelf, as if looking for something in particular. "Well I guess it is silly. I mean, living together after only a couple of days, and we haven't even been out on a formal date yet. Kind of weird."

"Yeah..." I said, trailing off. I felt my stomach start somersaulting inside me again.

"Do dragons even date? How does that work, anyways?" Gabriel mused thoughtfully.

"Well sort of. We're starting to, just look at my brother and *Kiarra*," I said, spitting her name out with venom.

"Well, so...you want to go out with me?" Gabriel said, trying to sound confident but sounding a little shaky.

I gave him an odd look. "Go out with you? I mean, we're like, shopping together for food and you're going to leave your shampoo in my shower." I was confused.

"No, like an *actual* date. Before I knew who you were, I wanted to ask you out anyways, then I found out who you were and I don't know...I felt like maybe I couldn't? I don't know, it's stupid. I mean, we've like kissed and stuff and—"

I cut him off. "Well, what did you have in mind?"

Gabriel beamed. "Really?"

I elbowed him jokingly. "Sure if you can come up with something to do around here," I said. "There's not a whole lot."

"I can do that," Gabriel said, suddenly appearing thoughtful. "Seven o'clock tonight, your living room?"

I smiled. "I'll be there."

Chapter 12

I tried to inquire more about this *date* but, he remained tight lipped. On the way back, we drove past the frontage road to Kit's place and I insisted we stop by quick to check on her to make sure she was feeling better.

Kit's small little cottage off a frontage road sat on about an acre of land at the end of a long, windy driveway. Trees of different kinds gathered on the landscape, haphazardly placed by Mother Nature years and years ago, and the little red house just sat in a convenient opening. Between the trees were carefully placed gardens and shrubberies, many of them she used in her Witchcraft. The path leading up to her house was lined with many fragrant herbs, with container gardens in her windows in boxes and up the small steps to her front door.

Kit, who had a handful of cats as well (and she insisted that against the damn stereotype that it wasn't because she was single, she just liked cats and she would have had them even if she was married) and a couple of them were on the front stoop, sunning themselves in the late autumn sun. A gray striped tabby immediately *yelped* at our presence and darted off, but an orange longhair didn't seem to mind us. He stretched his front paws and yawned, looking bored and rolled over on his back. He made no effort to greet us, yet his wiggly tail indicated he wouldn't be objected to one of us petting him. Or her.

"Everything looks kind of...off," I said, observing her neglected front stoop. Besides the cats, there were a couple of empty cat food bowls she always kept full of food and water for her outdoor preferring cats and the occasional stray that dropped by. The potted herbs and plants that lined the stairs leading up to the door were wilted and yellowed and appeared that they hadn't been watered in a few days, and there were a handful of newspapers in front of the door, untouched.

"*Mrow?*" A rather despondent sounding black cat said at my feet, bumping my ankles with her nose. I recognized her as one of the outdoor cats that didn't really care for me (or anyone, really).

"Awwww, what's up kitty?" I asked, leaning over to pat her head. She allowed one pat before bumping one of the food dishes with her head and sitting down in front of it, letting out a rather wistful *meow*.

I exchanged glances with Gabriel. "I don't remember it looking this neglected the other day..." I mused. I didn't wait for Gabriel to answer me, I opened up the black storm door to rap repeatedly on the main door. "Kit? Kit, it's Leo! Are you here? Everything okay? *Kit!?!*"

There was no answer, so I tried the doorknob. It didn't open.

"I can fix that," Gabriel said, nudging me aside. He placed his hands on either side of the doorknob and concentrated momentarily. I heard a *click, click* and he turned around and smiled triumphantly.

"How'd you do that?" I asked, in awe.

He shrugged, nonchalantly. "Well, what is metal but really fragments of earth, right?"

"Sweet..." I said, grasping the doorknob and twisting.

"You also didn't leave the door unlocked the other day, I totally opened it," he said, mischievously.

"You did not!" I exclaimed, as he dodged a playful punch from me. He snickered, and followed me inside as I pushed the door open.

"Kit?" Her house was pretty much the same as the last I saw it. She was a fairly neat person, but there were used pots on the stove, plates and cups in the sink. I pointed to a pantry and instructed Gabriel to find the cat food and feed the cats while I investigated.

"Kit?" I called, wandering the halls of her little house, wandering past pictures, paintings of cats and shelves of unicorn knick-knacks and the occasional cat. Her bedroom was at the end of the house. I entered and switched the light on as I went in. Her bed was unmade, but empty. Her altar on the opposite wall looked untouched, I recognized some herbs and a candle she'd used a couple of days ago, she didn't change them out yet.

"Huh...." I pulled my cell out and dialed her number. "Learn to Fly" by Foo Fighters started playing from her nightstand (an ironic choice of ringtone for me, of course...). "Great...wherever she is, she has no phone." I exhaled in frustration. Other than her not being there, and a few things out of place nothing really looked out of the ordinary. I mean, she'd been sick so it stood to reason a few things would get neglected.

I rejoined Gabriel in the kitchen. "She's not here. And she doesn't have her phone with her."

Gabriel wore a very subdued expression. "Something isn't right, and I'm not just talking about the cats not being fed or some dry plants. It feels...wrong."

"Wrong?" I questioned.

"Like, empty. You know how I told you before there's energy...*everywhere*," he explained. "Well like in your apartment I feel your energy. It's in the objects you touch, your clothes...like an essence."

I nodded. "Okay?" I prompted.

"Here? I feel nothing. *Nothing*. And I've felt her energy before, at the shop. Many times. And even when I came to pick you up that one night after dropping her off. Even from outside, I could feel something. Faint, but it was there. There is *nothing* here!" Gabriel paced back and forth through the kitchen, pausing here or there with his eyes shut. "Nothing!"

"That's...odd. What does that mean?" I asked.

He shrugged. "I'm not sure. I mean, at the shop I felt a dark presence. Evil. Your energy is...powerful but overall, pleasant. Without anything to sense I can't tell...*anything*.

"It could be a block of some kind. Perhaps some warlock? Or perhaps she's even more powerful than I thought, and she casted out all energy, somehow."

I gasped. "Kind of like that.... *thing* that was after me, huh?"

Gabriel paused reluctantly, not wanting to agree with me. "I am not going to say for sure, but..."

"Shit! Dammit I need to find her! How could this happen? Do you think it got her?" I pulled Gabriel out the door, slamming it behind me, startling one of the cats, and pushed him into the truck. "To the shop—that's the only other place I can think of she'd be, besides the hospital." I swallowed nervously.

Gabriel didn't argue, he just cranked up the engine and peeled down the driveway. On the way I began calling the nearby hospital. She wasn't there and since all the hospitals in the region operated by the same provider, if she wasn't coming up she wasn't at any of them, yet, she wasn't there. They instructed me to try calling back in about an hour if I hadn't found her, perhaps she just hadn't been processed yet but doubtful.

We sped into the coffee shop and were met with an empty parking lot. Gabriel drove me right up to the front door so I could peer in.

The lights were off, nothing appeared to have been moved at all, no one had clearly been there since we left the other day.

"Where is she, then? I can't believe she forgot her phone..." I sighed, feeling troubled. "If that—that *thing* got to her..." I buried my face in my palms and groaned.

Gabriel, who was currently back on the road to my place, reached out his hand and rested it on my leg. "I'm sorry, Leo. I know you're worried. I'm sure she's fine, maybe a friend came and picked her up and took her out. If something bad had happened to her there would be some sign of it...a struggle, something left behind. But there's just nothing there. Her car isn't there either, perhaps she just left somewhere."

I considered this. "You're right, but when you mentioned— "

"—I shouldn't have said anything, I'm sorry. I'm probably just exaggerating. Hell, she's a witch, she probably just banished all the lingering energy in the house and it worked a little *too* well. She'll be okay," Gabriel said, his thumb tracing circles on the top of my leg.

I nodded slowly. "Yeah, you're right. She probably went out with her coven and did some magic thing and she just left her phone. It is strange that she forgot to feed the cats, though..."

"Or did they just eat it all?" Gabriel offered.

"Maybe," I said. "They seemed awfully insistent for cats that have just eaten." I snorted at the thought, "But some cats are just like that, anyway. Ugh, I hope she's okay. I should have left a note."

"Do you want to go back?" he asked.

I shook my head. "No...no. We can just drop by tomorrow again. To check on her."

"Okay." He didn't remove his hand but he continued to drive the rest of the way, in silence. I leaned my forehead against the cool glass and shut my eyes, feeling a wave of fatigue over me. I closed my eyes momentarily as the scenery spun by me, making me attempt to blink the dizziness away.

"Are *you* okay?" he asked with concern.

"Yeah..." I said. "Just a little tired again. A lot going on you know..."

"I know," he said. I didn't look at him, but I could hear the smile in his tone. It wasn't a long ride, but I felt myself nodding off, fatigue winning the battle. Finally, I just gave in. Gabriel inquired again if I was in fact, okay, but I didn't answer. I just smiled, and without thinking about it grasped and squeezed his hand. He grinned at me, as I opted to lean on his shoulder to snooze and not against the cold, hard window. It was only a brief moment as I inhaled his now familiar scent and drifted off.

Upon arriving back at my place I was still feeling pretty groggy so I was instructed to go lie down. I was a bit afraid, because of that evil entity dream like thing that had *haunted* me in my sleep, but Gabriel surmised that since whatever it was disappeared after he flung the moonlight at it that the *thing* had an aversion to light. So, at least, there's that. I opened up my blinds wide to let the sunlight pour in and felt reasonably safe to nap. Gabriel said he'd be nearby (not like there was little choice, my apartment wasn't that large) on his laptop doing some "work" as he was falling behind. I slept without incident, thankfully, although I did have a slightly strange dream. Gabriel and I were at the nearby lake, enjoying a picnic in the summertime when suddenly it was dark, and little black tendrils started growing out of the ground. I woke up then, and that was the end. I was pretty sure it was just my imagination messing with me, and there wasn't anything going on since I woke up feeling fine and actually decently rested.

Until I realized that I was supposed to be going on an actual "date" in about two hours, and my brain went into panic mode. How the hell was I supposed get ready for a date!?! Especially when he was in the next room?

This required a nice, cold pop. I hesitated, before stepping out of my bedroom, looking down at my scrubby attire.

So far he has only seen me in crappy sweats and yoga pants and my dirty black jeans and casual shirts for work. I frowned. I didn't think sweats were typically date attire, especially the gray sweatpants and charcoal "Hogwarts School" t-shirt.

I put a hand to my hair. Currently it was in a messy braid that hung to the side and down over my chest. I hadn't a drop of makeup on, and I hoped I didn't appear *too* bedraggled. But, at this point he'd seen worse. Considering we hadn't been on an actual date yet, that was somewhat regrettable.

The thought brought me to some of the movies I'd seen, where couples become too comfortable with each other and they get bored and turned off when the other stops caring and just *farts* in front of the other, or doesn't care to close the door to the bathroom when they go "do their business".

"Oh, crap," I muttered to myself under my breath, putting palm to face and making a groaning sound.

"What did you say?" Gabriel piped up, from the next room.

I yelped, quietly, didn't think he could hear me. "Oh, nothing. Just uh…stubbed my toe."

"That sucks!" End of conversation, apparently. I could hear him clacking on his computer keyboard, and alternately typing on his phone.

Feeling a pang of desperation, I darted for my phone that I had tossed on the remains of my charred nightstand and started flipping through my very small list of contacts. Kit was the first person I could think of so I called her first, hoping she'd be home now and would answer. It went straight to voicemail. I tried again…no luck.

I sighed in exasperation. My brother would be of no help. Maxxus? I considered this for a moment before deciding that wasn't wise. I landed on Madison's entry and started to text her, but second guessed myself.

Madison was young, and a bit bossy. Judging from the fact that she was 17 and claimed to of been in love a handful of times already this year, I kind of had to doubt that she was the best person for the job of guiding me onto what I should do on a first date. Besides, she'd already seen us together at the grocery store, confiding in her that I hadn't been on an actual date yet might get me to appear a little—wantonly.

Emily Burton's name was right above hers, my other co-worker. Emily was beautiful, her hair and makeup always appropriate and not overdone yet always immaculate. As far as I knew, Emily had had a steady boyfriend for a time, and been out with a couple of guys. She was a bit more reserved, and patient. I decided to try her.

Emily, it's Leo. I need to borrow your beauty expertise.

Instead of texting, she actually called me. It barely rang for a second when I answered.

"Emily?"

"Yeah. Surprised to hear from you! What's going on?" she asked, sounding a bit timid. "Not often my boss calls me when I'm not late for work!" she said, with a nervous chuckle.

I had to laugh back. "Don't worry hun, this is strictly girl stuff, not work stuff."

"Oh. Well then, happy to help, but I don't know what *I* can do. You already look so pretty all the time," Emily said.

I softened. Sweet girl, that Emily. "Aw, that's nice of you to say. But I'm going out and I want to look extra special."

"Out? Like on a *date* date?" Emily squealed excitably.

"Mmm...yeah. A date." My ear erupted with cheers and girly giggles.

"Oh! That's so cool! Who with? Oh, I bet it's that hottie with the glasses that keeps drooling over you at the shop, huh?"

I had to grin at that one. "Yeah, that's the one," I replied.

She shrieked again. "Oh, yay! He was so cute! You guys would be so cute together!"

"Well, not if I don't make a decent impression which is why I called you. Madison is good at makeup but not good with secrets...I feel kind of silly that I even have to ask, but I'm not good with hair or makeup, and I don't have a lot of time either. Normally I'd call Kit but she's not answering her phone." I tried to hide the concern from my tone, not wanting to alarm Emily as to Kit's unknown whereabouts when I didn't know anything myself.

"Oh! Of course! Well...hmm...you have internet, right? Duh, who doesn't? Let me get out my laptop here...let's see what I can find. I don't have a ton of time since the dance is tonight but we'll figure something out."

"Thanks, Emily." Over the course of the next twenty minutes, Emily had me sit down and peruse this *Pinterest* site I'd never heard of but she swore it'd change my life. She had me look up "date hairstyles" and said she did the same, so hopefully we'd both come up with the same entries.

"I know most guys like the natural look and some of these are pretty high maintenance anyway so let's keep it simple." She instructed me to a photo with the girl in the picture, the front pieces of hair were twisted back and joined together in the back of the head, fastened with a neat design of bobby pins (which I could never do, but, she insisted that I didn't have to). The back of the hair was teased up and slightly poufy, and she claimed it was really easy to attain this but as she described and I read what was going on, I was quite confused.

Emily exhaled, trying to gather patience. At work, I normally just wore my hair long and straight or in a big, chunky braid down my back. I wore minimal makeup, just concealer, some eyeliner and mascara and lip gloss. In the dragon realm, makeup was non-existent. Obviously. So this was all fairly new territory.

She found a tutorial online and made me watch it, it appeared like something I could do except when I asked her about the stick in the woman's hand, I swear, sweet patient Emily actually sounded like a dragon when she growled. But she guided me through how to use it—it was a curling iron—I had one I just hadn't really ever used it much.

Another five minutes of hunting for tutorials on how to apply cat-eye makeup, flawless foundation and lip gloss, I had to swear to her that I would send her a "selfie" of my face before I stepped out in public. Then we discussed attire.

This was a bit more difficult, seeing as how I didn't have much. I had to describe to her everything in my closet in detail. Her audible dismay was very obvious. At one point she even insisted on coming over and loaning me some items of hers (although she was smaller than me, she swore she would have things that would fit me...I was doubtful) but I stretched the truth and told her my apartment was a huge mess and I was embarrassed to let her see it. Truth was yeah, it was a mess but I couldn't care less if she saw it or not. I didn't want her to see Gabriel camping out in my living room, comfortably lounging on the couch with his feet up, laptop in his lap, chewing tentatively on the earpiece of his glasses as he worked (yeah, I was spying on him through the crack in my door. Yeah, he looked pretty damn adorable while concentrating on...whatever the Hell he was concentrating on....)

I pulled the item she mentioned out from the back of the closet: I had never worn it, I almost forgot about it. Kit ordered it online, claiming the orange would just look *so* stunning with my hair and skin, while Madison claimed no one looked good in orange (it was more of a reddish, rusty orange, Kit had insisted). I never had any reason to wear any sort of dress.

"I could try it," I said, the phone cradled between my ear and shoulder as I held the hangered dress up to myself.

"Now...shoes. Do you have *anything* besides damn Converse or Doc Martens?"

"Umm..." I tossed the dress down on my bed and peered into the back of the closet, behind a handful of boxes to the sole pair of dress shoes I owned: a black pair of sparkly gladiator sandals with a slight platform heel. "I have one pair," I said, and I described them to her.

"Good. Perfect. You're gonna look so hot, he isn't going to be able to stand it." I had to swear again to send her a picture with my phone about five times before I could get her to hang up.

But before I could get started...I still needed that pop!

"Get a good nap in?" Gabriel chimed, as I tried to discreetly head into my kitchen.

"Pretty good," I said, reaching in the fridge for my drink. "Working hard, or hardly working?"

He snorted. "Well, a little of both, actually," he said, closing his laptop and setting it aside. "Still feeling up to going out?" he asked, a mischievous raise to his brow.

I popped the top of the can and took a sip, stifling the urge to belch afterward, causing my face to twist up in a grimace. "Feel great," I said, my tone strangled as I resisted the urge to burp. Belching as a dragon was...quite scary and usually required actual fire.

"Really?" he said with a chuckle.

"So what are we doing, then?" I questioned, leaning against the fridge and casually crossing my feet—one over the other—trying not to appear too eager.

Gabriel smiled impishly. "You'll find out."

"Uh-huh...you have *no* idea, do you?" I retorted.

He pretended to be wounded. "Come on now! Have you that little faith in me? After all we've been through?"

I snorted. "Right...well before we do *whatever* it is you have planned...need to grab a shower or anything before I hole myself in there for a while?"

"I can wait until you're done," he offered.

"No really...this will take a while. A long while. Trust me."

He scoffed and took the hint. It was interesting to see how male humans lived as opposed to female ones. Well, I only had myself to compare to but as depicted on TV, women tended to spend hours primping, plucking, curling—whatever.

Gabriel was in and out in about ten minutes flat, and came out looking fabulous.

It wasn't fair. Not fair at all.

"There," he said. "Sorry it took so long; your shower is pretty nice."

"*Long?*" I shook my head.

He chuckled. "Let me finish up some stuff here." He dove back into his laptop as I took my leave to the shower.

It was a nice shower, I had one of those rainfall showerheads with just the right amount of pressure. After undressing I paused a moment in the steam, inhaling the scent of his shampoo and soap and musing at how outrageous it was that there were *men's* shower supplies adorning the shelves of my shower: a bar of fragrant, musky soap next to my fruity-scented conditioner; a black bottle of shampoo next to my own. I smiled a little to myself.

If nothing else, at least I was getting to experience this point of humanity for myself, something I didn't think I'd ever experience: male companionship.

It took me about thirty minutes to shower and moisturize afterward (being a dragon, in human form we didn't have a ton of body hair because we were scaly…the downside is I suffered from dry skin most days that required lots of lotion to fix), another twenty or so to blow dry my hair with the adequate volumizing technique as was shown in the YouTube video I watched, another fifteen to curl some soft waves in my hair (I could only do the front and ends, it was just taking too much time and I had a difficult time operating the iron behind my head—I hoped Emily wouldn't scold me for it). All I had was a bottle of cheap hairspray to set it—product wasn't something I used in my hair, often. But, Kit swore it was good for taking out t-shirt stains like coffee which was mostly why I kept it around.

The makeup went a little easier. Using mineral makeup on my face that thankfully had little smell to bother my sensitive dragon nose, a little blush and simple eyeliner (I couldn't do the cat-eye wing thing that Emily suggested, even from watching the video I couldn't figure it out so I just settled with a simple line) put on some pale peach shadow and some mauve lipstick and finished off with mascara.

All the while I could hear Gabriel in the kitchen, banging around. He was talking to someone on the phone, I assumed it was Daniel from the way he was speaking. After about a half an hour of swearing, banging and clanging around did a wonderful aroma of garlic and herbs start to waft from the kitchen.

I was beginning to feel kind of high-maintenance. This was going to be around the third time he'd cooked for me, and I hadn't done so once for him. Of course, I had been serving him coffee for weeks but I was paid for that.

It smelled divine though—whatever it was and I didn't have any idea what we were going to be doing, although I was already impressed.

I glanced at my computer clock; I had about fifteen minutes before I was meeting him for our date (which just seemed so cheesy, making a *grand* entrance into my living room), which was just enough time for me to get that dress on and then spend the next ten minutes after that trying to work the straps on those damn shoes.

I paused as I was pulling the dress over my head, and looked down at my underwear: plain white bra, high-cut gray underwear with faded pink flowers on them...I wrinkled my nose. They didn't feel very...*date* like.

Not that I thought anything was going to happen, but I'd watched enough movies, seen enough TV to know that you did *not* want to be caught with your granny panties on. So I rummaged through my "delicates" drawer for something a little more acceptable.

"Really?" I asked myself, cursing because the sexiest pair of underwear I had was a pair of pink boy shorts and a pink cotton bra with white lace around the edges—again a gift from Kit; something she bought for herself but the bra was too big, claiming it was marked wrong. "Thank you Kit!" I said to myself, changing out of my grungier underthings and replacing them with the cuter ones.

Once I was fully dressed, I eyed myself in the mirror and was shocked at what I saw. I hardly recognized myself. One might describe me as pretty but humans' views on that were so varied, I wasn't sure if I'd fit that bill. But I definitely looked different.

I remembered to snap a shot of myself for Emily, begrudgingly. Dragon's *hate* selfies. I grabbed my phone and took a quick shot of myself in the mirror and sent it to Emily, who promptly responded with a simple: "*Hot!*"

"Here goes nothing," I said to myself, suddenly feeling my heart flutter. Not sure what was making me nervous: the impending date or my state of dress. Maybe Gabriel wouldn't like it? Perhaps he didn't like orange? I fingered my hair. Maybe I did my hair wrong?

I shook my head. "Shut up, Leo. It's just a dress." Okay so the dress made me feel weird—exposed. A bit like wearing traditional dragon robes. I inhaled, forcing the sudden feeling of bile rising in my throat down. I exhaled and forced myself to step out of the hallway.

Gabriel had his back towards me in the kitchen, frantically stirring something over the stove, with his phone perched between his shoulder and ear.

"*No*, Dan, I don't know if I used free-range beef. I see cows alongside the road all over here, they all look pretty free to me! So sorry I don't have your culinary skills or— "

"Am I interrupting?" I inquired meekly.

Gabriel chuckled. "Oh, just my brother, he—" he swiveled around from his spot in the kitchen, his mouth fell open in surprise.

"Leorah?" His tone was a mixture of surprise, and uncertainty. He allowed the phone to fall from his ear to the floor with a metallic *thud* that either killed the phone or hung it up; I heard no further noise from it.

I let out a small giggle. "Hopefully this will work."

"Leo—I—you," he stammered. "Holy shit, Leo, you look amazing!"

I smiled, feeling the heat in my cheeks, and had to look away from his stare of admiration.

"And I'm still not dressed yet," he said, setting something down on the stove with a *clink*. "I hope you don't mind, I figured since I don't know the restaurants here I'd just make something, then we can go somewhere." He motioned to a place set at the bar, with two place settings across from each other with my mismatched plates and silverware. There was a small daisy in a small glass between the two, with two tealights in two small dishes on each side.

I felt my heart swoon a little: a candlelight dinner! How totally Hollywood rom-com and cliché …

…and utterly adorable.

"Sit down!" he prompted, pulling out one of the chairs and motioned for me to sit. "I'll be right back!" He took one last glance at me and smiled nervously, before grabbing his backpack and darting off for the bathroom.

While I waited for him to return I glanced around the apartment. He didn't just have candles on the table, but a handful of them strategically placed in mismatched, clear glass glasses (that I forgot I had) around the kitchen and living room. Strategic in that they were perched in spots that would be difficult for my cat to reach.

Not only that but he had picked up a bit...not intrusively but organized my little piles of clutter, and wiped stuff down. I grinned to myself.

"Sorry," Gabriel said, re-entering the room a little hurriedly.

My breath caught momentarily upon seeing him and my heart jumped into my throat. He was dressed in boot-cut dark blue jeans, and an athletic fitting black t shirt with no slogans on it; which was unusual for him. The sleeves were short enough for his bicep tattoos to be fully visible; the tribal design on his right arm that extended to his forearm, and the flames on the other, surrounding what I assumed was Celtic writing. I wanted to ask him what it meant, but I was too busy trying to force myself to *not* drool. It was simple dress, but a far cry from the baggy jeans and sweatshirts he normally wore.

He bit his lip uncertainly, looking down at himself. "What? I know, I could do better but my dressy stuff— "

I cut him off, "You look...hot." I had to look away so he couldn't see my face set on fire with that confession.

The corners of his mouth turned up and his face flushed. He also wasn't wearing his glasses and you could see the glint in his playful, hazel brown eyes. "Let me get you—well," he awkwardly tried to reach for my plate, getting rather close to me, his forearm brushed my bare shoulder, sending electrical tingles down my arm. I could smell the aroma of his spicy soap in my shower on him.

I handed him the plate and he took it and his own five feet over into the kitchen. "I'm sorry, I know I bragged about my brother's pizza recipe but after arguing for about thirty minutes about not having the right ingredients, I decided spaghetti was the better option. I hope that's okay," he said, putting a plate together of noodles and sauce, garnishing it with parsley and a piece of garlic toast and setting it in front of me. "My brother insisted it was a bad idea, because the sauce is messy and if you spilled it—"

"It's great, one of my favorites actually," I interrupted his insecurity. "If I spill the washing machine is just right over there—" I said, pointing down the hallway.

Gabriel relaxed and smiled, setting down his own plate and sitting down to it. "Good. It occurred to me that even though we're shacking up together, I don't know that much about you. Like, your favorite food, your favorite color— "

"—*anything* but pink!" I exclaimed with a chuckle.

"No, I suppose not," he replied with a grin.

"Well," I said, twirling my fork into the noodles and winding up a good bite, "ask me anything you want to know. Just prepare to answer the same question."

"Fair enough," he said, as he started to take a bite himself before abruptly standing. "Almost forgot!" He went to the fridge and produced a bottle of red wine and a corkscrew. "I ran out quickly while you were showering—I hope you don't mind. Just the store around the corner."

I smiled. "Why would I mind?" I asked as he removed the cork and set two plastic goblets on the table.

"Sorry for the cheap plastic, but you didn't have any wine glasses, I noticed," he said, pouring me a glass first and himself second, before setting the bottle down in the middle. "Daniel assured me it was better 'slightly chilled', though I don't know if I believe him."

"It is, and generally straight out of the bottle, too," I said, with a laugh.

He snickered. "That explains the lack of wine glasses," he said.

I took the noodles and smeared it in a pool of sauce and took a bite. "Oh! It's really good!" I said, in between bites. Then I felt stupid…talking with your mouth full was probably *not* very attractive.

He beamed. "Good. Spaghetti is your favorite food?"

I considered this. "Hmm…I think so. With a side of raw wild boar and opossum liver sauce. Mmmmm!" I said, exaggeratedly smacking my lips.

Gabriel cocked a brow. "You're kidding, right?"

I grinned devilishly. "Yes." We chuckled. "Yes, spaghetti and meatballs is probably my favorite, secondly only to triple chocolate cheesecake. Oh, and Mountain Dew, but that's not really a food. More like an *ambrosia*."

He laughed. "I'm more of a Coke person myself."

"What!?!" I pretended to be in shock, clutching my chest and making weird choking noises.

"Stop!" he said, tossing a paper napkin at me. "Above all those I prefer coffee. Well, I'm sure you figured that out," he said, between bites of his spaghetti.

"What do *you* like? In case I get extra ambitious and attempt this…*cooking* thing?" I said, taking another bite. It really was quite good, just the right amount of fresh garlic, onion and basil. A little sweet, a little spicy, and full bodied. "Although I don't think I could do *this* good."

"I don't think I could again either. I'll have to just get Daniel for that," he said with a laugh. He took a sip of his wine between bites and looked thoughtful. "I really think I'm just a burger type guy. I love a good hamburger. There are some great spots in the Cities that have this cheese filled one. It's called a Juicy Lucy."

I narrowed my eyes in a grimace. "Really? That sounds gross."

"Maybe but it's not. It's *so* good. They've even been featured on Food Network before, at least according to my brother," he said. "You'll have to try one sometime."

"Maybe we'll go up there sometime?" I asked rhetorically, hopefully.

He nodded. "Definitely. That is if the whole date-thing works out," he said, with an insecure laugh. "I mean; I know I didn't do the greatest job—"

I scanned around the living room again. The candlelight, the breeze blowing in softly from the window, the sheer white curtain looking ethereal in the dim candlelight…the extra care he showed to keep the candles from my cat (even now, I could see her from her pillow on the floor eyeing the dancing flames on the wall, a look of needing to pounce in her naughty green eyes). I felt a warmth in my chest, that emanated outwards and upwards to my face, reddening my cheeks and causing me to smile. "It's wonderful, don't sell yourself short. Remember, not only have I had *no* dates to compare you to, but I can tell you tried very hard, and that counts for a lot."

He snorted. "So I could have like, decorated with garbage and put porno on and it would have been okay? Since you have nothing else to compare to?"

It was my turn to playfully throw the napkin at him. "*No*. This is very much out of a Hollywood romance. For short notice, I'm pretty impressed. And confused where you got these candles."

He flushed. "Ah, well believe it or not, they were mine. Sometimes I just light them and do magic things with the flames. Helps to keep my magic on edge, you know? Working with the elements and stuff. For the others, I just go outside or turn on the sink and it's all right there. Fire, I need a little help sometimes."

I considered this. "You mean you weren't hoping to romance some woman when you came down here, and that's why you had them?" I teased.

"Ah well, you should have seen the stack of them I had *before* I found you," he teased right back.

"Touché!" I chuckled, taking a bite of garlic toast and swooning at the flavor. "Oh! That's good!" I said, putting a hand over my mouth so he couldn't see me rudely chewing my food as I spoke.

He grinned. "That was all mine. Daniel doesn't believe in eating bread."

My mouth fell open in mock horror. "No bread? That's like…a dragon's staple!"

"Yeah he's all…*healthy* and stuff," he shuddered.

I laughed. "Yeah, dragons don't do healthy. We eat what we want. Or who…" I added with a wink.

"Not Daniel…he'd drive you nuts. Don't eat this, don't eat that, that's bad for you…blah blah blah," he said, rolling his eyes, making the motion of flapping jaws with his hands.

"That's okay, if he pisses me off, I'll eat him," I said with a wink.

"I don't think you're kidding either. I saw that dragon form. That was…*impressive!*"

"Was it everything you dreamed?" I retorted, mockingly with a slight roll of the eyes.

"More! I mean, there are pictures of pink dragons, ones that have been passed down in books and other various artworks. *None* of them hold a candle to you. It was…absolutely amazing," he said, sounding slightly giddy. "Tough and strong but still…majestic, like an eagle but bigger! Not scaly or scary at all, but just…" he cut himself off, laughing uproariously. "I must sound like an idiot. Or some sort of stupid fangirl."

I narrowed my eyes. "Hey. What's wrong with a *fangirl*?"

"Nothing!" he insisted quickly. I chuckled.

"Those wings…you described them as little, and fragile. But they so are not…they're like butterfly wings. All those iridescent colors in them, sort of like the sparkles you breathe…they just embody magic. I'll bet they serve more of a purpose then you know," he said, shaking his fork at me.

I frowned. "Well, that remains to be seen." I fell silently taking another few bites of my dinner, a swig of wine. I didn't know why, but the subject of my wings was a bit sore for me. Of all the things I could ever be picked on—and was picked on—the state of my wings hurt the most. Sure I couldn't breathe fire, but not being able to fly? I mean, it still keeps me from doing *anything* normal and dragon-like. *Everyone* knows dragons can always fly.

Gabriel cleared his throat to break the silence. "So, you never did answer my other question?"

I looked up. "Which one?"

"Favorite color? You hate pink, but what *do* you like?" he asked.

"Probably green. Can't get much different then green, you know?" I said, with a laugh. "How about you?"

"Red. Or black, but mostly red," he answered, after a moment's thought.

We spent the rest of dinner discussing favorite shows, movies and books and teasing each other over our choices. I laughed at him for geeking out over *Lord of the Rings*, and he taunted me for my obsession with 90s music. He told me that his current favorite band was a group called "Imagine Dragons" and I just rolled; he even used one of their songs as the ringer for his cell phone. I bet they weren't even dragons at all. He said it was ironic, yes, but had nothing to do with his ancestry's dealings with dragons now or in the past, he just liked them.

We finished dinner and rose to continue on with the next part of the evening which included getting dessert out and about.

"We should blow these out," he said, as he leaned in and started to exhale.

"Wait—let me!" I said. I sat back and closed my eyes, concentrating on the light breeze that was blowing in through the curtains. I exhaled slowly, imagining the candle in front of me extinguishing but sitting far enough back to make sure my blowing wasn't actually blowing them out, it was the magic. I imagined the room filling up with dancing sparkles.

"Open…your…eyes," Gabriel said, hushed.

I did so, slowly. I watched the sparkly mist I exhaled just a moment ago, dancing on the breeze, snuffing out each candle in turn: first the one directly in front of us, then the ones behind us on the coffee table…on a shelf over the couch….

A giddy smile spread across my face. "Oh! I did it!"

"You're definitely amazing. Only been a couple days trying," he said, reaching over and grasping my hand.

I looked down at his hand touching mine, and felt a shiver up my arm and down my spine. I wanted to say something—every nerve in my body was itching to make some sort of sarcastic comment to break the uncomfortable tension seizing my body—but I forced myself to say nothing. I tried to force myself to look into his face, into those amazing, deep eyes but I couldn't make myself do so, his gaze was too penetrating like he was going to see right into what I was feeling...but I couldn't allow that, since I wasn't even totally sure what I was feeling.

I didn't have to make the decision to stare or not to stare. Gabriel, his hand still on top of mine, came around the small table to stand right in front of me. I could feel the energy from his body—whether it was magical energy, or what it was I couldn't tell—and I was very aware of his proximity to me. He pulled my hand into both of his, and gently tugged, prompting me to slide off the chair. I did, and with one decisive move, pulled me into his body. I let out a startled noise, and again I felt the urge to make a snide comment but he didn't allow me, he leaned over and touched his lips to mine gently.

I slowly let my arms inch around his neck, tracing up his stomach and chest as I did so, feeling the strong presence of him, and pressed my body closer to his, feeling his heart pulsing, his chest rise and fall rapidly.

He kissed me again, a bit more intensely this time, snaking his arms through mine and firmly pressing his palms on the small of my back, nudging me even closer, making the kiss deeper, and more intense. My breath caught once more in the back of my throat, feeling the total proximity of his body to mine...his heat, the weight of him...the sensation sent tingles up and down my spine and jump-started my heart. Without realizing it, I kissed him back, harder, more feverishly and he responded in kind. His lips parted slightly as did my own in response, his tongue demanding entry resulting in a deeper, more insistent kiss.

I don't even know if he realized it, but his hands began trailing lower down my back, and lower still as we were kissing pretty roughly now, tongues mashing together, me biting his lower lip until they landed firmly on my ass, causing me to gasp in surprise and tense up.

Abruptly, he stopped. He pushed me away and immediately gasped, smashing his palms onto the sides of his face. "Oh my god. Crap, Leorah...I'm sorry, I got carried away, I—"

I waved him off. "It's okay. I just wasn't.... *expecting* that?" I didn't know what I was expecting. I'd seen the movies, read the books, watched the TV shows.... obviously when kissing someone pretty intently like we were, things get grabbed. Or pulled. Or bitten.

"No, that was a really jack-assed thing for me to do, I—" I cut him off again, this time pushing him towards the couch.

"What are you—" he began hesitantly. I pushed him again, and he fell onto the couch as I stalked him, staring him down intently. He looked nervous and excited at the same time as I slid into his lap and wrapped my arms around his shoulders. I hope I did it right, I saw girls in the movies do it all the time. Being romantic or flirty wasn't exactly something that came naturally to me or any dragon—but especially me. I don't really know where it came from, or why all of a sudden I felt so bold. I just knew I enjoyed the sensation. I liked the way it felt when he was next to me—the closer, the better. I loved how it felt when he kissed me, even more so when he acted abashed, like he did something wrong.

And all I knew is I wanted to do it more. Like something carnal was arising in me, something I didn't know existed. And the couch was more comfortable because in my human form, Gabriel was about six inches taller than me and it was straining my neck.

I forced myself to stare intently into his eyes. He smiled slowly, pushing back the hair that had tumbled into my face, cupping my face with his palm, and I couldn't tell who started it, but our lips met again and we started kissing yet again, slow at first but growing more intent.

My hands fell to his waist, searching for a comfortable spot to rest, my fingertips brushing inadvertently against a small sliver of skin that was exposed, his t-shirt rising up. It felt hot to the touch, I grazed a trail of hair. Intrigued, I allowed my hand to slip under his shirt further, feeling that trail of hair go up his stomach, across his chest, back down to his waist and assumedly, under his pants. I stopped when my fingertips scraped against the top of his pants, and that simple action seemed to do him in; any restrain he was using had flown right out the window. He yanked off his shirt from the bottom and pulled it unceremoniously over his messy hair and onto the floor nearby. Like they had a mind of their own, my hands instinctively reached out and wrapped around his shoulders, scratching at his shoulder blades—dragons liked to scratch when they become hot and bothered. Apparently, I was no different. Gabriel didn't seem to mind though, and he let out a quiet moan. He rolled me over onto the couch where he slid his body sideways between me and the couch cushion, his mouth still mastering mine skillfully. I allowed my leg to bend to him, nuzzling his upper thigh.

His fingertips brushed my calf and trailed upwards, leaving little electrical sparks along the way. I giggled a little at the sensation.

"Oh, the dragon is ticklish," he said, smiling as he moved his kiss to the side of my mouth, then along my jawline. All the while my dress had inched up my leg and now stopped mid-thigh and his touch stopped at the end of the hem, as if debating on what to do, where to go. His hand moved up towards my hip, his lips trailed heated kisses down my jawline and tenderly kissed the soft spot along my neck right under my ear, and I felt my eyes roll back in my head. "*Oh god,*" I whispered, not really realizing it had come out.

"She's got a sweet spot, too," he said, a flirtatious lilt in his tone.

"I guess I do," I said, feeling the strangest thing at that moment that I think I'd only felt slightly once before, an extreme heat that started between my legs and resonating upwards and downwards all at once. The feeling was blissfully relaxing and intensifying at the same time, this time causing me to let out a low moan that I didn't realize was coming out until it did.

Seemingly feeling a surge of bravery, Gabriel's lips moved from the spot on my neck and began trailing further down to my collarbone, and his hand on my hip not so gently this time raised up and rested on the spot under my breast and paused there. I could feel the electricity of his touch, even through the gauzy fabric of the sundress. Even though he appeared confident I could see the hesitation in his eyes. It slowed him down only slightly and after a ragged pant, his mouth was over mine again, biting my lower lip gently, and trailed my hands down his stomach slowly, finding the waistband of his jeans. I was about to unlatch it when Stone Temple Pilots "Interstate Love Song" started blaring, indicating that my cell phone was ringing.

"Oh my—Kit!" was my first thought. I pushed Gabriel off of me and jumped up, the strap of my dress hanging low on my shoulder and down my side, my boob half popped out of the neckline. I readjusted myself as I dashed into my bedroom for my phone I'd tossed on the bed. I didn't even notice the number, I just poked at the screen and hollered into it, "Hello? *Hello? Kit?*" Silence on the other end, then dialtone.

"Shit," I cursed, clicking the screen until I pulled up the last called number to see if it was Kit; I didn't know if it was or wasn't, it was one I didn't recognize. "Fuck!" I tossed the phone in frustration down on my bed and crossed my arms over my chest.

I gasped, feeling my exposed skin. "Holy hell…" Away from Gabriel's intoxicating presence, I could finally think more clearly without his woodsy, musky scent penetrating my brain. I was still breathing rapidly, still felt the heat between my legs but it was quickly subsiding.

Holy shit, what was I about to do? Where did that come from? Was I really just minutes away from having sex with Gabriel? I've only known this dude for a few days! Dammit, Leo, what the fuck are you thinking? Not that it was a big deal. As a dragon I didn't get diseases and whatnot like humans would, from being promiscuous. I could get pregnant, but, it wasn't my fertile time. Dragons could be aroused at any time, but our *fertile* times as females only arrived once or twice a year and it was marked by a heavy dose of pheromones, a musky scent and a cranky disposition; cranky because it *hurt*. I'd listened to Kit regale tales of her human menstruation and honestly, it didn't sound all that dissimilar. Cramps, bloating and swelling, headaches—we got them too.

Aside from that time though, it wouldn't be surprising for dragons to get it on after only meeting once; however I'd attained a bit of human behavior of course and it just felt wrong. It was also scary how *drawn* I was to him after only a short time. Dragons *rarely* felt that sort of magnetic pull to someone so soon, if *ever*. And that was disconcerting to me. But perhaps dragons could and did feel that way towards other humans; it's just that no one remembered feeling like that in recent history since it just wasn't done. My gut told me to *chill* but my body simply wanted to let go.

I fanned the heat from my face, feeling a sense of panic, when there was a light knock on the door.

"Leo? You all right?" Gabriel asked from the other side, as he peeked in.

I nodded. "Yeah…" I sheepishly smiled and pointed at the phone. "It wasn't Kit."

"I'm sorry, but that's not what I meant," he said, stepping in all the way, his shirt still off.

Oh, those tattoos…his skin…felt so good—I shook my head. "No—I mean, yes! I'm fine just a little—"

"We…probably got a little carried away, huh?" he said, looking down at himself. "I'm sorry, I don't know what was…the wine, your dress...*Gods* you look so fucking beautiful, and I loved kissing you so much I just— "

"—I liked it too...but it's probably a little too soon," I said. "I'm not even, uh...I mean..." I blushed.

"I am really sorry, I mean...it's been a really, *really* long time for me and being so close to you the past few days, well I—"

"It's *really* okay," I insisted. "I kinda egged you on so...kind of like you know, just eating one potato chip. You have one, you have to have more because they're so good."

"So...I'm a greasy, salty piece of potato?" he retorted, pretending to sound wounded.

"No! I mean—" he just laughed.

"Clearly we're both hard up and we need to chill," he said, shaking his head and laughing. "So, I say...ice cream for dessert. You wanna?"

I smiled. "Yeah...sounds good."

He outstretched his hand, "Come on," he said. I stepped towards him and put my hand in his, and he led me back out to the living room where he proceeded to pick up his shirt.

"Aw, does that *have* to go back on?" I protested.

He shot me a look, but smiled. "Sorry, don't think that Dairy Queen will serve me with no shirt on."

I cocked a brow and bit my lip. "Well, if there are girls working there and see *that*, I'm sure they actually will anyways."

He snickered and pulled his t-shirt over his head. "I doubt I'm their type," he said, with a chuckle. I grabbed my phone and my purse and we headed out for some *cold* ice cream to chill ourselves out of our hormonal fire fit.

The weather was still fairly warm for a late September evening, the temperatures being in the 60s with a light wind, the scent of dried leaves and campfire in the air indicating that autumn was just around the corner. Thankfully, despite the warm temperatures, the Dairy Queen was fairly slow for a Friday night being that it was Homecoming. There was a young teenaged girl and a gentleman in his mid-twenties working that night, the blonde teenager seeming mopey as he dictated to her instructions and she complained about not getting to go to the dance, being stuck at work.

We each ordered large sundaes and decided to take a walk around the nearby lake so we got into his truck and we rode the short distance over (while artfully attempting to not spill our melting ice cream) and parked in a nearby lot.

Willow Lake Park was dotted with weeping willow trees all over the landscape, giving the ambiance a somewhat ethereal appearance as they swayed in the wind, tickling the grass below that was losing it's green for a fall faded yellow and brown, the Parks department clearly abandoning general maintenance for the season.

"It's really a very pretty park," Gabriel commented, between bites of his ice cream, as we walked along the path surrounding the small lake.

"Yeah, it is," I agreed, admiring the sun low in the sky painting it a purplish-blue, though not low enough to cause the myriad of rainbow colors sunset generally brought.

My phone began playing Stone Temple Pilots again, and I thrust my ice cream at him while I rummaged for my phone in my handbag.

"Kit?" Gabriel asked simply, and I shook my head at the unfamiliar number.

"No." I frowned, hitting silence and shoving the phone back into my purse, ignoring it. "Kit knows I don't answer strange numbers…and there's no voicemail so it can't be her."

"I'm sorry," he said, with a sigh, as I took back my ice cream. We walked quietly for a few moments, I scarfed down large bites of my treat feeling comforted by the cooling sensation in my throat, and tried to mentally will it down to the butterflies still flapping around wildly in the firepit that was my stomach.

"We…we should probably talk about what happened," Gabriel said, breaking the ice a few moments later.

"What's there to talk about? We messed around, it was nice but it's probably too soon," I said, with a nonchalant shrug.

"Is it, though?" He stopped in his tracks in front of a wooden bench, setting his treat down on the arm and leaning against the back of it, appearing on the verge of something thoughtful.

"Isn't it?" I questioned, feeling confused.

"Well, I know how I feel about you," he said, pulling the ice cream out of my hands and setting it down, placing my cold palm between his.

"And, how's that?" I asked expectantly, shuffling my feet.

He grinned. "You're amazing. You're funny, and smart, *a great kisser*—" I chuckled nervously at that one, "—and passionate. I've never seen anyone get into the things you get into, with such zeal no matter how small or large they are. You're absolutely *gorgeous*, both your human and dragon forms are. And the thing is you're totally unaware that you are which gives you a kindness and humility."

I snorted. "You figured all this out over the past few days?"

"Well, that and the many times I've stopped into the café," he said. "I kept trying to find excuses to keep going back in there and talk to you, besides just ordering coffee. Like the time I asked about the Homecoming game? I just heard your co-workers talking about it, I don't give two shits about football." He laughed. "I certainly never really played it. That was more my brother's thing."

A slow smile spread across my lips, but I didn't say anything as I processed his flattery.

"You've been faced with all this adversity, and you still wake up every day and smile. It doesn't get you down you just keep right on going," he said. "I think I'm pretty confident when I say I'm totally crazy for you. Like…insane. I count my stars every day that the pink dragon we've been waiting for ended up being someone as amazing as you."

I had to bite my lip to keep myself from smiling too widely. "Yeah?"

"Yeah." He cupped my chin in his hands and leaned in and planted a soft kiss on my cheek. "Regardless of what happens with the dragon thing, I know I want to be with you. I'm secretly a little glad that that *thing* came around the other night because not only was it an excuse to get closer to you, it was a reason for me to stay around you all the time. I know that will get old and that's not healthy but for now, I'm going with it."

"It is kind of an exceptional situation," I said, nodding my head in thought. I smiled, looking up into his brown eyes. "I want to be with you, too. But…it just feels surreal, I suppose. So soon. But it's nice to feel these things for real, instead of just in movies."

He chuckled. "Yeah, it is! Nice to know someone who's a bigger nerd then me!"

I pretended to feign offense. "Nerd? I'm not the one who decorated his room to look like the starship *Enterprise*!"

He raised a brow at me. He didn't need to say anymore, and I just laughed. "Okay, okay."

Gabriel's face turned solemn. "When I saw you there, not breathing, looking like the life was drained out of you…it scared the shit out of me. I haven't ever been that afraid even when my brother had his mysterious seizure and he's the person I feel closest to in my life. Ever. All I wanted to do was help you feel better—"

"—and you did," I insisted, recalling the security I felt, waking up to him next to me.

He grinned. "Good." I smiled back, and wrapped my arms around his hips and laid my head against his chest. I closed my eyes, feeling his steady heartbeat and inhaling once again that intoxicating scent of him—this time not quite so heady.

I was enjoying standing there in the moment, feeling his arms wrapped around me, staring out at the sun beginning it's decent over the lake when my phone started ringing again and I groaned, pulling it out of my purse and seeing that unfamiliar number on the screen.

"Same damn number, what the Hell?" I asked, rhetorically, lifting it up to show him the display.

He grumbled. "Give me that." He touched the screen and held it up to his ear. "Hello, who the Hell is this?" he asked, appearing stern to match his tone. His face softened into seriousness. "Oh…you. Yeah, she's right here." He handed the phone to me. "That dragon guy—Max."

"Maxxus?" I was uncertain, grabbing the phone. "Is that you?"

"Oh thank the Gods you're okay!" Maxxus' voice sighed over the phone. "I thought something was wrong."

"Wrong? Why would something be wrong?" I asked, feeling a sudden surge of panic

"Well, the portal was used, but I didn't see anyone go through it. I felt it open and shut but… nothing was there. I shifted and came through to see if it was you, or some kind of weird spell or…*what*? I didn't know. And when you wouldn't answer your phone…"

"Wait—so that was you all three times?"

"Yes. Oh I'm sorry, I didn't mean to freak you out, I just can't be caught talking to you…if the Court knew with those orders out for you…" he trailed off, and we both shuddered, knowing fully well what the Court did to dragons who disobeyed (torture was putting it mildly). "So I came across and found a car in the clearing, just abandoned there. I wasn't sure if it was yours or not so I figured I'd better make sure you were okay."

"Well, thank you," I said. "So, you can't figure out who opened the portal?" I asked.

"No, there was nothing there but that car and the abandoned phone. I wasn't sure if—"

I cut him off. "What kind of car?"

"Umm...I don't know. I don't know cars very well but it's this round looking thing and it's yellow."

I nearly dropped the phone to the ground, Gabriel deftly catching it.

"What?" he mouthed, concerned.

"Yellow car? Round? Are you still there with the car?" I questioned, feeling my heart start racing again and this time *not* for fun reasons.

"Well, yeah. Why? Do you know it?"

I swallowed nervously. "I think it's Kit's car."

Gabriel's eyes widened. "Oh shit..."

Chapter 13

I instructed Maxxus to stay put and after I inhaled the rest of my ice cream—literally—and part of Gabriel's in the truck, we arrived in record time.

"What do you think it means?" he asked, as we came upon the clearing.

"I don't know," I said. "An open portal but no one crossed it? Kit's empty car nearby? I hate to think of the possibilities."

"Kidnapping?" he offered uncertainly.

"I'd think so, but Maxxus said he didn't see anyone cross, just felt it open and no one was there. Even if there was, it's unlikely that Kit would be able to enter it by herself. You have to have a magical signature or something similar to trigger it's opening. Even if Kit being a witch gave her magical ability somehow, I doubt it would be enough to trigger the opening," I said, as we pulled into the clearing.

Maxxus was standing before Kit's yellow vehicle in his human form, appearing to be examining it somehow. He turned around when he heard us pull up and slam our doors shut.

"*That* is him? That big green dragon guy?" I'd never seen Gabriel look intimidated—not even by Maxxus' dragon form—but for some reason something about Maxxus in his human form daunted him.

I raised my eyebrows at him. "Yeah? So?"

"He looks like a goddamned movie star," Gabriel muttered under his breath, but I didn't have time to react.

"I can't even smell anything," Maxxus said, with a sigh, running a hand through his wavy dark blonde hair with a touch of natural ginger highlights throughout. He was tall, and lean with a five-o-clock shadow dotting his strong jawline. As a green dragon who used earth magic, he was kind of a bloodhound when it came to scents. "I smell no one or nothing. It's very odd." He said, pausing to look me over. "Gods, Leorah…you look…"

Gabriel cut him off, shortly, "So how do we know you aren't just lying about no one going through that portal? Leo, do you *really* trust this guy?" he scoffed.

I shot him a narrow-eyed look. "Gabriel...Maxxus was a student of my grandfather. My grandfather does *not* mentor dishonorable dragons!"

Gabriel scowled. "I'm going to go into the car, see if I can sense anything." He turned on his heels in a huff, and opened the driver's side door and got in.

Maxxus chuckled. "I angered the human."

I rolled my eyes. "He's fine, it's just been...an *odd* few days."

He smirked. "Yes, I suppose. You know, he's already claimed you. He sees me as a threat, I think that's why he's so cross with me."

"*Claimed* me?" I exclaimed with incredulity. "I belong to no one! Besides, how can you tell?"

He smiled mischievously. "I can smell the hostility on him. The kind one has when he feels his mate has been threatened."

I coughed, and Maxxus laughed. "Well, maybe not exactly a mate but his jealousy is quite apparent. But Leo, you really do look beautiful," he said, halting his laughter. "A far cry from those ridiculous rags you tend to wear when coming over."

I crossed my arms across my chest and narrowed my eyes at him. "Stop, or you'll piss Gabriel off more than he already is," I said in a hushed tone.

He chuckled. "So, curious, how do you open this thing?" he asked, knocking on the hood. In response, the hood popped open causing Maxxus to jump back quickly. Gabriel popped his head out of the door and said, "There. Really not that hard."

I had to stifle a laugh, while Maxxus—trying not to look pissed—gazed at the inner contents of the Volkswagen. "I'm not sure what I'm looking for...but I'm looking..."

I snorted. "I better see if Gabriel sees anything."

"I looked," Maxxus said, looking confused while poking at random car parts under the hood. "There's nothing there."

Gabriel clamored out of the car, shutting the door behind him. "Of course you wouldn't find anything, that's my specialty. You might be a big, green, scaly monster, but I have my own set of talents, thank you."

I shot him a warning glare. "Seriously?"

Gabriel's face softened, and he sighed. "There's no trace of her. No keys, no purse...but something isn't right."

"Right?" I echoed.

"What do you mean?" Maxxus asked.

"Well, there is the residue of some sort of spell...I can't tell what exactly but there was a spell cast inside, and not a witch spell either. This was much more powerful than any earth witch could conjure. Kind of like those storms, Leo," he said.

"I didn't get anything like that, how can you tell?" Maxxus questioned, genuinely intrigued.

"It's a sorcerer thing, I don't think a dragon can tell, but I don't know many dragons, obviously," he said. "But since we draw from the energy in the world around us to create our magic, we can just tell where it is and what kind, usually."

"What kind is this?" I asked.

He shrugged. "I'm not quite sure, I haven't encountered magic like this before. But it's powerful, I will say that."

Involuntarily my palm covered the gasp coming out of my mouth. "Oh...is Kit going to be okay? I mean, is there any way to tell?"

Gabriel sighed again. "I don't know for sure, but...it doesn't feel like death magic. Energy wasn't taken away, but it was...*displaced*? I don't know how else to describe it."

Maxxus let out a low groan. "This is concerning. I don't suppose you could touch the portal or do...whatever it is you do and see if it's the same thing that opened the portal?"

Gabriel's eyes held a glint of victory, but he just remained solemn. "I could try," he said, nonchalant. He started to walk but hesitated. He turned to me and said, "Where is it, again?"

I looped my arm through his and led him over to the bushes, Maxxus trailing behind us.

I pointed at the slight shimmer near the greenery and stepped aside to let Gabriel do this thing—whatever it was. He moved his hands around the portal and appeared deep in concentration.

"What does he do?" Maxxus inquired to me quietly.

I shrugged. "I'm not quite sure."

"Huh. Curious, how did you meet him anyway?" he asked.

"Uh...he was a customer of mine at work," I said, conveniently leaving the knighthood part out of it.

"Interesting…how did it come up that he can…well, you know," he mimicked Gabriel's hand gestures as if he was summoning a fireball.

"Ummm…" I hesitated.

"I recognized her tattoo," Gabriel called back, breaking his own concentration. "Information handed down from sorcerer to sorcerer for generations," he said, with confidence. Maxxus still cocked a suspicious brow but let it be.

"So?" I prompted.

"Hard to tell. I mean I feel something but…could just simply be the portal being active. Without knowing how portals work…it's hard to tell. I'm not versed in the arcane magics," Gabriel heaved a heavy sigh. "I don't know, Leo. I can't tell one way or the other if it's Kit."

I frowned. Feeling frustrated, I sat down on the ground with a *thump*. I remembered then I was still wearing a (thankfully, *long*!) dress and crossed my ankles over one another.

Maxxus, who was wearing a long, black trench jacket, quickly took it off and laid it down on the ground. "Here, don't sit in the dirt. You're better than that."

I rolled my eyes but reluctantly scooted backwards on the jacket. Gabriel snorted and scoffed.

"Shut up, wizard boy," I warned, pointing a stern finger at him.

He feigned offense, but chuckled.

"So can we get back to my friend, here?" I asked, running my fingers through my carefully manicured hair. They got caught in the twist and bobby pins. Feeling constricted, I pulled them out, taking a small chunk of hair with it and tossing it on the forest ground. "I have no idea what to do. Where is she? Why is her *car* here? Why would she even be here?"

"I don't know, Leo." Gabriel sat next to me on the ground, being careful not to allow a single inch of himself touch Maxxus' jacket. "Looking for you, maybe?"

"She doesn't know I come out here," I said.

"Well, perhaps she followed once. I know I was able to follow you that one time," Gabriel offered.

I considered this. "Maybe."

"Well at least we know she couldn't get across by herself, if she indeed is there," Maxxus said, reluctantly joining us on the ground, folding his long legs under him. "Perhaps someone from Court found her, looking for you."

I snapped my fingers. "Maybe. That makes more sense."

Gabriel frowned. "Hey, wait—I thought you were guarding the portal. Wouldn't you be able to see who got by you? You said no one was there." He narrowed his eyes suspiciously. "Unless you're lying."

"No, you're right, except it was between Nicodemus' and my shifts," he said. "We would notice if a dragon—err, a *person* came over, but perhaps they are up to something I'm not aware of. I know some of them are quite proficient in magics of trickery."

I looked at him oddly. "Trickery?"

"Illusion," Maxxus explained.

"Yeah, but why would they do that?" Gabriel questioned.

Maxxus scoffed. "Well, Leo I know you'll be surprised...but Court isn't *exactly* what it seems. There's been a lot of dissention lately."

"Yeah but...what would they want with Kit? I mean, even to get to me, seriously, to risk exposure to a human?" I shook my head. "Something doesn't seem right."

"No, it does not." Maxxus heaved a heavy sigh.

"So, who's watching the other portal on the other side?" Gabriel asked.

Maxxus smiled. "Your Grandfather, actually."

I perked up. "Grandfather? Really?" I started to rise, by Maxxus pulled me back down.

"Not a good idea, Leorah. The second you cross that portal, guards will be all over the top of you," he said. "Both him and your brother have been coming by regularly to make sure you aren't mistreated if perhaps you *do* get over, although they both know there is little chance you'd come. But, he just wanted to be sure."

I stuck my lower lip out, defeated. "Fine. That sucks. So close yet so far."

Gabriel spoke up. "Do you really think they'd kidnap Kit?"

Maxxus shrugged. "I don't know what the threat is against Leo, but if it's bad enough, they just might."

Gabriel and I exchanged doomed glances.

"Please. Go back and see if you can find anything out," I requested, giving him a slight nudge.

"You do know they won't tell me anything, knowing that I'm associated with your grandfather, right?" Maxxus asked.

I nodded. "But someone, somewhere had to of seen a *human* if she was brought over, right? Who else could it be?"

"Worth a shot," Gabriel said.

Maxxus nodded, rising to his feet and reaching out his hand for me. Gabriel glared, but Maxxus ignored him. Reluctantly, I took it and allowed him to help me to a standing position although I didn't really need it, knowing that Maxxus was bound by dragon traditions.

"I will do what I can," he said, as I handed him back his jacket.

I half expected him to bow or something equally as ridiculous, but he simply waved as he turned and headed towards the portal. Before he stepped through, he turned to me. "Do be careful, will you?" It was a solemn statement, not a question.

"You too," I said, with a nod.

Gabriel said nothing, he just stood there with his arms crossed over his chest, looking stone-faced and gruff.

Maxxus gave the sorcerer an inquiring once over, but said nothing further. He gave a small smile and a slight nod of the head before stepping through the portal and disappearing.

Gabriel snorted. "What a— "

I immediately turned on him, angry. "What the *fuck* was all that?" I challenged, meaning to give him a small shove but I actually made him stumble backwards on his feet.

"What the fuck, Leo?" Gabriel regained his balance, brushing off some dust he kicked up on himself.

"Don't throw my swear words back at me!" I fumed, glaring at him. "What the Hell was with the attitude with Maxxus, Gabriel? Huh?"

"That? Oh my God Leo, you are kind of oblivious. He was like—" Gabriel stammered, trying to find the appropriate words, "—well, with all the *royal* shit, and the jacket and—"

"—he's a *gentleman*, Gabriel!" I fought back. "I know, it's an odd concept for humans to understand, but we have manners and protocol over there. Not that anyone has ever displayed them for me, but…still…" By now I was standing on my tiptoes and pointing my fingers in his face with each word, trying to emphasize my anger.

"So, why him, then?"

I threw my hands up in exasperation. "Okay, let me explain things to you. My grandfather is an Elder. Which means he's older than ninety percent of all the dragons out there. Even older then the King and Queen. Well, they aren't very old but that's beside the point. In our Court, an Elder is a very valuable member of Dragon society...if the King and Queen were to both die at the same time, and they do not have anyone appointed to secede them, the Elder would be responsible for appointing the next successors. Which, would be my grandfather. As a direct descendant, that kind of makes me some sort of a big deal. Had I not been pink, I would be revered to a degree. I might even have an official title! But regardless, they are required to show me a certain amount of manners—it's our protocol."

Gabriel's demeanor softened. "Oh, I'm sorry. I didn't know, I'm sorry. I just thought he was flirting with you."

I squinted my eyes at him. "Unbelievable..." I stalked off away from him, towards Kit's car.

He wasn't far behind. "Leo? What are you doing?"

I was opening up the driver's side door again to re-open the hood.

"Hot-wiring the car. I need to get it out of here," I said dryly, pulling the hood release knob under the dashboard, causing the hood to pop open.

"Um...you don't hot-wire a car from under the hood, it's on the dashboard," Gabriel said hesitantly.

I re-emerged from the car only to glare at him. "Oh." I climbed back in the car looking for...whatever it was you use to hot-wire a car with. I started feeling around the dashboard for...whatever. I'd only seen this done in movies before, surely there had to be something that would stand out.

"And...you don't need to do that, anyways," he said. "I can do the magic-thing and start it for you. You know...electricity and all." He gave a little awkward smile.

"*Oh.*" I leaned back against the driver's seat, purposely knocking my head on the headrest and sighed.

Gabriel knelt next to me on the ground, and dared to rest a palm on my leg. My first reaction was to shoot him another dirty look.

"What does it matter if he was flirting with me, anyways? He's certainly had every opportunity to do so for the past year or so, and...nothing. Like I said, even though Maxxus likes my grandfather, any kind of dragon having a relationship with me is social suicide. It doesn't matter anyway; we've been together all of like...*five* minutes."

Gabriel exhaled. "Leo, you're right. I don't know what came over me. I don't have any place in being jealous, now or ever. But I'm not going to lie...there's just *something about him* I can't stand!"

Despite myself, I let out a small chuckle. "Why?"

"Seriously? Did you look at him? Guys like him made life *miserable* for me growing up. Tall, good looking...looks like he could be an *actual* Disney prince, and acts like it too! God, my brother would be *falling over* himself over him!" Gabriel laughed, leaning against the open door frame.

I had to laugh. "I suppose, I never really thought about it, actually."

Gabriel appeared thoughtful. "Wait...you said, 'We've been together all of five minutes,'."

I bit my lip so he couldn't see the smile forming. "I guess I did, huh?"

"So...I mean...we're going to..." he stammered, motioning back and forth between us, blushing profusely.

I shrugged. "We can see what happens," I said, wanting to scream inside but trying to remain calm. "I can't predict what's going to happen...I mean, the whole dragon thing, I—"

Gabriel cut me off by leaning over and placing a tender kiss on my lips, silencing me. My eyes slid shut as I enjoyed the sensation, flicking the fire that was lit and extinguished earlier inside me awake again. I started to kiss him back, but pulled away, remembering I was still sitting in Kit's abandoned car.

"Shit, what a crappy friend I am. Making out in my best friend's abandoned car when I don't know where she is."

Gabriel put his palms on my shoulders and looked at me intently. "We'll figure it out. Somehow. We'll find her."

I nodded slowly. "I hope so. In the meantime...what do we do?"

Gabriel shrugged and shook his head. "Not sure...call the cops and report her missing?"

I considered this. "Maybe. Maybe she was taken somewhere and they drove her car here, and she's just somewhere else."

"Could be," Gabriel said hopefully.

"But, I don't want the cops finding her car *here*," I said. "Too close to the portal. I doubt they'll find it, or even be able to see it but since we don't know what crossed..."

Gabriel nodded knowingly. "I see what you mean, but I highly doubt that they're going to be looking for her car out here...or even *find* it even if they do. Just in case it is part of a foul play we don't want to tamper with the crime scene."

"Crime scene?" I yelped, but he was right. "Okay...I guess." I sighed. I climbed out of her car and shut the door behind me. As I did, I had a thought: "Finger prints!" I said, wiggling my hands. "Won't they find my fingerprints everywhere on her car?"

"Yeah but.... you're her friend, right? That's pretty reasonable," he said. "Did Maxxus touch the car?"

"I think so," I said.

"Hmm...." he was thoughtful, scratching his chin. "Too bad?"

I shot him a glare, and he held up his hands in surrender, laughing. "Okay, okay! Well in all seriousness...he's a dragon so it'll be nearly impossible for him to be found even if they find the car and dust for his prints, right?"

"Probably," I said.

Gabriel sighed. "Well, I can help on the outside but the inside? Shit out of luck unless we want to ruin the car," he said.

I nodded, shutting the door and stepping away. Gabriel took a few steps back from the car, and closed his eyes, with his palms together as he always did when he was conjuring an element. After a moment, I saw drips of water coming from his hands and he slowly spread them apart, his eyes deep in concentration, muttering something to himself. He pulled his hands apart slowly further and further until a large, formless water puddle formed between them. He pushed his hands towards the car and seemed to be scrubbing the car with the summoned water, starting with the front, moving along the sides and the back finally tossing it on the roof of the car before letting it disperse, causing the water to splash all over the car and pour down the sides before pooling on the ground below.

I grinned. "That's fucking *awesome*!" I said, as he stopped next to me and I wrapped my arms around his waist, giving him a small, appreciative hug.

He wiggled his brows. "Watch this now. You can help with this part, actually."

"How?" I asked, stepping back as he clasped his palms together again.

"You'll see," he said, pulling his palms apart again, and while I didn't see anything I felt a slight breeze blow across my shoulders.

"Oh!" I let out a giggle, excited at the prospect of doing magic again. I closed my eyes and exhaled, imagining my breath being carried along a strong wind blowing through the clearing. I felt the air grow more intense, as it blew my skirt up around my ankles and knees, and shot my hair in different directions. I opened my eyes and was watching Gabriel spin the wind into a small spiral and moved it across the car, drying the drops of water on it.

I grinned. "Never gets old."

Gabriel smiled back, taking another pass over the car with the tiny summoned tornado and finally allowing it to disperse, but not before shooting a quick gust of wind at me again with a sharp gesture of his hand, causing my skirt to nearly blow up to my waist if I didn't immediately push it down with my hands.

"Damn you!" I laughed, as the wind dispersed, letting my skirt fall back and my hair rested along my back and shoulders again.

"Sorry, *Marilyn*," he retorted with a snicker. I gave him an odd look of *"Huh?"* and he just waved me off. "Best I can do. Some fingerprints might survive but…hopefully that got most of them, and what's left hopefully it made them hard to find or indeterminate."

I nodded, looking over the sparkly, clean yellow Beetle. "Looks good. Kit would be thrilled," I said, with a wistful laugh.

What if whatever had invaded my dreams last night…. what if that has Kit? I must have looked worried, because Gabriel wrapped an arm around my shoulders and pulled me under his arm. "We'll find her."

I just nodded, and allowed him to walk me back to the truck and help me inside. He got in on the driver's side and we drove off, leaving Kit's treasured car in the clearing, hoping it would stay safe for her when she was found. Knowing how much she loved that car, something must have really gone wrong to get her to just abandon it here.

I so hoped she was okay.

I had just hung up with the police after making my missing person's report on Kit. I sent the cop I spoke to a picture in my phone of Kit and all the information on her I had; I also told him she had a sister—Melanie—who lived in the Cities. I'd never met her, but she should probably be contacted. I didn't know when she'd return and I needed someone to make some legal decisions or whatever on the shop, to make sure until she returned it didn't go belly up. They said they'd search for her but made no promises; it'd help if I could give them any information about her. I tossed my phone in frustrated defeat on the coffee table and scrubbed my face with my hands. I was going to have to go to Kit's tomorrow and see if I could find any information on Melanie or any other family member she might have. All the while dodging whatever threat might be after me tonight, *or* avoiding any possible contact with the Court that was surely searching for me. Besides Braeden and my grandfather, no one besides Kiarra had any idea where I lived…and I wasn't confident that she wouldn't spill the beans.

"So much for our date," Gabriel said, with a heavy sigh leaning back against the couch.

I glanced over at my wall clock: 9:23pm, it read. "Well, what did you have planned?"

He shrugged. "Well, we were going to walk around the park, watch the sunset, and while I didn't really have a lot of notice to look into what there was to do out here—took hours' worth of effort just to figure out how to make that spaghetti—I figured we could find a private corner somewhere in the park…and…"

I raised my eyebrows. "…and, what?" I asked, a playful smile spreading across my face.

"Well, I was going to say try your hand at some magic, but if you want to think dirty thoughts…" he trailed off, a flirty lilt in his voice. "…well, I won't stop you."

I rolled my eyes, and gave him a playful shove. "I think you got enough of that earlier, don't you think?"

Gabriel puffed out his lower lip. "Okay, I guess. If that's my only other option."

I smiled, and an uncomfortable thought occurred in my mind. "Hey so…when it comes to…*that*…" My cheeks lit on fire at the thought and I just stopped mid-sentence.

"What? Magic?" he asked. I shot him a pointed look. "Oh. *Oh!* You mean, sex?" he let out a nervous peal of laughter.

"Yes, that's what I mean. I take it by your laughter it's not a comfortable subject, and I will drop it," I said, with a sigh. I reached on the coffee table for the remote and dismissed him.

Gabriel leaned over and grabbed my hand. "I'm sorry…yeah it's a little uncomfortable but I mean, I can talk about it if there is something you want to know. Not that there is much to tell…" he added under his breath.

I chuckled. "So, I mean…we're both in our twenties…in human years anyways," I said with a laugh. "I imagine you have…before?"

Gabriel groaned, slapping his hands against his face with a *smacking* sound. "Ugggh…. yes, I have."

I forced a smile. "You have. Well…how many times?"

Gabriel exhaled uncomfortably. " I did some stupid things, after I graduated college. My first time was with…" he sighed again, recalling something he clearly didn't enjoy, "someone I met at a club. I think her name was— "

I cut him off, "—I don't want to know her name!" I insisted.

He smiled slightly. "Okay. Well, I knew her first name only, anyways. For a short time with some friends I frequented some local clubs…and I met this chick at one and we…" He sighed. "It was in the back of her *car*. How romantic is that?"

I snorted, avoiding his eyes. I was desperately trying not to think of him entangled in the back seat of some car somewhere fogging up the windows, but it wasn't working. I became very interested in the buttons on the remote control I was currently holding. "Is that the only time?"

Gabriel smiled sheepishly. "Well…no. But it was the stupidest. I did have a girlfriend for a long time. We met in my college calculus class, I was supposed to tutor her because she was having issues…well it lasted for about two sessions before we hit it off and…" he stopped mid-sentence, shuffling his hands uncomfortably in his lap.

"How long were you together?" I asked, trying to muster up some sympathy for him but was finding it hard as I'd never experienced a break up before.

He exhaled. "Nearly two and a half years. We broke up about nine months ago…I proposed to her, she said no…that was pretty much the end of it." He forced a smile to lighten his mood. "What can you do?"

"She said *no?* Why?" I asked, incredulous.

He shrugged. "I don't really know, except that she kept thinking I was hiding something from her…she thought I was cheating but really, it was just…" He clapped his hands together and produced a small lightning spark from his hands.

"You never told her about all that?"

He shook his head. "I just…I knew she'd just take off on me anyways. She was a super religious person, never missed a Sunday in Church. I don't know how it worked. I don't know why I ever *thought* it would work in the first place. We were very incompatible anyways, but I proposed to her on a whim one night after we got into another fight...well, it just wasn't meant to be."

I frowned. I was trying to get a mental picture of him making out with some other woman out of my mind and it was making me partially ill. I tried to hide my dismay by reaching over and trying to give him a sympathetic grasp of the arm. "I'm sorry."

He shrugged it off. "It's okay. I mean it should have ended like, six months into our relationship anyways but...I was just afraid I'd never find someone again."

I choked down the rage welling up in me like a deluge at the thought of not only someone *touching* him that way—which was totally irrational—but someone breaking his heart. Instead I tried to smile...I kissed my fingertips and held out my palm and blew gently... literally blowing a kiss at him, complete with pink dragon sparkles and all.

He smiled. "Now *that* makes it all better," he said, reaching over and pulling on my arm, urging me to lean into him. I knew if I did, I would probably become very relaxed and drowsy and I wanted to fight the urge...but I couldn't for long. I gave in, and leaned into his body, resting my head on his chest, his arm draped around my back. His free hand pushing my hair out of his face and smoothing it down my side.

"So...how about you? Ever date? Have a boyfriend...even a human one? You ever..." he trailed off.

I snorted. "No...relationships aren't something I really understand. It's only been recently they've been marrying out of *love*," I said, with a sour expression, thinking of my free-willed brother and his fiancée. "But, there really was no dating. It was *'Hey, I like you, let's mate.'* They'd either agree or disagree and if they agreed, they'd have a relationship for a while in private before being bonded—married—and that's it. When I came here...there were many things I didn't understand. Traditions, friendships, holidays...*relationships*. I didn't even know if it was possible for me to date a human—or a *sorcerer*," I added, when Gabriel opened up his mouth, assumedly to point out his distinction.

"No one? Really? *Nothing*? I mean...even over here, the most ridiculed of people find someone," Gabriel said. "Not even Maxxus?"

I let out a disgruntled groan. "As I've said, being associated with me is social suicide. My family, it has taken them *years* to rise above the stigma, mostly due to my grandfather and his reputation. But anyone else? No. I never had a friend—besides my brother. No one was ever nice to me. I cannot describe to you how terribly awful it was for me over there." I felt the pinpricks of tears nick my eyes, begging to escape down my face. I blinked rapidly, hoping that they would just *go* away. I cried enough about my life over the years, I didn't want to do it anymore. "Even if Maxxus did have a *thing* for me—which I doubt—I wouldn't do that to him."

He exhaled. "Shit, Leo...I can't imagine." With an index finger, he hooked my chin and urged my face towards him. "Well, I will promise you this: as a friend or a—whatever--I will never allow anyone to hurt you like that again...even if it kills me. I swear, until the day I die—and then after that I will find someone willing to do the same for you again and won't leave this Earth until I do—no one will hurt you again. Ever. Again." He looked into my eyes with such solemnness it nearly made me shift uncomfortably at the serious nature of his oath, except his brown eyes were so intense, like getting lost in a dream, I just felt a smile spread slowly across my face. And, in true Leorah fashion, I retorted with sarcasm:

"*Friend*?"

Gabriel blinked, taken aback. "Well, I— I mean...well...."

I roared with laughter. "I'm sorry, I just couldn't resist!"

Gabriel grinned. He leaned over and kissed me softly on the cheek. He traced down my cheek the trail of the single tear that had escaped my eye with a gentle fingertip, looking sad. "Enough of this sadness. Even with the shit that is facing you ahead, you will not be alone. No matter how bad it gets...you won't be alone. You have me. Eventually, you'll have Daniel—and he's a force to be reckoned with. You have your grandfather. We'll all figure it out. And anyone that gets in our way...we'll deal with them. Okay?"

I nodded slowly, "Okay," I said in a small voice.

"Good." He leaned down and planted a soft kiss on my lips, and when he pulled away, he chuckled. "Okay, now...let's forget about this sad crap and relax. What's on TV? Anything good? Have any fangirl crap you want to expose me to? Get it over with while all your idiosyncrasies are still cute?"

I sat up and pretended to act offended and pushed him in the chest. "Knock it off!"

He laughed, and pretended to reach for the remote which I promptly snatched away from him. "Mine!" I turned on the TV and nestled back into Gabriel's arms and flipped through the channels. I think I finally landed on some local news but I didn't care...after a while I relaxed and drifted off anyways so it didn't matter.

After a time, I awakened, my eyes fluttering slowly trying to adjust to the surroundings.

It was...dark...like the dark woods at midnight. I was barefoot, padding through the leaf litter slowly, with trepidation...only it wasn't leaves...it felt like...walking on silky, soft moss, damp and cold.

"Hello?" I asked. I heard a cackle in the distance.

I stopped in my tracks, glancing around me again. What I had thought were trees, were dark wisps of steam lifting up from the ground. I looked up at the sky—again, no stars, no moon. Just darkness, blotted with black and shades of dark purple...almost like a Northern Lights with no color.

"Gabriel?" I called. I know last time I happened to yell out, and he heard me for real.

The cackle sounded again, this time much closer.

"Hello?" I asked, my voice disappearing into the wispy woods, no echo at all. I swallowed, feeling the darkness start to surround me again.

I inhaled deeply, and tried to remember where I was—where I *really* was: in Gabriel's arms, on the couch, my cat snoozing at our feet. There was no darkness. My fear was only in my imagination.

Right?

I swallowed, hearing the cackle again, this time raspy and low, a word on the non-existent wind: *"Leorah."*

I gulped. "I don't know who you are, but go away!" I yelled out, trying to sound forceful and confident.

"Leorah."

I heard nothing else but the silence, and felt whatever was speaking—whatever it was—getting gradually closer to me.

Feeling my heart racing, I inhaled again, stretching my arms out on my sides. I wasn't going to let whatever this was get me, again. I imagined the sun, the way it looked as we were walking around earlier today by the lake.... stretching out before me, touching everything with warmth...lighting the world aglow in pinks, oranges and purples. I imagined this very same scene around me, and I exhaled, pushing my hands out forward as if pushing my thoughts of sunshine towards this unforeseen entity.

I heard a low, mangled scream in the distance. Finally, a panicked, raspy, "*Leo!*"

My eyes flew open, and I shrieked in the darkness.

"Leo? Leo!"

I blinked, my eyes taking in their surroundings, mainly Gabriel's panicked face before me, his hands on my shoulders, shaking them. I reached out and touched his cheek, rough from the shadow of his facial hair, the coarseness tangibly bringing me back to reality.

"I was there again...but...*not*," I said, struggling to properly describe.

"What do you mean?" he asked, grasping my shoulders tightly, as if afraid to let me go, afraid I'd slip away, looking incredibly alarmed.

I stammered, "I...I don't know. It was like before but...different. Farther away. But not as dark...not as evil. But I could feel it there, somewhere...but it wasn't like last time. It was..." I bit my lip, struggling to find the words.

Gabriel pulled me to him and hushed me. "Geez, I can't believe I almost lost you again and there was nothing I could do!"

I shook my head. "No...no it wasn't that. It was...different somehow. I was scared, but I didn't feel like I was going to die."

He exhaled lowly, an angry growl on his breath. He gave me a tight squeeze and stood up, gently helping me lean against the couch. "Where is that book that your grandfather gave you?"

I pointed at my backpack near the entryway. He produced it gingerly, opening it and leafing through the pages carefully.

"What are you doing?" I questioned.

"I don't know what we're dealing with, that much is clear," he paused, glancing at the clock on my wall: it was slightly after midnight. "And, whatever it is, it's not allowing you to sleep at night, so it has something to do with the dark. Somehow. Whatever the *fuck* it is. Whatever it is, it's not something that has been around for a good, long while because no one seems to know what it is—at least, no one I know. So perhaps whatever it is, there might be a clue in here; maybe it's something we haven't seen in a long, *long* time."

"You read Gaelic?" I asked, as he scratched his chin, setting himself in the recliner, leafing carefully through the pages.

He shook his head. "No. But I might recognize something in here, somehow. All languages are tied together, having roots in other, older languages. I might be able to pick *something* out."

I leaned back into the couch, with a pathetic whimper and sigh.

"This...this is not Gaelic," he said, after a moment.

"How can you tell? I thought you couldn't read Gaelic," I asked, putting my hand to my chest, feeling my heart leap around under my ribcage. I breathed in and out slowly to try to quell it.

"This alphabet...it's not Gaelic. It's not anything that can easily be recognized. It almost looked like...well, nothing I've ever encountered before." He shut the book carefully. "Almost like some kind of hieroglyphics..." He set it down on the coffee table and exhaled with an audible, frustrated groan. "*Fuck*! How in God's name am I supposed to be a Knight if I can't fucking help you against something that is threatening you?" He pounded his fist angrily on the coffee table, causing everything on it to shake and rattle. "*Fuck*!"

I stuck out my lower lip. My muscles were still feeling shaky, but I stood up slowly and went to him on the chair. I lowered myself into his lap and nuzzled my forehead against his neck. "Maybe you're just supposed to be here. You know what I was thinking of when I was there?"

He paused before answering shortly: "What?"

"You."

Gabriel's expression softened. "Really?"

I nodded, with a smile.

"So, you were able to control yourself this time?" he asked, I could see his eyes light up with anticipation.

I nodded again. "A little."

"Up up up," he said, urging me to stand. He got up, and grabbed my hands. "This is good. Perhaps whatever this is...it's a dream thing. A dream spell, that only affects you in your sleep. That means there is something we can do, we can teach your subconscious magic, as there is certain magic one can do on the dream plane." Feeling a sudden sense of giddiness, he pulled me into the bedroom and sat me down on the bed.

I cocked a brow, and smirked. "Right now, really?"

He rolled his eyes, and snickered. "Stop! I need your computer; I need to look up stuff on the internet. Okay?"

"Sure," I said, with a laugh. "Go ahead."

Before Gabriel sat at my computer, he took a moment to open my blinds up wide, letting the moonlight pour in and turned on every light he could in my room. "Just in case you fall asleep again," he said.

"What are you doing?" I questioned, climbing under the covers and leaning against the headboard, pulling the blanket up over my chest. Suddenly, my bed was starting to feel extremely inviting.

He paused in his furious typing to peek over his shoulder. "Tired?"

I puffed out my lower lip and shook my head. "No…" but I couldn't fight back a yawn.

"Try to hang on for a little bit. I might be able to find something that can help you," he said.

"How?"

"Google!"

I frowned. "How is Google going to help? You really think people go around talking about evil dream things…especially if it's something that hasn't been heard of in years?"

"You'd be surprised what you can find on the internet," he said with a laugh. "Just because dragons haven't heard of it, doesn't mean someone else hasn't had a crazy experience that might help."

I breathed out, blinking repeatedly, eyes suddenly feeling very heavy. "I hope you find something soon, I'm really tired."

"Can you hang on for a few? Some of these topics look promising," he said. "Dream demons…there's spells and whatnot to help ward them off."

"Dream demons?" I asked in disbelief. "But, I'm not dreaming…am I? You said it yourself that you could see the room, dark and the light from the moon you brought down helped ward it off."

Gabriel swiveled around in the chair, sitting backwards, casually resting his arms on the headrest. "Yes, but that could have been a coincidence. Maybe you really heard me and that's what woke you up, stopping the demons from doing…*whatever* it was they were doing."

"But, that first time I couldn't control a thing that I was doing. This last time I could…it didn't feel as malevolent. How do we know they are the same?" I asked.

Gabriel bit his lip, thoughtfully running his hands through his purposefully messy hair and mussing it up further. "I don't know. Were there any similarities?"

I considered this. "Those...tendrils. Like...black smoke from the ground but...not." I groaned in frustration. "I don't know how to explain it. Kind of...snake like? But, not. Ugh, that's no help."

"Hmm...I wish I could just see inside your mind, dammit. Would you mind grabbing my phone from the other room?"

"Sure," I said, reluctantly rising from my warm, comfortable bed and stumbling woozily into the other room, where I grabbed both phones from the coffee table and brought them into my bedroom. I set them both on my desk next to him, and peeked momentarily over his shoulder, reading the screen he was currently on.

I cocked a brow. "Incubi?" I read on further and my mouth dropped open, describing an incubus as a male demon who had sex with females in dreams. "No! That's not what's happening!"

Gabriel snickered. "I know, this is just a place to start, don't worry," he said. "First thing I looked up was 'dream demons' and this came up."

"Are there such things?" I asked, covering my open mouth with my palm, feeling slightly horrified.

Gabriel shrugged. "I have no idea, honestly."

I let out a little *yelp*. Gabriel patted my arm reassuringly. "Well, there's about a bazillion spells to ward off those little fuckers even if there are, so, no worries." He grabbed his cell phone and began texting.

"Daniel?" I asked, almost rhetorically. The entire time I knew him, I'd never seen him correspond with anyone else, so it was probably a stupid question.

He nodded. He also grabbed my phone and started poking at the screen. "Putting his number in here...just in case for some reason...well, you should have it anyways, even though you've not met him. Seers were often employed by the Order, and obviously, he'll be ours."

"How convenient he's your brother," I said.

He nodded. "Yes, it's pretty rare too to have two people with our different skills in one family.

"Hmm...wonder when I'll get to meet him?" I pondered aloud.

"Soon, I'm sure," Gabriel said, setting both phones down and going back to his computer research. I stood there for a few moments, watching him pull up screen after screen on dream demons, spells to ward them off, things like that. I rested my chin on his shoulder and let my arms drape over his chest, as if holding everything up was too much to bear.

"That tired, huh?" he asked.

"Yeah. I've not slept so much in probably a good five years or so then I have this week," I said, with a wide yawn.

"Well, you've been through a lot," Gabriel said. "I think tomorrow we'll work on some more magic. I think I can get you to call from the sun and it can help provide you with energy. It should help you feel better."

I peered out at the crescent moon outside my window, and the thousands of visible stars twinkling in the inky sky on this clear, autumn night. "I don't suppose there's moon magic that would help with that?"

He shrugged. "Yes and no. I mean, the moon basically is reflecting the sun's light back at us, but it's not true fire magic…the sun will be much more potent. The moon is generally used for relaxing and purifying."

"So you do spells and stuff too?" I asked.

"A little. Many times they're helpful in sorcery, though I can't claim to be as proficient in them as a witch would be."

I sighed, thinking of Kit. "I'm sure she could help." I didn't even need to say her name; I knew he knew who I was talking about.

"We'll find her. First things first…we need to make sure you're safe."

"Yeah…" I sighed again, reaching my arms over my head in an exaggerated stretch and a yawn. I looked down at myself a moment, noticing I was still in my orange date dress. I snorted. "Glad I broke out the dress for tonight," I said, dryly. "I think I'll take a shower and wash up."

Gabriel paused in his research to take one last glance at me. "Aw, but I like the dress," he said. "You really do look so pretty."

I flushed, suddenly feeling very vulnerable, flipping my hair forward and down over my chest. "Shower time." The curls were half unraveled in my hair and I'm sure my makeup was a fright. I grabbed a pair of gray yoga pants and a gray tank top that read *Starfleet Academy* in blue letters emblazoned across it, new underwear and debated on a bra. I didn't want to wear one to bed, but…I wasn't entirely comfortable with Gabriel seeing me without one, even though I'd be fully clothed. I grabbed for a zip up blue hoodie to throw over the top and headed for the bathroom, where I took a long shower. I washed out my curls and the hairspray, and scrubbed the makeup off my face with a washcloth. I sighed, seeing the last traces of our date wiped off onto the wet fabric.

At least for a few hours, I could pretend to be a normal woman. Not a dragon, not anything special or magical. Just a girl on a date with a boy, having a good time.

I had a feeling we'd never have a "normal" anything. Our relationship as it was hadn't started typical or normal...there was little chance it would continue as such. I at least hoped that after we figured out...*this*...whatever it was, we'd have time to be a little normal again. Soon.

Gabriel was still doing research on the computer, but this time he had a small arsenal of things on the desk he swore might help: some sea salt (nothing seemingly magical about it, just some stuff I purchased for margaritas from the grocery store), some white candles, a bottle of water, a glass of milk, some random herbs and spices and a stack of papers from the printer.

"What the fuck?" I asked, watching him sprinkle something into the glass of milk, eyes closed and concentrating.

His eyes flew up. "Dammit, I'm trying to concentrate, Leo!"-

I rolled my eyes. "Sorry," I said, trying to hide a laugh.

"It's fine, I think I'm about done. For now."

"What did you put in there?" I asked, motioning towards the dots that were now floating in the white liquid.

"Oh. It's just sage. That coupled with some positive reinforcement might make a nice nightmare-warding potion," he said.

I stared at him as if he just told me to drink more water when I was drowning. "Milk? If that's the case, then why does *anyone* ever have bad dreams? Pretty sure most people drink milk pretty often."

He clicked his tongue and shook his head. "Leo, what have I told you? Magic mostly is about intent. It's my *intent* that you have a peaceful rest so not only am I using these herbs which are supposed to have purifying properties but I'm infusing it with my energy. Since I only want the best for you..."

I waved him off. "Whatever it takes, I guess." He handed me the glass and I chugged it down, tasting the hint of Earth as I swallowed but of course, not noticing anything different then a normal glass of milk.

"Did you hear from your brother?" I asked.

"Yeah. He isn't sure about the dream demons or whatever but, he said he'll try to find something out," he said.

"How?"

"He has his ways, I guess," he said. He stood in the chair and stretched out, reaching a hand for my wet hair hanging down my shoulders.

He smirked playfully, brushing it over my shoulder and down my back. "You know, the wet hair is pretty hot too."

I grinned as he allowed his hand to linger on the bare skin on my collarbone. He trailed his fingers down slowly to the top of my cleavage, leaving a sensation of electrical shivers behind with each touch. "You know," he began, with a lilt in his tone, "I know we got a little carried away, but I really enjoyed...*earlier.*"

My cheeks pricked with heat at the thought. "I'd be lying if I said I didn't either." I wound my arms around his waist and stood up on my tiptoes, but in my human form I still wasn't tall enough to kiss him without him leaning over. He took the hint, and our lips met in the middle. I allowed one solitary kiss before I felt the fire burning in my center again, and pulled away, leaning my cheek on his chest. "I'm tired." It was a convenient excuse, but I really was tired.

He chuckled. "I know. I'll just do some...*things* beforehand. Do you want me to...umm..." he motioned for the bed, stammering. "I'll be a perfect gentleman, I promise. Or I can sleep on the floor, it's up to you."

I shook my head. "No, you can sleep here," I said, climbing into my bed myself and pulling the sheet over me. "I'd feel better if you did."

"Okay," he said. He turned away, for his arsenal of crap on the desk and started placing things in random spots that made no sense to me, and chanting every now and then, occasionally sprinkling a splash of water here or there.

I shook my head, bewildered. I unzipped the hoodie, figuring it was safe with the blanket over me. I couldn't sleep with sleeves on, they bothered me. I tossed the hoodie on the floor and rested against my pillow.

I was about half asleep, after watching his serious face purifying or cleansing the room of nightmares and I grinned to myself at his furrowed brow or his hushed muttering. Finally, he seemed satisfied and sat down on the bed. My eyes flew open for a minute as his weight shifted my position. He pulled his black t-shirt over his head and tossed it on the ground. I knew he had several more tattoos on his back and shoulders, lots of Celtic and tribal designs, surrounding a sequence of four circles entwined in the middle, forming one simple yet intricate design. Curious, I reached out and gingerly traced each circle with a fingertip, "What does this mean?"

He peered over his shoulder at me. "Oh, that's called the Celtic Wheel of Balance," he said. "Each circle represents one of the four elements all coming together in the middle, with the strongest element of all."

"Spirit?"

"That's right," he said.

"How come it's not colored in like the rest of them?" I asked, noticing one green circle assumedly for Earth, a red one for fire, so on. "And, what about arcane?"

"Lots of magic users don't believe arcane is an actual element; it exists between elements...sort of. Even so, the black outline can represent that. As for spirit, until recently, I had no idea spirit had a color," he said, throwing me a warm smile over his shoulder. "But I'll have to change that, because now I see that it does."

"And what color would that be?" I asked.

"Pink, of course," he replied, with a tender smile.

With that declaration, my insides melted. "Be careful, or I might start liking pink, finally."

He grinned widely. "Well, you should like yourself," he said.

I laid my head back down and patted the pillow next to me. "Sleepy time," I said, dreamily.

He chuckled. "Sec. I need different pants." He briefly left the bedroom and came back in moments later wearing a pair of black pajama pants, and he crawled into bed with me, pulling a spare blanket from the foot of the bed over him.

"You really don't have to do that," I insisted.

"No, actually, I do. Being that close to you in a bed...I am not sure if I can control myself," he said.

I shot him a playful half smile. "Who said you had to?" I asked, reaching out and running my fingers down the length of his bare arm.

Gabriel swallowed, and coughed. "Come on, Leo. Don't you want it to be more...special?"

I shrugged, continuing to brush my fingers over the lines of one of his tribal tattoos. "It would be."

Gabriel smiled wryly, and exhaled a large breath. "Seriously, you're killing me here."

I pulled myself to my elbows and crawled the short distance to him on the bed and leaned over him, my hair cascading over my face and onto his chest. I could hear his heart beat more rapidly, as I leaned in and lightly grazed the side of his neck with my lips, working my way up gently to the soft spot under his ear. I heard him audibly simper. I could tell he was fighting to restrain himself as he slowly wrapped his arms around my middle.

"I don't understand, you were so nervous about this before," he said, somewhat breathless.

I tossed my hair back over my shoulder with a hand, and let it linger as my fingers trailed slowly down my chest and rested in the crook of my ample cleavage (for the first time, I felt quite thankful that I had been blessed with larger boobs in my dragon form, and curves even though most dragons were built rather slim in their human forms). Gabriel swallowed again, grabbing my hand in both of his and bringing it to his face, placing a very passionate and yet very pointedly controlled kiss on it, his brown eyes staring at me with an eager sparkle.

"Well, see I was...but I think I'm over it now" I said , pushing aside the blanket and climbing on top of him as he lay there, straddling his waist with my own center, feeling the raging fire stoke itself as I did. "I've never had the opportunity to experience it, but dragons are quite carnal which is half the reason why they get married in the first place. Hell, even then it doesn't stop them from sleeping around because once that fire gets lit, it doesn't go out until someone *puts* it out," I said suggestively, getting a certain satisfaction out of seeing Gabriel fight his wanton desires so desperately.

He let my hand drop and bit his lip, hard. I could tell it was painful from the wince in his eyes. His hands wandered to my waist, his fingers carefully meandering under the cotton of my tank top. I grinned playfully and took the hint, and wrapped my arms around myself to grasp the top and start pulling it over my head. I got about halfway up my stomach when two strong hands stopped me, and pushed them down.

"Stop. Seriously." He said, giving me a warning tone. "I took it too far earlier, and I don't want you doing something you're really not ready for...as much as I want to..." His hands were back at my waist again, carefully lifting me up and urging me to climb off of him.

"But— "I blinked, the hot fire that was raging now suddenly turning to nausea and pin pricks of tears welling in my eyes, feeling my pride severely injured. Didn't this always work in the movies, seduction? Suddenly, I felt offended and...disgusting. I glanced down at myself, my tank top hiked up and the neckline yanked down, showing a bit more flesh then I was suddenly aware of that I was showing. I grabbed for my covers and yanked them over me.

"Leo... I'm sorry." Gabriel let out a frustrated groan, slapping his face with his palms and grumbling to himself. He tried reaching out to me but I slapped his hand away and quickly turned away from him on the bed and pulled the blanket all the way up to my neck and using the edge of it, trying to wipe away the tears that were furiously falling down my face.

He sighed. "I'm really sorry, I'm just trying to do the right thing." I felt the bed shift as he leaned over me and kissed the back of my head softly before rolling back over and laying back down on his side of the bed.

I blinked a few more tears out of my eyes before I felt the urge of drowsiness take over and I willingly gave into it.

Chapter 14

I was awakened abruptly that next morning by the sound of a loud rapping on my door. I quickly sat upright, glancing over at the alarm clock on my broken nightstand: 4:35 AM. I looked around, the sun just beginning its ascent—just a twinge of morning light in the sky.

I rubbed the sleep out of my eyes and shoved Gabriel, who had inched ever so closer to me over the night. He still looked adorable asleep and I felt a sudden pang of guilt over the night's activities—or lack thereof. He was just trying to be a gentleman, and I got angry over it.

Gabriel snorted himself awake, confused. "What? Are you okay?" he asked, but was answered by the sound of the heavy knocking on the door again. "—the hell?" He tossed the covers off of him and tiptoed stealthily to the door. I saw no need, as the knocking was so loud they were likely to not hear the footsteps inside anyways, human or dragon.

"Leorah?" A voice—slightly familiar—sounded from the other side of the door, but decidedly feminine.

"Kit?" I asked. I dashed towards the door, wishing I had a peephole. I was about to open it, when Gabriel pulled me away.

"What if it's someone coming to take you back?" he asked in a hushed panic, and I paused.

"But it sounds familiar, what if it's Kit?" I asked back, trying to keep my voice in a whisper.

He shook his head. "It's not, I don't recognize the voice at all."

Perhaps he was right. Another rap at the door. "Leorah? Open up, it's Kiarra. I need to talk to you, it's important."

"*Kiarra?*" I mouthed in surprise and slight disgust. Gabriel grimaced.

"What if it's something about your brother?" he offered.

I considered this. "Uggh, I guess we'll find out." I stepped back and motioned Gabriel towards the door. "You do it. If she's got some evil weird juju about her— "

"—I'll fireball her, don't worry." Gabriel twisted the doorknob and peeked his head out the door.

"Kiarra? Everything okay?" he asked.

"Where's Leo?" she asked. I could see the top of her head as she tried to peek through the crack in the open door.

"Sleeping. It is kind of the asscrack of dawn, you know," Gabriel replied dryly. "Is everything okay?"

"No, it's really not but...look I can explain just let me come in. Please," Kiarra pleaded from the other side of the door, trying to push it open but Gabriel was fighting it.

"Look, I'm really not sure if I should, with everything going on—" he began.

"Someone from the Court has located where you live, Leorah, and they're coming after you. Today. I came here to warn you, and help you escape," Kiarra said.

I winced, taken by surprise. Gabriel looked back at me and exchanged an appalled look. I nodded and he slowly opened the door.

"How do you know that?" I asked, the second she stepped in. Gabriel shut and locked the door after her.

Kiarra stood there for a moment, looking quite bedraggled from her generally super-model looks in a pair of faded blue jeans and a black boyfriend style sweater that hung well past her waist. Her black hair was in a messy knot on top of her head, her chocolate skin was dull with fatigue and she carried a large blue backpack that she hoisted off her shoulder and heaved to the floor. "Ugh, that portal travel always makes me feel so groggy," she said, brushing herself off.

"How did you *know*?" Gabriel prompted again, much more sternly this time, brown eyes narrow, stepping into her personal space and making her look very uncomfortable. His hands were dangling at his sides, in balled fists, but I could see the smoke coming from them as he involuntarily (or maybe voluntarily) created sorcerer's fire in his palms.

Kiarra looked at him with alarm, and held up her hands in surrender. "Seriously, I'm a friend. I know you're suspicious of me, but, it's not for the reasons you think."

"Spill," I said, motioning towards the recliner chair for her to sit in. Gabriel relented and stepped back. I grabbed his forearm and urged him to sit with me on the sofa. He sat first and I draped my legs over his lap (both for comfort and to weigh him down; preventing him from standing up and shooting plasma balls at Kiarra's pretty face) and he hugged my knees to his chest, and we both stared at her with anticipation. I didn't have any real reason to not let him blast her good, but I didn't want any more scorch marks in my apartment; the damage deposit was expensive.

"Okay, let me start from the beginning."

"That'd be helpful," I retorted dryly.

"Okay well…as you know, The Court hasn't always been exactly honest with you—or any of us. I'm guessing by now, you've figured out how to do magic, yes?" she began, and I nodded reluctantly.

"A little."

"More will come," she said assuredly. "Well, long story short an underground organization was formed underground to help maintain the integrity of dragon society against those who sought to do harm and unravel our way of life— "

"Sounds kind of like the FBI, or some spy thing," Gabriel said, with a chortle.

Kiarra smiled. "Yeah, that's kind of what we are. Anyways, we're called the Loremasters. No one knows about us but other Loremasters and now, you.

"Part of my mission was to infiltrate the Court, and make sure everything stayed on the up and up because we all had suspicions there were corrupted members out for their own personal agenda— but we knew that long before I was even born. So, when I was of age, I became somewhat of a double-agent and infiltrated the Court, as an entry level member. I didn't have much to report, until I met your brother."

My mouth fell open, my eyes narrowed, feeling a sudden surge of anger. "I knew it! I knew there was something up with you, you're just *using* my brother!" I tried to stand up and confront her, maybe with fists but Gabriel hugged my legs closer to him and refused to let me stand.

"I know how it looks," she said. "But I swear, my feelings for him are real. It started off as a job, but I genuinely fell in love with him and we do intend on getting married, for real."

"Does he know about all this?" I asked.

She shook her head. "No, not yet. I felt that it was more important that you know what was going on first, because my *real* job is to first and foremost make sure you are protected."

I exchanged glances with Gabriel. We said nothing, but he wrapped his arms a little tighter around my legs. The air in the room was palatable with tension. Kiarra—if telling the truth—was revealing something huge, and she wasn't done yet.

Kiarra *ahemed* pointedly. "Anyway, my point is that, I know that Court issued a warrant for your return to Anarach and since I knew your brother, they assumed you'd come more willingly with me."

"But, why do they want me?" I asked. "I've been here for two years now. It's never been an issue before."

"The official edict states you're here illegally," Kiarra said, with a wry face.

"Illegally? Hell, they were only too eager to *push* me through the portal!" I protested. "The Queen especially! I remember pleading with her to leave and I barely had to speak and she granted it. 'Be gone, granddaughter of Aleron.'" I scoffed.

"It wasn't the King or the Queen that issued the warrant, I hear," she replied.

I cocked a brow. "Oh? Who did?"

She shrugged. "Not sure. Someone in the House obviously. Also the fact that you and Gabriel have connected is sending off warning flares at the Court. It's a threat."

Gabriel and I both began to speak at the same time. I said, "A threat? Why?"

"Well, there are members of Court that are old enough to remember the Order and their mission to help dragons...word has it that they've reunited again and, essentially, shit is hitting the fan," Kiarra explained.

"But—how would they know? The only ones that know are, you, my grandfather and Braeden. Surely none of you would betray me?" I mused out loud.

"Of course not, but...I'm not sure you haven't been watched—either over there, or here," Kiarra said.

I raised my brow. "How would they do that?"

She shrugged, with a sigh. "I'm not sure. No one is. But the fear is since you're reunited, you are planning something against the Court."

I laughed out loud. "What?? What the Hell do I want with the Court?"

"I'm guessing since you and Gabriel have finally met, and you've probably practiced magic. No one is more of a threat to a corrupted government then a powerful pink dragon and his—or her—Knight of the Order," Kiarra mused. "One of them must have sighted something pretty big in order to summon you home. And I don't know what they intend in doing with you, all I know is I was instructed not to harm you, so they need you unharmed…so far. But don't think they're not below severely harming you, because they will," Kiarra said, stone faced.

I nodded slowly. "So…. now what?"

"Well, we need to get you some place safe," she said.

I snorted. "Where, though? I have some evil entity following me around in my dreams, trying to kill me and now I have members of my own *Court* trying to capture me. There really is no place safe!"

Kiarra smiled smugly. "That's…not exactly true."

Gabriel considered this. "I could take her back to Canada with me, I suppose. It should be safe there."

She shook her head. "I have a better place: Castle Danger."

I gave her an odd look, as if she just told me to spread butter on my toes. "What now? And where?"

Gabriel spoke first. "I've heard of that. Actually I think I saw signs for it on the drive down here. But…as far as I know it's all camping and there's really not much there. Just some cabins and that's pretty much it."

"Ah, that's what we want you to think," she said, smugly.

"Wait now—who is this *we*?" I asked.

"The Loremasters. It's where they are headquartered. To the ordinary human or even dragon, you can drive through Castle Danger and not notice anything out of the ordinary. As far as the rest of Minnesota and the rest of the area is concerned: it's just a fabulous place to go camping, along the giant Lake Superior. But hidden in the woods is a secret realm where the Loremasters live and work, and take in threatened magical beings to keep them safe."

My eyes widened. Gabriel swore under his breath.

"You're not serious?" I asked, incredulous.

"I am serious as a dragon bite," she replied. "Outside of the Loremasters, hardly anyone knows we exist and you cannot access the realm unless you've been imbibed with a potion to grant you access by a very powerful Alchemist."

"There's Alchemists too?" I asked, my voice barely an audible squeak.

She nodded with a grin. "Oh yes. Usually witches or sorcerers that specialize in potion making. It's pretty damn fascinating actually." She glanced at a wristwatch she was hiding underneath the sleeve of her oversized sweater. "Shit, we need to go. They are going to come looking for us within the next few hours."

"Wait!" I leapt up and pushed her down into the chair. "I can't just *go*! I have a home here..." I glanced around wryly, wrinkling my nose. "Okay, so it's not the greatest, but it's all I have. I have a friend that is *missing*, I have a job and I have—my cat!" I exclaimed, pointing at Sona who was padding around suspiciously. She yelped and darted out of the room.

"Leorah, I'm afraid you have no choice." Kiarra, who the couple times I met her was the cheeriest, perkiest thing I believe I'd ever met—cheerier then a songbird on a spring morning when all you really just want to do is sleep—sounded solemn and controlled; appearing serious. She reached out and grasped my hands in hers and squeezed reassuringly. "If you don't...no one can protect you once you get caught. They want something from you, and I can promise you, it's not good."

"My grandfather can do *something*; I know he can..." I started, not feeling entirely convinced about that myself.

Kiarra shook her head. "He can't, not this time. Believe it or not, I'm the only one that can help you right now. Well, me and the Loremasters."

It was Gabriel's turn to interject suspicion. "Wait wait wait...how do we know *you* aren't the one after her. I mean...what a coincidence about all this, huh?"

I pulled away, back towards him. He grasped my shoulders with his hands tightly and I leaned back in towards him.

Kiarra heaved a weighted sigh. "I know how this all must seem. I know. I wouldn't believe it myself, but you're going to have to trust me this time. You know what trouble I'm going to get into if they find me here, helping you? I won't even get a trial, I'll just be killed, instantly," she said, with a dramatic snap of her fingers to prove her point.

"Not if you're really working *for* them. Or the...evil thing," Gabriel said, struggling to find a term for the evil dream entity.

"The Loremasters can help you figure out what you're up against. They have records and memories of everything that ever existed throughout time. If one could have come to you themselves, they would have but for now, I'm their best option. Their *only* option." Kiarra sighed again. "Look, you're a pink dragon. Your magic lies in the spirit element...I'm sure Gabriel here has explained this to you at least a little bit, but I know you have no idea truly how powerful that element and you are. I do. One of your abilities should be to sense whether or not someone is telling you the truth—it's how you determine whether or not to side with someone or battle them, it's one of the *many* powerful and sometimes scary skills pink dragons have. I don't know quite how you do it, but from what I've heard you just close your eyes and read your gut—it never lies to you. It will *always* be honest with you. Try it, now, and it will tell you that I am in fact telling you the truth. I am your ally."

I hesitated, considering her words.

"How do you know so much about a pink dragon's powers?" Gabriel asked, the very question that was forming in my own mind.

Kiarra sighed again; a conflicted groan. "Okay, what I'm about to tell you needs to remain a secret. I mean it. It's the entire reason I joined the Loremasters. It's the entire reason I tried to get in close with you, why I seemed too eager to meet you at first." She paused, as if struggling internally with something.

"Well…what?" I prompted impatiently.

She inhaled and exhaled again quickly. "Cyril—the last known pink dragon—well he wasn't crazy at all. In fact, he was very sane, and powerful. And, he was my grandfather."

I winced, as if dodging a punch of ice to the face. I felt my heart leap up into my throat, and I tried to choke it down like a sour drink of spoiled milk.

"What!?!" Gabriel managed to ask for me, dumbfounded.

"But—Cyril had a dragon that was stillborn. He didn't have any other dragons…did he?" I asked, second-guessing myself. It wouldn't be the first or the last time my knowledge of my own society failed me.

"That's true, the dragon that would have been my aunt died at childbirth. But what no one knows—what he hid from everyone—is that he paired with another female at a later time, when he was exiled. He refused to assist the corrupt leaders of the Court at the time, so he was exiled…sent to Earth to live out the remainder of his days. He wasn't alone though, another dragon named Philomenia went missing around the same time. They had three dragons together, one of them was my father. The kids re-assimilated into dragon society, once he was found, and assassinated. I still don't know how he died, but he left behind a trunkful of journals, books, dictations about life and his powers, knowing fully well what the Court and

Kingdom were doing to his good name, and the name of all the pink dragons that would come after him. I've been studying them for years, so I know something about how your magic is supposed to work. Well, I know how his worked and there should be many similarities."

I narrowed my eyes at her, still feeling suspicious. "How do I know—really?"

"Just listen to your instincts, Leo. They will never lie to you, even if others do. Listen to them, what do they say?" She turned to Gabriel now and said, "And you, can you detect whether or not I'm using any magic at this time?"

Gabriel closed his eyes for a minute, and opened them again slowly. "I can't read any magic. At least, none that I'm aware of."

"Leo, just try to use your magic and let it tell you whether or not I'm telling the truth," she said earnestly.

I breathed out. "Okay...I don't know what I'm doing though." Gabriel pulled my hand into his lap, stroking the back of it with his thumb. I glanced into his honest brown eyes, and he nodded.

I bit my lip, and closed my eyes. I concentrated on Kiarra, and replayed the words she told in my mind. *How am I supposed to tell if you're lying?* I asked myself, taking a deep breath. Suddenly, I was overcome by a wave of peace...light shrouded my vision and warmth—like summer sunlight—touched my fingertips, feeling like a trusted friend I hadn't seen in a while. All at once, I knew that Kiarra was in fact telling the truth. I don't know how...but I just knew.

My eyes flew open. The light dissipated, but it lingered for a moment around Kiarra's form. I just nodded at Gabriel.

"She's telling the truth." I said confidently.

"You're sure?" he asked, squeezing my hand.

I nodded quickly. "Yes. I can't tell you how I just— "

"—if you say so, that's good enough for me," he said. He leaned over, and planted an affectionate kiss on my cheek before standing. "Well...what do we have to do?"

Kiarra let out a low whistle. "Wow, that was intense," she said with a laugh. "You're strong, for sure."

"You felt that?" I didn't know what she felt, exactly.

She nodded. "The energy in the room—it was intense. Like fog. You could almost slice it with a knife."

I chuckled. "Well...what can I say?" I asked rhetorically with a nonchalant shrug.

"How long will it take for us to get there? Your Castle place?" Gabriel asked.

"Oh, not long. It's just a portal ride away." She produced a vial from her pants pocket—it was small, but it was almost like looking at bottled lightning—you could see the electricity crackling in it. It was powerful, whatever it was. "All I have to do is throw this into a portal before we jump in, and it will re-direct the path to Castle Danger, and destroy the entrance portal behind us so no one can follow."

"You're going to use the one in the woods?" I asked, with trepidation. That would make it very, very hard to come back.

"Well, I kind of have to. It's the closest portal to us, the next one being hours away. We could drive but...we don't have that kind of time," she said.

I groaned. "What am I going to do—with my life? How long are we going to be gone? And what about my cat?"

"Bring her," Kiarra said. "Castle Danger is home to many, many animals, both domestic and wild. Many people who seek the safety of the realm have animal guides and familiars that stick with them. So, she'll be right at home."

I breathed in relief. "That's good. But what about—what about Kit? And my apartment?"

"Is it really worth your life?" she asked.

Gabriel shook his head. He wrapped his arms around me tightly, and nuzzled my cheek with his own. He leaned over and whispered, "It'll be okay. I'm with you. You have to do this."

I nodded, and forced a smile. "Okay...I guess I'll pack."

"I'll start shutting stuff down," he said, kissing my cheek again and pulling away.

"I'm still worried about Kit," I said, and I briefly explained to Kiarra the situation with my friend. She didn't have much to offer but a sympathetic "I'm sorry" and reassured me that Kit's yellow beetle was still parked outside the portal. She said the Loremasters could probably help.

I didn't completely unpack my bag from the other day when we were heading back towards the dragon realm, but there were still quite a few things I wanted to add now, especially knowing that it would be harder to return.

Kiarra followed me into my bedroom and offered to help me, urging me to pack only what I truly needed and practical items. As I packed, she told me more about the Order—things I already knew but things that no one else did, so another fact to prove my instinct was correct, even asked me if Gabriel was part of the O'Donnell bloodline. She said according to one of her grandfather, Cyril's books about the Order that because the Knight and the dragon had to work so closely together, an unshakeable bond was formed and sometimes, they fell in love. The stronger the bond though, the stronger the connection with magic. She said quite frequently, the bond between knight and dragon was so tight that if one lost their life prematurely, quite often the other died shortly after, no matter if it was a dragon or human that went first. The notion made me slightly nauseous, being that close to someone that you literally couldn't live without them. I couldn't say that about Gabriel yet, in fact I wasn't one-hundred percent sure how I felt about him, other than the fact I was incredibly disappointed we didn't consummate our relationship last night, and that being around him made me feel more calm, more confident. But love?

I knew I had fallen for him pretty good, for me to even consider sleeping with him. I'd *never* allowed another to ever get so close to me so soon. It took me nearly six months to speak to Kit about something that wasn't work related, and another month or so before I agreed to go out to dinner with her or do something outside of work. I have never fallen for anyone this fast, it was strange that I did now but, perhaps that's how it worked? How would I know based on *no* experience?

I guess I'd find out sooner or later how I felt about him exactly. Or, perhaps I already knew, but I didn't want to admit it to myself.

She also told me more about her grandfather's magic, how he was able to heal, how he could use compulsion on most sentient beings aside from basic amplifying or dispersing the four elements. I did have to ask her about his wings—did he have the flimsy, iridescent looking wings? Could he fly?

She said he didn't have those type of wings and that like any other dragon, he could fly, and she wasn't sure why mine were different. But if anyone would know, it'd be the Loremasters. The same went for my 'evil' entity that kept haunting me, so to speak.

I didn't know why all of a sudden I was divulging these things to her; maybe it was the fact that suddenly, she wasn't that perky, cheerleader type that made me sick to my stomach. She wasn't the person that was taking my brother away. She wasn't exactly a friend, but she was someone with answers and I couldn't afford to burn that bridge, yet.

She did keep checking her phone, though and tapping her foot anxiously. She was nervous about something—more than just being caught by the Court helping me. I called her out on it, as I was shoving the last bit of clothing and toiletries in a wheeled suitcase I was opting to bring this time. I had no idea what this new realm would have in store for me even though she assured me there would be food, water and everything I would need. Still...better to be safe than sorry. I should have asked about Mountain Dew and *Star Trek,* I thought, regrettably to myself.

"Your brother," she said, with a wry smile. "Any moment he's going to know they're after me, too."

"They aren't going to hurt him, are they?" I asked, worried.

She shook her head. "No, they'll give him a truth serum and they'll learn he really doesn't know anything. They'll just think I was with him to get to you...he'll think I betrayed him." She sighed. "It'll be awhile before I can tell him the truth, but at least he won't be harmed."

I frowned, watching her dark eyes well up with tears that she refused to let fall down her face. "You *do* care about him, don't you?"

She chuckled, pressing her fingertips to her closed eyes and squinting, trying to pressure the tears to stop presenting themselves. "Pink dragon instinct?"

I shook my head. "No, sister instinct. Don't worry, I'll make sure he understands."

She looked up momentarily and smiled half-heartedly. "Thank you."

A few more minutes, I had everything packed. Gabriel had shut down the water coming into the apartment and pried all the windows shut . He said he had cast some sort of enchant on the place to keep people out (like landlords that would be wondering where missing rent might be, although Kiarra assured me I'd be able to still get online via the internet and make some sort of payment or...something. Though with no human income, I didn't see how it was possible). Gabriel himself packed up his small amount of clothing and his laptop and had helped gather Sona in her carrier—again (she was not happy about that and even nipped him lightly on his palm) and her bag of food. I sent them ahead to my car while I locked up, pausing for a moment before shutting out the lights, feeling mournful at the thought of possibly losing my first place of my own, wondering if I'd ever be able to come back to it...all my collections, my tchotchkes and all my crap...two years of normality all possibly gone in a day. I closed the door behind me and stuck the key in the lock, turning it and hearing the deadbolt tumble and lock with a *click*.

"So how did you get here, then?" I asked, climbing into the driver's seat of my purple Neon and turning over the ignition.

"Well, Maxxus had put me in contact with one of the rogues, and he hooked me up with a cab driver—another rogue who was familiar with driving dragons to and from the portal," Kiarra replied.

"And we're just going to leave my car there in the clearing? Kit's car is already there, someone might think something is up," I said, beginning our drive to the portal

"No, we're actually going to drive it right into the portal," Kiarra replied.

Gabriel and I exchanged smiles. "Cool," I said.

When we arrived at the clearing, Maxxus was standing in the middle in his human form, apparently waiting for us to arrive. He rushed up to the car the second he saw us.

"What took so long?" he mouthed, pointing at the imaginary wristwatch on his arm.

I pulled into park and got out of the car, Gabriel and Kiarra following suit.

"What are you doing here?"

"I had to get her over safely," Maxxus said, nodding towards Kiarra, "and prevent any more of them from coming over. No small feat, might I add. There are two dragons knocked out on the other side, we need to *get outta here*!" he exclaimed, motioning towards the portal.

"Wait, wait!" I held up my hands. "You're coming with us? No. No no no..."

Kiarra came up beside me. "We don't have a choice. They'll be after him now too. Had he simply let me over—okay. But he's attacked members of the Court on an official mission. He's committed treason. He's one of us now."

I raised a brow, and crossed my arms over my chest. "One of what? Idiots?"

Maxxus chuckled, briefly reaching out a long arm and grasping my shoulder before Gabriel came up beside me, glaring daggers at him. "Just another member of Leo's army," he said, with a laugh.

"But—why?" I asked, dumbfounded. "You might never be able to come back here, again. You could be exiled!"

Maxxus just shrugged. "Well, at least I'll be in good company," he said, nodding to Kiarra who just smiled and nodded. "Besides, your grandfather is one of my favorite beings ever—he took me on when many wouldn't, and has been more loyal to me then my own family ever has been. I owe it to him to try to keep his granddaughter safe."

I let out a low growl, begrudgingly. "Fine. Get the hell in the car." I turned to Kiarra. "What do we do now?'

"Climb in, and I'll throw this—" she held up the small vial containing the swirling blue liquid inside, "—into the portal. We wait until it shifts and we'll have about one minute to get in before it implodes on itself, destroying the portal for good. So everyone, get into the car, and Leo drive about twenty feet to the portal and be ready...I'll jump in and you floor it. We need to be quick."

One more look at Maxxus and I shook my head at him. I couldn't believe he would do this. He shrugged and just climbed into the back of the car, folding his long legs uncomfortably into the backseat.

Gabriel didn't appear happy, but he kept his mouth shut as we climbed in and I crept the car carefully forward, with Kiarra in the lead, ready to toss in the vial.

"It's going to make a loud *pop* sound, like a firework and you'll see it change colors. After it turns blue, that's our cue to drive in as fast as possible!" Kiarra yelled to us, and I came to a stop just before where she was standing.

"Ready?" she asked. I kept my foot heavy on the brake, gripping the steering wheel so hard my knuckles were turning white. I nodded.

"I wonder what this is going to do to my car?" I mused under my breath, as Kiarra tossed the vial into the portal's opening. She quickly dashed back to the car and climbed in beside Maxxus who's tall form was crouched uncomfortably in the back, Gabriel looking rather smug at his discomfort.

We heard a loud *bang* and the portal lit up like a floodlight in the dark, first changing bright yellow, then red and orange before fading and shifting to an easy, calm blue color.

"Go!" Kiarra said, and I slammed my foot onto the gas pedal. I could feel my tires spin a few times before catching grip in the dirt, and it hurled us into the blue portal, Gabriel nervously grabbing at my thigh and looking a bit uneasy as I glanced over at him momentarily as we sped in. I didn't even think about how a portal shift would affect a human. Hopefully since he was magical, it wouldn't have too much of an ill effect on him.

I felt a sudden sense of disorientation, like being spun around too many times before the piñata and being stopped suddenly and told to smack a tree. There wasn't much to see, or time to see it because just as quickly as we were hurled in we were hurled out, into another clearing nearly equal to the one we had just come from. I had to slam on the brakes to prevent from hitting a small tree and we skidded and came to a stop about at a 90-degree angle from how we entered.

We watched the portal we had just come from make a few hissing and popping noises before eventually just fading into a puff of steam and dissipating into the air.

No one spoke or uttered a sound. Finally, I released a breath I didn't realize I was holding in the form of a guffaw and said, "That was it?"

Kiarra let out a little giggle from behind me. "Why what were you expecting?"

I shrugged. Gabriel and I shook our heads at each other with a laugh, and I glanced around us. "So this is the safe spot?"

"Well, not *here* exactly," Kiarra said. "Do you really think it would be a great spot for a portal inside the middle of a town?"

"Town?" Gabriel repeated uncertainly.

"I concur, what kind of place is this, exactly?" For the first time since declaring his allegiance to our…cause as it were, Maxxus appeared just a shade apprehensive.

Kiarra grinned knowingly. "You will love it. You can be whoever you are, whatever you are…no one will bat an eye," she said, specifically towards Gabriel.

"Me?" he placed his hand on his chest, aback.

"It's a place of magic," Kiarra explained. "Where outcasts and mythological creatures that have nowhere to go for whatever reason, they all belong here, and they all co-exist like a community. Some cook and prepare food, others craft, grow crops, some entertain...it's a beautiful, peaceful existence." She took her phone out and glanced at it briefly before shoving it in the kangaroo pocket of her sweatshirt, "it's nearly 3pm...the marketplace should be beginning soon."

"What's that?" I inquired.

"Exactly what you think it would be, vendors selling their goods. Jewelry crafted by the finest jewelers...one of them a green dragon, actually," she said with a nod towards Maxxus, who just ran a hand through his wavy hair briefly, nervously smiling. "Crafters selling blankets, flowers, artisan bread...anything you can think of. There is no money here, only bartering for goods and services. You will all enjoy it immensely."

I looked at Gabriel, and then at Maxxus again with anxious glances. Our moment was ruined by the sound of Gabriel's cell phone chirping from his pocket.

"What the—I get service out here?" he mused under his breath, glancing at the screen. He poked at it, and spoke: "Daniel?"

I mouthed "*His brother*," to the others who both nodded.

Gabriel's mouth fell open. "You're here. *Here?* What do you mean you're here? Wait a minute, I'm putting you on speaker." He touched the phone and set it on the middle console. "What do you mean, you're here, Daniel?"

"I mean, I'm here! Castle Danger, Minnesota—where you are. Although...I don't see anything but a lot of trees and...more trees and...oh look! Another tree!" Daniel's deep voice closely resembling Gabriel's but each word was a bit more articulate and almost overly-pronounced sounded surprised and sarcastic at the same time.

"Why are you here?" I asked, awed.

Daniel's tone turned from surprised to silly. "Well, am I speaking again to the one and only beautiful famed pink dragon?"

I snorted. "Well the jury is out on beautiful," Gabriel shot me a glare to which I stuck out my tongue at him and crossed my eyes, "but yes, that's me."

Daniel let out a little laugh. "Oh! I'm so excited to *finally* meet you! It would have happened already but the way my brother is—I think he wants you all to himself!"

Gabriel forced a smile and sunk back in his seat, cheeks flushing red. Kiarra chuckled and even Maxxus managed a smirk. "Shut up, asshole," Gabriel warned.

"Oh shove it, bro. You mad?" Daniel's voice was sing-song in his torment. "Anyways, so I had this *vision* a few hours ago, and the majority of what I remembered was seeing this green sign and highway numbers...the sign for Castle Danger, and I felt a sense of urgency. The fact I'm able to tell you this means I'm supposed to be here so...the question is why? And where the hell are you?"

My phone chirped then. I pulled it out of my bag.

He magical? It was Kiarra, not wanting to be heard while Daniel was on the other line.

I looked away from the phone and nodded. I replied back simply *"Seer."* She nodded, that was enough.

"Daniel, my name is Kiarra. I'm a dragon first and foremost, and Loremaster and I have taken both Leorah and your brother and another comrade to the haven of Castle Danger for their safety until we can learn and eliminate the threats against them. If you can give me your relative location, I can come get you through a portal."

Daniel described his location and Kiarra seemed to know where it was even though he described little more than trees and the position of the sun. She said he was nearby, coincidentally and she instructed that he would see a shimmer suddenly about fifty paces to the west of him, and that was his cue to step on through. She exited the car and started running off into the woods.

Maxxus reached out and grasped Gabriel's shoulder. "You are sure that your brother can be trusted?" He glanced at me as well. I nodded my head. If Gabriel trusted him, so did I. Perhaps that was a naïve stance to take, but my instincts told me it was the right thing to do.

Gabriel gave him a brief nod. "He knows all about dragons—probably more than I—and he's a Seer. He doesn't have any magic besides the visions that we know of, but he's a strong fighter and has had my back every time I have had even the smallest tiff. I know he'd do the same for Leorah. Just because he's not an official Knight, he's still obligated to serve them and the dragons however he can."

Maxxus opened his door. "I should see if she needs assistance." He ran off after her into the woods.

"So..." Gabriel reached over and grabbed my hand, giving it a gentle squeeze. "Are you sure you can handle my brother?"

I laughed. "That's the least of my worries right now," I said. "I'm pretty sure I can handle him. I'm not sure if I can handle...all this. A strange place. New people and...beings." I sighed.

"We'll be fine." Gabriel said. "It might be interesting to be able to practice magic openly, if it is as Kiarra says. I wonder if there will be other sorcerers there," he mused.

I shrugged. "Sure sounded that way."

Gabriel beamed. "That will be nice for a change."

I wanted to share his joy, but inside I was still nervous and frightened. Frightened for my missing friend and nervous for myself at this stage. So much had happened in the past couple weeks.

A *yeowl* sounded from the floor of the car behind us. I peeked over and discovered Sona, disgruntled but okay had woken from her catnip coma in her little crate. I reached my hand out and rubbed her velvety nose with my finger. "Soon, kitty.... you'll be able to get out soon."

She snorted and turned around, presenting me with her backside before letting out an angry *meow* and tried to fall back asleep.

"She sounds unimpressed," Gabriel said, with a laugh.

"Well, all I see is trees so far. We could have hidden in the woods back home if this is all it is," I said, peering out the window again, watching for Kiarra and company to emerge again through the woods.

Before I could speak again, Kiarra emerged with Maxxus and someone on a black motorcycle (the engine was shut off), wearing a leather jacket and a black helmet with red flames adorning the sides. I assumed this was Daniel, taking long strides on either side of the bike in his black leather chaps.

"Chaps? Really?" I didn't realize I said this out loud, narrowing one eye. Gabriel snorted and guffawed.

"Yes, that's my brother." We both shook our heads and enjoyed a brief laugh before climbing out of the car from our respective sides.

As we emerged, Daniel paused for a moment before taking of his helmet, and kicking the kickstand down to prop up the heavy black bike. He tossed the helmet aside (which Maxxus politely picked up and hung by its strap on one of the handlebars) and came bounding over to us like an excited puppy.

"Oh my *God*!" he exclaimed, giddy. "It's you, it's *really* you!" He said to me as I outstretched my hand.

"It's you?" I retorted, not sure how to react to the sudden adoration.

He pushed my hand aside and wrapped his extremely thick arms around me—I almost felt like I was in a vice—and he lifted me up and spun me around, grinning from ear to ear. It was nearly like being next to Gabriel except Daniel was a couple of inches taller, with the same strong jawline, dark shadow of facial hair, very broad muscular shoulders and carefully coifed, manicured wavy black hair that was slicked back with closely-shaven sides.

"You have blue eyes," I observed, surprised. Not sure why I was, really...all Gabriel ever mentioned about his brother was that he was *cut*, being that he was a personal trainer and I could see that. There was a resemblance but they each had different smiles. Gabriel's was sly, more hesitant and playful. And of course, the different eyes. Daniel, when he grinned it was a confident smile from ear to ear.

He set me down and brushed the rumpled sleeve of my sweatshirt. "Yes! We're not identical twins, as you can see...surprised my silly brother here forgot to mention that," he said, seeming to over pronounce each word. He shot his brother a mock scowl who in reply just flipped him the bird.

He looked back and me and grinned. "You know, you're just as beautiful as I saw you were—even more so in person."

"You saw me? Where?" Did Gabriel take some secret photo of me I wasn't aware of. I shot daggers at him but Daniel quickly dismissed that idea.

"No, no...nothing like that. I had visions of you. I didn't know you were *the* dragon but I knew you were special somehow. Recently I figured out who you must be, I had a vision of you before my brother left for Pineville. Now I really just thought at the time he was meeting his Princess Charming but this is *so* much better!" Daniel reached out and brushed a tendril of my strawberry hair back over my shoulder, while peering at my exposed neck.

I instinctively started to raise my hand to cover my dragon's clan mark but just let it fall. Clearly Daniel had seen it already if he knew where to look. "Just what I thought it would be. Beautiful." He brushed my hair gently back over my neck. "This really is quite an honor."

I heard Gabriel chortle behind us. "Don't weird her out anymore then she already is, Dan...okay?"

Daniel rolled his eyes. "Okay, okay. I supposed we should get this show on the road here, eh?" He did turn towards Maxxus briefly, giving him an approving once-over. It wasn't unusual in the dragon kingdom for the same gender to be attracted to one another, so

Maxxus took it in stride. "How exactly do you fit in with this rag-tag group here, if you don't mind my asking?"

"He guarded the portal where I went between realms," I explained. "He's one of the Court guardians."

"Was," Maxxus said, with a wry laugh. He held out his hand for Daniel who took it firmly and shook. "Maxxus."

"Daniel O'Donnell...*Seer* at your service," Daniel said, with a little bow.

I gave Maxxus a pitiful smile but he waved me off. "Don't worry, I'm here because I want to be. It's the right thing to do."

Daniel nodded in approval. "Good. We'll need all the help we can get."

I raised my brows expectantly at Daniel who just bit his lip. "Sorry, can't say anymore."

I sighed.

"So, what now?" I asked to Kiarra, as Gabriel and Daniel exchanged the official "man" hug where they grasp each other's forearms and lean in briefly while patting each other about three times on the back with the free hand. *Humans*. Pffft.

"Well, the town is in a little way, about a mile. We can drive in most of the way but there's a little carport with a handful of cars parked there and then we walk in the rest of the way," Kiarra explained. "We can shift while Gabriel and Daniel park the vehicles."

"Shift?" I asked, the taste sour on my tongue. "We have to shift? Why?"

"It's tradition, newcomers to Castle appear for the first time in their natural forms, as a gesture of trust and honesty."

I grumbled, crossing my arms over my chest and sticking out my lower lip. "I don't wanna."

I heard Maxxus attempt to stifle a laugh—unsuccessfully.

"Oh *stop*!" I said to him, but couldn't help smile as well. "My human form is natural. It's natural to any dragon," I protested.

"Oh come on, Leorah!" Daniel grasped my shoulders and looked me in the eyes, although I tried to avoid his stare. "Do it for me. I've never seen a dragon before looking like...a dragon. I've waited a long time...please?"

"Fuck. *Fine*." I relented, still refusing to look into Daniel's face.

"Oh good!" Daniel clapped his hands together excitedly. "Let's do this! Lead the way, Kiki!" he said, turning to Kiarra who just blushed.

I handed Gabriel the keys and insisted he drive, I was feeling a bit overwhelmed—again—and my cat was howling from the backseat. I instructed Maxxus take the front passenger seat as I was sure it was fairly uncomfortable for him being so tall cramped in the backseat, even for the short ride we were embarking on. Gabriel behaved himself but kept his lip bit and refused to look anywhere but the forest.

I leaned against the cool glass of the window and closed my eyes momentarily.

"This must be rather hard for you, huh?" Kiarra mused from next to me.

"You could say that," I said, putting my fingers to my temples and rubbing circles.

"Do you think she'll be safe there?" Gabriel inquired from the driver's seat.

"From the Court? Definitely. They have no idea it exists," Kiarra replied.

"Well that's good but from the…evil dream demon things."

"Dream demons?" Kiarra asked, uncertain.

"No…we don't know what it is." Gabriel said, with a sigh. We were driving at a snail's pace, Daniel straddling his motorcycle and walking it beside us. The ground was bumpy and overgrown with leaf litter and shrubberies but the landscape around us began to change. Abundant pine trees gave way to willows and birches, Kiarra insisted there was a reason for this; both trees had magical properties that enhanced the magic that surrounded and cloaked the hidden respite of Castle Danger.

I explained my dream visions and Gabriel piped in whenever he could and as we finished, Kiarra appeared very alarmed.

"There's no time to waste, we need to get to the Loremasters. Fast." She said, sounding urgent.

"So you know what it is, then?" I asked.

"No, not for sure. But I know who will…" Kiarra pointed at an overgrown tent off to the right that was covered in ivy and moss and instructed Gabriel to park inside. There was only one other vehicle parked—an old, army-green colored Jeep with no windows or doors. It was dusty and clearly hadn't been driven in a while.

Gabriel parked and Maxxus and Kiarra emerged from the car and began stripping off their clothes.

"Umm..." I said, as Daniel's eyes flew open wide when Maxxus lifted his shirt over his head, revealing a very trim but slightly muscular chest. I punched him lightly in the arm. "Don't stare!" I whispered to him, admonishing, but I had to admit my gaze lingered a bit too long on his lightly defined muscles as well.

"What?" Kiarra piped.

"Well...humans are modest and so am I...so..." I nodded behind the tent.

Maxxus chuckled, seeming embarrassed. "I am sorry; I didn't even think of it. Ladies first...."

I wrinkled my nose but begrudgingly followed Kiarra behind the tent. Gabriel had grabbed out our backpacks from the trunk and handed them to us.

"Robes really would be easier," Kiarra said, as we ducked behind the tent, tossing our bags on the ground. "This is a pain; don't you think?"

I shrugged. "I rarely shift anymore."

"You don't feel like you...need to?" she asked, pushing her pants down and stepping out of them. I spun around so I couldn't see. "You don't need to be embarrassed, you know."

"I know, but you remember I've been mocked for years for my form so you'll forgive me if I don't seem excited to change into it," I said dryly.

"Huh. You know my grandfather had similar aversions," she said. I heard the backpack zip open and shut, and a few moments later heard a growl and felt the energy in the air as she shifted to her dragon form—a rather attractive shade of deep blue with a wide wingspan and light blue eyes. "Ahh..." she sighed, with a smile of her toothy dragon mouth. "That feels better. Next."

I grumbled some more as I stripped down to my birthday suit, shoved the clothing items in my backpack and willed the change. I felt my appendages tingle as they changed to four feet with pink skin, and the slight disorientation as the rest of me shifted into my pink dragon self. Shifting was about the only time a dragon was vulnerable, and the thought made me insecure. I was relieved when it was over.

I stretched my iridescent wings to the side and up again, letting out a low growl.

"Admit it. That does feel good," Kiarra said, smiling.

The corners of my mouth turned up slightly. "Okay. A *little* bit."

Kiarra stared momentarily. "Those...wings. They are amazing like...well I don't know what. I have never seen anything like it."

I snarled. "No one has," I said.

We emerged from behind the tent, me following behind her, looking down at the ground as I walked. There was a gasp, and I felt warm human hands on either side of my face. I looked up, expecting Gabriel but it was Daniel who gazed into my eyes tenderly.

"Do not ever walk with that ashamed look. Forget what you knew in the past, the reality is you are amazing. Walk with your head held high, and make sure everyone who ever doubted you never forgets the name Leorah, got it?" He said it with such earnest and conviction I almost believed him.

"Something you've seen?" I asked.

He smiled. "I didn't need to have a vision. From everything my brother says about you, there's no doubt you're bound for greatness. He doesn't speak highly of just anyone. We're behind you, in all that you do. So if nothing else, remember that—you have friends, and a family. Okay? That alone should give you something to hold your head up on high for, right?"

I nodded. "Right."

Maxxus emerged from behind the tent then, in his very large, formidable green dragon form, and he towered over both Kiarra and I (she was larger than I, not surprising...most were), and Daniel fetched all our packs from behind the tent and slung them over his shoulder. "Shall we?" he motioned for Kiarra to lead the way.

Chapter 15

"It's just another two hundred paces or so," she instructed. "Well, for you," she said with a chuckle. Gabriel grabbed Sona's carrier and another bag from the car (Kiarra insisted we could get the rest later) and we followed Kiarra into the town.

Gabriel stayed by my side as we walked. We couldn't hold hands or anything, obviously since right now I didn't have them but he did wrap his arm around one of my wings that I held out at my sides. "They feel...like silk almost. So cool..." he mused. "I do hope you learn not to hate them, someday."

"As do I," I replied. I had to admit to myself, I did enjoy watching Gabriel's reaction to me in my dragon form. So often I was looked upon with scorn, and it was thoroughly nice to be myself—all myself—around someone. Even as a human I often had to hide who I was, really. I think he got the message because he nudged me with the side of his body. I grinned my dragon grin (which probably looked more like a snarl) and nuzzled his neck with the end of my nose.

"Oh my *gawd* stop! Just stop!" Daniel's excitable voice chimed in from behind us, Maxxus bringing up the rear. "That's just too cute."

"Shut up, Daniel!" Gabriel threw back at him. I just snorted a low growl, causing a steam of sparkles through my nostrils.

Kiarra chuckled from her position as lead. "Just a little further."

I began hearing sounds of life as the trees finally gave way to a handful of rather small, simple brick buildings.

"This is the outskirts of the town. The nymphs generally live closest to the forest because they fall ill when they're away from the woods for too long," Kiarra explained, shouting back at us.

The dwellings were nothing more than four walls, a couple of windows and doors with a wooden roof. There were a couple small children outside chasing after a small furry creature—I couldn't tell what it was—and they stopped in their tracks to stare at us as we walked in.

"Whoa...." one of them—a small boy with bright green eyes and hair so blonde it was nearly white—said as we walked past.

"Oh! Look! A fairy dragon!" the other one—a girl with the same white hair and eyes brown like a tree said, with glee, pointing right at me.

I looked around nervously, and tried to smile. The girl started slowly walking up to me.

"Hello. Who are you?" she asked out of curiosity. She was reaching out for something, but pulled her hand back nervously.

I let out an anxious cough. "I—um...I'm Leorah. Leorah James. What's your name?"

"Willow," she said. It was a moment before I could figure out what she was staring at: my wings. "What are you?"

"I'm a dragon. Ever seen one before?" I asked, feeling a bit calmer.

"I have but never one the color as you. Are those your *real* wings?" She asked, reaching out again.

Feeling a smirk on my face, against my better judgment I squatted down on my haunches to allow her access to my wings. She squealed in delight, and reached out carefully, stroking a section of my wings with her fingertips. "Wow! Leif, you need to try this!"

The boy—watching carefully from behind the girl—stepped forward slowly. I stretched out my wing a little to give him easier access. He swallowed anxiously, but reached out and touched my wing as well.

"Oh...it's...cold! And...smooth. Like water!" he mused.

Willow nodded. "Yeah! But they're strong—even though they look like fairy wings!"

I grinned. "You know many fairies?"

Willow smiled. "Yeah, my best friend is a fairy. You should meet her sometime! I bet she'd love you!"

"That would be fun," I said. The two children pulled away, and I folded my wings up back at my sides and stood back up.

"And, what are you, a Nymph?" Gabriel had been hanging back in fascination. He handed a very calm Sona over to Daniel who gently set the cat down on the ground nearby; she was glaring at him fiercely. She was not a happy cat.

Leif nodded. "Yeah. What are you?"

Gabriel looked expectantly at Kiarra, who just smiled and nodded. I knew what he was going to do. He held his palms together and after a brief moment, a small blob of water appeared between them.

Both children gasped. "Wow! How'd you do that?" asked Leif, his brown eyes wide.

Leif reached out, and Gabriel nodded. The boy ran his fingers through the water. "It is just water. That is so cool."

"Aren't there any other sorcerers here?" Gabriel asked the two children.

"Yes, but it's still always cool!" Willow insisted excitedly. Gabriel beamed widely.

From slightly behind me, I heard Daniel make a sniffing sound. I stepped back slowly. He was wiping his nose with the back of his hand, and he blushed when I caught him.

"I'm sorry," he said, in a hushed voice, from behind his palms as they covered his face. "It's just...after years of being ashamed of who he is, it's nice to see people...see him for the amazing person he is."

I smiled knowingly, watching the happiness radiate from Gabriel's face as the two children crowded around him as he conjured random elements and shaped balls of earth into different shapes. "I can relate," I said quietly.

Daniel gave me an earnest look, and placed his palm on what would be my upper arm. "I have a feeling you really do relate."

Kiarra came up beside Gabriel. "We need to get to town, now. You can come see us whenever you want, okay?"

The children nodded. Willow bounded up to me, pulling on one of my legs. "Can I have a ride sometime?"

"Ride?" I asked, confused. "Just like...around the woods?"

"I mean *fly*!" she said excitedly, jumping up and down.

I tried not to frown. "We will see." I didn't want to break her little heart and tell her that I couldn't fly.

She hugged my leg. "Bye, pink dragon!"

"'Bye, Willow."

We left the children to play outside in their yard, running and squealing around and continued on further into the town.

There weren't a lot of people out around this time but what there was is fairly interested in our presence. We came to a small village block, dotted with trees, tall and sprawling gardens and small, modest houses in all different materials...some looked like dirt or clay with flat roofs, others brick like a regular house you'd see in a city, some were like log cabins…there was no real rhyme or reason.

What people—and I use that term loosely—were out and about were murmuring and tittering about to each other and staring at us. I saw an orange dragon speaking to what I assumed was a yellow dragon in human form—he was young but shirtless and he had a tell-tale yellow mark of his clan on his right bicep. Across the gravel street was a rather stunning couple with multi-colored hair and—I'll be damned—*wings*.

"Are those…?" I whispered quietly to Kiarra as I nodded acknowledgement to them.

She grinned, and nodded. "Yes. Fairies."

I bit my lip and tried to contain my excitement. "Wow!"

Gabriel whispered to me: "See? I told you!"

The dragons were behind us now, whispering.

A couple of short—very short, *little people* short with blaze orange hair and musical laughter emerged from one of the gardens.

"G'day!" Both male, they made little bows as we passed. I nodded at them and tried to smile.

"Leprechauns?" Gabriel questioned Kiarra, quietly. She nodded. "Wow…" he said, trailing off, amazed.

Before we reached a two-story stone building, with regal gargoyle statues out front and a heavy wooden door, I gasped as something I never thought possible emerged.

"Oh my…" Standing on four hooves with snow-white fur and a silvery mane stood a horned horse—a goddamned *unicorn*—with a horn on its forehead that shimmered pearlescent in the afternoon sunlight.

"Afternoon, Donovan," Kiarra greeted.

"Kiarra!" he greeted in reply. "Good to see you back. I see you have friends?"

I stood there, mouth agape. I took a brief glance at my companions and saw the o's of surprise on their wide-eyed faces as well.

Kiarra nodded. "These here are the only reasons I left Castle Danger…"

Donovan the Goddamned Unicorn trotted up to me. He was shorter and smaller than I, but not by much. The top of his horn was nearly eye level with me, but his very presence was much larger than

I, if that made sense. Maxxus towered over him by nearly double but even he was in awe.

Donovan bowed his head at me slightly. "So you're the one. We've been waiting for you for a long time. Do let me know if there is *anything* I can do to assist you, will you?"

"I, uh, I mean," I stammered, dumbfounded. "You're a friggin' unicorn."

He chuckled—more like snickered and whinnied—but it was meant as a chuckle. "I guess my appearance may appear overwhelming to your kind. Yes, I am a Unicorn. Yes, there are others but not many left. We're scattered all over safe-havens like this one here around the world. I do hope we'll get to know one another as you stay here, yes?"

I nodded. "I would…like that."

He smiled—inasmuch as a horse could smile and let out a nickering sound. "Very good. I'll let you get to it. Finnian is waiting for you." He bowed again first at me, then towards my companions and trotted along his merry way along the gravel road.

"Really? A unicorn?" I was still at a loss, so I let out a peal of giggles.

Gabriel chuckled at me. "Ain't that a surprise?"

Kiarra just grinned. "Let's go see Finnian, and then I'll show you to where you're staying. There are guest quarters on the other side of the Square where you will all stay. I have a cabin nearby with a spare bed and an underground lair if they are not comfortable enough or if anyone wants…just until we know how long you all will be here. Then you will get assigned an actual stead where you can build your own home."

"Build?" I wrinkled my nose and snorted. "I don't build."

She laughed. "Sure you don't. But between an earth dragon, a sorcerer and yourself…I think you can conjure up enough magic to make suitable homes for all of you," she said, pushing open the large door.

"Umm…how am I supposed to fit through that?" Maxxus paused and wondered aloud.

I wondered the same thing. The door was large, and heavy but it was large enough to barely fit myself, was about the size of Kiarra— and there was *no* way Maxxus in his dragon form would be able to fit through. Actually, I didn't think there would be enough room for us all inside, period.

She smirked. "Trust me. It's magic."

I glanced back at Maxxus and we shrugged our faces, since we couldn't actually shrug shoulders.

Kiarra stepped in first and I watched somehow as the door magically appeared to adjust to her size. I raised a brow, watching the door shrink back down to normal and paused before I stepped through. It didn't have to move hardly at all for me and not at all for Gabriel or Daniel but opened wide for Maxxus.

Upon standing inside, we were in absolute awe.

The simple stone building outside was a grand, beautiful atrium inside, with a water fountain in the middle, shiny, sparkling marble floors and walls at least twenty feet high and long, winding staircases that led to separate areas of the building.

"Holy shit!" I mused out loud, hearing my curse echo through the walls. I bowed my head in shame, for some reason it felt wrong to be cursing in such an amazing building.

Needless to say, the inside was at least twice if not three and four times larger than the building appeared outside. I was about to comment but I didn't have to; Daniel did it for me.

"Ohmygawd, *really*? What kind of magic is this?" He elbowed his brother. "Gabe, can you do this? What *is* this? How did they...." He trailed off, bewildered.

"I don't think I could do this...how on earth?" Gabriel was just as awestruck. "It's like the damn T.A.R.D.I.S!"

I glanced at him and grinned; appreciating the reference. He just chuckled and winked back at me knowingly; it's always fantastic when another geek understands your geek references.

"It's spelled this way. Hard to explain how it works, but they take space from another dimension and...oh forget it. I don't even understand it! But even I still think it's awesome, no matter how many times I've seen it. Probably some sort of really complicated arcane magic," Kiarra said. "This way." She nodded down a hallway that headed east, dotted with different colored marble slabs and many pieces of fancy artwork on the walls. The hallway was so large that Maxxus comfortably moved through them, not hitting a single wall or painting.

We came to a room at the end of the corridor, and Kiarra didn't knock, but pushed the French-style doors aside and we entered a room that looked very much like a typical office, with a desk in front of the window, file cabinets and bookshelves filled with books everywhere.

The only thing that wasn't typical of an office was the tall, dark and wavy haired *God* perched on the desk, one of his long legs was tucked underneath him, and the other was resting on a chair seat. He was leaned over some kind of...something (a paper maybe), tapping a pen on his heart-shaped lips.

I tried hard to keep my jaw shut, but it was hard. Until I saw this man, I didn't really believe that a man could truly be *beautiful*. Gabriel was hot, Maxxus was gorgeous but this man was *beautiful*; like a sculpted work of art.

Clearly that observation wasn't lost on me: next to me. Daniel was muttering, wide-eyed, "Sweet Jesus..." and watching him intently. Gabriel and Maxxus both appeared to be uneasy.

I fixed my face to be serious. But it was hard.

Then he looked up, his eyes stared directly at me, the color of the Minnesota sky in the afternoon on a cloudless day. He smiled, and I swear, his eyes changed color...to somewhat of a spring green. And I was toast. I felt my knees start to buckle under me.

Kiarra must have sensed my troubles, because she came over and let me lean on her. "Don't look directly into the eyes," she muttered into my ear, "they'll bespell you."

"No shit," I said out loud. Everyone jumped, but the man on the desk just grinned. It was a wide, intoxicating smile but it wasn't bespelling like the eyes.

"Sorry about that," he spoke in a proper British accent. "You must be Leorah, the last pink dragon and company. So glad to meet you." He slid off the desk on onto his feet, bowing at the waist slightly before me. "I am Finnian, Head Loremaster of Castle Danger. Welcome!"

I smiled. "Thanks?" was all I could offer, desperately trying to avoid his gaze although I could swear they again changed color to a stormy gray.

"I generally wear contacts so that doesn't happen when I know newcomers are coming, but you are a little earlier then even I expected," he said, turning to the others. "My apologies," he said to Gabriel. "My eyes are a little—*enchanting*. Part of it is a Loremaster thing the other is just—well nevermind."

Gabriel forced a smile. "I didn't say anything..."

Finnian smirked. "I know..." he said with a wink. He and I exchanged a look and I just looked away innocently.

Finnian crossed the room to one of the file cabinets and pulled out some long, black velvet robes. "I know how you dislike your dragon form. I do hope upon your stay here you'll learn to overcome that discomfort, but for now...I want you to feel at ease. So please feel free to change to your human self."

I exhaled nervously. "Thank you." He handed the robes to Gabriel. He pointed at a second door in the office. I just noticed yet again how large the room was...large enough to fit three dragons the sizes of various semi-trucks, a seer, a sorcerer and a yeowling cat plus Finnian. It was the size of a library, and looked it too, now that I thought about it. It had just about as many books.

"You may feel free to release your feline...all animals are protected in Castle Danger, no harm will come to her, and she cannot leave our borders," Finnian said, nodding towards an uneasy Sona in her carrier, still being carried by Gabriel.

Gabriel looked to me, and I nodded. He set the carrier on the ground gently and released the latch, and Sona cautiously padded out, sniffing the air around her.

Finnian leaned over and allowed her to sniff his hand. She did, and bumped his fist with her head before laying down and rudely bathing herself in front of everyone. Finnian just snickered. "She feels at home...that's good."

He began describing his role and purpose as a Loremaster to those that remained, while I disappeared into the room attached to the office/library.

Another room that was larger than appeared, it was a bathroom with a large stone shower and a rather formidable bathtub before a window overlooking the grounds below.

Gabriel let out a whistle. "Not too shabby..." he said, setting the robes down an ivory colored chaise and winking at me before shutting the door behind me.

I let out a relieved breath, and willed myself to change back into a human, feeling a slight squeezing feeling as everything squished down to size. I was left on all fours on the marble floor, and I quickly stood up and reached for the robes. I held them up to admire; they were embroidered in silver along the edges with Celtic knotwork and vines, and appeared to be very carefully and lovingly made; no detail went untouched. I draped them over my shoulders, and latched the silver buckle at the neck and noticed unlike typical dragon robes, they had buttons down the front and sleeves. I also noticed a small pair of shorts remained on the chaise.

"Huh…it's almost like they were waiting for me." I stopped at that thought, before I grabbed them and slipped them over my legs. For all I know, they just may have been.

The robes fell over my body and surprisingly weren't matronly as most robes were, they hugged every curve but draped tastefully so not to reveal too much. They also had a large hood I could pull loosely over my head. I pulled my hair out and let it fall down my back. It was unfortunate I had no shoes but the floor was smooth and cool and felt good on my feet (after switching back from dragon, my human feet always felt a little sore after putting up with all that extra weight).

I emerged from the bathroom and joined my friends who were listening intently to Finnian talk.

"Did I miss anything?" I piped up, re-joining them.

Finnian smiled and clapped his hands together, looking pleased. "Oh they fit. Marvelous. Hildie will be so thrilled!"

"Hildie?"

"She's one of our town seamstresses, she makes ceremonial robes and dresses and all things of that sort," Finnian explained.

"What is she? Does she have some sort of powers to make things?" Gabriel questioned, while looking at me, I watched his eyes trail the length of my body. I tried to hide my enjoyment at that.

"Well, she's a dryad so…I assume so," he said, as if that explained it all.

Finnian explained a little more about the Loremasters, and about the history of Castle Danger as a magical safe-haven…it actually stood here longer than the actual unincorporated town did, but the earlier loggers of the area as they were being shipped in on boats looked at the rock formations and in the early fog of morning, they appeared like castle turrets overlooking the immense lake…hence the name Castle Danger. They took on the name themselves when it was named by humans figuring it was appropriate. But the safe-haven had actually existed for hundreds of years prior—this one and a handful of others scattered over this world (and a few more on a couple others—meaning other *planets*. I was so stunned I couldn't even speak at that one. Fairies and nymphs were one thing; *aliens* were another!), originally beginning as a safe place for the Loremasters to look and watch over history, and keep their records of happenings; later they became havens for mystical creatures who were threatened or being persecuted.

Finnian glanced at the wall clock overhead. "Well, it's almost time for Market. I do hope you'll come, after you get settled in of course," he said, nodding towards Kiarra. "Kiarra will show you to where you'll be staying, and I've already sent some one off to fetch the rest of your bags from your vehicle."

"How did—" I started, but just threw up my hands. "I'm sure you know pretty much everything."

Finnian smirked. "Nearly everything. I know you're plagued by something very frightening, but I'm afraid I cannot tell you what it is—yet."

"Yet?" Gabriel sounded hopeful. "You mean, you think you can, eventually?"

Finnian nodded. "These dreams…they are not normal; they aren't anything we've seen in a while. A *long* while. I will have to enter your mind to see what it is for myself before I can say anything else."

"Enter my mind? Like a Vulcan mind-meld?" I asked, swallowing nervously.

Daniel whooped. "Oh my god she's like a female Gabriel.…"

Gabriel glowered at his brother and punched him playfully in the shoulder.

"Whatever it is seems to happen while I'm sleeping," I explained.

"That is curious…but not unheard of. Whatever it is I suspect will have a difficult time getting through our borders, but if they're attacking in the dream-dimension well…that's another story. After you've settled in, would you mind terribly if I tried? I assure you, it won't be painful, it will feel like you're asleep and in a dream that I just happen to be in."

I nodded. "Yes. Please."

"Is it safe?" Gabriel asked cautiously.

"Oh, quite…for someone inexperienced it would be quite dangerous but I've been doing this for…well a long time," he said with a laugh. "Kiarra?"

"Are you all ready?" she asked us, and we nodded.

"In honor of Mabon, after Market we are serving a feast in the town square followed by music and dancing today…not everyone follows the traditions but even if you don't, it's a lot of fun. I hope you'll consider going to that as well. It's a good way to meet a lot of the people of our town."

Living on Earth for so long, I completely forgot about Mabon...which is basically a minor fall holiday in the Pagan calendar. A lot of dragons were moving away from the old traditions but we still celebrated the bigger ones...Mabon usually warranted an official dinner at the palace, some spelled wine and the castle walls would be decorated in reds and burnt oranges and sunny golds.

"Do I have to be in dragon form?" I asked.

Finnian grinned. "Only if you wish to."

I cheered. "Yay!"

He snickered. "It is nice meeting all of you. Do let me know if the accommodations aren't acceptable, we will find you something more to your liking."

"I'm sure it will be fine," I said as Kiarra led us out the doorway, back down the expanded hallway and outside again.

"It's just a little ways away," she said, leading us through what I assumed was the outskirts of town. We encountered no more people or...magic beings but just backsides of brick and wooden buildings until we reached a long, log cabin type building with a handful of doors on the outside placed every few feet or so.

"There are hallways connecting all the rooms, like a hotel," she explained, as she hovered her hand—or, her front foot—in front of a doorknob of the first door and it opened automatically. She stepped aside and I was the first to step in.

Although the outside looked about the size of a small motel, the inside again was much larger. I stood in a rustically-decorated living room, complete with a log-trimmed sofa (it was like a cushion set on stripped, sanded and polished birch logs), a tall stone fireplace and all the amenities of home like a fridge, a wood burning stove, cabinetry, etc. The one thing I noticed—no electricity. Or it didn't seem to have electricity. I wasn't quite sure how the fridge was powered, then....

"The guest rooms are totally empty, so you have your pick of however many you want. Share, or not—there is plenty of room. There are two bedrooms to each living space, with full sized beds, bookshelves, a desk and even wi-fi hookups," Kiarra explained.

"Wi-fi?" Daniel echoed my surprise. "But there's no electricity?"

Kiarra chuckled. "Well, there is...it's just powered by magic and spells. We're not hooked up to any power grid. Most here in Castle Danger choose not to use modern conveniences—the Loremasters don't have much of a choice, they kind of have to—but most of the residents choose not to, although they can at any time if they wish. We have plenty of oil lamps, lanterns—whatever is needed to make you comfortable," she said. She crossed the other side of the room to a door that opened to a long hallway, and opened it. This exit didn't seem to require any magic. "As long as you're in the building, you will not need any magic to enter. But once you leave you will need to be attuned to the doorknob to allow entry. I will do that with each of you before Market if you should decide to go of course. No pressure. I am going, however so I will need to have you attuned before then, if that's okay?" She looked at each of us in turn and we all nodded.

Sona came patting through the doorway and leaped up on the plush green velveteen sofa and curled up with a satisfied sigh. I chuckled.

"Okay, clearly this is Leo and Sona's room...the rest of you just pick wherever you want with whoever or no one, whatever," Kiarra said. Daniel and Maxxus shuffled out the doorway, leaving the rest of us behind.

"I'm staying here, obviously," Gabriel said. "I'll sleep on the floor if I have to."

"You really think it'll come to me here? There seems to be a lot of magic protection here, I don't know—" I began, but Gabriel cut me off.

"No. Even Finnian said himself he wasn't quite sure what it was. So until we know for sure, I'm not taking any chances. I don't care if it's decent or not— "

It was Kiarra's turn to cut him off, "Gabriel, you don't have to be defensive, we don't have the same rules and hangups in our society as humans. You wish to stay with Leo, no one will even bat an eye, I assure you." I glanced over at the rest of the group and sure enough, no one was batting an eye but Maxxus did have a curious look on his face. I mouthed a *"What?"* at him and he just forced a smile and shook his head, indicating *nothing* or *never-mind.*

Gabriel crossed his arms across his chest and fixed his mouth in a thin line, appeased. "Okay, then."

"Relationships are different to magic folks. Some are polyamorous. Others are not. Some have been together for years, others only a few days. Some bounce around with each other, some stay within their race and others don't care. It's...whatever makes you happy. Plus, even though the Order is new to you, Leo—we've all known about it for some time. So we're aware of Gabriel's function to you, if nothing else. It is all completely fine," Kiarra explained.

I frowned. "Sure wish someone had clued *me* in on all that," I muttered under my breath. Kiarra heard me but she pretended not to notice.

"Well...I'll start with the other boys and get them attuned. You get settled in. Your things will be here shortly," Kiarra said, disappearing through the doorway. "See you in a bit," she said, leaving Gabriel and me alone in the room.

"Wow...so..." Gabriel said uncertainly, throwing himself down on the couch. "This is...something, huh?"

I crossed my arms over my chest and observed my surroundings. The colors were warm and comforting, maroon and rust reds, pine green and everything appeared so rustic. You could almost feel the energy from each piece of furniture, each piece of artwork. I tip toed across the room and held my hands over a glass oil lamp, the globe around artfully formed and colorful on top of an iron base. I closed my eyes and let my hands hover a moment. I could almost *see* the person who made it...small, colorful wings, small, feminine features and a pretty smile, with sky-blue eyes. I smiled at the thought. Then my eyes flew open. Wait...I couldn't really be seeing who made this could I? I've never seen anyone here before, how could I—

Gabriel cut my train of thought off. "What are you thinking about?"

I let my hands fall to my sides and shrugged. "Oh. Nothing. It's a nice little lamp."

His brow wrinkled, unconvinced. "Right."

My feet were starting to get a little cold, and I could feel the hardness of the wooden floor under them. I was really wishing for some sandals right now. I glanced down at my feet and caught a glimpse at my boobs under the slinky fabric. It was fairly unforgiving in the modesty department, and you could see my nipples quite well. Sure, many of the beings here didn't have the same hang ups as I did but suddenly, I was very much wishing for my bra, new underwear and my black flip-flops. I crossed my arms back over my chest to hide my chest, and I sauntered to a room that was attached on the west side.

It was simple a room, with its own little wood burning stove (I took it that no one used natural gas or propane heaters here) and a full-size bed with handcrafted navy blue quilt, with stars sewn on to it and fluffy pillows. The same bare, polished logs that made up the frame of the sofa and tables in the next room made up the walls of this bedroom, except for the opening on the north side. Gold drapes adorned each side. I peeked outside, under me was a gravel path, alined with wildflowers and willow trees. A human (at least, they appeared to be human) appeared with a wooden wheelbarrow with bags of flowers and vegetables sticking out of them. A small child joyfully trailed behind her, they both had the same blonde hair and golden skin. The adult paused and turned my way. She caught my eye and offered a nod and small smile.

I responded with a little wave, and she and the child continued on their way.

"Well, at least everyone seems friendly," I said under my breath. I pulled the curtains shut over the window, blocking out the afternoon sunlight. I heard a light *thud* and swiveled around to see its origin.

"I'll be damned..." My backpack and duffel bag along with a bag of Gabriel's and his laptop case magically had appeared on the bed. I called to Gabriel.

"What the—they weren't here when we got here, were they?" he asked, amazed and I shook my head.

"No, they weren't," I said in confusion.

Gabriel grinned. "*Awesome*! Must have been a spell!" He clapped his hands together, giddily and opened up his case, producing the computer and setting it on the bed. "Looks fine. Wow!"

I just shrugged, not quite sure how to react to all this new sorcery. However, I did smile to myself, seeing how happy it made Gabriel; like just a short while ago, when he was openly able to perform magic for the little boy on the outskirts of town. I reached for my duffel bag and unzipped it, relieved to see that my stuff too was unscathed. I rummaged for some new underwear and my sandals at the bottom. I pulled them out happily, and went back in for a new t-shirt and jeans.

"You're not going to wear that?" Gabriel asked, sounding disappointed, his lower lip slightly puffed out.

I smiled wryly. "Why?"

"Because it's...well..." he coughed uncomfortably, his eyes involuntarily betraying him as they trailed to my breasts.

I shrugged. "Well, it *is* comfortable, except for the lack of underwear."

"There's no underwear?" Gabriel let out a groan, covering his face with his hands and uttering a few unintelligible words. He threw himself down on the bed. "I can't take it. Just…take me. Now."

I raised a brow. "Really?" Feeling mischievous, I sauntered over to him on the bed, unbuttoning one of the buttons near the neck as I sat next to him, exposing some of my human flesh to him.

Gabriel reached out but I swatted his hand away. "Ha. Forget that, Kiarra will be back any second," I said, leaning over to place a kiss on his forehead. He tried to grab my waist and pull me back towards him but I yanked myself away.

"Tip on dealing with dragons? Do *not* start something you cannot finish. It's not a pretty picture," I advised, leaning over him and grabbing my clothing. I headed for the small room next to this one which I assumed was the bathroom, leaving him to swear and groan. I laughed, shutting the door behind me. "We *do* bite!"

It was a bathroom, with a claw-footed tub along one wall, a small bowl sink next to that and a mirror over it, shelves lining both walls. I assumed this was a combination of a bathroom and closet, and there was s door that undoubtedly led into the second bedroom. I peeked my head in momentarily, it was essentially the same bedroom except with the furniture on opposite sides to this one, with green and red linens and trees on the quilt instead of stars.

I pulled my head back in and noticed a stack of linens already taking up two of the shelves. I reached for one, and noticed it was the same soft velvet as the robes I was already wearing, though this time in a deep midnight blue. Under was another set in deep purple, and red, and a couple more in white.

I grabbed the set of red and tossed into the bedroom at Gabriel on the bed. "Here. I'll wear these if you were those."

He held them up in front of him. "Really?"

I nodded. "Do you have a jacket or anything?"

He groaned and slapped his palm against his forehead. "No…"

"Well, there you go. They're deceptively warm," I said. I shut the door behind me and pulled on my own underwear, twisted myself into one of my ugly beige bras (*when all this was over, I* really *needed to get new underwear* I thought to myself) and pulled on my jeans. I took the robes off momentarily to pull on my t-shirt and thought again. The luscious fabric felt *really* good against my skin. I tossed the tee on the floor and was satisfied with the jeans and sandals (and of course, underwear). For some reason, the robes felt a little more appropriate for this town (and I was pretty sure there wasn't anyone with a t-shirt that said "Real Vampires Don't Sparkle" on it, and being I wasn't 100% sure if there were vampires here or if they really existed, I didn't want to accidentally piss one off. I liked my blood inside my body, thank you very much).

I exited the room to see Sona pat in, looking content, tail upright and twitching on her end. She jumped up on the bed and made herself comfortable on one of the pillows.

"Perhaps we'll be switching rooms," I said, with a laugh.

Gabriel appeared in the door frame, the red robes draped over his broad shoulders. He scowled. "Is there another color? I feel like *Little Red Riding Hood.*"

I snorted. "There's green."

He considered this and nodded. I grabbed for the green ones and we exchanged.

"These really are nice," he said, rubbing the fabric of the sleeve with the opposite palm. "Whoever made these really put a lot of work into them."

I nodded. "Yes." There was a knock at the door to the hallway. I figured it was Kiarra and I hollered for her to come in.

"We found more robes and—oh," I said, surprised to see the tall stature of Finnian in the doorframe.

He gave me a pleasant smile and nodded at Gabriel who joined me. "Would you mind if I spoke to Leo, alone for a moment?"

Gabriel appeared hesitant and opened his mouth to say something, but I shot him a pointed look. "Umm…I'll go see where my brother is staying. Be right back," he said, disappearing out the doorway but not before shooting Finnian a stern look.

Finnian chuckled. "I'm sorry," I said, "he's—"

"No need, no need," Finnian said, sitting down on the sofa and gesturing for me to sit next to him. I did. "Are the rooms to your liking?"

I nodded. "They're very beautiful."

"Do you have everything you need? Anything you need—we can procure for you. Just let me know, and it's yours."

"But I don't have any money here, and—"

He waved me off. "Leorah, as I explained, we do not use currency here. Just barter and trade for goods and services. You might not feel your purpose yet, but you will. Just your magic alone could be a great deal of help to a lot of the people here."

I bit my lip and looked away, ashamed. "Um...well I'm not sure about that. See, I just found out that I even—"

He waved me off again, a bright smile on his jovial face. "I already know about your situation. Remember, it's my purpose to know. You've been using magic your whole life, you just don't know it because you've been told not to. You just need some confidence and a few pointers and you'll pick it up in no time."

I looked at him uncertainly. "Right. And you know this...how? How do you know all this...stuff? Are you a Seer, too? What exactly *is* a Loremaster? Are you human? Fairy? *Alien*?" I tried to add a jesting tone to the last word but I'm sure it didn't come out that way, because for all I knew, maybe he *was* an alien.

Finnian chuckled. "Well, yes, I'm human. Partially..."

I raised a brow. "How does that work?"

Finnian grinned easily but ignored my comment. He reached out his hand slowly, and attempted to touch my cheek. I fought the urge to pull away.

With soft fingers he gently caressed my cheek. "Very dark. Very dark indeed." I watched in amazement as his eyes changed from gray to a deep brown.

"May I...look into your mind?" He asked. "I sensed the dark magic when you first entered, but I couldn't be sure what it was. I conferred with Ceceline, she fears it may be a kind of magic we haven't seen in sometime. A very frightening, evil magic."

I put a hand to my mouth and gasped but nodded. "Will I feel it?"

Closing his eyes, Finnian smiled. "No, you won't feel anything." He cupped my cheek with his palm and shut his eyes. I sat there, still as a statue, intently watching his beautiful face. His eyes twitched under the lids, like he was in rapid-eye movement sleep; his lips formed muttering words but nothing came out.

It felt like forever, but finally, he pulled away. His eyes flew open, looking alarmed, in a pale blue. "This is...worse than I feared."

"What?" I squeaked.

"You've been touched by the Shadows."

"Huh? Shadows aren't dangerous!" I glanced at the ground to see the dark silhouette of myself on the couch, sitting down.

Finnian managed a wry smile on his frightened face. "Well, no, our shadows aren't dangerous. I speak of being in the shadow realm..."

"Shadow realm?"

Finnian let out a sigh. "Long ago as you know, dragons chose to separate themselves from humans not only to protect dragons but humans as well as some dragons wanted to dominate the human race, use them as slaves and," he paused, shuddering, "a food source."

I grimaced. "Ew."

"Yes," he agreed. "These dragons were banished to an empty realm, the shadow realm. Realms are basically just layers of different places, layered on top of one another. The realm where you go when you die, Earth that we live on right now, the dragon realm, and in between both those realms lies a small, unhabited realm that is hard to get to, even harder to leave. It is dark and desolate…anyone who goes there is consumed by Shadows. It's basically devoid of energy, of life. Some people have called it the void realm as well."

I winced. "That…does not sound good."

"No. You turn dark and evil. But, you turn very powerful. If you can find someone to do your bidding on the other side, you can be very destructive," Finnian explained.

"How do they do that?" I asked.

"Well, there are only a few times they can get through…'in between times'. In between dark and light, awake and asleep."

I gasped. "Is—is that what is happening to me?"

"Not entirely. My guess would be that they've recruited a Dreamwalker. From what I saw of your mind there was no portal, there still needs to be an actual portal between realms—between *any* realm," Finnian said. "But the Dreamwalker would still be bound to shadow realm "rules" as it were. So you must have been half awake, half asleep…and it was chased away by light. Either by the light itself, or by the fact that the light woke you up, this I can't tell."

Feeling a sudden shiver, I pulled the robes tighter over me.

Finnian placed a comforting hand on my shoulder. "Don't worry, I think you'll be safe here. We should be able to put a spell on you to ward off dream invaders just in case."

"But—why me? And how?"

"Well, that is an easy answer. It's an ugly world to live in but if they can figure out how to break down the barriers, they could easily wreak havoc on all realms—Earth and dragon. Someone like you on their side would guarantee the scales tip in their favor," Finnian rested his hands in his lap and adjusted his long body. "As for how…well, I'm sure they have someone here that has marked you somehow. It would have to be someone close to you in order for them to get close enough to place a strong enough shadowmark on you."

I jumped up from my seat. "Oh my *god*! Kit!" I described to Finnian everything with Kit, how Gabriel felt the dark presence at the shop, about the storms and her going missing.

Finnian exhaled slowly, resting his head in his hands and scrubbing a hand over his face. "Yeah, that's probably how they got to you. The question remains: how did they get to *her*? And…it doesn't make sense, if she went through that portal, she would have gone to the dragon realm, yes?"

I thought back to the time I went through the portal, and it was already energized but neither Maxxus nor Nicodemus had seen anyone go through. I told Finnian.

"That certainly is…curious. And you're sure these two are trustworthy? Do you believe they'd tell you the truth if someone had come over or not?"

Immediately, I nodded. "Well…Maxxus of course. Nicodemus is bound by honor and codes and tradition, I don't think he would lie. It could mean his job."

Finnian shrugged. "The portal was destroyed, correct?"

"I think so, at least that's what Kiarra said would happen," I replied.

"If she used the potion we gave her, then yes, it was. More or less. Hmm…" Finnian scratched his chin in thought. "What I don't understand is, the storms. Even if someone from the shadow realm had come over, there is no way they'd have any Earth magic. The Shadow consumes every part of you, you turn into a shadow."

"What if they were controlling someone else?" I offered.

"Perhaps…" Finnian drummed his fingers on his thigh. "I think it's more likely that it was someone else. There is…another force out there, after you."

It was my turn to facepalm myself. I slapped my hands against my face and groaned. "*Fuck*!" I glanced up, sheepishly. "Sorry."

Finnian patted my leg, and stood up with a grin. "Don't worry. I can appreciate a good F-bomb. We will figure that out, too. Likely it's a dragon—or a lot of dragons—who have a chip on their shoulder about you. Probably working with a nasty warlock. In the meantime, the market is happening soon, and then the festival. You will be there?"

I hadn't discussed it with the others, but I nodded. "Can't speak for anyone else, but it sounds fun to me."

"Great," Finnian said. "You had better save me a dance."

I snickered. "I...don't really dance."

"Don't worry, it'll come to you. Like your magic. Farewell." He waved and went to open the door to let himself out but instead it opened and he stepped back, as a glowering Gabriel stepped in. Finnian greeted him warmly, but Gabriel let out a grunt as he closed the door on Finnian.

"What's that about?" Gabriel inquired grumpily.

"Bad news. Looks like we're dealing with an old force that hasn't been seen in a thousand years," I said, with a sigh, as Gabriel sat down next to me. The door opened and shut again, and Daniel let himself in.

"Mind if I—oh, hell, I'm going to anyway," Daniel said with a laugh, setting himself down on the matching chair next to us. He tucked his legs under him and sat cross legged. I was about to inquire about how he did that comfortably with his being so tall, but Gabriel interrupted.

"What?"

I sighed, and explained to him what Finnian told me, about the shadow realm. I looked back and forth and saw both brothers' eyes widen.

"Oh...shit."

"Why now is my question," I said, shaking my head, feeling stress build up in my neck and head.

"You are the first pink dragon in centuries, they're probably after your power," Daniel explained, sounded rather knowledgeable.

Gabriel raised a brow at his brother. "Something you already know?"

Daniel grinned sheepishly. "Maybe? Look at it though—when was the last time Finnian said we have seen anything from these Shadow dragons? 998 years ago?" I nodded. "Well...when did the last pink dragon live?"

"Fifteen—wait. Oh wow." Gabriel wrapped his arm around my shoulder and pulled me in close to his chest. "He supposedly died almost one-thousand years ago...."

"Don't worry, that's what we're here for." Daniel said, sounding rather confident.

I gave him a wry smile. "I wish I had that confidence."

He patted my leg and chuckled. "Trust me, I have enough for all of us."

Chapter 16

The little hidden village of Castle Danger was amazing—like stepping back in time, or into a Renaissance Festival complete with all sorts of colorful, crazy characters you wouldn't believe were actually real.

We had spent about an hour or so wandering around the Marketplace, viewing and sampling the local faire. Of course, Kiarra was a regular so she had a general shopping list of things to gather. Her barter was her water magic, she could water crops, clean hard to reach objects, making her rather useful around the town. She knew everyone, and everyone knew her and she was greeted with warm smiles.

Gabriel, Daniel and I followed closely behind her, in awe of the makeshift market in the center of town (and the center of the town held the Loremasters building, a library, a school surrounding a square dotted with trees and flowers). Several booths were covered by canvas and wooden frames, others just sat in chairs with crates of goods like vegetables behind them. Artists, jewelers, weaponsmiths and metal sculptors, a butcher selling various meats which, I won't lie, being a dragon I lingered at a bit longer than the others. Farmers were also selling their flowers and crops, vendors selling tapestries and clothing…it was all overwhelming.

Kiarra explained to me that generally every couple of days they had a Market and generally it specialized in one thing or another: food, or clothing or art but every other week they did one where everyone gathered so everyone could gather everything at once so this one was a bit more overwhelming than most.

What surprised me most, was that everyone already seemed to know me. Each vendor—no matter what species they were—gasped a little when they saw me and seemed to struggle for words before offering a friendly smile. It was far from the disgusted greetings I was used to getting.

A booth selling jewelry and small trinkets spoke to me. I paused, fingering the stones artfully wired on to chains that hung from branches the vendor had fashioned into jewelry stands. Gabriel and Daniel were a couple booths down, admiring some swords that were being sold by what I assumed was a green dragon who had made them. I wondered if Maxxus could do anything like that, being green himself. It occurred to me that not only wasn't Maxxus present for the market but for someone who just gave up an awful lot to assist me in my time of need, I didn't know much about him. I frowned. I would have to rectify that.

"Something troubling you, dear? The necklace not to your liking?" An older woman with a weathered face but beautiful, sky-blue eyes, wearing a bright colored scarf tied around her long, brown hair, salted with white and on her ears hung large brass hoops. She reminded me a bit of a Gypsy, and I wondered if that is what she was indeed.

I noticed that in my daydreaming I was fondling a beautiful pink crystal prism, hanging from a woven chain. I turned the stone to see it catch the late afternoon sun's rays, and rainbows danced delightfully on my hands. I smiled. "No, actually. I was just…thinking about something else. But this is really quite lovely."

A pleasant smile spread across her face. "How appropriate. A pink crystal for the pink dragon."

I raised a brow, a question burning on my tongue. I opened my mouth to voice it, but wasn't sure if I should.

"Go ahead, dear. Speak your mind. I can tell something is on it," she said insistently.

I exhaled. "Well…I'm just wondering. I've been here a total of about four hours now and everyone seems to know who I am…but I don't know anything about anyone else, including what everyone is. There are *unicorns* and faeries here! I had no idea this stuff existed! Yet everyone already seems to know who I am. It's a bit…"

"Unsettling?" she offered when I couldn't supply the right word. I nodded. "Yeah."

"Amongst us are a great many seers and prophets. Your face has shown up in many of our visions. You're like an old friend to many of us," she explained, with a warm smile.

I forced a smile. "That's great to know…but…I don't even know *myself*, how can everyone else know me?"

"We know you're capable of great things," she explained. "Even if you've been told in the past that you aren't capable of anything."

"So, can you tell me what you've seen of me? And if it's not rude of me to ask...what are you?" I asked.

"Not rude at all. Why, I am human but also an alchemist. That's someone who is able to imbue everyday objects with magic and potions...things like that. I also have the Sight on occasion but, it's rare and fickle," she added with a laugh.

"An alchemist? So you do actually have powers?" I asked. I thumbed the pink crystal, feeling a certain buzz about it. A relaxing force, almost.

"I do, after many years of learning and teaching the craft." She nodded towards the crystal I was still holding. "Take it, dear. It's clearly calling to you"

I dropped it quickly, letting it clink against another behind it. "Oh no. I couldn't. I don't...I don't have anything to offer you. I'm supposed to have magic but I know nothing about it." I frowned sullenly.

"Perhaps not now, but you will. I have seen it," she said.

I perked up. "You have? What did you—I suppose you can't tell me."

She shook her head. "I see the dark. And... I see your friends. Everything is sort of cloudy right now when I try to call it."

I blinked. It was cryptic at best. "The dark...what is this you speak of?"

She shrugged. "That I cannot say. It could be figurative or literal, I don't know. Negativity, maybe. But I've seen your faces long before you ever arrived here, even if I didn't know your names. I wish I could say more..."

I nodded knowingly. "I know, you can't."

"In time....in time." She gently pulled the crystal and it's chain off the branch and held it in one hand, and reached out for my palm. She gently pried my fingers open and let it slide into my open hand and placed them shut. "This is yours. You already pulled the energy out of it. It needs you. You are one. Take it. It could never be suited for anyone else."

I grasped the cool metal and smooth stone and placed it over my heart. I felt a tingle, a surge of...happiness. "I don't know how to thank you."

She smirked. "Dear, just your name will do. Knowing that this old woman isn't just seeing make-believe in her mind is compensation enough, believe me."

I chuckled. "I am Leorah. On Earth I go by Leorah James. Back home it's...well."

She chuckled, with a flourish of her hand that meant she understood. "I have heard Dragon spoken. It sounded like shrieks and grunts. Leorah is good enough." She explained, with a nod of acknowledgment. "I am Esmè Romanov. Please, come and see me again sometime. I always love the company."

I smiled warmly at her, opening up the chain and pulling it over my head and letting the pretty crystal rest on my chest. I grasped it with a palm and felt its positive energy. "Thank you, again. This is just what I needed."

"Anytime, dearie." She waved, and began tending to the next customer behind me.

I glanced around the market for Gabriel. I grinned to myself as he was surrounded by a handful of children, summoning water balls in his palms and shooting them at some bushes that were nearby. The kids of all different species (one had wings, another had pointy ears—fairies? Elves? *Vulcans? Oy...*) giggled with delight but still didn't look as enthralled as Gabriel. His grin was ear-to-ear and his brown eyes positively sparkled, even through the lenses of his glasses.

I decided to leave him be. I scanned for some place to sit and noticed Maxxus sitting at a picnic table outside of the market, where several people (and one unicorn) had gathered to eat or drink or just chat. Maxxus, however sat by himself, his hands folded on the table as he looked around solemnly. I dodged customers and made my way over to him.

"Leo," he said, surprised as I sat across from him at the table. "Why aren't you..." he gestured off towards Gabriel.

I took a glance back at him, he had now advanced to balls of Earth (mud, really) and the kids were daring to stick their hands in them, gleefully squealing as they got mud on their fingers. "I think I'll let him be for a moment."

Maxxus smiled half-heartedly. "It must be nice to finally be able to be who you really are after so long."

I shot him a knowing look of *"Duh"* and he chuckled. "I guess you would know about that, huh?"

I sighed, leaning in towards him to speak to him easier over the cacophony of the voices at the market. "Maxxus, really. What the *fuck* are you doing here?"

He winced. "I told you. I'm here to help protect you. I'm a guard. It's my purpose."

I narrowed my eyes at him. "But—shit, Maxxus...you gave up *everything*! You're a fugitive, now! You know very well what could happen if they catch you!"

Maxxus just shrugged his broad shoulders and looked away. "It was the right thing to do." He turned back to me and stared at me intently. "I am confident in you, that whatever lies ahead you will succeed and put things back the way they are supposed to be." He snorted. "Going after a dragon who hasn't done anything? If they've done it to you, think how many others they've done that to? No..." he shook his head, his mouth in a solemn line. "That's not what I signed up for." He folded his fingers together and rested his hands on the table. He shot me a smile. "Besides, I'm really not giving up much. Being a guard was so damned boring. This is sure to be more entertaining."

I smirked. "I thought the King and Queen were decent?"

Maxxus shrugged. "I don't know them well, but I don't think they are necessarily the problem. At least not the whole problem. Some of the House is...well a bit too narrow-minded for my taste. Bad influences."

I snorted. "You got that right." I sighed, glancing around us, the market, and the town. "Can you believe this?"

Maxxus shook his head. "This is...definitely worth it. I could find solace here, finally." He gave me a half-smile. "I think you could too."

I shrugged. "Maybe. But is there *Star Trek*?"

Maxxus threw his head back and laughed. "If not, I'm totally out!"

"We're still on for that marathon, you know. I have my phone...it's on." I said, patting my chest (I had tucked my phone in my bra, as the robes didn't have pockets...that was something I was going to have to look into).

He grinned. "Are you sure he—" Maxxus gestured towards Gabriel, "—will be okay with that?"

"Okay with what? I do what I want." I said defiantly, crossing my arms over my chest.

Maxxus chuckled. "Evil forces be damned, no one crosses Leorah, right?"

I shook my head from side to side. "Nope!" We both laughed a moment, and Maxxus grew silent.

"Your grandfather...he's probably worried sick," Maxxus said, with a sad sigh. He scratched at a knothole in the wood atop the table mindlessly.

I frowned. "Yeah...I wish I could talk to him."

Maxxus looked up. "You know that's too dangerous, right? If they catch you..." he shuddered, "I can't even bear to think what they might do to him."

"I do know. I would never risk it."

He gave me a somber face. "I am sorry. I can't bear to see either of you be hurt. You know I hold him in the highest esteem. He...turned me into a great dragon, when so many just dismissed me. My family included."

I bit my lip to hide my pitiful look. "I know what that's like."

"Only one other dragon refused to write me off. One other..." he trailed off thoughtfully, looking away towards the trees as if clearly recalling a memory. I sat silently, waiting for him to share it with me. When he didn't after a moment, I just let it go.

"That is also part of the reason I'm here. To be there for you when he can't. He would want it that way," Maxxus explained somberly.

"You sure? You sure he'd want you risking everything?"

He was nonchalant. "I did what I had to do. Someday, you'll understand why." He smiled and looked away. I eyed him suspiciously, but didn't press.

Maxxus was clearly a dragon of many secrets and I wasn't going to get any answers today.

I felt a cool breeze then breeze across my neck, sending cold shivers down my spine. "Wow...that came out of nowhere." I pulled the hood up of the robes some and pulled the neck higher towards my hair line.

Maxxus stood up, looking at something behind me. The breeze turned into a gale at that point, blowing my hair out in all directions. I struggled to pull it in and away from my face. I pulled the hood over my head and had to keep it in place.

"Leo...my god." Maxxus darted around the table and directly in front of me. A loud clap of ominous thunder sounded then, causing the marketplace goers to jump and scream, startled. I had to grab

Maxxus by the elbows to shove him aside—a futile attempt because he was solid as a rock—to see what he was shielding me from.

My mouth fell open, seeing the pitch-gray and black clouds roll in from out of nowhere, and start swirling just outside of the market place.

"Oh my god..." was all I could utter, feeling stunned at the frightening sight. Just moments ago it was sunny and joyful with a warm tickle of a breeze. Almost like that storm I encountered at that truck stop.

"Oh...fuck." I said. Maxxus kept trying to push me in back of him but I kept shrugging his arms off to the side.

"Leo—get back. This is *not* normal," he insisted.

"No shit," I retorted, sounding more snidely than I had intended.

"*Leo!*" Gabriel dashed up to me at that moment, with Daniel hot on his heels. He grabbed my hands and pulled me closer. Maxxus relented and stepped back.

"It's.... it's the same thing that was in Pineville, isn't it?" I asked him, feeling the trepidation shake my tone.

Gabriel nodded fervently. "Shit, Leo, this is bad. We're supposed to be safe here. There are safeguards in place, I thought."

"Everyone!" Finnian had leaped up on a table at that point, attempting to address the frightened and dumbfounded people in the marketplace who were speaking frantically at one another, some of them walking rather quickly in the opposite direction of the storm and others just staring in awe at the sudden storm front. "Take cover, quickly in your homes! Anyone that can harness the weather, I need you, quickly."

I swallowed the bile raising in my throat, and rubbed my forearms with my palms, trying to calm the hairs that were standing on end. Most people scattered frantically, assumedly to their homes, a handful stayed behind in the square, looking frightened but determined.

"Can you do anything?" Daniel questioned his brother, panicked.

Gabriel stared open-mouthed at the twister that was starting to form, at the lightning that was shooting straight out but not touching the ground. "I.... I don't know what I can do. I can summon it...I can't make it disappear."

"Can you...summon it to you and send it elsewhere?" Daniel questioned as Gabriel just stared blankly.

"But this is not natural. This is magic-made, right?" I pulled on his robes and forced him to stare me right in the face instead. "*Right*?"

Gabriel looked away from the storm momentarily. "Yes...I feel the energy. It's..." Gabriel shuddered, and he didn't have to finish his sentence to know what he meant.

"That's what I thought." I inhaled deeply, and pulled away from Gabriel.

Maxxus grabbed my arm. "Leo! What are you *doing*?" I pulled away.

I pointed at the square, at the various sorcerers and witches throwing their hands up at the swelling storm, shooting random magics at it and having no effect. "This. I can end this. I have to. It's here...for me."

"What the—" Maxxus began, looking at Gabriel accusingly.

I glanced at Gabriel and he nodded and left them behind to protest. "If it doesn't work...be prepared to like, summon up a big wall of earth!" I said to the magic users. I wasn't sure how good Maxxus' magic was, but surely he could do *something*.

"It's not working!" shouted one male sorcerer in the square frantically, as the storm grew. It was near the ground now, the twister, and beginning to toss aside brush and leaves and dirt as it made its way toward town.

"Do something! It's nearing houses!" cried another magic-user, who had just finished chanting and pushed something invisible towards the oncoming storm. It had no effect on the twister and almost seemed to strengthen it.

I made my way to the center of the square, ignoring the protests of Maxxus and Daniel alike. Gabriel shoved past the sorcerers and joined me.

"Are you sure about this?" He asked me earnestly.

I nodded. "Just...if it doesn't work...use my magic or whatever to try to blow it in the opposite direction."

He nodded.

"Leorah!" I heard Finnian's voice call out, but I ignored him as I walked slowly, closer to the storm, feeling the rain pound against my face, the wind whipping my hair all around, and slap at my robes. I felt the crystal pulse, and grasped it momentarily, feeling a surge of confidence.

I can do this. I did it before.

The wind howled, and almost seemed to growl at my presence and answered with a strong blast of wind that nearly knocked me over if it hadn't been for Gabriel, anchoring me with his hands at my waist.

"You may be stronger in dragon form," Gabriel said.

I nodded. I glanced down at myself, thankful I had chosen to wear the robes. The garments underneath would be shredded and I'd be naked again underneath but this was no time for modesty. The size and intensity were twice that of the truckstop storm, and I felt a quick pang of guilt, knowing that it was probably seeking me out—or whoever conjured it was, anyways. I closed my eyes and willed the change into my pink dragon form.

I growled, feeling the pull in my bones and skin as they became larger, my hands became feet, the sharp tingle as my wings shot out of my back. Feeling suddenly liberated, I roared, staring at the storm through my dragon eyes. I shook myself briefly, re-adjusting to my other form. Gabriel grabbed for the robes that had blown off of me, not able to withstand the size of my neck and clutched them to his chest. He nodded at me once and mouthed, "*You got this. I'm here.*"

Several gasps sounded out behind me, but I ignored them.

Feeling a sudden determination, I closed my eyes in concentration. I exhaled, feeling the sting of the potent glitter streaming out my nostrils. I took one more glance at the storm and shut my eyes again. I pictured the storm in my mind again, imagined the sparkles that shot out from me penetrating the funnel, causing it to shrink, dissipating the rain, quelling the wind that blew around me.

"More, Leo!" Gabriel shouted. I barely heard him, but I managed to breathe out again, this time with a loud, rebellious growl that made a couple people yelp behind me somewhere but I paid them nevermind as I blew the sparkles, my glittery fire towards the storm, imagining it smaller, picturing the clouds swirling in the sky calming.

I opened my eyes momentarily to peek at the storm, it had dissipated somewhat, but not enough.

I stalked it, causing the ground to rumble under my feet, exhaling once again, feeling the burn of the "fire" leaving my nose and mouth, getting as close as I could to it as I breathed directly into it, willing it to go away.

The rain pelted against my rough skin and the wind howled once more ominously at me and I finally felt it lessen, the funnel soaking up into the sky.

There was a hand on my side, and I noticed Gabriel beside me. He had conjured some wind of his own, and was pushing it up towards the cloud cover. I exhaled again at his hands, and he pushed it further into the funnel and it lessened to nothing more than a slight gust as it fully dissipated. With a wide gesture, he used the wind to push aside the remaining clouds, causing them to part and sunlight to penetrate the grounds once again.

There was an astonished lull of silence in the square. I spun my head around on my large neck to see everyone was all right, and all I heard was a joyous peal of laughter and Gabriel's voice unintelligibly speaking as my vision before me went blurry and I felt my dragon's knees turn to rubber and give out under me and everything around me went black.

My head felt like a ton of bricks as I attempted to lift it, but winced at the pain shooting from my eyes and promptly let it fall back down to an...unfamiliar surface.

"Leo?" a quiet but worried voice I heard barely from next to me. I felt a warm palm on my front foot. I grimaced in my mind—not sure if it was actually being juxtaposed to my face—noticing that wherever I was, I was still in my dragon form.

I felt an itchy sensation underneath me. I shifted uncomfortably and struggled to do so, my limbs not quite listening to my brain as I told them to stand, sit or just *move*. I struggled to lift my head again, raising it a bit higher this time and forcing my eyes open. Everything around me was blurry, but I could make out a large wooden structure with a window on top that allowed the reassuring, bright sunlight stream in.

"Is she awake?" a familiar voice questioned from nearby. I didn't hear a response, so I tried to utter, "She's trying," but I think it came out like a garbled mess of growls.

"She's awake." The voice chuckled and I recognized it to be Kiarra from nearby.

"What was *that*?" Gabriel questioned, sounding somewhat horrified.

"That was dragon basically for *'Screw you'*," Kiarra replied with a laugh.

"Wow..." was all Gabriel said. "Not what I was expecting."

I forced my eyelids open, finally, my vision still blurry. I winced at the sunlight streaming in but quickly my irises adjusted. I struggled to get up to a sitting position at least, as whatever I was laying on was incredibly scratchy and uncomfortable.

"Where the fuck am I?" I questioned, looking around me to see hay bales and stalls around. I must have been speaking in Dragon again because I caught Gabriel's dumbfounded, open-mouth stare.

Kiarra snorted. I turned my head to see her standing nearby, next to a unicorn that was occupying one of the stalls. She was stroking his white mane with one hand and feeding him an apple with the other. The unicorn snickered and whinnied appreciatively. "You're in the barn, dear. The guest housing isn't magically equipped to handle a being of our size. We'll have to fix that, I guess."

I pulled myself up a little higher, shaking my head and neck, feeling strands of hay fall off me.

"You okay?" Gabriel had hunched down next to me on the ground. He reached out a hand and touched my nose. I bumped it and grinned, feeling my head throb but relieved that I was regaining some mobility to the rest of my body.

"I...think so." I glanced at all the hay around me, but noticed a pillow that someone had placed carefully under my head. It only took up my forehead but I was thankful for it. I groaned, and rested my head against the soft cotton again. "How did I get here?"

"Maxxus." Gabriel nodded behind me, and I carefully and slowly craned my neck to see Maxxus in his dragon form, in a laying position, his sleeping head resting peacefully on his front haunches, a hushed growl as he breathed in and out, causing steam from his nose.

"The second you collapsed, he was in his dragon form immediately. Just like that," Gabriel said, with a snap of his fingers for emphasis. The resentment that had been once in his tone before when he spoke of the green dragon guard was gone, replaced with appreciation. "He just...lifted you up with his head and knelt down and got you on his back. Finnian took us to the barn with the unicorns and he set you down here, and you've been out for about twelve hours."

"Twelve *hours*?" I repeated in astonishment. I groaned. I managed to raise myself to my knees, but it was a struggle. I closed my eyes and willed myself to change back into human form, suddenly wishing myself away from this itchy hay and into the soft bed I was really wishing I could be sleeping in in my guest quarters, but nothing happened.

"Esmè said that might happen," Kiarra said, patting the unicorn and sitting on a hay bale nearby.

"Esmè?" Oh. The alchemist gypsy who gave me the crystal.

She nodded. "Yeah. She cast some sort of spell on you, and placed that crystal nearby you and said because of the drain in magic and the healing spell, you might not be able to shift for a while, until you're fully rested."

I groaned. "How can I be fully rested in this damn barn?"

I heard a whinny. "Hey, we like it just fine!" hollered the unicorn that Kiarra had been tending to nearby.

I tried to roll my eyes, but couldn't—our eyes didn't quite move that way in our dragon-forms. "No offense," I offered, and the unicorn just *neighed* crabbily in response.

"Have you all been here all night?" I asked.

Gabriel nodded. "Well... I have. Maxxus too. He refused to switch back into his human form and go to bed in the rooms. The only time I left was when I left to check on Daniel. Shortly after you blacked out, he had another vision."

I gasped. "Oh no...is he okay?"

"Oh, yeah he's fine," Gabriel replied.

Maxxus let out a loud growl, and I felt guilty as I looked over at him, knowing that he had once again stuck his neck out for me and I still barely even knew him. It seemed an extreme reaction for someone who just admired my grandfather. But he must have been dreaming, as he seemed to be still asleep.

"I'm fine," Daniel piped in, entering from the large barn door. He sat on a bale of hay and looked at me with concern. "How are you?"

I just uttered an unintelligible growl and Daniel just chuckled. "That good, huh?"

"Meh," I turned to Gabriel. "Did *you* sleep?" I asked him.

He shrugged. "You were vulnerable...perfect time for the Shadows to strike. Thankfully, they stayed away last night."

Kiarra rolled her eyes. "Yeah...when I came in here you were curled up to her like a little puppy. It would have been cute, if not for the growling."

I snorted. "Sorry."

"I didn't say it was *you* growling," Kiarra replied with a laugh, standing up. I laughed, Gabriel rolled his eyes. "I said I'd tell Finnian when you were awake. Someone else will come by with another healing spell, and he wants me to start magic practice with you as soon as possible."

"You?" I replied, unabashed. "Shouldn't it be Gabriel?"

"He'll be there too...but no one else knows anything about pink dragons other than me," she said. "At least, what your powers are or what they could possibly be. Feel better," she said before disappearing out the large barn door that opened and shut with a creak.

I glanced at Gabriel and snorted. "Well...there you are, then."

Gabriel smiled wryly, but was tapping a finger on his chin, appearing to be far away. "How is it that these Loremasters supposedly know everything, but yet, Kiarra is the best person for the job?"

I raised a brow, intrigued. "Hey now...there poses an interesting question."

"And...where was she when the damn storm was flying overhead, huh?" Gabriel scratched his chin. "I remember seeing her at the market but...during the storm. Nowhere to be found."

I couldn't answer that. "Are you saying..."

He threw up his arms. "I don't know what I'm saying!" he exclaimed in exasperation. "I just know that *none* of this makes any goddamned sense!"

"Now, that we can agree on," Daniel said, with a chuckle. "Now that Sleeping Beauty has awakened, I'm gonna go get some food. What is it that dragons eat? Side of cow? Pork ribs still on the pig?" he kidded.

I groaned. "Pizza...would be fab. And Mountain Dew."

He narrowed his eyes. "Girl, that stuff is horrible for you."

"But, it's good for the soul. Now..." I motioned my head for the barn door. "See if you can...*talk* to Kiarra while you're at it. Find out where she was." Daniel nodded and too disappeared out the barn door.

"Do we know for sure that the last pink dragon is really her Grandfather?" Gabriel mused.

I shook my head. "I don't think she's lying. I don't sense it off her but, I'm not too knowledgeable with the empathy yet," I said, dryly. "I just wish I knew what else I could do...or if I'll ever be able to do *anything* without being rendered a total invalid afterward." I groaned, closing my eyes and willing another shift again. It didn't come as I wouldn't think it would but it still didn't stop me from cursing a whole string of swear words in Dragon.

The big barn door squeaked open then, and Esmè poked her head in. "Hello? Can I come in?"

Gabriel motioned with a hand for her to come, and she did. She looked tired, her hair in a long ponytail at her neck and she looked like she was still wearing pajamas.

"Long night?" I questioned, at her long gray nightgown, blue fuzzy slippers and long pink robe, tied tightly at the waist. She carried a cloth bag and set it down next to me and pulled up a stool nearby.

She chuckled at her attire. "Healing is serious business. Especially from magic wounds."

"But...I wasn't cut."

She shook her head. "No, but magic injuries in a different way." She picked up her bag and rummaged through it, pulling out a small water bottle filled with green liquid. "Open...this will help you feel better."

I squinted at it. "What is it?"

"Potion."

Gabriel reached out his hand. "Mind if I...??" he nodded towards to bottle, and she handed it to him. "Certainly," she said.

Gabriel eyed it carefully, swirling the liquid around in front of his face, peering inside. He grasped the bottle in his hands and closed his eyes momentarily before handing it back. "Just checking."

Esmè smiled warmly. "Of course. I would expect nothing else from a Knight." She uncapped the bottle. "Open, please."

I did so, reluctantly, and she poured the warm liquid on my tongue. It was bitter, but not terrible, almost like a dark, burnt coffee. I swallowed it quickly, it burned like a shot of vodka down the throat but not entirely unpleasant.

I half expected to be able to stand up and start dancing, but I felt no different. "I...don't think it worked."

Esmè patted my knee that stuck out, my front legs curled under me. "It takes a couple of minutes. Oh...I have something for you." She placed the bottle back into her bag and pulled out something pink. "My companion made these for you, after seeing you last night. She would be so honored if you would keep and wear them, sometime." She handed it to Gabriel, who lifted it up by the corners and pink velvety material tumbled down.

"Robes?" I commented, rhetorically. They were pretty and surely as soft and alluring as the black ones but...I hated pink.

"These are a little different." Gabriel turned them around, and on the back was a familiar symbol embroidered in silver.

"My—my mark. How...?" I had no hands right now to finger the supple fabric so I nosed it instead.

Esmè smiled. "She is very talented, is she not? Between her and Hildie they could create an entire Castle Danger fashion line!"

Gabriel folded them up in his lap and smoothed the cloth with his hands. "They are very nice."

"Yes...thank you," I said, feeling a pang of guilt. "I...don't even know who she is."

"Oh it's okay. You can meet her when you're feeling better." Esmè reached into her bag for one more thing: a plastic bag full of little objects that resembled vitamins. "One more thing."

"Vitamins?" I asked, uncertainly.

"Sort of. They are specially made, with magically cultivated herbs for restoration for a dragon's tough system. I'll come by with some more, later. You'll find them useful, I think, whenever you use magic to help gain your energy back until you learn to harness that power," Esmè explained. She held them in her hand and I opened my mouth, again. She tossed them in and I swallowed all six of them with little problem.

"You made these too?" I asked.

She nodded. "My brother farms the herbs and I use them in my work. Potions and magic concoctions..."

"Oh. Well...thank you very much," I said, trying to smile but I was sure it came out awkward and terrifying.

"You are welcome." She stood again, patting Gabriel on the shoulder in acknowledgment who just smiled and nodded. "I will be around again in a couple of hours, if you're still here. If you need me...well Kiarra or Finnian should know where to find me." She smiled again before disappearing out the barn door.

Gabriel exchanged a glance with me. He held up the robes again. "Feel like you can shift, yet?"

I closed my eyes a moment. I still felt weak, but gradually getting a bit better. "Soon, I think."

"You don't *have* to, you know," he said. He came and sat next to me in the big pile of hay, leaning against my side. "I know this is a part of you, too."

I snorted. "Yes, pink scales. So sexy, eh?"

Gabriel reached out a hand under my rather large dragon chin, and pulled my face with some effort towards him. "You're a pretty dragon," he said, smiling innocently.

I chuckled. "Right, right. Okay...tie those robes on. Let's see if I can do this. If I'm lucky I'll shift right under the robes and no one will see a thing."

"Aww, damn," Gabriel chided with a big cheesy grin on his face. I glowered at him with intimidation and quickly Gabriel stood, and draped the robes over my back, moving in front of my and tying the cord around my neck, loosely.

"Thanks." I felt a surge of energy then and shut my eyes and felt relieved when I was finally able to shift.

I opened my eyes, so glad to look down and see my bare feet in the hay and my hands sticking out. "Thank god."

I heard a rustling from next to me, and a pained sounding growl. I glanced at Gabriel who shrugged and we peered around the stall wall to Maxxus sleeping in the large stall next to us.

He had shifted his body so the opposite side was facing us, revealing a rather large, gaping wound on his dragon stomach.

I gasped, horrified. "Oh my *gods*, Maxxus!" I screamed in alarm. I was at his side in mere seconds, kneeling down on my human legs. I looked around for any indication of what happened, but noticed the edges of the wound had begun drying, but were still oozing blood out slowly, so the injury probably happened a while ago.
Like...yesterday. Say...in a tornado.

Gabriel winced. "There's an imprint; a magic one. I would say this happened yesterday during the storm."

"And no one bothered to find out if he was okay or not?" I scolded. I didn't know what to do. Panicked, I shook his neck rather hard to wake him. "This is why he must have shifted, yesterday and won't shift back. He won't bleed as much in dragon form, nor will it hurt as much."

Maxxus snorted, and slowly lifted his head up to look at me. His eyes were tired and glassy. He tried to force a smile, but he ended up grimacing instead. "Leo...you're okay."

"I am. But *you're* not! What happened?" I gently placed my palms around the wound, moving them around the gape in his scaly, dragon skin.

"I'm sorry, man. We didn't notice this yesterday. We were—" Gabriel started, but was cut off by a growl from Maxxus as I touched the wrong spot on his side, sending pain shockwaves through him. I yelped.

"Oh, I'm so sorry!" I pulled away, and placed a hand on the back of his neck instead, running my fingers over the scales up and down in hopes of calming him.

"It's…. okay," he said, with labored breaths.

I whimpered. "Oh…" I felt tears prick my eyes, as I glanced back at Gabriel. "Go back and get Esmè. Or Finnian. *Someone*!" I insisted. Hearing the panic in my tone, Gabriel nodded and ran off.

"It's not okay. How…how did this happen?" I stammered, feeling panicked.

Maxxus groggily craned his long neck, awkwardly placing his large dragon nose in my lap. His eyes were so sad and pained.

I put my hands on either side of his face and looked straight into his eyes. "We'll fix this. You'll be okay. All right?"

He tried to nod, but winced instead.

I frowned. "I…all because of me. You shouldn't even be here! You— "

"St…t..op." He managed to mutter, narrowing his eyes slightly.

"Oh…there has to be something I can do!" I patted the spot between his eyes and walked on my knees in the hay back to his wound. It was still dripping blood, slowly…I noticed a spot where the hay under him was red from bleeding. I felt so helpless. I sighed, leaning my head and cheek on his side. "I wish…I wish this didn't happen. I wish you were better." I gingerly touched the skin area around the gash, hoping that some kind of magic would start shooting out my splayed fingers.

A handful of sparkles from my breath landed inside the wound. Maxxus let out a growl, but I felt him relax slightly under my palm. I gasped. The wound had closed ever so slightly.

I pulled my hands away and stared at my hands. "Oh my…I think I can…I think I can heal!" I scooted myself in the hay directly in front of his wound, placing my hands gently on either side. "I can heal you…I know I can. You need to heal. You…. you will be healed. You will…" I closed my eyes, taking a deep breath and blowing gently and slowly on the wound and all around it. *You will heal. The cut is getting smaller. And smaller. You're not bleeding anymore. You're not in pain. It's healing.* I concentrated on this mantra for a few minutes, concentrating so intently through the guilt I felt, feeling a stray tear fall down my cheek.

Maxxus gasped, and let out a growl before releasing a sigh. "Oh...oh, that's better."

I opened my eyes and to my absolute joy and relief, the wound had closed and scabbed over. No more blood seeped from it. I let out a squeal of joy, leaping up. "I did it! I...I can heal!"

Maxxus grinned. "You did do it. How...did you know?"

I shook my head. "I don't know. I just...felt so helpless. I exhaled and I was wishing you felt better....and I noticed the wound healed slightly. Oh!" I wrapped my arms around his neck in a hug. He rested his nose on my shoulder and I felt relaxed, allowing his dragon cheek to nuzzle mine. He lifted his head slightly and we swapped a brief look. My breath hooked in my throat under his intense look as my heart fluttered slightly. *What the fuck is this?* My mind questioned as I fought to tear myself out of his penetrating stare. *Panic. It had to be the panic.*

"Thank you," he said, weakly but not pained any longer. I nodded slowly, not wanting to be the one to break under the weight of the gaze.

The barn door flew open at that moment, causing me to leap back in a startle. Gabriel with Finnian in tow came dashing in. Momentarily I felt off, almost guilty. Maxxus let out a low growl and he too stepped backward.

"He's hurt! He's...." Gabriel stopped, staring confused at Maxxus, at the spot where he had been wounded. "He's better?"

Finnian pushed past Gabriel who stumbled slightly to peer down at the gash in Maxxus' side. He turned back to look at Gabriel and I in turn. "You said this was gaping? And bleeding?"

Gabriel pointed, dumbfounded. "It...it was."

Finnian turned to me, looking pleased. "You did this, didn't you?"

I chewed on my lip, feeling nervous. Finnian's gaze was penetrating, causing me to shift my feet and look anywhere but those compelling eyes. "Yes...."

"You can *heal!?!*" Gabriel exclaimed. He grabbed my shoulders and looked me square in the face. "You healed him? Really?"

I nodded.

"How did you do that?" Finnian questioned.

I shrugged. "I just...I just felt so bad that Maxxus got hurt trying to protect me; bad that he's here because of me...I just...I just wanted him to heal."

The corner of Finnian's mouth upturned slightly. "I knew it."

"Knew what?" Gabriel asked.

"I knew you could do it. Can you finish it?" Finnian asked, nodding towards the scab.

"No!" Maxxus' tone was still weak, but firm. "No. I'll be okay. She...will wear out again."

"Actually...I feel pretty good," I said, with a smile, suddenly like I had drank a gallon of coffee, with a burst of energy. I knelt down again and with more confidences, held out my palms around his wound and exhaled, willing the scab to be replaced with skin...this time I didn't close my eyes as I breathed out. Maxxus twitched slightly, but didn't appear to be in any pain as the scab lessened and was gone, leaving a scar in his scales behind. I ran my fingers over his smooth, cool skin. I tried to imagine the scar being replaced with his green scales but nothing happened. But at least he was healed.

Maxxus sighed. He threw his head back, with a smile. "Amazing!" I jumped back, as the dragon next to me suddenly became human, hunched over in the hay. I blushed and turned away. Gabriel pulled the robes off of himself and draped it over Maxxus' naked human form quickly.

"Thank you," Maxxus said, tying the cord around his neck and adjusting the robes over his front. He paused a moment before turning around. He chuckled, spinning around. He had part of his abdomen revealed through an opening in the robes, revealing a shiny, pink scar. "Amazing, Leo! There's like, nothing left!"

I reached out slowly, gingerly, ignoring Gabriel's glower as I touched the area I had healed. It was warm and smooth and injury-free. "I...I'm sorry I couldn't stop the scar."

"Sorry? Leo, you *healed* me! The scar is nothing." He let his robes close all the way, beaming at me proudly. "I will wear it with honor."

Under Gabriel's sour gaze I resisted the urge to give him a huge, relieved hug. I just smiled and nodded at him.

Finnian appeared smug, thumb and index finger stroking his chiseled chin thoughtfully. "Well...I will send in Esmè to see you, have you checked over just to make sure everything is as it should be, but I suspect she will find nothing."

"No need." Maxxus had a moment of joviality and did a short burst of dance before crossing his arms over his chest and appearing serious, once again.

I stifled a laugh as Gabriel narrowed his eyes, fighting back a smile himself.

"You're sure you're okay?" I asked again cautiously.

Maxxus in a moment of bravery grasped my hand in his, bowed slightly and softly kissed my knuckles. A nervous shiver shot up my spine. I heard Gabriel audibly glower but I ignored it, hoping my face didn't betray me and blush at his chivalry and strange display of affection. "Your grandfather would be so proud of you."

I felt my knees melt, at the mention of my grandfather. I felt grateful that Maxxus was indeed okay, but my lower lip trembled momentarily thinking of how worried he must be; not knowing where I was. Where *we* were. Maxxus was like another son to him. He always regretted we weren't closer, Maxxus and I, but he knew I feared to tarnish the green dragon with my reputation. Once my brother actually suggested he believed Maxxus and I would make a good match but I was horrified—I didn't even give it a moment's thought because of what it could do to him. My parents' claim that my mere existence held them back from the throne wasn't a lie. They tolerated me because they had to. Choosing to be with me? More than social suicide; it was social *murder.* Maxxus overcame way too much to have to put up with someone like me. Even if I wanted to, I couldn't entertain the notion. Braeden knew that.

Gabriel coughed, interrupting our moment and Maxxus blushed sheepishly and pulled away.

"That certainly was a lot of blood," Finnian observed nodding towards the spot in the hay where Maxxus' dragon had been resting, a pool of blood, some dried in with the hay.

"It was." Gabriel said. "Which reminds me of how dangerous this magic is, and that we need to find the source of it and fast before it injures someone to the point where *no one* can heal them."

Finnian gestured his hand flippantly. "Oh, that's easy. I know where it came from."

"Where?" I demanded, urgently.

"I did it," Finnian said, hands crossed over his chest appearing without a care in the world. He was looking at the pool of blood and mumbling, "I must get someone in here to clean that up."

"*You* did it?" Gabriel hollered, his hands balling up into fists. But that was nothing compared to the rage I felt fuming inside.

"You? *You?!?!*" I felt my heartbeat accelerate, the fire inside burning out of control like a forest wildfire, burning my face and cheeks as the heat rose. A pair of hands were grasping my shoulders but I shoved them away, determined and angry. "You caused this? Why the hell would you do that? You *nearly killed my damn friend*! What the hell were you thinking? You risked your *entire town*! Are you some kind of psycho? Some masochist? What the—" with each word I spat venomously, my raging tone grew louder and louder until finally words weren't enough to properly display my anger. With a tribal yell, I charged into Finnian's towering form who had appeared rather nonchalant but his expression rapidly changed to one of surprise as I slammed my body into his, knocking him into the bare ground. I straddled Finnian's body with my own, my legs on either side of his torso like vices, attempting to squeeze the air out of him. I grabbed his shoulders and shook them, his head jostling as I did so.

"Leorah, just—" for the first time since I encountered him, Finnian did not appear composed and confident. I caught a glimpse of trepidation in his eyes which has changed from bright blue to a muddy yellow.

I couldn't get the image of his smug face out of my mind as he announced that he had caused the raging storm that nearly killed Maxxus, that scared the entire town. All I could think of was wiping that smug grin off of his face. I panted rapidly, clenching my teeth, my hands squeezing his shoulders I imagined choking the wind out of him as I exhaled, sparkles escaping my nose and falling over Finnian's now extremely fearful face.

"You...*you*..." words were escaping me now, and I began lapsing into dragon curses which sounded feral and intimidating with their growls and roars.

Finnian's eyes grew large as he gasped for breath, I saw the color escape his cheeks as he struggled to speak, my resolve choking out any words out of him he could have possibly uttered. As his face turned white as a sheet and then a telltale shade of blue, he struggled to bring his hands up to my forearms, attempting to pull them away from his neck. I felt a sense of triumph watching his air leave his lungs, his face turn color as he began to lose consciousness. I grinned, as I spoke in dragon something along the lines of "*You're dead, asshole.*"

I felt various hands around my body, arms attempting to pull me off. Voices around me, pleading. I heard none of them as I wickedly watched the life drain from Finnian's face, the eyes roll back into his head.

"Leo! *Leorah*!" I think it was Gabriel's voice I heard, and both he and Maxxus' strong grips on my arms and shoulders that it took to pull me off of Finnian.

Maxxus—who since he was a dragon was just physically stronger—had my arms pinned behind me, holding me close to himself, was speaking dragon into my ear.

"You are no murderer, Leorah. Your grandfather wouldn't want this for you. Aleron would be disappointed."

It was the mention of my grandfather's human name that eventually pulled me out of my bloodlust. To nearly everyone, he was just "Elder" or "grandfather" even if you weren't technically his grandchild.

I winced, and relaxed in Maxxus' grip as Gabriel was kneeling next to Finnian, helping him to sit up as he choked and gasped for air, the color slowly returning to his momentarily-not-so-beautiful face right now. "Oh, balls...."

"Are you okay?" Gabriel was asking Finnian, helping brush off the dirt and hay from his clothing. Finnian rubbed his throat with both hands, still coughing.

Maxxus' grip on my arms loosened a bit but he didn't let go.

"I am...fine." Finnian replied, between coughs and gasps.

"Oh my...." Feeling suddenly weak in the knees, I felt my legs turn to rubber and give out underneath me. Maxxus had to tighten his grip on me again, this time wrapping his arms around my body to keep me from tumbling to the ground.

Gabriel left Finnian to catch his breath and darted over to me. "Leo?" He placed hands on either side of my face, staring into my eyes intently. He stroked my hair out of my eyes, as I struggled to stand, Maxxus still needing to keep me propped up.

I struggled to glance around him at Finnian who was regaining composure on the ground. He was sitting up now, running his hands through his disheveled hair and brushing the wrinkles out of his black button up shirt.

I struggled to speak, but Finnian held up a hand, shushing me. "I will be fine. You had every right to do what you did," he spoke hoarsely.

"But, I—" I protested. The raging fire was completely doused by guilt and remorse at what I had nearly done.

"Clearly, you're even more powerful than I had thought," Finnian said, his voice raspy, between small coughs. He managed to get to his feet now, and stand.

"You're okay?" Gabriel asked him tonelessly, and Finnian nodded.

"Good." Gabriel glowered at him through narrow brown eyes and pulled his fist back and let it go, connecting with Finnian's cheek. Maxxus and I collectively winced as we heard a telltale *smack* of knuckle against skin, and Finnian's cheek was instantly changing color. "It may not be a good idea to kill you, but you definitely deserve an ass-whupping for that bullshit!"

Maxxus, ever calm and collected piped up then finally. I struggled to be released from his grasp and he finally relinquished his grasp, but his hands remained hovering on either side of my arms in case I tried to give murder another go again. "Perhaps you should explain to us what you were thinking, causing that storm," he said, through clenched teeth.

"Yeah!" I said, setting my mouth in a thin line, crossing my arms over my chest.

"And...how did you do that, anyways? Do Loremasters have sorcerer powers or anything? Or—" Gabriel began, as Finnian held up his hands in a gesture of surrender.

"I am sorry, friends. I know it's hard to explain or to understand, but I needed to coax the magic out of Leo, to see what she was clearly capable of. Upon learning of this new threat by the shadow realm, it sets the realms—all of the realms—off balance. Sooner, rather than later we are going to need her assistance in helping restore the balance between our realms. I know her magic has been squelched since she was a young dragon, and I needed to know if she was truly capable of great feats of magic; if it was possible even. That perhaps she may be strong enough to ward them off indeed." Finnian wiggled his jaw from side to side and with a grasp he pulled his jaw back into alignment with a sickening *crack*. I fought the urge to gag. "Ah. That's better." Finnian gave one of his stellar, bright smiles. His eye color shifted from the muddy brown to a pleasing shade of blue.

"But..." I began to protest. "Does that mean you caused the storm back home as well? Was that you?"

Finnian shook his head. "No, that was *not* me. Nor do I know who it was, either. Someone very powerful, or with some very powerful friends indeed, I had to pool together many resources to cast the magic to summon this storm. *This* particular storm was concocted with potions and some assistance from another sorcerer such as yourself. I do not have elemental powers like you have, Gabriel."

"But...why? Why not just train her, like you were going to have Kiarra do?" Maxxus asked.

"Wait—was Kiarra behind this? Did she help?" Gabriel demanded, his eyes narrowing.

"She was consult, only," Finnian explained. "I asked her about what sort of powers her grandfather had and she had told me about the storm back in the Pineville area and how you quelled it, Leorah. I had to see it for myself that you were indeed powerful enough with the right threat to summon magic you didn't know you had." Finnian rubbed his throat with his fingertips and chuckled. "Apparently, even I underestimated you. I didn't count on your friend getting hurt." He looked at Maxxus and with a slight bow of the head, said, "I am sorry about your injury. But I'm not sorry we now know more about the extent of Leorah's magic....as destructive as they are constructive, given the proper motivation."

I threw up my hands in the air. "This is ridiculous. You could have killed someone. I could have killed *you*!" I started to storm off out of the barn, but Finnian reached out for my arm, stopping me. I pulled away with such force that I nearly knocked him off balance. "Do *not* touch me."

"I apologize for my methods. It seems I have bitten off more than I could chew. But, I knew you would have the ability to stop the storm, especially with Gabriel's assistance here," he said. "I really am sorry. But we may not have the luxury of a lot of time. The Shadows could strike at any time, and we need to bolster our forces if we do not want to get taken over."

"They can do that?" Gabriel questioned, with a nervous swallow.

Finnian nodded solemnly. "I'm afraid they can. But, knowing what I know now, it's going to be a lot more difficult for them with Leo on our side. I'm sure they know how powerful she is already and that's why they are going after her...either to sway her on the side of the Shadows or to kill her entirely, I do not know." I swallowed nervously as Finnian continued.

"But it is imperative that we keep the balance between our realms. If the Shadows are allowed to come over in droves, that will mean the end of life as we know it...well, maybe everywhere," Finnian explained.

I shook my head, still frustrated. "Surely, there had to be another way."

Finnian ignored my statement. "Well. Kiarra will meet with you this afternoon. I suggest you three go get a decent meal and some rest. There is a tavern and eatery nearby that serves a side of ribs that most of the dragons here really enjoy, with some great ale. I highly recommend you keeping up your energy. Afterwards, catch a nap before Kiarra is to work with you. We may have to work fast." Finnian nodded at each of us in turn. "Again, I apologize for my methods. I will see you later." Finnian turned on his heels and sauntered out of the barn, leaving the three of us behind to look at each other, bewildered as to what just went on.

"*Fuck...*" was all I could utter. No one disagreed with me.

Chapter 17

Since the Shadows tended to seek me out and have access to our realm—somehow—in the in-between times, I avoided sleeping during anything I could think of that might be construed as in-between: day and night, morning and afternoon.

Daniel made good on my request for pizza and Mountain Dew—apparently there were quite a few other mythological creatures that were addicted to it as well. He arrived at Gabriel's and my quarters triumphantly with a large, homemade, super cheesy pizza and a couple two-liters of Mountain Dew. I was extremely psyched and greeted him with a large—and rather surprising hug for both of us (seeing as how I wasn't much of a hugger). He didn't complain, yet hugged me back and lifted me into the air and spun me around.

Maxxus had insisted on following us back to our room, and I invited him to stay for pizza but he declined, insisting that Finnian's suggestion of ribs and beer sounded more enticing. Daniel decided to join him (even though Gabriel insisted he was a vegetarian) and with an eyebrow wiggle he followed him out the room and to—wherever the tavern was.

I chuckled. "Daniel has a thing for Maxxus?"

Gabriel scoffed. "Daniel has *things* for anything with legs. Even four legs, apparently."

I raised my eyebrow. "Apparently, it's a family trait."

He chuckled. "Touché."

I rummaged through the cabinets in the small kitchen, looking for plates or napkins or anything and produced two clay plates and hand-blown, blue glass glasses and brought them to the log coffee table in the center of the room and dug into the pizza promptly. Gabriel began pouring himself a glass of pop and began pouring one for me but I stopped him, reaching for the other two-liter, spinning the top off and drinking directly from the bottle.

"Okay, then," Gabriel said with a laugh as I struggled to keep a loud belch down.

As the fizzy drink burned down my throat I sighed with pleasure. "Oh my god...I needed that."

"Want me to leave you two alone?" he kidded, grabbing a slice of pizza for himself.

"No, I'm good," I said, wiping off my mouth with the sleeve of the robes I was still wearing.

Gabriel took a bite of his pizza and sighed. "So...another eventful night for you, huh?"

I groaned. "Yeah...really. I don't think it bodes well for me that my first night here in the safe-town was less than safe. And I was totally unconscious most of the time."

Gabriel shook his head. "I can't believe Finnian did that," he said.

I let out a low growl, folding up the slice of pizza and fitting half of it in my mouth as Gabriel laughed at me. "What? I'm hungry." I said with my mouth full.

"Still...I can't necessarily argue with his methods. Unorthodox but...at least we have a better idea of what you are capable of," Gabriel said, sounding grudged.

I wrinkled my nose. "Yeah, well...it's nice that someone has more confidence in my abilities than I do."

"Rightly so. *Look* at what you did, Leo," Gabriel said with a tone of awe, setting his pizza down. "You *healed* someone! That is..." he let out a low-whistle, "...that is pretty fucking amazing."

I shrugged. "I did what I had to."

"And, you're not totally worn out?" He questioned.

I was fighting the urge to yawn, but I choked it down. I was tired but not anywhere *near* as tired as I was after that storm last night. "Whatever Esmè gave me, it was effective."

"I see that," he said. "We will need to get more." I nodded in agreement, and we ate the rest of our pizza slices in quiet contemplation. At least, Gabriel was contemplative. My mind was totally blank as I devoured three slices of pizza, interrupted only by the sound of my phone buzzing. I noticed that after I shifted yesterday I had no recollection of it, and wondered who had thought to grab it and bring it to my room. I was beginning to inquire to Gabriel out loud when I noticed who was texting me: my brother. My brother for my grandfather and a text from Melanie Thompson—Kit's sister. The police must have managed to get a hold of her and given her my number. I didn't know much about her; Kit said they were estranged. They spoke a couple of times a year during holidays.

The text basically said that she hadn't heard from Kit yet but she'd contact me *ASAP* if she did hear anything; and I was to do likewise.

I tossed my phone down onto the sofa and rubbed my palms over my face. I still couldn't believe no one had heard from Kit, yet. I wanted to be more concerned about her, but in my position there wasn't much I could do. Gabriel pointed out that if I sought her out, whatever magic force that had touched her, looking for me (the Shadows, probably) might attack me next or possibly endanger her more.

Suddenly not feeling hungry, but tired, I decided that 12:30 in the afternoon was safe enough to lay down and take a quick nap, after a long shower where I scrubbed myself and my hair down to get the barn smell out. I pulled on a pair of sweats I had brought and a blue t-shirt and towel dried my hair some before laying down in the bed.

The night had apparently taken its toll on Gabriel as well, who was already curled up, breathing calmly under the covers. I glanced at the sunlight streaming in through the drapes and decided I would be safe, pulled the covers back and curled up next to him, resting my cheek on his chest and within minutes of listening to his steady heartbeat, I was asleep myself.

A rapping on the door awoke me from my slumber. I started, sitting upright immediately and smacked the back of my head against something.

"*Ouch!*" Gabriel cried out, covering his nose with his hand.

"Shit! I'm sorry!" I yelped, as he pulled his hand away momentarily, showing the blood that was collecting in his palm, dripping from his nose.

"It's okay," he said, with a groan, pinching the bridge of his nose with one hand and laying back.

The loud knocking at the door wouldn't stop, and I swore out loud. "Just a *fucking* minute, already? Shit!" I cursed, clamoring out of bed into the bathroom for a towel. I found one hanging next to the sink and quickly dashed back into the bedroom and pulled Gabriel's hand aside and gently wiped at the blood under his nose.

"Thanks," he said, flinching at the pain.

"I'm *so* sorry, that knocking scared the shit out of me. I guess I was really out," I said, apologetically.

"It's okay. I heard it just before you and was sitting up to go get it when you, well..." he flinched again as I tried to apply more pressure to his nose to stop the bleeding.

I swore. "This is ridiculous." I closed my eyes, picturing the blood ceasing and the pain leaving his face, and concentrated my magic.

A moment later, Gabriel wiped away the last of the blood and looked more relaxed when I opened my eyes. "That's amazing," was all he said, with a grin. I didn't even have to blow my sparklies on it, somehow I had just conjured them like a sorcerer would have. Gabriel assured me that it was normal and it would get easier the stronger I got.

Pound pound pound.

"Shit, insistent, aren't they?" I grumbled, rolling my eyes.

He grumbled, with a flick of his hand I heard a *click*. "Come in, already!"

I heard the door open and shut again and light footsteps. "Leo?"

"Kiarra," I said under my breath, feeling a hint of resentment (she did, after all know about the storm) as I jumped deftly out of bed onto the floor. I grabbed for a ponytail holder I had apparently left on the nightstand and was twisting my hair into a messy bun on top of my head as I stormed into the next room to see her standing there, looking innocent.

"Leo...." Gabriel was after me, clearly sensing my frustration. "Don't..."

"I'm sorry, I guess you were sleeping, huh? I was just worried—" she began, as I stalked right up to her and got in her face.

"What is the big *idea* with that storm, huh? You know Maxxus—" I growled angrily.

Kiarra took two hesitant steps back, holding up her hands. "I know. I *know* Leo, I'm so sorry. It got out of control, the witch who made the storm potion made it a little too strong, I'm sorry."

I stepped back myself, resting my hands on my hips. I glared at her a few minutes longer. "Well...fine. Whatever. But...why?"

"Finnian is right, that we needed a true test of your powers. We knew you wouldn't be able to sit idly by as the town was threatened, which proved to us that you do have the blood of a hero in you, you haven't been Shadowtouched yet, although they certainly have tried. We didn't know any other good way to properly test you but things just got out of hand. I had *no* idea Maxxus would be foolish enough to jump in front of a flying branch to protect you; it wasn't even going to *hit* you or anyone else, he just reacted. Everything you did..." she smiled, "It was truly, truly amazing. Like the things my grandfather described in his journals. The powers of pink dragons *truly* are unrivaled by anyone in the dragon realm. Really."

I softened my gaze. "Did...could your grandfather do this stuff, too?"

She nodded. "Well...mostly. You do appear to be *much* stronger than he was, although we haven't quite figured out why, yet. We suspect it has something to do with your wings. Or at least the magic in them."

"My *wings*?" I asked reaching back and patting my imaginary dragon wings on my human body. "Why would that make a difference?"

"We are not sure yet, but it's the only difference between you and him that we can tell so far," Kiarra explained. "Other than your upbringing, things weren't much different. Well..." she paused.

"Well *what?*" I demanded.

She bit her lip. "Your wings. Your wings are completely different."

"My wings?" I repeated uncertainly. "But...they're just wings. Wings that don't work."

"Precisely. I don't believe there has ever been another *dragon* period with wings quite like yours," Kiarra said. I tightened my face and Kiarra quickly said, "I know you don't like talking about it. But it's true. To my knowledge—or anyone *else's* knowledge—there has never been another set of wings quite like them."

"But, what does that mean?" Gabriel interjected.

Kiarra shrugged. "I don't know, really. I don't even know *how*. They are iridescent, like a fairy's or perhaps—"

"—so you're saying I'm part *fairy?*" I retorted, incredulous.

"No, just that they look like it. But, they're strong. Stronger than they look," she said, with a chuckle at her own unintended joke.

I rolled my eyes and groaned.

"Sorry, sorry," she said, laughing. "But...we do know that a fairy's wings are meant to help amplify magic, as well as fly. We are guessing that's what yours are for, as well."

Gabriel considered this. "It's an interesting theory."

"But," I began protesting, "if they are like a fairy's wings, and fairies can fly then why can't *I* fly."

Kiarra's eyes glinted with a hint of mischievousness. "Who said you can't? I think that you can."

I narrowed my eyes. "Come on."

"No, really. In fact, that's one of the things that we're going to work on. Right now." Kiarra grabbed for my arm and I allowed her, tentatively. She looked at Gabriel. "Coming?"

Gabriel nodded. "This I have to see."

We followed Kiarra through the town square. Several human-appearing people and one orange dragon in actual dragon form were seated at the tables, laughing and talking. One of them—a demure, spritely thing with pointy ears and long, *long* golden blonde hair caught sight of us and nudged her companions and pointed. A male gasped (he looked entirely human), and the other male (another with pointy ears and similar golden blonde hair) stood up and cheered. "All right, pink!" he shouted. Even the orange dragon bowed his head in a sign of respect.

My cheeks flushed and I hung my head. Gabriel gave a small wave for me and pulled my arm through his and guided me through the remainder of town, through a chunk of pine forest and into a clearing. "They don't even know that it was their own leader who caused it," Gabriel muttered under his breath.

"Where's Maxxus? And Daniel?" I asked, standing in the center of the clearing and looking around my scenery.

"Last I saw they were still whooping it up at the tavern," Kiarra replied. "Finnian wanted to come, but I assured him that for the time being, it was *probably a* good idea for him to remain elsewhere."

I snorted. "You think?"

Kiarra smiled. She had a floral printed crossbody-bag hanging at her side, that she pulled off and tossed on the ground. She rubbed her hands together in anticipation. I had to fight the urge to roll my eyes again. "Okay…Finnian and I were talking about you, and we developed a theory."

"Theory?" I retorted.

"Yes," she replied with a nod. "Now, your wings look like a fairy's. But, if you look at a fairy and their wings, it doesn't even look like it should be possible for them to fly. Small, light wings on a body that's not aerodynamic or anything. A fairy flies because she wills it."

I cocked a brow. "Wills it?"

"Yes. She flies because it's the magic that allows her to fly, not because her wings were necessarily built for flying," Kiarra explained.

Gabriel tittered this time. "Does she have to think a *happy thought*?"

I chortled. "Pixie dust!"

Kiarra stopped talking and allowed us to giggle and laugh like a couple of school kids in the back of the classroom during sex education when they thought no one could hear them. She lifted her brow at us after a moment. "Are you finished, yet?" she asked, rather sternly, crossing her arms in front of her. Gabriel and I composed ourselves and tried to appear solemn.

"Yeah. Yes. Keep going," choking back peals of laughter. Gabriel poked me in the ribs and tried to look admonishing which nearly set me back off again.

Kiarra sighed audibly. "*Anyways*…we think it's a similar concept with you. Since your magic is rooted in spirit, it could be the same concept. You were always told you couldn't fly, or practice magic, so you just…didn't."

Gabriel snapped his fingers. "Actually…that does make a bit of sense. Like the healing—she didn't know she could, but she thought she might and was desperate. We thought there was a possibility she might be able to heal and we were right."

"Could your grandfather heal?" I questioned, finally serious.

She nodded. "My grandfather was extremely powerful. Not all pink dragons are as—or were as—powerful as each other. Some had better control of their powers. Others just didn't have the abilities. But they *all* had spirit magic, probably the most powerful of all the elements because there is a bit of spirit in just about *everything* so, in that case— "

"—a spirit user could potentially have control over anything," Gabriel finished.

She nodded. "To a degree, at least. But your best bet is still to enhance say, like an air user's magic. But I wouldn't be surprised if you could at least when we're done, light a candle or something like that. Maybe," she said with a wink.

"Is that what your Grandfather could do?" I asked.

"He says he could in his journal," Kiarra replied.

"Hmm," I said, with an approving nod to Gabriel. "So…you really think I can fly?"

"Yes," Kiarra said. "And, since flying is key for a dragon, I think it should be lesson number one. Because sometimes magic isn't enough; sometimes you just have to *haul ass*."

I let out a raucous laugh. For some reason, it was really strange hearing Kiarra—who'd been akin to a bouncy cheerleader when I first met her—swear like a sailor. I grinned. Nothing like curse-words to make me feel more at home.

"So, *Sensei*, what do you want me to do?" I questioned.

"It's simple really. First, you need to *believe* you can. You need to believe you can fly," Kiarra said seriously, but it still sent Gabriel into fits of laughter.

"*I belieeeeeeeeeeeeve I can fly…*" he sang, off-key.

I snorted and continued, "*I believe I can touch the sky!*"

Kiarra narrowed her eyes at us, but the corners of her mouth were upturned into a smile. "Yeah, yeah," she said, rolling her eyes. "Shall we? Oh, first…Leo, it would be helpful if you could shift. Obviously."

I groaned out loud. "*Fine…*" I crossed my arms over my chest and looked at them pointedly.

"Well?" Kiarra prompted.

Gabriel snickered, and turned around. "She's modest."

"Oh geez…" Kiarra muttered, but complied.

Glad for the robes, again, I closed my eye and willed the change. The more a dragon shifted back and forth, the more it became old hat, like blinking your eyes and sneezing. Actually, it was more like sneezing: uncomfortable and uncontrollable at first, but when it was over, it was such a relief.

I felt the tell-tale pull as my human limbs turned into dragon legs and the rest followed, with my "fairy" wings shooting out of my back. I turned my head to look at them momentarily, and gave them a couple of flaps, causing a breeze nearby that rustled Gabriel and Kiarra's hair.

"Safe now?" Kiarra asked, not waiting for me to answer. She yanked a pair of robes out of her shoulder bag, tossed them around her neck and shifted herself while Gabriel just stood in awe (her private areas shifted underneath her clothes so nothing was exposed—for that I was grateful, Kiarra's human form was ridiculously gorgeous, that of a runway model), shaking his head.

"I don't think I will *ever* get used to that," he said.

I started to comment, but Kiarra cut me off. "Okay, like I said. You need to believe that you can fly. Do you believe you can fly?"

I began to snort a laugh but took a deep breath and staved it off. I lifted my head proudly. "I can fly," I said, rather meekly.

"No! No, you have to truly, truly believe it," Kiarra instructed.

"Leo…maybe it's just like healing, or conjuring wind…or wanting to kill Finnian," Gabriel joked, but his expression turned serious. He came up to me and I lowered my head, to better look into his eyes. "You believe you can, you will it. You exhale your magic dust and…picture yourself flying."

"Well, let's try floating a little off the ground, first. Don't want to get ahead of ourselves, here," Kiarra interjected.

I nodded, with a short growl. I glanced once more into Gabriel's earnest eyes and took a deep breath. I shut my eyes.

I can fly. I can do this. Dragons were meant to fly. I can too. Just a little. Just float a little off the ground. I imagined myself feeling weightless, hovering off the ground a couple inches and I exhaled, blowing the dust towards the wings outstretched on my back. I flapped them gently to catch the dust, and exhaled once more, catching more sparkles between my wings, and flapped them ever so slightly harder.

I heard a gasp. "Leo…look." It was Gabriel's voice.

I opened my eyes and looked down. My feet were hovering about a foot off the ground.

I gasped myself, shocked. Suddenly nervous I allowed my wings to stop flapping and in a moment of fear, fell to the ground with a small *thud*. I let out an *ooph* and a growl as I fell to my knees.

Kiarra stood beside me, smiling like the Cheshire cat. Gabriel threw himself at me and attempted to wrap his arms around my neck. "You did it!"

I blinked a little, feeling my heart beat rapidly. I glanced back at my wings again and looked back at him with a nervous smile. "Well, sort of."

Kiarra gave a growl of approval. "Good start, *good* start, Leorah. Seriously, that was awesome!" she praised. "Now…try again and see if you can't go a bit higher."

I nodded. *I can do this. I can fly too.* I repeated the process with a bit more determination, exhaling a bit more and beating my wings slightly faster. *Just get off the ground. Off the ground, Leorah.*

"Should this really be so easy?" Gabriel asked Kiarra in a hushed tone. I heard her *shush* him, reminding that I could easily hear him.

"Dragons were meant to fly, Gabriel," was all she said. "The rest of the magic probably won't be so easy."

Still shutting my eyes, afraid to look, I imagined myself floating a bit higher, flapping my wings a bit more furiously and exhaling. I opened my eyes, then, to see both Gabriel and Kiarra craning their necks to see me as I hovered about twenty feet in the air. Gabriel looked positively elated, and was nearly jumping up and down in his shoes.

"Oh my…" was all I could say, looking around me. I was about leaf-level with a handful of nearby young birch trees. I grinned. "Cool…" I exhaled again, much larger with a bit of a roar and beat my wings much harder. I easily floated to the tops of the birch trees and was now rivaling some tall pines that stood behind them.

"Don't get too cocky, Leo!" Kiarra shouted back up at me, but it was hard to hear her over the repetitive sound of my flapping wings.

I scoffed. "I got this!" I shouted back, as a gust of wind came out of the sky, pushing me forward. I struggled against the current as it wanted to push me forward, and blew my dust away and I started losing altitude. "*Shit!*" I growled, breathing out furiously, flapping my wings.

Gabriel shot a gale of wind underneath me, keeping me aloft with a wide gesture of both his hands. I exhaled more furiously as the two currents fought each other and felt my wings go slack as I began falling. Gabriel pulled more air seemingly out of nowhere and made a swirling motion with his hand, causing the wind to swirl under me. Kiarra added to it by inhaling and shooting out a mist of water from her mouth, and it mixed with Gabriel's wind to form a cloud. Gabriel pushed it under me as I tumbled, and I let out a relieved gasp as the cloud "reached" up beside me on all sides and cradled me before I slammed into the Earth.

Gabriel's eyes were intent and narrow, as he gestured with his hands, slowly, bringing the wind and me back down to the Earth, pushing it down. When all four of my feet touched, he spread his hands wide and with a final push at the palms, dispersed the wind around us, and it calmed.

I grinned sheepishly at him and Kiarra who just shook his head. Gabriel wiped a bead of sweat that had formed on his forehead with the sleeve of his robe and let out a low whistle. I hadn't realized that he had been working so hard to keep me afloat.

"Sorry," I said to him, pulling a Sona and gently bumping my forehead against his side, being cautious not to knock him flat on his ass.

He stumbled slightly, but recovered quickly. He patted the top of my nose. "That's what I'm here for, eh?"

I sighed out of frustration. "Where did that come from? Was it conjured?" I asked, a tone of anger in my voice.

Kiarra chuckled. "No, silly. There's *always* wind. You will have to learn to fly against it."

"Uggggh..." I grumbled. I tried to facepalm myself but I couldn't get my dragon foot up that high so I settled for an f-bomb under the breath, in dragon.

Gabriel rubbed the side of my face with both his hands and leaned his head in. "You'll get it. This was only your first time! You did great."

I looked at Kiarra, who nodded. "Try again?"

"What do I do with the wind?" I questioned. This really should be common sense for me, but I seriously had *no* idea. The laws of physics and what not didn't have a place in dragon lessons growing up, and I tried to picture how an airplane would fly. Of course, those have huge engines. I just have…dragon power. I groaned at the thought and hung my head.

"It's okay…" Gabriel said, another comforting pat.

"You have to adjust your body for the wind. If it's coming in back of you, you make yourself bigger to the wind, to block it. That is, you start flying upwards slightly, and let your feet fall a bit. If it's coming forward, crane your head down and let it fly against your back. All while flapping your wings harder until it passes. Like this." I watched as Kiarra effortlessly flapped her solid wings and lifted off into the air, high above the pine trees now. A gust of wind blew from the sky again, and her wings beat harder as she craned her long neck up, kicking her front feet slightly like she was pumping a swing. "Or, like this," she said, spinning around in the air so the wind was blowing against her back. She lowered her neck *oh so slightly*, beat her wings a little harder to compensate, but she stayed aloft. The wind passed, and she hovered level again. "See?"

I sighed.

"I got you, if you fall," Gabriel said, forming an invisible ball of air between his hands for emphasis. He winked at me.

With a slight nod, he stepped backwards. I closed my eyes again, summoning up my confidence. *Be one with the wind, Leo.* I involuntarily whimpered, thinking of the falling sensation again.

"I *got* you." Gabriel said with conviction in front of me. "You can do this."

I nodded slightly. Okay. I can do it.

I squinted my eyes shut, and stretched out my wings as far as they could go. Another gust of wind came from up high and I pulled my wings in tighter, feeling it blow across them. *No! You're a dragon! You can do it!* "Screw you, wind," I mumbled under my breath. I forced my wings out through the wind, fighting the recoil, I beat them harder. Faster. I inhaled deeply and exhaled and bent my knees slightly to gain some height.

I tried not to yelp as I felt a current of wind underneath me. I opened my eyes, startled, but relaxed when I saw it was Gabriel pushing the wind under my legs. He nodded. "Do it!"

Feeling a burst of confidence, I flapped harder and exhaled again. Once. Twice, catching the sparkles in my wings and craning my neck, pushing myself up higher, and higher. I dared a quick glance around me, as the ground grew further away until I was level in the air with Kiarra. I exhaled and allowed my wings to catch the dust and slowed the flapping slightly, to hover with her in the air.

"Good!" Kiarra praised, with a toothy, dragon grin (which to anyone else it would probably look like a snarl—all our expressions really looked like snarls, really…if you get used to us you do find a difference between them, though).

I beamed, feeling confidence as I felt Gabriel push another gentle gust of wind underneath me.

She caught on to what was happening, and she looked down at him. "Stop the conjuring, now. See if she can float on her own."

"Okay!" he shouted back, but it was lost in the gale of wind that came from in front of us. He pulled back his wind just as the other wind blew. I yelped, trying to exhale quickly and pull the dust back to my wings, but the wind pushed it away from me. I beat my wings harder and hung my head low to make myself a bigger blockade to the wind, but it just blew stronger and I felt my wings just give out, no matter how much I flapped, they just couldn't hold me up, and suddenly I was very aware of the ground beneath me and just how far it was. I knew I wouldn't die, but it *would* hurt. I wondered if I could heal myself…?

My musing was cut short by another gust of wind from the other direction that sent me tumbling forward, head down, tail overhead.

I heard Kiarra curse as she tried to fly under me but wasn't fast enough, the wind was strong for her too and she was having trouble staying up.

I looked pleadingly at Gabriel who was getting closer, rapidly. He held his arms out wide and narrowing his eyes in concentration, pulled all the air he could from nearby and pushed it underneath me, just in time to catch me before I slammed against the ground, headfirst.

I cussed, feeling him gently lower me the two or three feet to the ground, and I landed on my side as he dispelled the wind around us.

Vexed, I kicked the ground under me with one of my front legs and let out an angry, low growl.

Kiarra landed with grace next to me and knelt down on all fours. I hung my head, feeling ashamed. It looked so *easy*! Why couldn't I do it? If it wasn't for that pesky wind, I'd have it! I chuckled with contempt, shaking my head. *Silly dragon…you can't do anything about that.* I squinted my eyes shut, as Gabriel sat down cross legged in front of me. I buried my nose under the bend in my leg and sighed, feeling pity for myself.

Gabriel rubbed my forehead with a hand, and I dared to open one eye to see the piteous pout on his face. "I'm sorry. I wish there was something I could do."

My eyes flew open again, and I whipped my head up. Perhaps there was. "Well, you *are* a conjurer, are you not?"

He lifted a brow, curiously. "What are you getting at?"

"Well…can you push the wind away from me when it comes? Just until I get the hang of it?" I asked, pleading. I didn't realize just how badly I wanted to fly until now; my dragon soul was craving more. The sensation of being weightless, of being off the ground felt right, even if the wind did not.

Gabriel breathed out. "As long as you're near the ground, I could help. The second you get over those trees, though, I can't reach you."

I grinned. "So, come with me."

Kiarra let out a disturbed noise. "Leo! You can't possibly think that's a good idea! You know what you're asking?" Humans riding dragons was frowned upon, but it was hard to believe she held the same prejudices.

"So? He rides on my back, at least until I get the hang of it. No big deal," I replied with nonchalance.

Gabriel bit his lip, and exchanged a look with Kiarra. "No...I think she's getting at that I could fall."

My face fell, crestfallen. "Oh, yeah. Of *course*."

Gabriel frowned. He scoffed. "Fuck it. I know you won't let me, and you won't get that high until you really get the hang of it, right?" he asked me, almost pleading but trying to sound confident.

I grinned. "I won't go that high."

"I can just break any fall with the wind...right!" He leapt up to both feet with conviction. "Sure, let's try."

"You can't be—" Kiarra began, but we cut her off with a stare-down. "Okay, okay," she relented. "Whatever you want."

I growled with defiance. "Damn right," I mumbled. I raised myself on all fours, and bent my knees and lowered my head to the ground to allow Gabriel to climb on.

He paused at my side. "Umm..." he said, looking confused. He laughed, attempting to grab spots that weren't there to help pull himself up. "This isn't exactly like getting on a horse." He stepped back thoughtfully for a moment, rubbing his chin between is thumb and index finger. He snapped them together then. "I got it." He tossed the robes over his back, and exposed his chest, and more specifically, the string that wrapped around the neck and hood of his sweatshirt. He gave it a strong yank with both hands and pulled it all the way out. "Bridle."

Kiarra snickered. It was one thing to have a human ride you, it was another thing *entirely* to wear a bridle or saddle. But, I didn't care. I nodded at him and lowered my neck again, allowing him to tie the string around my neck. It barely made it around enough to tie, but he managed. "We'll find something better for next time. For now, this will have to do." He gave a couple yanks to make sure it wouldn't come off. "Oh, sorry...that hurt?"

I chuckled. "Did what hurt?" I kidded. I felt no more than a light tug.

He laughed. "Okay, good," he said. I knelt down again, craning my head backwards to watch him awkwardly grab the string and pull himself up slightly. "Here," I said, lifting one leg out to allow him to climb it, giving him height to throw his leg over me. He nearly tumbled off the other side, but I braced him with my wing and tightened them around him briefly, to allow him to balance his legs on either side of me. He scooted his backside back and forth to find a comfortable position.

"Okay, then," Gabriel said, nervously. He fixed his face up bravely. "This is…odd. But not bad." He said. "Softer than I thought it would be," he said.

"Are you saying I got big junk in my dragon trunk?" I asked with mock incredulity.

Gabriel gasped. "Oh—no I didn't mean that, I—" He was interrupted by the sound of Kiarra cackling uncontrollably, and it was very disconcerting in her dragon form. Sort of like she was a lion, getting strangled.

"Awkward," I just said, shaking my head. "I was kidding!"

Gabriel bumped me in the back of the head with his palm. I just cackled.

"Geez, dragons laughing is a *really* strange sound," Gabriel said, with a hesitant laugh.

"Sort of like a cow getting beat against a rock?" I suggested.

"Something like that, though I've never heard of someone beating a cow against a rock before so I'll just have to take your word for it," he responded sarcastically.

I snorted. "Are we ready?" I asked him. The moment I said this, I felt his legs tighten nervously on either side of my chest. "It'll be fine. Right?"

He nodded, his mouth in a firm, straight line. He grabbed the string in both hands and gripped tightly. "Y-yeah."

Kiarra shook her head. "First time for everything," she mumbled. "Just remember, you'll be slightly heavier now. It might be harder to take off."

I hadn't considered that. Some of my conviction started to leave, but Gabriel's joke helped lighten my mood, "What, are you saying I'm fat? You guys weigh like, what? A ton in your dragon forms? I feel like a feather to her." Kiarra wore a look on her face that said, "*If I had hands, I'd be facepalming right now.*"

I laughed loudly. "Ready?" I said, between chuckles.

"Yeah."

I flapped my wings and exhaled again, and flapped harder. I tried to push off the ground with my legs like I was going to jump, and I was airborne again, about halfway up the tree line.

I twisted my head to give Gabriel a glance. "You okay?"

Gabriel was concentrating (on what, I wasn't sure) so he just nodded, his forehead crinkling in thought.

I flapped a little harder and gave a big exhale and we flew higher and higher still, well over the tops of trees. Gabriel's nervous *gulp* was barely audible to me: I felt his weight shift as he briefly looked down at the ground. "Shit..." was all he muttered. "How you feeling?" he shouted to me, as a small burst of wind came from the clouds.

I braced myself and exhaled more dust, and out of the corner of my eye I could see one of Gabriel's hands give a wide gesture, the other hanging on the sweatshirt string for dear life. He pushed a gust of wind against it, and I remained unscathed.

"Cool!" I said, feeling a burst of confidence. I lowered my head, and flapped harder. "Hang on!"

Gabriel let out a curse, and tightened his grip as I picked up speed. I didn't gain altitude, but I was flying around the clearing, a bit faster with each pass around Kiarra, Gabriel fighting the gusts of wind with his own as I flew.

I giggled joyfully. "I'm flying!" I kicked my legs and I flew a little higher. Gabriel's grip tightened a moment, then loosened as I gained my bearings.

I looked down myself at the trees, mere toothpicks in the ground as high as I was flying, Kiarra's dragon form was a large spec on the ground. I swiveled around to catch a glimpse at the center of town: the market was just beginning. "Here we go!" I said, and lowered my wings slightly to allow the air to pass over, gaining a little speed as I flew over the trees, to the market.

"They're so small!" Gabriel mused, out loud. Every now and then he shot a burst of wind in various directions from his hands, and I flew the perimeter of the market. I was high enough so no one would really notice me unless they looked up. Dozens of people wandered around, and chattered, I caught random laughter and yells as vendors hawked their goods (food and crops, today, apparently), everyone looking like ants as I looked down.

"Leo—careful!" I heard Gabriel shout, but before he could get the words out, a massive gust of wind blew across the area, flying everyone's hair back and to the side, and vendors were chasing various things they were selling as they blew off their counters and into the Square.

It took me by surprise and knocked me slightly to the side, and I felt Gabriel slip. His legs tightened on either side of my body, and he leaned his entire body on my neck. "I can't fight this one, Leo!"

I blew out and flapped furiously, bending my neck down to allow the wind to glide over me, but as it did, we shook under the turbulence. Beating my wings as hard as I could I tried to stay aloft as the wind kept trying to push us down.

Gabriel kept shooting blasts of wind from his hand, underneath us to prevent me from falling to fast, but the people underneath us were growing larger as I slowly fell.

"We can't fall, Leo! You'll crush them!" he shouted at me.

I narrowed my eyes. I wouldn't fall. I would fight it.

With a newfound determination, I growled all the dust I could and picked it up in my wings, outstretched on either side as far as I could reach them. The growl must have been a bit louder than I thought, because a handful of people looked up, a couple screamed, sounding rather terrified. One ducked behind a vendor booth and cowered with a scream.

"Leo!" Gabriel cried, as we came near to flying over their heads.

"No!" I called out, beating harder and kicking my legs. I straightened my neck and just as I dipped, I caught my strength again and we flew back up to a safe distance.

"Phew…" Gabriel said, relieved. He patted my neck approvingly. "Good work."

I flew past the market and over the treeline, again, back to the clearing. Kiarra was hovering over the clearing, flapping casually like she didn't even have to think about it—and she probably didn't. I was *extremely* aware of my beating wings, of the way I jerked around as I lifted or bowed my neck and where the wind was as it darted across us (and Gabriel loosening and tensing his grip as I tried desperately not to toss him off the side).

"Nice save, girl," Kiarra said, with a nod of approval. "Let's bring it in for a landing." She turned and lowered herself to the ground with no effort, and I tried to mimic her movements: head down, legs tucked in, wings flapping slower. Gabriel assisted with shooting wind under me cushioning my jerky landing where I kind of thudded down, causing my front legs to bend and we skidded through the dirt a few feet; Gabriel clutching his arms around my neck. I could feel his jaw tense as he buried his face in my cold skin, and loosen again as we landed. Not gracefully, but safely.

I knelt on my knees and kept my head lowered, allowing Gabriel to slide off my left (well, more like slide and jump).

I straightened myself out after he was safely on the ground. The sudden realization of what I just did suddenly hitting me.

I flew. I actually *flew.*

Even in my dragon form, I could feel tears prick at my eyes (dragons in their dragon forms seldom cried) and my lower jaw quiver. A proud exhilarated feeling shivered down my back and through my wings. I looked back at them, rustling them slightly and giving a small grin. Maybe they weren't so bad after all.

Gabriel leaped in front of me, jumping up and down excitedly. "You did it! You flew!"

I nodded slightly. "I did..." I trailed off, turning around so I wasn't facing either of them. I didn't want them to see my joyful tears as they tumbled down my scaly face. I tucked my head under my wing as I began to sob, both terrified and relieved and happy.

"Leo..." Gabriel said softly joining me at the side, Kiarra on the other side.

"No!" I said, pulling away from his grasp. "No."

Gabriel and Kiarra hung back, but Kiarra said, "It really was great for a first time."

I nodded slightly, sniffling, snorting out my sparkles as I did so.

"Just like Harry Potter on the broomstick!" Gabriel offered, with a laugh.

I tittered, unburying my face and turning back towards them. "Ha," I said, trying to sound mocking. "I can't believe I did it. I can really *fly!*"

"You can. And you'll only get better at it," Kiarra said, sounding proud. She appeared sympathetic, watching happy tears roll out of my eyes. "I think that's enough for today." Underneath the blue robe she was wearing around her neck, she shifted back into her human form, Gabriel pointedly looking away from her even though as she shifted, the robes (thankfully!) covered all the key points.

Almost feeling reluctant, I lowered myself once again onto my knees to allow Gabriel to tie the pink robes around my neck, allowing them to drape over my front (covering *everything* in front, but if there was someone in back they surely were going to get a show!). I closed my eyes and I willed the change, again, feeling the familiar tense and squeeze of everything getting smaller and upright.

I heard a collective gasp from both of them as I finished and tried to pull myself to my feet...but instead I stumbled backward, feeling a heaviness I was unaccustomed to. With a yelp, I started feeling myself fall backward, pulled down by an unknown force.

Gabriel was quick, and grasped my hands before I fell. He helped steady me on my feet, all the while never ceasing to stop looking over my shoulder.

I wrinkled my forehead. "What?" I heard a flapping, like the noise of a bird's wings.

Kiarra, wide eyed just simply pointed behind me. "Leorah..."

I turned my neck quickly.

In back of me, my dragon wings remained, jutting out from my back and arched over my head and diving down, their edges barely scraping the dirt below.

I screamed, covering my surprise with my palm. I stumbled under the unfamiliar weight. Gabriel braced me once again, this time with the entire side of his body smashed into mine.

"Oh...my..." Dumbfounded, those were the only word Kiarra could mutter, both palms covering her open mouth.

"Try again, maybe it was just too much magic you used," Gabriel suggested, not sounding very convincing but it was a reasonable suggestion. "They're smaller than your dragon wings, though so you almost got it."

He was right, they were, but they were almost the size of my entire human form. I nodded though in agreement and kneeled again, willing the change into a human—a *full* human again, sans wings, and recalled the sensation of my wings being pulled into my back, leaving nothing behind.

I stood again, when I was satisfied, Gabriel swallowed, and simply pointed.

I looked over my shoulder again and yelped: my wings were still there.

"What the..." Kiarra muttered.

"Did this ever happen to your grandfather?" I demanded, my tone full of distress.

Shaking her head slowly in a *no*, Kiarra scratched her head with the fingers of her left hand. "We need to go see Finnian. *Now.*"

I didn't argue. Gabriel nodded, and helped fix the robes over my backside, biting the fabric over the spots where my wings jutted out with his canine teeth and ripping the fabric in long strips, allowing my wings to jut out comfortably and cover up my ass.

Kiarra stomped with a purpose through the clearing. Gabriel clutched one of my palms between his and pulled it to his chest with a comforting squeeze. He shot a worried look my way. I swallowed, and awkwardly followed behind him as we darted through the trees for the Loremasters main office in the center of town.

Chapter 18

Kiarra barreled through the French doors to the Loremasters' office, like an outlaw barging into a saloon. "*Finnian!*" she bellowed in such a low, roaring tone that nearly made *me* jump, as I was so used to hearing perky, giddy Kiarra.

A door attached to the office opened and Finnian emerged, wiping his hands off on a towel.

Kiarra said nothing. She simply pointed at me.

Finnian's jaw dropped. The towel fell to the floor, as his hands covered his open-mouthed, shocked expression. "Oh my…"

"What's wrong with me?" I whimpered, crossing my arms over my chest, as if holding myself would prevent the anxious trembling. It didn't. Gabriel placed two strong hands on my shoulders and grasped, sending his strength to me.

Finnian shook his head slowly, his wide eyes changed from the pleasant blue they were to a pale golden color. "I haven't seen anything like this before," was all he could remark. He stepped forward towards me, and reached out to one of my wings, folded against my back like an angel's wings were typically depicted. I shied away momentarily, causing the wings to rustle against each other. The noise startled me. I turned slightly to allow him to touch a wing.

He rubbed a palm along the outer side of my left wing, intrigue on his face. "Fascinating…" he mumbled to himself. "Does it…hurt?"

I thought a moment. It didn't hurt, but it was a bit uncomfortable if not heavy. I shook my head no. "Feels really weird, though."

"I imagine so," he said, touching various spots on the wing.

Kiarra tapped her foot impatiently behind him. "Well?"

Finnian shook himself out of a mesmerized daze, and swiveled on his heels to face her. "Right. I'm simply at a loss. What were you doing before this happened?"

"Flying," Gabriel offered. "Kiarra was helping her to fly. Me too."

Finnian arched his brow. "Really? Were you successful?" he asked me.

I nodded, with a small smile, my moment of triumph still fresh in mind but regrettably trumped by the winged nuisance on my back.

Finnian smiled widely. "Excellent. Besides the wings, how do you feel? Drained magically? Emotionally?"

"We thought that maybe she might have exhausted all her magic, and she wasn't able to shift fully into a human, leaving her wings stuck out, basically," Kiarra hypothesized.

"I would agree with you, but...they did shift, at least a little. Leorah, your wingspan is about twice what they are right now, correct?" Finnian questioned. "They look a little small for a dragon, yes?"

I nodded. "Yes, they are smaller."

"These are suited for a human's size, like fairy wings," Finnian said. He backed himself towards the desk and leaned against it, knocking several knick-knacks and pen cups over. It didn't faze him, he just rested his chin in his palm and drummed his fingers against his jawline.

"You don't think—" Kiarra began, but Finnian interrupted her with a flourish of his hand.

"Ceceline? Come, quick!" he hollered, to no one in particular. A door opposite the wall creaked open and emerged a short, voluptuous woman with white hair piled on her head artfully, piercing blue eyes and porcelain skin, ruby lips standing out like a sore thumb. She wore a set of bright red robes, which kind of made her appear to me like a candy cane. I almost laughed at the image, then I remembered why we were here...best not to piss off the lady who might have information.

"What?" she asked, in a melodic voice that sounded much younger than she appeared. Her face was lined appropriately, slightly crinkled around the mouth and eyes. I guessed she would be about fifty or so, but I knew these Loremasters lived quite a bit longer so it was anyone's guess as to how old she was. Her gaze trailed to me, and she gasped. "Son of a bitch," she cursed. She grinned, shamed. "So sorry," she said, covering her mouth with her hand briefly.

"Ceceline, this is Leorah. The pink dragon," Finnian said, motioning to me.

"Dragon?" She appeared more surprised this time. "But—"

"The wings, we know. What we don't know is why she can't shift out of them," Kiarra rolled her eyes impatiently.

Ceceline bit her lip. She narrowed her eyes, and I could see her eyes fall on Gabriel momentarily, as they shifted from blue to gray. Gabriel shifted uncomfortably under her gaze. I coughed out loud, pointedly.

"Hello? Dragon with a problem here!" I said, waving my arms wildly.

Ceceline turned away from Gabriel to me, and Finnian repeated to her what we told him about flying, my magic, etcetera. Ceceline just nodded thoughtfully.

"Well...I certainly have *never* seen another dragon who couldn't shift out of her wings. Can you move them, dear? Are they functional?"

I hadn't tried. As habitual as moving an arm, I outstretched one of my wings carefully, fluttering gently. The stretch in the wing felt quite pleasing, actually, so I outstretched the other.

"Clearly, they work," Finnian said unnecessarily.

"Quite," Ceceline responded, shortly. She reached out to touch the serrated edge, and rubbed her palm alongside it. "They are dainty but not fragile. Peculiar...a fairy's wings would be rather flimsy."

"So, no idea? And how do I get rid of them?" I demanded, feeling under scrutiny as both Loremasters poked and prodded and smoothed hangs along my wings.

"Well, dear, do you really want to? Imagine the possibilities. How handy it would be to fly in human form, wouldn't it be?" she said, hopefully. I scowled.

"How am I supposed to live with these things? They're...weird. How am I going to sleep?" I asked, feeling rather exasperated.

"You can't shift out of them? You're sure?" she questioned.

I frowned. "Don't you think I would if I could?"

"Okay, okay. I get it," she replied, with a laugh. "Dumb question, but I needed to know for sure."

Finnian suddenly slid across the desk he was leaning against, sending various items and papers tumbling to the floor as he landed in the chair and began furiously rummaging through drawers, obviously looking for something. Ceceline gave him an odd look but turned away and ignored him.

"Leorah, dear...I can sense magic in a person. Will you allow me—" she hovered her hand near my cheek. I nodded and she pressed her warm palm onto my face and closed her eyes. Almost immediately, she opened them and pulled away quickly.

"What? What did you see?" Gabriel insisted, trying to wrap an arm over my shoulder but finding it cumbersome with my wings. He settled for my waist instead and pulled me a bit closer to him, as close as the wings would allow.

"Magic. Very powerful magic. *Neither* of you is aware of *just* how powerful this magic is," she replied, intently.

"The Shadow?" I gulped.

She shook her head. "No. I sense the darkness but, it's faint. Hardly there. Just an echo, almost. What I sense is your magic. And the magic emanating off of him—" she said, pointing at Gabriel. She let out a nervous laugh. "I understand why they are gunning for you. Power like that on their side..." she trailed off, with a shudder. "I can't even think of the possibilities."

"Me?" Gabriel was taken aback. We exchanged wide-eyed glances.

She nodded. "Oh yes. You aren't any regular sorcerer indeed."

"So what do you think it is?" Finnian asked, peeking his head up from the mess of paper and folders he was creating on the desk and floor around him.

"I can't be sure, I have some theories but I need to be sure," she said. "Would you mind giving a bit of your blood, dear?"

"Huh? Why?" I asked.

"I want to make sure there are no other mythological beings in your bloodline," she explained.

"Is that even possible?"

"Oh yes, it is. As you've seen, many of the people here look fairly human. A nymph could have been posing as human and impregnated a human, or whatever the case may be. It could be...*generations* ago and you got the magic mix of mythological DNA," Ceceline explained.

I squeezed my eyes shut. "Ugggh...just what I need. To be even *more* of a freak."

Ceceline smiled warmly. She turned to Kiarra. "Dear, would you mind getting a syringe and wipe from the infirmary?" Kiarra nodded, and set off on her mission.

"Another explanation could be just a magical, evolutionary one. To be able to use one's dragon wings as a human gives you...many advantages," she said.

My cheeks flushed sheepishly. "Well...maybe not. I can barely fly."

She was taken aback. "Oh? That is...that is something indeed." She crossed her arms over her chest and drummed her fingers on a forearm, thoughtfully.

Kiarra arrived moments later, with a tall, lanky woman who was carrying a tray of first-aid items.

"She refused to let anyone else draw blood," Kiarra said, with a chuckle.

The tall woman chuckled. "Hell no. That's what I'm here for. You'd probably give her Ebola or taint the results." She turned and looked at me, and I was surprised by her pale eyes, against her snow-white skin under a shock of jet black hair in a pixie crop. She grinned at me, revealing two sharp, pointy canine teeth. "You must be the dragon in question," she said, setting down her tray on Finnian's unkempt desk. She groaned in annoyance. "Really, Finn? What the hell is this?"

Ceceline waved her off. "Oh, you know him...just having a *moment*," she responded scornfully.

"Shut up!" Finnian retorted, his head buried in a filing cabinet. Even in my uncomfortable situation I couldn't help but chuckle at him.

She turned back to me, with a square packet that she ripped open and stepped towards me. Wide-eyed and hesitant, I involuntarily stepped back. "You're..."

She rolled her eyes. "Okay, let's get this over with. Yes, I'm a vampire. No, I do not attack people or steal their blood. It's a viral mutation that attacks people with certain genes, and here I am."

I forced a smile. "I'm sorry, it's just—"

"I know, I know," she said, dismissing my apology, as if she was used to hearing all this before. "I am Evie, by the way."

"Leorah." I responded. I gingerly held out my arm. "So, you really don't drink blood?"

"Well, I do but I do *not* forcefully take it from anyone," she replied, ripping open the back and pulling out an alcohol wipe. The smell burned my nostrils and I wrinkled my nose. "I know, it's strong. Sorry. I know how sensitive dragons are to smell."

I nodded.

"So, you are a vampire who drinks blood and here you are, taking blood from her?" Gabriel finally piped up, looking just as shocked as I felt.

She snorted, wiping off a spot on my upper forearm and tapping the area with a finger, apparently looking for a vein. "It's not what you think. Before I contracted the virus, I was a nurse. I live here now because, yes, the bloodlust around humans is hard to deal with. I have never attacked anyone, and I never will. We just don't do that. But here, I don't have to deal with any of it, I have no taste for magic blood. Like yours," she said, nodding at me. "Or yours, sorcerer." She raised a brow at him, and he smiled sheepishly.

"Sorry...you have to admit though, it's a little weird," he replied, with a nervous giggle.

"No more than throwing fireballs from your hand," she said, with a wink towards him. She reached for a rubber tourniquet on her tray and tied it around the lower part of my bicep, tapping the area underneath again. "Perfect." She reached for a syringe and needle. "This will just be a slight pinch." Deftly, she maneuvered the needle into my skin. I didn't even wince at the mosquito-bite feel. She pulled the plunger out and extracted blood from my arm. It was only a few moments before it filled up, and she pulled the needle out carefully, replacing it with a gauze pad with a sticky back. "Easy peasy."

"Thanks?" I said, rubbing the area with my hand.

She snickered. "Sure. I will go take a look at this and see if I find any magical markers," she said. She paused. "No, I won't drink the rest when I'm finished."

I laughed. "So, how do you get blood?"

"Blood banks and such. I have some inside friends in the business who legally obtain it for me. If they can't for whatever reason, I find someone who can compel and obtain it that way. But never from the person; always a willing donor into a bag or vial," she explained. "I hate to do it, but I have no other choice. The virus makes it so that our bodies just don't replace blood very fast, so it's like a transfusion, sort of. I still eat regular food too. I just run the infirmary here to give back to the place that gives me refuge and so my six years of nursing school don't go to total waste," she said. Evie nodded at Gabriel and Ceceline. "I'll get back to you guys." She put some sort of cap on the syringe, placed it on her tray and carried the tray out the door, pushing the door open with her backside.

"I'll be damned...." I said. Gabriel and I laughed.

"That was unexpected," he said.

Ceceline was bored with our tittering. "I suspect she won't find anything, but just in case. In the meantime, I suppose you really want them gone, yes?"

I nodded. "Any ideas?"

"No...but perhaps with some rest, rejuvenate your magic you'll be able to fully shift back into your *fully* human form," she said. "Finnian and I will continue to search for something in our files, but I believe this is unprecedented."

I sighed, feeling defeated. "So I just have to deal, for now?"

Ceceline nodded. "I'm afraid so."

I groaned.

"Stop by and see Esmè, again. She might have some advice. Or, perhaps one of the fey can help advise you by how they get their wings to retract. Once you get them back in, it may just be a fluke," Finnian said, poking up his head from behind the desk again. "*A-ha*!" He yanked something out of whatever he was looking in—it appeared to be a large, brown folder with a string around it—and set it on his desk. "Pardon me, I have some reading to do. I will get back to you if I find anything."

"As will I," Ceceline said. She patted the side of my arm, stoic, but in an attempt to be reassuring before disappearing out the same door she had come in.

I swiveled around and faced Gabriel, looking defeated. "Now what?"

"I can take you to one of the fey," Kiarra said, giving me a sympathetic glance. I just shrugged at the idea.

"Really, I don't know why it's so bothersome," Finnian offered, plopping himself down on his desk and crossing his long legs under him. "I mean, they're gorgeous wings. I've seen websites where people pay hundreds of dollars to buy fake wings that aren't even *half* that stunning," he said.

I frowned. "They can take them off, though, right?"

"Yes...okay, I'm not good at offering comfort. Your friends are better for that." Finnian flashed us a wide smile before burying his head in the documents he pulled out of the folder.

Gabriel pulled my arm. "Let's go, Leo."

"I'll meet you at your rooms," Kiarra said. She pointed at Finnian who was clearly oblivious to our presence and I nodded.

"'Kay," I replied, pouting and allowed Gabriel to lead me out of the office.

We weren't in our room more than five minutes, when the door burst open and Daniel popped in. "I *knew* it!" he said, followed by Maxxus ducking in a moment later.

Maxxus stared in disbelief at me, but said nothing. He didn't need to; Daniel spoke for him.

"What the *fuck*?" Daniel was awed.

I groaned, as I attempted to toss myself onto the sofa. I let out a *yelp*, my wings pinching under my weight I jumped right back up. "Wonderful. Now I can't even *sit*!"

"What happened?" Maxxus questioned with concern. "Does...does it hurt?"

I shook my head. "No, just uncomfortable." I stood in the center of the room, looking for a place to sit. Gabriel noticed, and produced a barstool from the kitchen area and brought it into the living room for me. I sat on it, rigidly, having to maneuver carefully so as to not sit on the wings.

"You said *'I knew it'*, when you came in," Gabriel prompted his brother. "What did you mean?"

Daniel shrugged. "Maxxus and I were eating at that tavern—*to die for*, by the way—the ribs smelled divine and although—"

"*Daniel*. Focus here. What did you *mean*?" Gabriel demanded, grasping his brother on the forearms, shaking him slightly.

Daniel narrowed his eyes down at his brother. "Chill, bro," he said, gently pushing him back. "I mean, that I had a brief vision. Not much, but there was a sense of confusion, and elation...and then frustration, and all I saw was her face."

Maxxus raised his eyebrow. "It was...weird. His eyes rolled into the back of his head and he got catatonic. *Very* odd indeed," he said, with a slight shudder, as if recalling something he didn't want to.

"Oh you get used to it," Daniel said, with a dismissive wave of his hand.

"So, you are like, clued into her, somehow?" Gabriel questioned. "That seems like an awfully vague vision for you to have."

Daniel shrugged. He brushed off a piece of lint from his blue muscle tee and ruffled his spikey hair. "I guess it's because of your connection to her, and my connection to you. We're linked psychically, maybe. But I knew we should probably find out what was wrong anyways. I see that I was right." He was eyeing the wings very curiously, I could almost see him fighting the urge to reach out and touch them.

I rolled my eyes. "*Go* ahead. You know you want to."

Daniel let out a chirp of glee, and ran his hands all over my left wing. "Marvelous..."

Maxxus stood back hesitantly, giving him a strange look. He appeared uncomfortable, out of place as he tried to find a place to stand, finally relenting to lean against the wall across the room, crossing one foot over another. He rubbed at his rust-colored goatee thoughtfully, as if pondering something.

"Everything okay?" I questioned him, acknowledging his pensive mood.

Maxxus shook himself out of a thought, and forced a smile. "Oh, yeah. I'm sorry. I should be asking *you* that question!"

I scoffed. "I'm wonderful, no worries. I'm just a dragon in human form that now apparently has wings. No big deal."

He smiled warmly. "How did it happen? They just...shoot out randomly or were you shifted or what?"

"She was flying," Gabriel responded proudly. "I helped, but only a little."

I chortled. "It was a lot more than a little, but yeah."

Maxxus' mouth opened in an *O* of joyful surprise. "You flew? Really?" One of the common conversations I had with him while waiting for my brother to fly in and rescue me from my shame was how frustrating it was not being able to fly like a normal dragon. He grinned. "Leorah! That's amazing!"

Even I couldn't help but smile. "Yeah...it kind of was."

"Then she shifted back afterward and the wings wouldn't go away," Gabriel offered, not wanting to be left out of the conversation. He tossed himself on the sofa with a sigh, and his brother followed suit.

Maxxus raised a brow. "Wow. That is...that is odd."

"No shit, Sherlock," I retorted dryly. I glanced up at him, who looked a little wounded at my sarcasm. "I'm sorry, I'm just...a little edgy."

His face softened. "No, it's okay. I just...I don't know what to say. Sorry?" he offered.

"It's fine," I answered with a laugh. "It's fucked up, that's all I can say."

"Well, if you can fly in your dragon form—is it possible to fly in human form? Wouldn't that be a kick?" Daniel asked.

I shrugged. "Maybe. And none of the Loremasters have any idea why or how it happened, but they're 'looking into it'," I said dryly, making quotation marks in the air with my fingers.

"What good are they, then?" Maxxus scoffed, with a laugh.

"I don't know, actually." I heaved a heavy sigh, resting my elbows in my lap and resting my head in my palms. I whined out loud. "This is uncomfortable!"

"Give it some time, maybe you'll be able to shift *out* of it," Maxxus offered.

"But, wouldn't it be awesome if they worked?" Daniel said, looking mischievous. He jumped up from his spot on the sofa, grabbed my arms, pulling me reluctantly off the stool and out the door to the field just outside the guest rooms

"What are you doing?" I grumbled unhappily.

"Well…you were flying before. Can you fly now? Logic stands to reason…" Daniel said. Gabriel and Maxxus both emerged from the doorway.

I just stood there, outside, feeling rather exposed. There was no one around but a couple of kids in the distance but I just felt…strange. *Odd.*

"Well?" he prompted.

I shrugged. I outstretched the wings, and my arms along with them and closed my eyes, my face pointed up at the sky. I took a deep breath, and exhaled. Without even having to think about it, my wings started beating, like they were their own separate entity and I was suddenly feeling weightless.

"Shit." That was all I heard before I opened my eyes, looking down at the top of Maxxus' head, from about seven feet off the ground (his human form was well over six feet, for sure). He covered his mouth with his hand, eyes agape with emotion.

Gabriel grinned as well. "That is just flippin' awesome."

I looked down at the ground, and back at the wings which were steadily beating. In my human form it actually felt a bit more effortless, flying did, my feet dangling in the air. I grinned despite myself.

I scanned out the area around me, a couple of kids—I would guess young sorcerers or witches—were nearby in the woods, messing around with elements. One boy would pull up a tuft of dirt and earth with his hands and "throw" it at the other one, the other would respond by tossing a puddle of water, summoned by his hands. They were giggling gleefully at each other, their clothes and hair muddy and mussed but they didn't have a care in the world. I felt wistful, watching the two boys play, and just be themselves. I didn't know what they were—human, fairy, but it didn't matter. Not here.

I found myself flying nearer to them, my feet kicked out behind me and I was horizontal with the ground. One of the boys caught my eye and just waved.

"We're doing magic!" he called excitedly, conjuring up a ball of water from seemingly nowhere and throwing it at his companion, just as the red-headed boy (I was guessing they were brothers but I had no idea, actually) was speaking under his breath, some kind of rhythmical incantation. Suddenly, spires of fire began shooting up around them in a circle. I gasped as the boys screamed, and clutching one another.

The other boy—a cute little brunette—pleaded at me through wide brown eyes. "Help!"

The spires of fire were growing higher, taller and edging in towards the boys. I looked back at my boys—Gabriel and company—and realized that they didn't see what was going on. They were intently discussing something. They wouldn't be able to see anything, anyhow, the fire concealed by the shrubs and trees alongside the edge of town.

One of the boys shrieked as one of the fire spires roared and began shooting ash and sparks around, the boys had to duck to barely avoid them.

I summoned up my courage and flapped my wings harder. I didn't even think to exhale my dust—not that much would come out (not enough to fly faster, anyhow—not like in dragon form) but it didn't matter, I gained altitude and speed anyways.

I heard one of the boys shout my name, suddenly realizing what was happening and the three of them began running towards us, but they wouldn't arrive in time, the fire was inching in towards the boys quickly.

I shot my fist out, demanding that I fly upward and my wings and body responded correctly darting up over the flames and down in the center of the creeping flames.

"Are you okay?" I asked, landing deftly in the center like I had been flying as a winged human my entire life.

The two boys in tears just threw themselves at me, and I wrapped my arms around them, and shielded them with my body. My wings spread out and over them as well acting as another barrier from the heat of the fire that was all too close. I wasn't sure if I could grab them and fly out. I clutched them close, one under each arm and began beating my wings again and willed myself to fly upwards. My feet began to hover off the ground, but I could only get as far as my tiptoes before realizing my wings couldn't handle the weight of the three of us.

"I can't fly out!" I shouted, at no one, nearly into a panic. The heat was beginning to prick at my skin, causing beads of sweat to drip down my forehead. My blood pressure started to raise and my heart beat about a mile a minute as my eyes darted back and forth in between the boys and the fire.

I heard a *hiss* and I peered around one boy that had buried his face into my side, sobbing uncontrollably. The other boy was coughing uncontrollably. I covered his nose and mouth with my palm, and he grabbed it, pushing it tighter against his face. I caught a glimpse of Gabriel between the flickers of flames, rapidly shooting water balls at the flames, to no avail. It just wasn't enough.

"If I could...." I thought to myself. I wasn't sure if I could grasp his magic through the fire.

"Leo!" I watched as Maxxus shifted into his dragon form, and began to barrel into the towers of fire.

Without thinking about it, I held up my hand as if to push him away. My wing came up with my outstretched palm and somehow, even though Maxxus was currently trying to barrel through the fire, he stopped dead in his tracks. He kept trying to run against the invisible force but wasn't getting anywhere.

I glanced momentarily at my hand. Somehow, I was preventing him from entering.

One of the little boys screamed, as a spark flew at his leg, scalding a hole in his pants. He cried out in pain.

"No!" I breathed out, trying to blow out the flame. The dust danced around the fire momentarily before squelching it out. The boy breathed a short-lived sigh of relief.

Since Maxxus couldn't get in, I watched him from the other side, breathe out with a loud growl a huge flame of green "fire" at the ground, causing a mound of earth to jut upwards. Gabriel saw this, and summoned a large water ball and tossed it at the earth, causing a large splatter of mud that momentarily dissipated one of the fire spires before it shot up again this time a little smaller. The two of them joined forces and began shooting their own magics at it, not having much success. The fire was too strong, nearly out of control.

Clearly, it was up to me.

"Stay close. If something happens to me, those two on the other side are trying to get you out. There will be a small window of time when the fire is low enough to jump out, but you'll have to be quick!" I shouted at the boys. One nodded, the other one just wrapped his arms around my leg.

It's like the tornado, Leo. The storm. You just...will it gone. Imagine it getting smaller. Picture a cloud of rain pouring over us, putting it out.

I bit my lip and inhaled deeply, ignoring the smoke entering my lungs. I sputtered briefly but breathed in again, fighting against the burning. I looked up towards the sky, at the cloudless blue above and imagined a rain storm suddenly overhead, dropping a monsoon of water, all around us. I closed my eyes and exhaled, throwing my sparkled mist at the sky.

I felt my wings outstretch wide, and a cool breeze floated in from above us. I pretended to grab it with both hands and pull it down and over the flames. They hissed and roared in protest, the wings I hadn't wanted cooperating, beating quickly, helping to push the air outside and all around us.

I heard a crack of thunder. I looked up at the sky and out of nowhere, a gray cloud was swirling. I fought back a joyous and relieved laugh. I shut my eyes again, picturing the cloud dumping a deluge of water all over us.

At first, it was only a trickle. I breathed out again, feeling the spatters of rain touch my wings. In response, the wings outstretched as far as they could, I felt the pull on my shoulders.

I felt the tension in the sky, the cloud was ready to release its storm but it needed coaxing. I opened my eyes, and willed it to release its water.

As if responded, the sky opened up directly over us, and poured rain all over us.

The fire sizzled and hissed in response, and was lessening but it wasn't nearly fast enough it was still inching way too close, nearly touching the feet of the little boy on my right.

I gasped. My wings folded over the two boys as a shield and I looked up at the sky, feeling desperation and anger. "More!" I called out to no one in particular, but it responded by releasing a torrent of water. I closed my eyes once more, imaging the rain pouring over us, over the fire and stomping it out furiously. I threw my hands up and slammed them down, and the wings followed suit as if commanding the water to shoot out and at the flames. More hissing, more popping as the flames were reduced to steam. I opened my eyes the flames a mere circle around us now.

Gabriel summoned a wall of water from the rain pouring down, and threw it at the base of the fire in front of him. The fire sputtered and fizzled out completely.

"Now, Leo!" I wasn't sure which of the men shouted this at me—Maxxus I believe, as I could barely hear Gabriel's human voice over the roar of the flames. I released my hold on the rain and bent over the boys, wings reaching out on other side again and down, wrapping around the boys clutched to my side, protecting them from the heat of the flames that remained and ran them through the opening in the circle.

Daniel was immediately ready, pulling the boys away from me and lifting them effortlessly and holding them against his body. I nodded a *thank you* to him.

"Leo!" Gabriel pointed at the ring of fire, which was starting to grow again.

I swallowed nervously, relieved that once the boys were out of immediate danger, but this fire needed to be contained or else it was going to engulf the entire town.

I ran in between both Gabriel and Maxxus, who were still trying to throw their own magics at the base of the fire and having nominal success combining the summoned earth and water as mud.

"We just need more!" Maxxus hollered, not taking his eyes off the spire of fire that he was trying to contain. It had been only a couple inches high just a few moments ago, but now that I wasn't concentrating on the rain above me, it was beginning to dissipate.

"Leo, can you shoot this at the sky with your magic? Everything you got!" Gabriel called to me, spinning his hands around each other, causing a large ball of elemental magic to combine with each other—a ball of water and wind and electricity—a plasma ball. "To strengthen the cloud over us!" he explained, as I was about to open my mouth and ask why.

I nodded.

"On three..." Gabriel aimed the ball of energy above him, pushing it delicately, slowly. "One...two..." I inhaled and summoned my will to shove it at the sky with *everything* I had.

"Three!" Gabriel shouted, pushing it towards the sky.

I exhaled, pushing my magical dust at the sky. It was struggling to reach the cloud overhead and the ball of energy Gabriel had summoned was beginning to disperse.

"It's not enough!" he yelled.

Feeling a sudden urge of determination, I beat my wings rapidly and jumped into the air, gaining altitude quickly. I didn't even have the time to look under me as I shot up into the air, nearing Gabriel's energy ball. My wings beat steady as I got close enough to nearly wrap my arms around it, and they slowed for a moment, allowing me to hover with it.

I felt the energy from the magic tingle at my skin, waking up my nerves, causing every hair on my body to stand on end. I placed a hand on either side of it and it responded by resting in my grasp. It felt...powerful. Strong. I fought back the urge to smile at the surge of power welling up inside me. *Focus!* I yelled at myself in my mind.

I glanced up at the sky, the cloud above me was beginning to separate. I pulled the energy ball close to me for a moment and, exhaling my dust into it, shoved it with a push into the sky.

The cloud seemed to explode then, in a burst of wind and water. Thunder crackled, a bolt of lightning darted out and touched the ground nearby momentarily, shaking the earth like a volcano eruption and the sky opened up and dumped buckets and buckets full of rain and hail rapidly.

I leaned forward slightly, allowing my wingspan to cover me shielding me from the oncoming pea size hail. A crack of thunder boasted from the sky, almost as if speaking to me, announcing its arrival. I glanced down momentarily at the fire below, it was rapidly going out as the rain and hail pelted the earth below me. A gust of wind blew from the cloud, threatening to knock me from my flight. It would be a hard landing if I fell.

"No!" I told it with determination, pushing my hands out in front of me as if to stop the gust of wind from hitting me. It stopped and pushed against my hands. I felt the energy of the air, frustrated it was contained. I smiled, feeling triumphant that I had conquered it.

"Down there!" I demanded, like it was a person with an identity. I pushed it down towards the ground, and combined with the rain it swirled downwards like a brief tornado, stifling any flame left behind on the ground, spinning the flame into submission. I looked down at it from above, my wings keeping me comfortably aloft in the air. I watched the wind pull the flame up into its funnel and suffocate it (which seemed odd, like the opposite of what should have happened). I just watched it, entertained and mesmerized by the wind and rain dancing around each other, attacking the ash and spark on the ground.

"Enough, Leo!" a voice boomed from the ground. I glanced briefly to see Maxxus had been tossed about twenty feet from where he had been, struggling to get up from the ground. Gabriel was nearby, face down into the ground, making his body smaller as if trying to hide from the storm. I let out a cry of surprise, and glanced back down at the storm.

"Enough!" I told it, and spread my hands apart, inhaling and exhaling the dust again, willing it to dissipate into the atmosphere above.

And suddenly, it stopped. The winds calmed, the rain lessened to drizzle and eventually just ended, and the cloud above me parted and dispersed around me in a puff of steam.

I stood motionless for a moment, afraid to move and jinx the magic. I stared, wide-eyed at each of the boys in turn, all of them staring at me, mouths agape until one of the little boys whimpered. It was the one who had cast the spell went awry, who'd had a hole scalded into his pants. He bent over clutching the area with his hands. I dashed over to him and knelt in front of him, on my knees.

"It hurts!" he cried, tears of fear and pain trickling down his dirty, soot-stained face.

I gave him a sympathetic look. "Sit down. Let me see if I can fix that."

He nodded, carefully plopping his butt down on the ground and stretching out his injured leg in front of him.

I carefully pulled away the scalded fabric from the burn, and he cried out. Some of it had actually fused with his skin. I bit my lip. I motioned behind me, and called for Gabriel who was by my side in a second. He flinched, when I pointed at the burn.

"Some cool water should help." Gabriel summoned a ball of water between his hands. I poked out a finger and touched it, testing the temperature. "Can you make it colder?"

"I will try." He waved his hands around the water ball, eyes concentrating as he did. "Best I can do."

I touched it again, it was a little colder, but not much.

"Hmm..." I closed my eyes, picturing a snowball in Gabriel's hands, and held a palm out from my lips and blew gently, I heard the noise of a crisp winter breeze as I did.

I heard the tell-tale crackle of ice as the outside of the ball crystallized into ice. I tried not to grin at the awesomeness of it, since the boy was still whimpering but fixated on the cold ice ball in front of Gabriel.

"Can I?" I asked, putting my hands on the open sides of the ball, and Gabriel nodded. I grasped the water magic in my hand, gently and lifted it out of Gabriel's grasp and slowly moved it to the little boy's leg and exhaled, blowing the dusted water gingerly at the wound on his leg. I closed my eyes, imagining the water soothing the pain and cooling the skin and blew out again.

The little boy let out a sigh of relief, as the water had turned to snow and trickled over his skin. "That feels better."

I smiled at him warmly. "That was some crazy magic you did there. What were you thinking?"

He bit his lip, clearly embarrassed. "I'm sorry. My mother is a sorceress. My brother too," he said, nodding towards his companion, still cowering into Daniel who had picked up the little boy and was hugging him against his chest, patting his back. "I didn't get any powers, but my mom said I'd be a good witch if I practiced. I might even learn some magic, too, like them. It was a spell in a book of my mom's." He looked down at the ground, crestfallen. "I'm sorry."

"It's a good thing Leorah was here to save the day," Gabriel said, patting me on the shoulder. I rolled my eyes at him.

"Well...for what it's worth, it *did* work. A little...too well." I said, motioning towards the spot where they were playing, scorch marks in a circle on the ground, soot painted on the nearby trees.

He managed a half-smile. "I think...I think I'll wait and have my mom help me."

I grinned. "Now, that's a good idea." The snow had melted and trickled off his leg onto the ground below, leaving behind a severely reddened area, but it was obviously less painful, and the ice had hardened the fabric and it had fallen off easily. "Going to try one more thing." I placed my hands around the burn, splaying my fingers, and closed my eyes. I imagined the burn turning from red, to pink to white and fading away, his normal skin growing over it. I breathed out, my wings were shrouding over me, over my arms as if channeling the magic down my arms.

When I opened my eyes, no wound remained. Not a mark, not any redness...not even a scar. I raised a brow and exchanged a look with Gabriel.

"That tingled!" the boy said with a giggle. He peered over at his leg, pulling his pants up to his knee and exposing the area of skin that I had healed. He marveled at the fact that nothing was there. "It's gone! You healed me!" He grinned gleefully at me, standing up and throwing himself into my arms, nearly knocking me in a thankful bear hug.

"What *happened* here?" Kiarra piped up from behind us. We turned to see her, looking expectant, arms crossed over her chest.

"They had a little accident," I replied, the little boy avoiding Kiarra's stern gaze.

Kiarra frowned, but the boy piped up. "She fixed everything!" he said, pointing at me.

She glanced at the other little boy with Daniel, and he nodded, who gently set the boy on his feet. Kiarra outstretched her hands, motioning for the boys to come with her. "Well...Jackson, Davis...I'm going to walk you to your house and you're going to tell me *exactly* what happened, okay?" The boys—the one I'd healed appearing to be Jackson—turned back to us and waved, and placed their hands in hers. Over her shoulder she said she'd be right back.

I stood up, placing my hands on my hips, feeling self-satisfied. I beamed, but Gabriel, Maxxus and Daniel just stood there, staring at me, dumbfounded. Maxxus, robes still tied around his neck, shifted back into human form and wore the same human expression of shock and awe pointed at me.

It was Daniel who spoke first. "*Shit*, Leo!"

Gabriel stammered, apparently trying to find the right word. When none came, his brother spoke for him.

"You realize, that you conjured an entire *storm*, right?"

"I had Gabriel's plasma ball too, remember?" I retorted.

"Yeah but...it wouldn't cause *that* amount of magic. That was...insane!"

I shrugged. "It was just a little rain."

"Rain? Just a little *rain*!?!?" Gabriel exclaimed, thunderstruck. He slapped his palms against his face, making unintelligible noises.

"Leorah, it was an entire storm, not just a little rain," Maxxus offered, a little rattled.

"And you conjured it out of *nowhere*!" Gabriel finished, slapping the sides of his face and shaking his head. "Are you *sure* you've never done this magic stuff before I found you? I mean...there is no way you can be *that* powerful, just in a couple weeks' time!"

I crossed my arms over my chest and narrowed my eyes. "I already *told* you, I have never done this before in my *life* okay? Except that one time with that bully dragon long, long ago. I never have. Shit, what does a dragon gotta do to get peoples to believe her?" I grumbled under my breath.

"I know it sounds crazy but I really don't think she has," Maxxus piped up, coming towards me and offering a comforting hand on my shoulder. I jerked away and continued scowling. "Seriously, though..." he turned to Gabriel, looking stern, his blue eyes staring him down. "You have *no* idea what it's like for dragons up there who *don't* fit in. I couldn't do magic, either for a very, very long time."

I blinked, surprised. "What? Really?" I knew he had had a rough time, but I didn't know that's why. I just knew he'd had strife with his family; who were very influential in the Court. I'd always figured it was some deep-rooted argument or something of that nature. Not that he'd struggled with magic. *And why didn't I know about that?* Seems like something that would have come up in conversation with my grandfather, you'd think. Sure would have made me feel better to know I wasn't the *only* one who struggled with magic.

He nodded solemnly. "I was an embarrassment to my family. It wasn't until your Grandfather..." he trailed off, looking sullen, "...well, I finally learned but in the meanwhile, it was *hard* listening to all the ridicule. It was pure hell; I wouldn't wish the scrutiny on my worst enemy. So, why in the *fuck* would Leo be faking that she couldn't do magic, when if she could—it probably would have made her life a whole lot easier? Huh?" Maxxus' mouth was in a straight line, glaring sternly at Gabriel.

Gabriel puffed up his chest and squared his shoulders, glaring right back. He opened his mouth to speak, but stopped, softened his gaze and looked at me. "Leo—I didn't mean *that*. I just didn't think it was possible for anyone—*anyone*—to be that powerful right off the bat."

"She always has been, she just didn't know it," Maxxus said, sounding a little...boastful? He was still continuing his stare down, his fists clutched at his sides.

"I believe I may have some insight on that." A vaguely familiar voice chimed in from behind us. I swiveled around; it was Evie, the vampire, clutching a manila folder by her chest. She waved it in the air, indicating that she received some sort of test results from my blood. "Can we?" she nodded towards the door to our room, and I nodded as she waited for Gabriel to wave his hand over the doorknob unlocking the magic lock and pulled the door open for all of us to walk in.

"Sit down," I said, offering her a spot on the couch. I attempted to sit down next to her, but couldn't quite maneuver past the wings. I groaned, trying to push them off to the side. "Please tell me you have a solution?"

The others—Gabriel, Daniel and Maxxus—all sat around the room, in chairs or on the floor (Daniel was cross-legged on the floor, looking like a little kid on the "magic rug" awaiting story time). I noticed as Maxxus took a seat on the nearby velveteen chair, Gabriel made a big production of picking up the stool and moving it across the room—nearly out the door—as far as he could get. I shot him a dirty look briefly before turning to Evie, hopeful.

Evie sighed. "Well, I can't say that I do. But...let me just ask, have you *ever* gone and had your blood drawn anywhere? Like at a human doctor or...something?"

"What? No, of course not." I furrowed my expression. "Gods only know *what* they'd see; one weird cell and it's off to the laboratory to be a dragon guinea pig."

Evie laughed shortly. She pulled out a piece of paper and handed it to me.

I looked it over. It was a bunch of numbers and letters, with some kind of diagram. I handed it back to her with a shrug. "No idea what this is."

"Just a second." She produced another sheet of paper from the folder, and handed that to me. I glanced at it; whatever it was looked extremely similar to the first. "Well...what am I looking at? Seriously, whatever they are, they look the same." I thrust them back at her in frustration.

"That's precisely the point: you cannot tell the difference between them." She produced a *third* sheet of paper from the folder and handed it to me. I cocked a brow at the random letters and numbers—twice as many as the other two pages. "Okay, this is different."

She nodded. "Now, pick out which one you think is your blood results."

I snorted. "Um, obvious. This one." I waved the third piece of paper in the air.

She swiped it from me. "*Wrong*."

Out of the corner of my eye, I saw Maxxus shift forward in his seat a little more, as if suddenly intrigued.

"Wait, what? I'm confused."

"One of these papers contains your test results. The other a human's," she explained; her mouth was partially open, her tongue running along the bottom of one of her sharp fangs. I heard Daniel gasp *ever* so quietly. Evie glanced at him momentarily, who just smiled sweetly.

"Yes, I am what you think I am," she told him dryly. She turned back to me, her pale eyes playful as I scanned over both sheets of paper, looking for some sort of difference.

"I am not sure what this means?" I said, rhetorically.

"*It means*, Leorah, that your DNA is virtually indistinguishable from a human's. Meaning, you could go to a human doctor, have your blood taken and no one would be the wiser that you're anything *but* human," Evie said. "It's…fascinating really. I've never seen anything like it."

My mouth fell open. "But…how is this possible?"

"Does that mean she's *actually* part human?" Gabriel mused from the opposite side of the room. "That doesn't explain the magic part…"

Evie had to crane her head over her shoulder to peer at him. "Well…that we're not sure about. It's a possibility. *But*…there's more."

"More?" I swallowed the lump welling in my throat. "I'm some sort of like, demon?"

Evie snorted. "No, not a demon. At least I don't *think*."

I let out a little squeal, and she chuckled.

She pulled out another page and handed it to me. It was a picture…a bunch of red circles.

"What's this?" I questioned.

"*That* is a close up of some of your blood cells and platelets. As you can see—very human in appearance," she said. "But when you view them under *here*," she stood up momentarily to produce a thick magnifying glass from her pocket and handed it to me. "There. Look through *that*."

I held the glass in my hand—which was deceptively light—and positioned it over the picture. There, appearing next to the red cells were very, very faint circles and shapes of different colors, almost misty in appearance. "What the—?"

"The glass is spelled to detect magic. What you're seeing is the actual magic in *your blood.*"

"What?" Gabriel was on his feet in a split second, and grabbed the glass and picture away from me and looking for himself. Daniel jumped up and was peering over his shoulder.

"What does that mean?" I asked, my voice small and somewhat appalled.

"I'm not sure, exactly," she replied. "It's nothing anyone has ever seen before. Somewhere along the line, I cannot tell if it was in *you* specifically, or just your genetic line, someone infused your DNA with some extra, super powerful magic." She yanked out yet another page from her folder and handed it to me. She grabbed the glass away from Gabriel with a scowl and handed it to me.

I looked through it at the picture, similar to the one I already looked at: red cells, platelets, but it looked the same under the glass as without.

"And this." Another page. This one had at least triple the red cells, along with some other ones I could not recognize but again, the glass revealed nothing special.

"One of these is human—a sorceress, actually—and the other is dragon. Even though they are magical, there is no actual magic in the *blood*," she explained. "So, what you have is…something quite extraordinary indeed."

I let out a groan, covering my face with my palms and cussing. "Oh great…I'm even more of a freak than before!"

"But who could do this kind of thing? Or what?" Gabriel asked.

"I am not sure. It would be a tremendous undertaking indeed. Probably a whole *group* of someones, I would guess." We all handed her the pages back, along with the glass and she set them down on in front of her. "All I know is whatever it is…it's insanely powerful. I have *no* idea how you were able to not know it for so long, how powerful you are. I would imagine that there was a spell to make it lie dormant too until something triggered it. But what—I have *no* idea."

Daniel let out a noise, and gestured towards his brother. "It has to be."

Evie bit her lip with one of her pointy fangs. "When did you two meet?"

"A couple weeks ago," Gabriel replied.

"When did your magic start?"

"A couple—" I began, and Evie nodded knowingly. "Hey...whoa."

"Can't be a coincidence," she said.

I frowned. "Great. Well great. But that *still* doesn't answer the wing problem."

She shrugged. "I'm sorry, but that's all I know. Finnian said that he guesses the problem will fix itself. Just...go about everything as normal. Eat. Sleep if you can...maybe try shifting again. Replenish your energy; it should fix itself. We think. But *clearly* you are meant to be just as powerful in your human form as your dragon." She turned to Maxxus. "Your magic is less in human form generally, right?"

Maxxus smirked. "Well, mine isn't that great *anyway* but yes, in human form it's a bit less. Other dragons though have more control over it."

I gazed at him apologetically. He just gave a small smile and shrugged as if to say "*no big deal*."

"And as we just saw, Leo yours is just as powerful in human form as your other form," Gabriel said. Evie looked at him expectantly, and he explained briefly what had just transpired. She let out a low whistle when he was finished.

"I'd wondered what had happened as I was walking here." Evie tucked all her papers back into the folder and shoved the glass in the front pocket of the white lab coat. She turned to Gabriel. "Would you mind if I tested your blood too?"

"Me?" he asked, a surprised hand over his heart.

She nodded. "I'm just curious if there is anything similar to yours, maybe something there that would act as a trigger."

He shrugged. "I guess, sure."

"Right now, if you don't mind." He nodded.

I just stared, dumbfounded at the floor as he followed Evie out the door and to the lab.

Maxxus coughed loudly, getting to his feet. "Well...I suppose I'll go let you rest."

I peered at him momentarily. "What are you going to do?"

He shrugged. "Well, I didn't sleep much last night so...perhaps get to bed early. Maybe eat some more," he said with a chuckle.

"Well, why don't you come eat here? We'll all have...something. Whatever is around here, anyway," I insisted.

"No, no," he said, waving my suggestion off with a motion of his hand. "You need to get some rest yourself. I'll find some way to entertain myself." He gave a quick laugh. "Let me know when you get that—" he nodded towards my wings, which I hadn't noticed but were flapping ever so gently and slowly, almost like a nervous habit like twitching one's leg rapidly, "—figured out."

I stood and attempted to walk him to the door that led to the hallway, adjoining all our rooms but he was on a mission to get out the door. I stopped in my tracks in the middle of the kitchen area. He was about to shut the door behind him, when he stepped back in.

"Thank you, Leorah...for saving me." He said, with a warm smile.

I snorted. "Oh, it was only a small cut. Hardly life-threatening to a big ol' dragon."

He raised a brow. "It was a little more than that, and you know it. It hurt pretty badly."

I shrugged. "No biggie," I said, looking down at my feet instead of at him, suddenly uncomfortable with the praise.

"It was a big deal." He took a couple steps closer to me and paused in his tracks again. I looked up, his bright eyes were clearly fogged with conflict; his expression troubled.

"Is...everything okay?" I asked uncertainly.

He looked as if he wanted to say something but did not. He just smiled instead. "It'll be fine, Milady Leorah," he said, a lilt of regality in his tone that made me chuckle. He reached out for my palm and bent at the waist slightly, pressing his lips on my knuckles softly, and ever so briefly.

I knew I blushed under the gesture, but I tried to keep my expression neutral; knowing fully well for whatever reason Gabriel had a problem with him (which was just stupid) and his brother was still sitting in the living area, probably watching the entire thing.

He shot one more smile at me and disappeared out the door.

I stood for a moment, not quite sure how to react when Daniel piped up, "Well...that was *interesting*!" he said shooting me a suspicious grin.

Maxxus opened the door to the room across the hall, disappearing behind the door and leaning back against it, with a frustrated sigh...the wood felt cool and smooth against his skin.

He untied the robes around his neck and let them slide down his back to the floor, walking to the bathroom—a room that was nearly identical to the one he'd just been in—a room that Leorah was sharing with Gabriel, while he shared with no one.

He didn't have many clothes as he hadn't planned on actually escaping with Leorah—just making sure she was all right as she made *her* escape but, when things transpired how they did, he knew he couldn't leave her. He reached into the bag he'd had on the shelf and pulled out a pair boxer shorts that Daniel had helped him find at a goods store in town, and pulled them up over his legs.

As he stood up, he caught a glimpse of his bare-chested self in the mirror. He frowned...he had a body most human males would kill for: defined pectorals, flat stomach with a hint of muscle, broad shoulders and long muscular legs. Not a bad face, either; although...it did him no good. She didn't seem to notice. Still, he wasn't human, he was really dragon and although dragons should be equally as comfortable in their human forms as their dragon selves, Maxxus had still preferred his dragon. Probably because of his hard time with magic; it was easier in dragon form. But, while being here he was beginning to be more comfortable with it; especially because *she* was endlessly more comfortable in hers.

He frowned at his reflection. He should be happy that he was blessed with an attractive human form, he could probably attain many beautiful human females to distract him away from the pull on his heartstrings that he'd felt every day for years. Recently that pull strengthened into a full-on heartache that welled into his throat and caused him to gasp nearly every time he was near her. So many times he almost told her; but he just couldn't. He could distract himself but...it would do no good. Nothing would take his mind off of how much he loved her, how much he'd loved her in secret for years. *Years*. She barely even knew who he was, yet he thought about her *every single day* since...well since long ago.

He noticed the shiny, pink flesh that now marred the side of his abdomen. He laughed shortly, noticing it *almost* resembled a perfect heart shape, except the left side was a little jagged. The fingers of his left hand gingerly traced the outline of the scar, the wound that *she* had healed. He remembered clearly the look of absolute panic and terror on her face upon seeing his mortal injury, caused by a tree limb that had been barreling towards her as she was performing her magic: she hadn't seen it, she was too busy saving the town. He knew—he *always* knew she was meant for greatness; he just didn't know *how* great until today. He knew, long before anyone else—besides maybe her grandfather. That's why he didn't even hesitate: it took him only a split second to shift and throw himself in front of the sharp, spear-like limb that would have been a devastating injury to her in her human form; knowing no one else but maybe Gabriel would be fast enough to stop it.

And she conjured the magic—the magic a short while ago she didn't even know she had—and she passed out afterward from the sheer exertion of it, he didn't speak of his wound, even though it hurt (but less than it would if he was in human form) because all that mattered was her. He would heal, although it might take a while. He didn't want to take away from her accomplishment, from her recovery. It was stupid, of course but…when it came to her he often didn't think clearly.

The corners of his mouth upturned a little. *She* had healed him. She had been worried, scared even. Perhaps guilty, he didn't know. What little he knew of spirit magic, he knew that the user had to draw strongly on intent, and pure will…and especially since she didn't even know she could…it is remarkable indeed.

She had felt badly that she hadn't been able to heal the scar, even though she had healed the little boys; clearly more practice was needed but he really didn't mind. It was her, she did it. It would always be a reminder of the caring magic she performed on *him* and she didn't have to. She could have called for a witch or healer, but she took it upon herself to do it, somehow instinctively knowing she could. If the scar was all he had of her for now…he was okay with it. And he'd wear it proudly until the day he died. He smoothed his fingers over the shiny skin again and sighed.

This was all he could have, for now. Maybe ever.

For now, it'd have to be enough.

Chapter 19

I stood in the kitchen for a moment, motionless, in a moment of bewilderment before Daniel piped up behind me.

"So...what now?"

I shook myself out of a daze and swiveled around, the weight of the wings I was unaccustomed to nearly knocking me off balance. Daniel was up in a flash to catch me before I stumbled over. I shot him a pathetic half smile. "Thanks."

He placed his strong hands on either side of my shoulders, helping me regain my footing.

"You're gonna have to get used to those, darlin'. Even if you can shift out of them...well there's no telling when you're going to need them again."

I blew out an annoyed raspberry at no one in particular; just fate, really for this particular turn of events. I dragged my feet back into the living room and tried to toss myself on the couch, my wings of course getting in the way.

Daniel shot me an empathetic smile. "Oh, hon...stretch them out," he instructed. I lifted the wings up a couple inches, feeling listless and blah. "No not like that. Like a bird. An *eagle.* Be a proud, winged bitch!"

I snorted. "*Okay*," I agreed reluctantly, and I raised my wings up parallel with the sofa and stretched them out as far as I could go. The stretch felt nice as it did before and I involuntarily stretched my arms out over my head and back down, with a sleepy yawn as I did.

Daniel helped position the wings half over me, half over the couch so that I took up three quarters of it, and assisted me in leaning back, the wings still stretched out to the side but I allowed them to fall, and drape over the couch.

Daniel stood back, crossing his arms in front of him. "They really are quite stunning, you look positively majestic," he gushed, folding his tall body into the chair nearby. "If only I was straight..." he clicked his tongue and reached over to smack me in the arm, playfully.

I snickered, rubbing the drowsiness out of my face with my hands and letting out a whiny moan. "I don't *feel* anything close to majestic, that's for sure."

Daniel grinned. "Give it time, give it time. This is all…new for all of us."

I peeked through a separation in my fingers at him. "Well…at least you always knew who you were. Up until a couple weeks ago I was just a freaky mythological beast serving coffee and listening to my co-workers' squeal about their Homecoming plans and helping Kit run the coffeehouse." I exhaled deeply, allowing my hands to fall listlessly into my lap. "Now somehow I'm this wild magic *creature* with magic no one knows about, possibly spelled, possibly a hybrid of *god* knows what and somehow I'm supposed to do…'*something great.*' Ha! How am I supposed to do *that*?"

Daniel let out a wild laugh. "Trust me, I didn't always know who I was. I was the first born—by thirteen minutes but, still. I was supposed to get the sorcerer powers. I was *groomed* for it from the time I was little. The attention overshadowed my poor brother. Then when *he* got his mark…" he chortled shortly, his eyes distant as he recalled a faraway memory. "*Everyone* was shocked. But mostly—me. I had my first vision slightly after." He shuddered, remembering something terrible. "It was the worst thing I ever saw. Planes flying into buildings, people jumping out of windows…they thought I was crazy."

I frowned somberly. "World Trade Center attack?"

He glanced at me with sadness, his lower lip trembling. "It was a lot for someone so young to witness. And, I saw it all. *All*. Not how it happened, but *that* it happened. I was alone with Gabe at the time and he freaked out; called an ambulance and everything. He described it to the paramedics and they said they thought I had a grand mal seizure from the description of what Gabe said. *Scary* stuff. When I came to, my brother was sobbing and hyperventilating. They had to sedate him; he was so worked up. He thought he was going to lose me."

"Poor thing." I could sense the guilt and sadness in the room, radiating off of Daniel. "It wasn't your fault, though."

"It wasn't but still…I felt awful. Especially after the doctors ran their tests, and found nothing." Daniel sighed, folding his hands in his lap and shaking his head. "Our dad was pissed but, our uncle—Christopher—knew what happened. Thank god. A seer hadn't been born in years, but, there was a chance I was one. It was awhile before I had another vision but when I did—this time it was much smaller—I knew it was true."

I lifted a brow. "What was your next vision of?"

He chuckled lightly. "It was a little pink dragon at the edge of a field, crying. A group of dragons in the slight distance laughing. You were joined by a green dragon. You didn't want to talk to him but he just sat there, nearby, keeping his distance."

My face fell. I remember that day. "That was, I think, the first day I came back after Lorusto tried to toast me. No one wanted me to be there of course," I said, with a sigh. "But—I don't remember any green dragon being there."

Daniel gave me a look of confusion. "Are you sure?"

I nodded. "*No one* ever wanted to be around me."

"I see." Daniel turned away. "Well that's besides the point. We figured out I was a seer; Gabriel got his powers. And then I came out of the closet."

I gazed at him questioningly. "Closet?" Literally, I was picturing him in a bedroom closet, bursting out the door with his flair like usual.

"Yes, it's how we refer to people when they realize they are gay, and tell everyone else," Daniel replied. "As you know it's still sort of…frowned upon here."

I grumbled. "Stupid."

He grinned. "I agree. *Obviously*. You'd think people that believed in sorcery would be open minded. Hell no!"

"Your dad?"

"And uncle, yes. In fact, that's how we ended up in Canada," he groaned, scrubbing a palm down his face. "I was so stupid. I was *madly* in love with this guy—Jeremy. And since the rest of our family was being assholes; I followed Jeremy to Canada so we could get married. I was eighteen."

"Guessing that didn't up well," I mused, sarcastically.

Daniel let out a howl. "Oh no. But, Gabriel was there for me. Dad was pissed when we left the Cities. He didn't talk to us—well me—for about a year. He was really pissed though, about my being gay; not about us leaving."

"Family drama?" I could relate.

"So much," he said, with a dramatic hand flourish and roll of his eyes. "Well, college was cheaper there anyhow so we rented an apartment after Jeremy bailed and stayed. Gabriel went to school for computer technology and graphic design; I went to be a personal trainer. The rest is history. Our father took about two years to warm up to the idea of having a *son-in-law* someday. But at this rate, he won't have to worry about it," he said, with a laugh. "Not so much luck with the fellas."

I laughed. "I relate to that too!"

He let out a groan. "Ugh, even my gay friends—I didn't have anything in common with them. They all wanted to dress up and be in drag. Now, I love looking fabulous but—" he motioned to himself, "—I look great as is; drag isn't for me. I'm perfectly happy being just a gay male. My other friends…not so much. They thought I was weird because I didn't enjoy doing drag."

"Why is that weird?" I questioned.

He gave me a knowing look. "Because, there is a stereotype. Gay men like to wear dresses and makeup and be feminine. Everyone knows that, right?"

I gave him a strange glare. "I don't get it."

He chuckled. "You wouldn't but I imagine it's a lot like you—people thinking you should be one way, when you're not."

I sucked in a breath. "Yeah…I guess so."

"Yep. I mean I tried the drag thing. It was awful. I mean, I *rocked* it but while it was fun once or twice, it wasn't for me. I liked my motorcycle better. And a little bit of leather," he added with a playful wink.

"Scandalous!"

"Mmm-*hmmm*. I did this act to Def Leppard's 'Pour Some Sugar on Me.' Girl, it was fabulous! I had a pop I shook up and sprayed all over myself. It was *hot*! So many men chasing me after that!"

"That's good, right?" I groaned, adjusting my wings behind me again. They were definitely getting in the way.

"Yes, but they just wanted me for kink stuff. Because they *thought* that's what I'd be into." He sighed. "I had to reinvent myself. I had to change peoples' ideas of me. I had to reinvent what it meant to be a gay male. At least what it meant *for me*.

"Honey, you're in the exact same position. *You* have to re-invent what it means to be pink. People won't like it; you're taking away their comfort. Disturbing what they *think* they know, because the idea was popular. People thought I was a traitor because I didn't like drag. I wasn't really gay *enough*." He scoffed.

"That's ridiculous!" I exclaimed.

"Of course it is, but you have to do the same thing. Redefine yourself. Redefine what it means to be pink. You're strong, and smart, and caring. You're *beautiful* and have a heart of gold. I know this. And before long, when you start being true to yourself and just not giving a shit about other peoples' opinions of you, you're redefining yourself to the world. You are not Cyril the Mad. You are Leorah the Inspiring!"

I gave a hesitant smile. "I'm not sure I can," I said.

"I know you can," he smiled knowingly, reaching over and clutching my hand with a squeeze. "It will be okay."

"You know this for sure?" I raised my eyes at him, hoping for some sort of insight.

He shrugged with indifference. "I think it will…that's all I can say."

I smiled warmly at him before the guilt welled up again once more. "*Ugggh*…and I dragged all of you down with me. You know what would happen if the Court caught you with me? Even though you're human?" I shuddered.

"Let me guess…we'd be tasty with ketchup?" he jibed but I shot him a serious look and he stopped smiling. "You're…not kidding."

I shook my head. "Nope. Probably the worst out of all of us—Maxxus." I slapped my hands against my face again, leaning over my lap and crying out in frustration. "He has no pull in the Court, nothing to barter with. The way they'd punish him is…unthinkable. And for what?"

"I'm sure he has his reasons," he said, absently.

I looked up. "You've spent some time with him. What do you think?"

He smiled playfully. "Well he's gorgeous for starters!"

I smirked. "Yeah…I suppose so. Any…interest there?" At least if there was some sort of interest…something there, at least perhaps he could gain *something* from defecting from his entire life. I wiggled my eyebrows hintingly at him though, for some reason as soon as I said it I instantly regretted it.

Daniel guffawed. "Um…not so much. He's as straight as a ruler."

"Figured." I frowned again. "I know he is close with Grandfather but…it still doesn't seem like a good enough reason to leave everything behind."

Daniel shrugged again. "Maxxus is definitely a man—a *dragon*—with secrets, that's for sure. Secrets I can't even figure out. The entire time we were eating he just…ate. He barely spoke, but some small talk he was clearly very awkward with. Good looking company, but not the best conversationalist."

"Really? I always had no problem talking to him, he was always pleasant when I'd see him across the portal?"

There was a glint in Daniel's blue eye; one of mischievousness. "Have you ever thought of him…like *that*?"

"Who? Maxxus?" I snorted. "I barely know him. The most I saw of him before he took his position as a guard at the portal in Green Knoll—that's the dragon side—was maybe once in passing when he was accompanying my grandfather for…whatever it was they were doing. That is it."

"Doesn't take long, though, does it? I mean…look how long you've known my brother," he pointed out.

I bit my lip, feeling the telltale flush in my cheeks. "Yeah…I suppose you're right. What are you getting at with this, anyway?"

"I don't know…" he said with a smirk. The lock clicked then and the doorknob turned. "Look who it is!"

Gabriel glanced at him briefly and rolled his eyes. "I don't even want to know. What kind of shit is this guy feeding you?" he questioned me.

"Oh, all the good stuff!" Daniel kidded. "Like, about the time you were at the pool and your shorts fell down, and—"

Gabriel shushed him. "*Enough!*" I couldn't help but laugh at their brotherly repartee and smiled, but feeling suddenly wistful I looked away, thinking of my own brother.

"What is it?" Gabriel asked, awash with concern.

I waved him off. "Oh, nothing. Just…the day is getting to me."

Daniel checked a chunky black wristwatch on his left arm. "It is getting a bit late. Sun should be setting very, very soon."

"We should figure out what we're going to eat," Gabriel said, clutching his stomach as it rumbled audibly.

I patted my lap for my cell phone and reached under the robes and pulled it out of my pocket, tapping on it a message for Kiarra.

"Calling for Chinese?" Daniel kidded. "Oh...that sounds good. You don't suppose they have a Chinese restaurant here?"

Gabriel chuckled. "Maybe in Duluth. Besides, you don't eat that stuff."

Daniel puffed out his lower lip. "True. I suppose that's off limits, anyway, huh? Going to Duluth?"

I exchanged a look with Gabriel and we shrugged. "I don't know, actually."

My phone chimed again, indicating a response from Kiarra, hopefully instructing me on a good place to eat.

Don't worry about it. I will fix dinner. I have a ton of food from today's market and I need an excuse to cook.

I smiled. *That sounds good. Given that we're stuck with each other...might be nice to have some* fun*!*

Indeed. She explained how to get to her home in her next message and I agreed we'd meet her in about thirty minutes. I forwarded the message along to Maxxus, but after ten minutes and more my message went unnoticed or he just didn't reply.

"Did Maxxus seem okay to you, after this morning, Daniel?" I inquired, interrupting a bout of brotherly snickering and banter between the twins as I was on the phone.

"How would I know differently? He seemed okay if not all that chatty, at least," he replied.

"Hmm..." I trailed off, attempting another text message again to him again.

"What's up?" Gabriel questioned, trying to peek over my shoulder.

I shot him a dirty look over my shoulder and clutched my phone to my chest. "*If* you must know, I'm trying to send a message to Maxxus, to see if he wants to join us—*all of us*—for dinner at Kiarra's."

Gabriel fought a scowl, unsuccessfully. "You know, you are not responsible for the choice he made, right? I know the guilt you have is—"

Abruptly I was on my feet, getting right in his face. "*Excuse* me? Guilt? You think this is about *guilt?*"

"Gabe..." Daniel was behind his brother in an instant, trying to pull him away from me.

He pulled out of his brother's grasp. "No!"

I felt the anger swell inside my chest. "This has *nothing* to do with guilt, Gabriel. It has *everything* to do with Maxxus being my friend. Period. I knew him before you. Is that a problem, *Knight*? That I have another friend that's a male? Is *that* what this is all about?"

"When the male could be a goddamned runway model, yes!"

Daniel let out a low-whistle. "Low blow, dude. Low blow..."

I smirked and nodded knowingly. "I see what this is all about. It's about your *insecurity*. Well, dude...if you cannot handle that I have a male friend—a *good* looking male friend—and you're this jealous right off the bat...I do *not* think we can continue!" I shot daggers from my eyes at him. He looked sheepish, now with a smug grin on his face as he looked away, as I made him nervous with my stare. I raised my hand abruptly as if to slap him in the face—which I had the urge to do. Before I could land the blow, he winced and clutched his cheek, stumbling off to the side.

"What the—" he said, rubbing his jaw. Daniel had caught him before he tumbled over.

I gasped in horror, looking at my hand which remained in its raised position and had been nowhere near Gabriel's face.

"Bro...I think it's best not to piss of the dragon..." Daniel said in a sing-song voice in Gabriel's ear.

My hands fell and I was quickly at Gabriel's side; the rage I had felt quelled by the sudden remorse I had after apparently *mind* slapping him. I looked at him apologetically and I tried to reach out to him, to touch his reddened cheek but he pulled away.

I stepped back, feeling emotionally wounded.

"I don't think she meant—" Daniel began, giving me a look of sympathy. Gabriel just stood up, shot another angry look at me and stormed out of the room into the bedroom, where he slammed the door.

My lower lip trembled. "I...I didn't mean to—" I began, my voice wavering.

Without hesitation, Daniel wrapped his long arms around me—wings and all—and pulled me close. "I know you didn't, Dear. It's been...overwhelming for all of us, I think."

I nodded against his strong chest, involuntarily sniffing into his t-shirt.

"I haven't been around dragons much but I *know* it's not a good idea to make one angry," he said, stroking my hair over my wings which lay flat against my back.

I shook my head *no*.

"And...my brother is a *huge dick* for saying what he said about Maxxus. And trust me, I know a thing or two about huge dicks," he said, with a chuckle. I snorted at his quip briefly and continued to allow him to hold me. It was comforting, like Gabriel but there was no confusion involved about love or friendship; he was just...*strength*. A pillar of sanity in my crazy life. No question about it, Daniel was a friend, and confidante.

"*And* you," he said, pointedly yelling out the insult part for emphasis in hopes his brother would overhear him. "He is insecure, most definitely. After being picked on and tormented..."

I sniffled. "I know..."

"The way you jumped up to save him without hesitation really threw him for a loop," Daniel said.

I pulled away momentarily and stared up at him and his familiar features but somehow still different. "If it had been him—"

"—or any one of us, I know. You would have done the same thing. Or...anyone really. What you did for those boys...it was heroic. I can tell you care about Maxxus, too and that's a little intimidating for my brother," Daniel said, placing his hands on either cheek and looking me square in the face. "I can't imagine being in your position, right now." He leaned down and placed a brotherly, comforting peck on my cheek. "And I'm sorry for the way my brother acted."

I nodded, pressing my fingers to my eyes in hopes of stopping the tears from pricking them.

He patted my shoulder. "Now...go head over to Kiarra's. I'll drag the *jackass* over in a few, after I smack him around a bit," he kidded.

"Okay," I agreed. I left the comfort of my friend and headed towards Kiarra's.

I smelled it before I even saw it; all the delicious smells wafting through the small "neighborhood" that was home to a handful of mythological beings. Kiarra's home was *not* what I expected. The majority of houses along the way appeared like they were either 100 years old or more, or were little more than huts with straw roofs. So I was surprised when I arrived at a red-scalloped trimmed, white cottage-style house with a red front door and a "*Welcome!*" mat before it. I almost wasn't sure if I was in the right place—it was such a far cry from the sterile, cold homes dragons generally lived in, but when she emerged from the door, all smiles, I sort of figured that it was.

"Where's everyone else?" she questioned, her tone slightly disappointed.

I heaved a sigh. "Well...I couldn't reach Maxxus; he went back to his room saying that he was 'tired' and didn't respond. Gabriel is throwing a temper tantrum in our room, and Daniel supposedly is trying to smack him out of it."

Kiarra raised a brow. "Okay, then," she said with a laugh.

"They're supposed to be along soon. Or so Daniel says," I said with a roll of my eyes. *Men,* I thought disparagingly. Kiarra stepped back and invited me in.

The inside décor surprised me even more than the outer. It was a straight up country house, complete with chicken and cow paintings and figurines all over random, red shelves with hearts carved in them; a floral patterned sofa and matching chair and red-checked tablecloths over the end tables. I must have looked appalled, because Kiarra piped up:

"I just couldn't do a normal dragon house." She shuddered and wrinkled her nose. "Can you imagine the reaction if I had built this back home?"

I chuckled. "They'd probably eat it."

"Or burn it down!" She laughed. She motioned for me to follow her through a white door that sat on a single hinge on one side and it shut automatically when you pushed through it and we entered a kitchen, which was just as country as the rest of the house. I grinned, and pointed at the white curtains with pictures of fruit on them. "Those would really get a reaction."

She snickered. "Right? I just...had to pick the most obnoxious things I could find that would never fit in back home."

I shook my head, taking it all in, awed. "Wow...imagine Braeden's reaction when he sees this!" I said with a laugh, and noticed the cheery expression she had worn was replaced by a crestfallen one at the mention of my brother.

I groaned audibly and rolled my eyes, not at her but at my own stupidity. "I'm *sorry*. I'm just not doing well today."

She waved me off. "Oh, it's okay. You've been through a lot."

"Well...so have you," I insisted, and she shrugged.

"Yeah but, I signed up for this," she said. "You didn't."

"True."

She offered me a sympathetic smile and after a moment, clapped her hands together. "Well then...let's get to eatin' shall we?"

"Best fucking idea I've heard all goddamned day."

She certainly didn't disappoint and served a meal certainly fit for a dragon: meatloaf, the ultimate comfort food (absolutely to *die* for!), fresh squeezed lemonade, Caesar salad with low-fat dressing for the vegetarian, au gratin potatoes and several loaves of homemade bread and apple pie for dessert. I was practically drooling by the time she had set everything on the table (a blue and white checked tablecloth and mis-matched blue, wood backed chairs).

True to his word, Daniel did get his brother to calm down and they arrived just as I had begun digging in without manners or prejudice, suddenly noticing the empty pit of my stomach as it rumbled, reminding me just how hollow it was. Kiarra let them in and led them straight to the kitchen. I purposely pretended to be extremely engaged with my meatloaf (which, I kind of was, actually) and I couldn't be bothered with the entrance of new people.

I felt his presence behind me, hesitant. I took a long gulp of lemonade and ignored him.

Daniel coughed, pointedly. "Go on, ya douche," he said.

I heard an exasperated sigh and then a hand was placed on my shoulder.

"Oh, is someone there?" I asked feigning ignorance.

Gabriel groaned. "Shit...Leo I'm sorry. I was...way out of line."

I set my food down, not even bothering to use silverware anymore and turned to him, fussing momentarily with my wings. I positioned them so they were more comfortable at my sides. I raised a brow. "And?"

He sighed again. He pulled up an empty chair next to me and reached for my hand and hugged it to his chest. "I was a complete fuckwad."

"My words exactly!" Daniel chimed in, sitting opposite of his brother at the table in between Kiarra and I. He scanned the food choices cautiously and his sights lingered on the potatoes. "Oh, how I miss thee, carbohydrates."

Kiarra shoved them towards him. "One time won't kill you."

Daniel grinned widely. "YOLO, bitches!" he said, grabbing for the nearest fork and digging right into the dish they were served in, not bothering with a plate. "Oh my *god...*" he said, with a pleasured moan after the first bite.

I had to choke down peals of laughter, as my own mouth was full of meatloaf. I glanced at Gabriel and rolled my eyes. "Wow...he's nuts."

"Runs in the family, apparently." Gabriel sighed. "Really, Leo. I'm sorry. Of course you can have whatever friends you want. I won't lie, I'm totally intimidated by that dude."

"Dragon." I corrected. "Dragons don't take too kindly to the word *dude*. They'll be liable to bite your head off."

"Literally," Kiarra offered, with an innocent smile.

"*Dragon*, then," he said, with a slight grin.

My expression softened. "I am sorry, too, about the—" I raised my hand to my cheek and winced. "The magic slap."

Gabriel shrugged it off. "I deserved it. And for the record, it's not about you. I trust you. But, there is... something about him. Something I can't put my finger on about him that is totally bothering me."

"What do you mean?" I asked.

He shrugged. "I really don't know. I mean, don't you think it's rather odd that this random dragon you barely know is all of a sudden helping us?"

I narrowed my eyes. "I do know him, though. Longer than any of you," I said, motioning to everyone at the table. "And, like I said before...Grandfather trusts him. If he didn't, he wouldn't have chosen to mentor him. If he's okay with him, that's good enough for me."

"You certainly place a lot of stock in your Grandfather's opinion," Daniel said, in between mouthfuls of cheesy potatoes.

Kiarra banged her fork against the table. "Hey! For good reason, he is an amazing dragon." She gave me a sympathetic look. "He could be King probably but—" she trailed off, her cheeks flushed. I knew what she was going to say; but she was too nice to say it.

"Yeah, he is," I said solemnly as I cut a big piece of meatloaf off a bigger chunk off with my fork.

Daniel eyed it wistfully. You could almost see a string of drool escape the side of his mouth.

In response, Kiarra speared a large piece of it in her fork and smacked it down loudly on his plate. "YOLO, bitch, remember?"

Daniel's eyes widened at the large portions of what he deemed as unhealthy food on his plate. "Oh hell you guys are a terrible influence on me!" With reckless abandon, fork in hand he stabbed the large lump of seasoned meat and took a very large bite. He slunk back in his chair as he chewed slowly, savoring every bite. "Oh my god...I think I just came a little."

"Wow, you need a boyfriend," I quipped.

"Why bother, when I have this?" Daniel took another bite and sighed happily. We all giggled as he struggled to compose himself. "Good lord I'm going to have to run a million miles tomorrow to work this off. But *so* much less drama."

"Too bad you aren't a dragon," I said, with a wide smile, shoving a large slice of bread halfway in my mouth. "I eat all sorts of crap and never worry."

"Too bad," he said in agreement. "If I could eat like *that* and have those curves...damn girl. I'd pig out on all this stuff, every day!"

I winked at him with appreciation.

"So, why now isn't your grandfather king?" Gabriel questioned in between bites of his dinner.

Kiarra sighed. "Well, it was feared that since he has such close ties with Leorah, that somehow she'd influence him against the kingdom and well...you know the rest. Same thing goes for her parents."

I let out a low growl, assuring her that I did.

"How did he become Elder, then?" Gabriel asked.

"Nothing they can do about it. When a dragon lives as long as he has—they have no choice. That's part of the way we keep the royalty in check and *attempt* to balance out any favoritism there may be," Kiarra explained. "The King and Queen have a *lot* of pull as to who serves on the Court, but they have to have an equal balance of opinions."

I grumbled. "I honestly don't understand *how* any of my family was able to get positions in the Court with me in the mix." Disgruntled, I tore off a large piece of bread and gnawed it loudly.

"Gross; dragons are rude," Daniel said, wrinkling his nose.

I let out a low growl from the back of my throat, and tossed the rest of the bread at him. He yelped and brushed it off of him, whining about the dangers of more complex carbohydrates. I just chuckled and rolled my eyes. "You have no idea."

"I wonder who was behind the order to come after you, then?" Gabriel mused.

I shrugged. "Clearly there is something going on there we aren't privy to," I said.

Kiarra frowned. "Clearly."

Since the conversation had taken a slightly serious turn, we finished the rest of our meal in comfortable silence, and the rest of the evening went on uneventfully, thankfully. If you had been an outsider, we appeared to be a normal group of friends, gathered in front of the TV, trashing the cheesy movie playing on the Hallmark channel (I was surprised they got cable here but...whatever), laughing and giggling and drinking wine and beer and singing along to songs from Kiarra's iPod (to my delight, filled with plenty of pop and rock music from the 90s!). Minus of course the blasts of air Gabriel kept shooting at his brother whenever he thought he was cheating at poker or the fact that I had a big, awkward set of wings jutting out my back—we appeared totally normal. Honestly, it was probably the most fun I've had—wings and all—that I could recall in my lifetime. I'd never had the luxury of having friends, let alone a *group* of friends, even as ragtag as we all were.

No matter where we were, the more alcohol we drank—and I swore there was something about it because I was actually feeling a bit fuzzy—Gabriel and I somehow found ourselves sitting closer and closer together as the night wore on, like some sort of magnetic pull was between us.

I was slightly tipsy when Gabriel and I headed back to our room, stumbling and laughing through the town as we walked (me mostly tripping over the wings, to be honest). It was early in the morning or late at night depending on how you looked at it, and everything was fairly dark except for the balls of wispy light that hung low in the sky, over our heads darting around.

I giggled with glee as one of them flew face-level to me. I held out my hand and it landed in my palm, gently. It was nearly completely weightless and emanated a quiet tinkling sound like that of a handful of jingle bells. I gasped, noticing what appeared to be a female face, very childlike in the glow.

Gabriel was peering over my shoulder, and gasped as well. "It's a wisp!"

The wisp tinkled musically, flying around my head and pausing momentarily near my cheek. I felt a tingle, the wisp appeared to kind of kiss me before it made a musical giggling sound before it darted off into the sky with its friends.

I beamed, feeling a sudden surge of elation. I grabbed Gabriel's hand and pulled him towards me, wrapping my arms around his neck and pulling him down to my level. I playfully bit his lower lip lightly and he shivered, and grinned mischievously. He smashed his lips into mine and we kissed passionately there in the center of town, with the light of the wisps emanating around us.

One of the wisps—I can't say for sure but I had a feeling—flew around our heads, letting out a little tinkling, giggling sound that I swear sounded like a young, giddy girl. In the midst of our kiss I started laughing while pressed against Gabriel's mouth.

He pulled away suddenly and smiled wryly. "Come on it wasn't *that* bad was it?"

I laughed. "No, silly," I said, smacking him playfully on the chest, as the little wisp took one more swoop in between us, letting out it's little musical giggle. I pointed at her and grinned widely. "Hear that?"

Gabriel smiled widely. "They are quite amazing." Another wisp tinkled next to him quietly, daring to get closer to him. Grinning, he lifted up his palm and flicked open his fingers and lighted a tiny ball of light. The wisp, seeming momentarily startled, flew backwards a little before cautiously moving forward, almost as if it were nervous to examine it.

The little "she" wisp near my ear slowly joined the other wisp and they musically tinkled at one another. Gabriel and I beamed at each other over the light of the magic in his palm.

"They seem happy," I observed, watching as they danced happily around the magic.

Gabriel shot me a smirk and a nod. "Do your thing, Leo. Give them a show."

I raised a brow but smiled, not only at the wisps but the sexy half smile he was shooting at me in the dim light of the magic. "All right," I said. I closed my eyes briefly and exhaled, motioning with my hands to move the mist towards Gabriel's palms. When the magic of my spirit mist mixed with his, the ball of light grew wider, larger.

"Again," Gabriel said quietly, with a nod, not taking his eyes off the magic.

I breathed out again, giving more magic to the light and it grew even larger. "That's it..." he said, in a hushed tone, the little wisps floating backwards slowly to allow the magic more space. They were silent now and barely moving, and somehow I knew they were okay; only enthralled by the magic.

Gabriel spun his palms around the ball of light and after a moment, shot it upwards and opened his hands with a snap of his fingers the magic burst apart, showering us in thousands of little balls of sparkle and light, like one of those white firecrackers that fizzles and trails glitter down towards the ground.

"Oh, look at them!" I said, with a joyous laugh, pointing. The two wisps danced around each other happily, chiming melodically as they were joined by at least a dozen or so other wisps that had been hiding nearby somehow. They sang their little wisp songs and "danced", frolicking in and out of the magic.

Gabriel was grinning at this sight. His brown eyes sparkled with bliss as he watched the delightful sight of the wisps dancing around in his magic—well, *our* magic. Watching his handsome face, content at himself in the low light of the magic made my heart swell in my chest. I snaked one of my arms through his and he brought himself out of his dazed reverie. "I think I made them happy," he said.

I nodded, pulling him a little tighter to my side, careful to avoid slamming my wing painfully in between us. "I definitely think you did."

Gabriel and I stood there a few more moments, watching the innocence of the wisps dance playfully in the magic before he finally was able to pull himself away. By this point I was no longer looking at the wisps, but at him as he proudly stood there. He blushed when he finally noticed my heavy gaze on him. "Sorry...it's just a rare thing when I can openly do magic and have it appreciated, you know?"

I nodded knowingly. "Yeah, I think I do a little."

Glancing one last time at them, Gabriel wrapped his arm around my shoulders and leaned over slightly to kiss me gently on the cheek. Feeling this sense inside of pure elation and peace I sighed happily as I leaned my head against his chest and allowed him to walk us back to the guest room.

I placed my hand on the doorknob when we reached the quarters and paused momentarily for my magic to register before it clicked and opened up.

I stepped inside the quiet, dimly lit room and sighed. I fumbled around the wall for a light switch but, I didn't have to. With a wide motion of his hand, Gabriel had lit one of the oil lamps that sat on the coffee table in the middle of the room, and then the two on the end tables on either side of the couch.

"Showoff," I said, with a wide smile.

"Damn right." Gabriel turned around and stepped towards me, reaching out one hand and wrapping it behind my neck, pulling me gently into him. His other arm wrapped against my waist, using care to avoid a wing. "Where were we?" he asked, a lascivious lilt in his voice as he leaned over and brushed his lips against mine.

I sighed into the kiss, letting my arms coil around his neck, the fingers of my right hand lighting grabbing at the dark brown hair at his collar. My breath quickened as his lips parted slightly, gently biting my bottom lip. I gasped into the kiss and let out a little moan, involuntarily, feeling the heat rise up quickly inside.

"Oh Leorah, I want you so bad right now," Gabriel whispered in my ear, his other hand deftly trying to untie the robes that fastened at my collarbone.

Suddenly, my eyes flew open and dropped from his neck the heat and arousal I was beginning to fear quickly replaced with a sense of anxiety.

My breath quickened into fevered gasps, as I placed my hands at my heart, feeling it pound like a drum in my ribcage. A wave of nausea washed over me as I heaved heavy, gasping breaths and edged backwards on the bed even more, away from him.

"Oh god, Leo, I'm so sorry, I—" Gabriel said, his tone full of guilt as he stepped backward quickly from me.

I held up a hand to indicate I needed a moment. Keeping my eyes shut I concentrated on my breathing, willing myself to calm down. *What the hell was going on?*

My body warred inside itself, my lower half heated and willing to allow Gabriel to take me to bed, the other half panicked at the thought.

"Are you okay?" Gabriel questioned with concern. I felt his weight next to me on the bed as he sat down.

I took one last breath and opened my eyes slowly. His heady expression was gone; replaced with one of shame. I frowned and reached my hand out to gently stroke the five-o-clock shadow on his cheek. "Oh geez, I'm so sorry, I panicked, I—"

Gabriel raised his hand and shook his head. "No, it's okay. Given all that's been going on you're entitled to a little freak out." He patted my shoulder lightly before resting his hands in his lap and cringing, his face wrinkling in a grimace of pain. "I got a little carried away, and now I'm paying for it," he said, his voice squeaking slightly.

Feeling a twinge of guilt swell up in me, I moved away from him a little more. "I'm sorry, I shouldn't have allowed myself to get carried away if I wasn't ready." I bit my lip, regrettably, wondering what would happen.

So why all of a sudden, was I freaking out? The other day, I was ready to go and even downright disappointed to the point of offense when he shot me down?

"I don't know what's wrong with me," I said, rubbing my temples with my fingers and letting out a pained groan. "The other day, I was all—"

"Leo, it's okay." Gabriel assured me. He sighed and inched closer to me again. "I should have known better, but I just couldn't help myself. You looked so damn beautiful in that starlight and, the wisps made me feel so happy and for the first time in a while I felt so relaxed, I got carried away. Of *course* you're not going to want to sleep with me right now; look at everything that's going on! Your friend is missing, we're in some strange new place, your entire government is after you..." he trailed off with a dry chuckle. "Geez, I don't even know what came over me, exactly. I promised myself that I'd wait awhile before propositioning you like that again."

My head snapped up and I raised a brow. "Why?"

"So we can both get our shit worked out. Listen, Leo," he reached for and grasped one of my hands to him, placing it against his bare chest. My heart skipped a beat, feeling his warm skin underneath my touch but I took a deep breath and tried to calm myself. "I know how I feel about you. You're amazing. You're beautiful. You're.... *perfect*. But everything is complicated, and this," he said, motioning between us, "Will just complicate things right now. Don't you think?"

I let out a heavy, low groan. "Perhaps. I don't know what keeps stopping me. It just feels like...something is keeping us apart."

He ruffled his hands through his hair and gazed at me questioningly. "Something keeping us apart? Like what? The Shadows?"

I shrugged slowly. "I don't know. Maybe it's just my own anxiety getting in the way. Something just feels...*off*."

Gabriel exhaled a soft whistle. "Maybe it's just too much, too soon. Especially for two people—two *mythos*— with relationship problems."

I nodded. "Maybe."

Gabriel looked to me earnestly and opened his arms for a hug, sensing my insecurity. I allowed myself his safe embrace and snuggled into his chest. I guessed this was all I was ready for, for now.

"Besides...I have to admit, I'm sort of relieved," he said, with a nervous laugh.

"*Relieved?*" I asked in dismay. I pulled myself out of his hug and glowered at him. That's not something a female ever wants to hear from someone they've just come on to; relief that they didn't follow through with it. Nothing like saying, "*Oh, I wasn't that into you, really, after all*" to make a dragon—or person—feel just *great!*

"No, no. Not like that. I mean...it'd be your first time. I'm not sure I could live up to the pressure and would probably last all of five seconds after all," Gabriel said, his voice somewhat lighthearted but I could sense the truth behind the words.

I wrinkled my nose. "Yeah, that would be a problem," I said, with an uncomfortable laugh. "You know, most dragons just don't give two shits. They want to hit it, they hit it—no regrets."

Gabriel leaned closer to me and kissed my cheek gently. "I guess you're more human than you thought, huh?"

I turned to him and smiled. "Guess so." I reached up and traced his jawline with my fingers gently, gazing into his deep brown eyes, happy and *relieved*. His eyes shied away but he still smiled.

Involuntarily, I felt waves of fatigue wash over me. I tried to stifle a yawn but, wasn't successful. "I don't think I would have made it, anyway. All of a sudden, I'm exhausted."

Gabriel chuckled. "Well, get some sleep." He flung open the heavy curtain on the window with a flick of his hand and the moonlight came pouring in. Somehow, being this far up north, it seemed to be larger and brighter here. It was a comforting thought as I carefully snuggled underneath the covers, tucking my wings tightly against my back and pulling the blanket up as far as I could before it became awkward for them, I lay face down on the pillow. I reached my left arm out for Gabriel and found him sitting upright nearby. "You'll stay, right?"

He ran his fingers gently down my forearm, pulling my hand into his lap. "I'll always stay, if you want me."

"Good." Another comforting thought as I sighed and drifted off; happy that no matter what, I knew he'd always be there.

Chapter 20

My eyes flew open suddenly, only to be replaced with more darkness. It was hard to tell if I was really even awake or not.

"Hello?" I called out into the pitch black. I felt a shiver down my spine, causing my skin to goosebump when my voice didn't reverberate back.

A very faint mist began to collect at my feet. I stepped backward slowly trying to escape, but it just followed and became thicker.

I swallowed. "*Hello?*"

Footsteps. Very faint in the distance. Branches rustling, leaves crunching. "Hello?" a voice called out, faint but vaguely familiar.

I blinked a few times, trying to adjust to the darkness but there was just nothing to see. I felt around me and stepped closer to the voice cautiously. "Is someone there?" I called out. I noticed the closer I became to where I'd heard the voice, the denser the mist.

"*Leo?*" asked the voice, surprised.

I stopped in my tracks, listening closer to the voice. "How do you know me?"

More rustling, the footsteps grew near and quicker. "Leo! It's me!"

I paused again, trying to get the voice to register in my head. "*Daniel?*" I saw a figure part the mist before me; a strong, broad shouldered, familiar figure and I could barely make out his face in the fog that surrounded us.

"Yes!" I felt a strong pair of arms around me suddenly in a relieved embrace. "Holy shit, it really is you!" His hands patted my back. "No wings?"

I reached behind me, suddenly noticing they were gone. I looked down at myself, realizing that somehow, I was wearing a set of robes but nothing else, no shoes or anything—but at least, no wings. "I guess not."

"Where the hell are we?" he asked, nervously.

"I don't know...but this is like where I was attacked by that...shadow thing," I said, trying to gulp down the nervous fear that was rising in my throat.

He gasped. "Are we in the shadow realm?"

I shrugged. "I...don't think so. I was just asleep; I don't think you can get to it by dreaming."

"This is a dream?" He patted himself down. "Feels real enough." He reached out blindly, his hand running over my face. "Yeah. Huh. This is.... weird."

"Were you asleep?" I asked.

"Yeah, but not for long." Daniel reached for my hand and I clutched it, thankful for the anchor. "This is odd."

"Yeah. Usually by now...something has jumped out at me. Like...these little...things that crawl up your legs and arms." I shuddered, recalling the fear and emptiness I had felt as the dark tendrils crawled up my body like a hundred creepy spiders. I glanced around hesitantly. Besides the mist, and Daniel I didn't see anything else. "This is the first time someone else has been with me in the 'dream' or whatever the hell this is."

"I wonder...why?"

We jumped suddenly, hearing a terrified shriek in the distance.

Daniel grasped my arm. "What was that?"

"I don't know," I said, shushing him, listening closer for the sound again.

Another shriek. I started walking carefully and quietly towards the sound.

"Leo...are you sure we should be going after it? Maybe we should be running away?" he said nervously.

"There is...something about that scream..." was all I said, tiptoeing through the leaf litter, the mist that had surrounded Daniel was the only light we had, lighting our way and it wasn't much but it was enough to make out faint outlines nearby and illuminate that we were in fact walking on piles of leaves and brush through some wooded area somewhere.

"Help!" the voice was louder now, a little more terrified and then quieted to a panicked whisper.

I began walking a bit faster now, listening for the whimpering, dodging twigs and tree branches sticking out at me everywhere, Daniel on my heels muttering nervously to himself but I ignored it.

I was listening so intently for the noise; I didn't see the large mound at my feet. I stumbled over it and landed face first in the leaves and dirt.

The mound was crying hopelessly. I wiped the dirt off my face with the sleeve of my robes and looked at it. Daniel was right beside me, helping me stand up when I cried out.

Whoever it was lay in the fetal position on the ground, long light brown, wavy hair matted and messed, splayed out around her head like a disheveled halo, her clothes no more than torn, tattered rags (which looked like they could have been a white t-shirt and jeans at one time). The most disturbing thing about the image was the black, oozy tendrils that had attacked me before were completely enveloping her and she was trembling uncontrollably.

I knelt down, despite warnings from Daniel and reached out to touch her shoulder. The tendrils screamed and hissed as I gingerly touched her, with a finger.

She gasped, and laboriously lifted her head, revealing bloodshot blue eyes, rimmed with black shiners, cheeks pallid, lips dried and cracked like she hadn't drunk in about three days.

"L...Leo?" she asked weakly, trying to reach out to me but the tendrils growled and forced her hand back down.

I let out a cry of surprise, and then horror. "*Kit?* Oh my god, Kit!" I threw myself over her body, not caring that the tendrils were hissing at me. I growled, and shooed them away and reluctantly, they listened and continued to envelop her more, with each squeeze she shuddered and wheezed for breath.

"You know her?" Daniel asked, cautiously kneeling down at Kit's side, and attempted to stroke her hair which was the only part of her that wasn't covered in suffocating, dark tendrils.

"Yes. My friend...she went missing and we found her car by the portal. I assumed she'd been captured by the Court, and were using her to find me..." my lower lip trembled at the thought, and I couldn't fight the tears that stung at my eyes and fell on her body.

"Leo...what are you..." Kit began, but a tendril wrapped itself around her throat, cutting off her air supply.

"No!" I screamed, trying to shove at it with my hand. A small beam of light shot out of it and at the tendril and it screamed and recoiled back to the ground.

"Oh my god..." I pulled myself up to my knees and held my hands over my friend, closing my eyes and willing light to leave my hands and attack the dark tendrils. I exhaled and opened my eyes as a brief shock of bright electricity left my hands and attacked a tendril on her back. It too recoiled with a pained scream, but slowly began crawling back. I attempted this several more times, the electric light getting weaker with each shot I tried.

Daniel put his hand on my shoulder, as I unsuccessfully tried to shoot the light from my hands. I whimpered when nothing came, and the little bit I had freed her had enveloped her again.

"Leo…just go. There is nothing you can do," she panted, her voice raspy and strained.

"No! I can…I can—" I shook my hands, trying to shoot magic from them. "Work, dammit!" I sank back to my feet, defeated.

"You can't help her here…wherever this is." He pulled me back from Kit and I yanked away, throwing myself over her in a fit of sobs and rage.

"Kit!" I cried, "I'm so sorry! This is all my fault! I—"

I sat up abruptly and my eyes flew open, heart pounding so furiously in my chest I thought it was going to explode. I rubbed the sleep from my eyes with my fists and scanned my surroundings. I was no longer with Daniel, wherever we had been. I was sitting in the bed upright in the bedroom that I had fallen asleep in, and apparently, Gabriel had later at some time at least. He allowed me the blanket and, still shirtless was using the robes as a blanket; he pulled them up to under his arms and rested his head on a pillow, one hand tucked under and the other dangling off the side of the bed. I smirked briefly, watching his peaceful rest and nearly reached over to trace the outline of the geometric patterned tattoo on his shoulder when I suddenly was slammed with a realization that I had been dreaming. I gasped, noticing the moonlight was gone, and was instead replaced with the hazy oranges of the morning's impending sunset. "Shit…" I couldn't tell if it was night or day in—wherever we were—but if it was morning now, chances are that was hours ago. If it was in fact, for real. "Kit!" I exclaimed quietly, in a panic.

I reached out, fumbling for my phone on the nightstand: 6:15 AM.

I threw off the blanket that covered me, tossing it over Gabriel that still slept peacefully and stumbled out of bed clumsily, landing instead of on my feet flat on my ass in a tangle of limbs and robes draped over my shoulder. I winced at the sensation of air being briefly slammed out of me as I struggled to get to my feet.

"Kit..." I said, under my breath. *If that was you, I'm coming.* Somehow. I wrapped my arms around my chest to avoid the bounce of my nearly naked chest under the robes as I dashed into the bathroom next door where my clothes were. I frantically dug into the suitcase I had brought, full of clothes and toiletries, tossing things aside on the floor until I produced underwear, a t-shirt, a pair of black yoga pants and a heather gray sweatshirt.

I quickly pulled on the items, catching my reflection briefly in the mirror as I did. I barely had time to notice that just like in the dream, my wings had disappeared. No time to breathe in relief I just fastened the bra strap around my chest and shoved my arms through the straps, not caring if it was even on correctly before yanking the white t-shirt over my head, pulling on the pants and grabbing the sweatshirt and draping it over my arm.

I re-entered the bedroom, hunting on the floor for my sandals. I found them near the door and tried to balance against it while trying to get them on my feet and fastening the Velcro, I lost my footing and slid down the doorframe, bonking my head against the wood trim.

"*Fuck!*" I cried out in pain, rubbing the injured area at the back of my head.

My cursing startled Gabriel, who snorted and sat upright in bed. He groaned. "Leo. What's going—" he started, but I interrupted.

"Kit. I saw Kit." That's all I needed to say. He flung himself out of bed and rummaged around the room for his clothes, alarmingly alert for someone who'd just been sound asleep a few moments ago.

I tugged the sweatshirt over my head and began to dash outside before I paused. "Daniel..." Instead I dashed out to the hallway, intending to go to Daniel's room but the second I flung open the door, there he was outside of it, prepped to knock, looking panic stricken.

"Shit...it wasn't a dream." He took one look at the urgency on my face and knew it must be true. I nodded frantically.

Daniel hadn't even put on a shirt, he still carried it in his hand at his side and he wore a pair of plaid sleep pants and flip flops on his bare feet.

"But...how did we...?" he began to ask, befuddled. He jerked the gray *I Love Canada* shirt over his well-defined chest and crossed his arms over it, shaking his head. "I thought I was having a vision. But how could...?"

I seized his forearm and yanked him into the room, letting the door slam loudly behind him, probably waking up anyone else in the building who happened to be asleep.

"Phone?" I patted my body for my phone, realizing that I had left mine on the nightstand. He produced his from a pocket in his pants.

"Text Kiarra. Tell her we need Finnian. *Now.*"

He nodded vehemently and tapped into his phone. I didn't bother waiting for a response, I pulled him through the room and out the door leading outside.

Before the door could shut behind us, Gabriel emerged.

"Leo, what is going on?" he asked, confused. He ran his hands through his messy hair, wedged up on one side and attempted to smooth it out. Daniel looked between us momentarily, and raised his brow. I suddenly was aware of my own hair and its disorder and yanked it over my shoulder and tossed it back, not really caring. He opened his mouth to speak, but I cut him off.

"*Not now*," I said sternly, and the lilt of a smile wiped off his face. I began storming through the center of town, barely noticing the wisps had disappeared from the sky and the light from above was from the sun beginning its ascent into the sky for the day. Gabriel called to me again.

"I'll explain on the way." Gabriel and Daniel, both taller than me with longer legs struggled to keep up with my determined power walk.

"I saw Kit. She was in that…Shadow place." I explained, briefly. "Daniel was there too."

He nodded frantically. "I saw everything."

Gabriel blinked, confused. "How is that possible?"

I shrugged. "I don't know, but it should mean something because however it happened, we were both there. She's close, Gabriel. I know it. I *have* to find her; the darkness is getting to her. She's dying." I paused in my tracks to flash a look of desperation at him, tears prickling my eyes for real this time. I wiped one away as it fell. "It's all my fault. If I hadn't—"

Gabriel reached out and brushed my tear away with the side of his hand. He began trying to pull me into his chest for a comforting hug but I pulled away. "No. Must find Finnian. Hear back from her, yet?" I tossed my words over my shoulder at Daniel as I continued to storm through town to the main Loremasters office nearby.

"No," he answered back. We reached the building and I shoved the heavy doors aside with little effort and stomped down the hallway.

"Finnian? *Finnian*!" I yelled, not caring who I disturbed. We reached his "office" at the end of the hallway and I shoved through the doors. They slammed against the wall with such force that the surrounding walls shook.

Finnian was in his office but he appeared…catatonic. He was sitting cross-legged on his desk, amidst a mess of papers and various office items, his palms resting upright in his lap. His face was expressionless and I might have thought he was asleep if it wasn't for his eyes—they were open wide but there were no irises—they were blank. Fully white.

"Finnian! *Finnian*!" I demanded again, getting right into his face. No response. I slapped at the side of his cheek with moderate force and called out his name again.

"Finnian, goddammit! Wake up!"

He gasped, and he blinked in surprise revealing his "normal" pale blue eyes. He winced, surprised to see me.

"Leorah! What is—" I didn't let him finish.

"My friend is in the shadow realm!" I exclaimed, my face mere inches from his, my hands grasping his upper arm tightly and I realized that I was shaking him, and not slightly either. I didn't care, but I stopped and gestured to Daniel. "He and I saw her. She's there! We saw her! Sh— "

Finnian held up a hand, indicating I should pause. "Wait, wait now. Okay first things first." He looked at Daniel. "You were there?"

He nodded. "I guess, though I don't understand it myself."

His brow furrowed thoughtfully. "Have you ever dreamwalked before?"

"Dreamwalked?" Daniel repeated in surprise. "No! I mean…is that a thing? Can you do that?"

Finnian nodded intently. He slid off the desk to his (bare) feet, toeing around him for his shoes, apparently. "Yes. It is common for Seers to dreamwalk, especially with those they have a psychic connection to."

I placed my hands on my hips and narrowed my eyes. "Connection? I've only just met— "

"I know, it's outrageous but whatever, clearly you are *all* connected," Finnian interrupted, motioning between Gabriel, his brother and I.

"What does that even *mean*?" I groaned in frustration.

"It means that, especially in this case since he's related to the Knight—a sorcerer—that the three of you are bonded, at least psychically," Finnian explained. "A seer can dreamwalk into someone else's dreams when necessary. I'm surprised it hasn't happened before, though I can assume it's because that your magic has lain dormant for many years," he said to me. "But somehow, the three of you coming together has unleashed part of *your* magic too, Daniel."

Daniel's brow furrowed in confusion, and he opened his mouth to speak but once again he was interrupted. I let out a frustrated noise, slapping my hands against my face and rubbing feverishly. "Wait…psychic?" I bit my lip, sheepishly. Could he have heard Gabriel and I making out earlier? "How much can he see?"

Daniel smirked, crossing his arms over his broad chest and drumming his fingers on his forearm. "Well, I know what happened but it wasn't because I saw it. I can just *tell*."

Gabriel coughed, shifting his feet uncomfortably in his brother's knowing gaze. "Nothing happened!" he insisted, feigning innocence.

"Well, not *nothing*…" Daniel muttered, offering me a playful wink.

I stared him down sternly. "Focus, here, people!" I demanded, rapping on the desktop. The two brothers snapped back to reality.

"Are you sure it was the shadow realm?" Finnian questioned.

I nodded adamantly. "Yes. It was the same place you saw when you…did the mind meld *thing*," I insisted, struggling for words. "With the creepy tendril things. They had her captured. It was…" I trailed off, recalling Kit's helpless face as the Shadows drained her of her life force.

"How do we get there?" Gabriel demanded.

"Oh no…you can't go there," Finnian said.

"But—" I began to protest but he continued.

"*But*, remember how I said that realms kind of exist on top of one another?" he continued, looking directly at me and I nodded.

"I am guessing she is nearby, just in another realm," Finnian explained. He snapped his fingers, as if suddenly recalling something. "This woman—Kit? She's a good friend?" I nodded vigorously. "Is she magical?"

I shook my head. "She is a Pagan witch but as far as I know, she isn't magical."

Gabriel piped up. "I did sense some powerful magic off of her the couple times I've seen her. Not necessarily dark, but— "

"—she doesn't have to be magical but open to the *possibility* of magical," Finnian said. "I am guessing somehow, in her rituals or whatever, the Shadows who have probably been seeking out a connection to you, realized an opportunity to get to you through her. She probably had no idea what happened."

I swallowed. "So, they did possess her?"

He considered my words. "More or less. I would assume that the shadow realm is in the employment of a dreamwalker who has defected to their side, and through her connection with you, are able to get to *you* in the dream state—which is another in between, gray area. One of the *few*, slim times and places they can ever access us."

Gabriel let out a small noise, pointing out the window behind Finnian. The sun had risen a bit higher, the sky a brilliant blaze of orange, yellow and purple. "Between day and night. *Sunrise*!"

Finnian nodded. "Yes. "He glanced at a watch that had been tossed haphazardly on the desk. "Yes. We may be able to get to her, but we have to wait for the right time."

"How?" I demanded, clutching his arms and glaring directly into his eyes. They shifted color to the same muddy yellow that they did when I had attacked him and I could feel the energy wave off of him as he tried to appease me. I glared. "How?"

He coughed lightly. "Well, we can't go in there but…we can possibly rip a hole in between the realms—a temporary portal. But we have to figure out *exactly* where she was. I am guessing that she is nearby, like I said…a dreamwalker has to be in reasonably close proximity to its recipient in order for it to work. Can you remember…anything about where you were?"

I blew out, running my fingers through my tangled hair. "Oh Gods, I don't know. It was…the woods. Do you remember anything, Daniel?" I asked, turning to him.

Daniel tapped his foot on the ground. "Oh…I don't know. The woods. I remember bushes and leaves and trees. That's about it."

Finnian exhaled in frustration. "Well, that isn't helpful. This entire village is surrounded by woods." He thought momentarily, snapping his fingers. "Will you two allow me to look at your thoughts?" I nodded immediately, but Daniel was reasonably more hesitant.

I grasped his arm comfortingly. "It doesn't hurt, I swear. You don't even know he's doing anything."

"The second perspective might help me spot something you missed, because I'm more familiar with this area," Finnian continued. "People are more aware of their surroundings then you realize, only they are focused on other things but their eyes are still seeing things, storing things away for later."

Daniel nodded slowly. "Okay, then. Whatever it takes to get your friend back," he said, giving me a diminutive smile. I smiled wryly back, grateful.

"Okay." Finnian cleared off an empty space on top of the desk, and patted it. I gave him a strange look but he said, "It's easier if I don't have to bend over. You're a little...*shorter* than me," he said, with a jovial laugh.

I narrowed my eyes. "Perhaps I'll just change to my dragon. *She* will be taller *and* I'll let her eat you."

Gabriel choked back a laugh.

"Sorry, sorry," he said, holding his hands up in surrender.

I sighed. "Fine." I lifted myself up on the desk and shifted myself around so my legs were hanging off the edge.

"Oh, I see your little problem corrected itself," Finnian said, motioning to the air around me where my wings once were.

I shrugged. "I just woke up and they were gone."

"Interesting..." Finnian extended his hand and hesitantly touched my cheek. He pressed more firmly after a moment—after he was confident I wasn't going to bite him, I'm sure—and closed his eyes.

I caught a glimpse of Gabriel over Finnian's shoulder; his hair was still mussed and there were several telltale marks on his neck of the night's "recreational activities," before I lost my nerve. I guess I had gotten a little carried away to begin with. It was fun, but probably good that we had stopped. Despite myself, though, I began to smile at the thought, Gabriel flashing me a flirtatious wink.

Finnian's eyes flew open momentarily and he smirked.

I put my hand to my mouth and gasped, realizing that I had been thinking about *that*. "You stop that, now!" I admonished, shaking my finger at him.

Finnian just grinned and winked. "Naughty minx," he mumbled under his breath. I let out a low warning growl from the back of my throat, and he wiped the shit ass grin off his face and closed his eyes again, concentrating. After a couple of moments, his eyes began fluttering.

What's going on? Gabriel mouthed from behind Finnian. I just held up my hand, indicating it was okay. He shrugged and relented.

Finnian's eyes opened again slowly after another few moments, and he blinked a couple of times, his eyes changing from a blue to a deep brown. He glanced at my sympathetically. "She is in bad shape. I am so sorry..."

I nodded slowly, recalling Kit's desperation and misery. I sniffled, rubbing my nose with the side of my hand; the tears ready to fall from my eyes at his confirmation.

Finnian stroked my cheek, his mouth grimaced in a firm line, the corners downturned slightly. "I hope you know, that even if we get to her, it may be too late. She seems pretty far gone. But we—" he continued when I opened my mouth to protest, "—we will do our best."

I nodded again.

"I didn't see a lot of landmarks from your perspective, but that's not surprising, as you were so focused on your friend. However out of the corner of your eyes were a couple of trees and you didn't notice, but you stumbled twice over roots and rocks on the ground. That might prove helpful in locating her, especially if Daniel here was more observant." He patted my cheek again and turned to Daniel. Daniel was a slight bit taller than Finnian so he had to stretch his arm a bit to reach his cheek. Daniel bent, slightly to allow him better access.

Finnian firmly pressed his fingers to Daniel's right cheek and clamped his eyes shut; immediately they fluttered. I assumed Daniel's thoughts were clearer than mine. I was right and it was only a minute before Finnian pulled away. "I know where she is."

I smiled hopefully, clapping my hands together eagerly. "You do? Where?"

"There is a small clearing about three-hundred feet from the building where you all are staying," Finnian explained. "Sometimes residents here use the area for camping; I noticed the rocks and such as a campfire that had been used recently and the logs hadn't totally burned down. She is nearby."

"So, what now?" Gabriel asked.

Finnian drummed his fingers together, thoughtfully. "We will somehow need something or someone powerful enough to penetrate the veil that separates the realms. A potion, or a spell. But, the complicated part of this—"

"—more complicated than a potion?" I asked in disbelief.

"Unfortunately, yes. In order for us to get over there, and not be stuck permanently, we have to reach her in a dream state."

"What does that mean?" Gabriel questioned.

"It means that you—" he pointed at me, "—will need to be asleep. And you—" he pointed at Daniel, "—are going to have to dreamwalk her over to the shadow realm and you will have to coax her out that way."

Daniel swallowed, uneasy. "Me? I don't know how I did, that even! It just…it *happened*! I've never dreamwalked before—I didn't even know I could!"

"Well, that's where I will be helping you. Both of you will have to be asleep, and I will be inside your mind, Daniel," Finnian continued as Daniel let out a sharp noise. "I will be guiding you how to dream walk. Of course, I have no *idea* how to dreamwalk, so I will be seeking the council of one of the dreamwalkers in residence here. He'll have to be here while this is all going on, guiding me as to how to guide *you*."

I let out a small groan. "This sounds very complicated."

"Yeah, why can't we just open a portal and I go in, shooting light everywhere, killing off those tendrils and grab her and yank her out?" Gabriel offered.

Finnian shook his head. "Once you are in, you cannot leave. Not without being consumed by the Shadows."

"Then…how are we going to get Kit out, then? If no one can leave?" I asked, confused.

"I assume Kit is not there of her own will. You have to make the choice to cross into the shadow realm. She may still be shadowtouched, but if she didn't choose to be in the employment of the Shadows, there may still be a chance we can save her," Finnian explained. "Once you go over there of your own volition, that's it. You're stuck. It's all about intention."

I let out a low whistle.

"So, why couldn't Leo get her out when we were just there? She tried, but nothing worked to get those *things* off of her," Daniel asked, in disgust at the recollection of the tendrils covering her body.

"Not enough power. Keep in mind, you weren't really *there*. At least, not physically. Your subconsciouses were at that in-between state that allowed you to travel there, just not be stuck. That's what you will have to do again; without severely powerful magic, you cannot enter the shadow realm. But, in order to get her to leave Leorah will have to bolster her mentally enough to *want* to leave, and while the portal is ripped open, we'll be outside, shooting in magic and potions to help get the Shadows to disperse for long enough for her to escape."

"Want to leave? Why wouldn't she *want* to leave?" I asked incredulously.

"Again, it's all about intent. The Shadows are making her helpless, wishing for escape, or death. While she's there, all of her will is taken away. Otherwise, she'd be able to just stand up and walk out, since she isn't there of her own choice. The Shadows reside in our subconscious—more of that 'in-between', gray area—brainwashing, basically. That's why they're so dangerous, and you won't even know that's what's happening." Finnian sighed. "We need something to give her hope, to be able to coax her to leave. The Shadows will pull at her, and it will be painful. She will want to give up, and let them consume her. She will need a lot of willpower to be able to walk away."

"What happens if she can't walk away?" Gabriel asked the unavoidable question we all already knew the answer to.

"She will be consumed. Her essence will add to the power of the Shadows, strengthening them for whoever comes along next. That is what happened the last time they were able to penetrate realms."

"She'll...die?" I asked in a small voice. Gabriel came up to the side of me, and leaned his head against mine and threaded his arms through mine, comfortingly.

"I wish it was that simple." Finnian's voice spilled with dread, his eyes changing to yellow. "She will be in limbo. Her soul will be at unrest. She will never know peace. Her body may be gone, but her soul will not be free."

"Purgatory." Daniel offered, alarmed with a gasp.

"Bingo," Finnian acknowledged him with a nod.

"Oh *fuck*..." my voice shook, my lower lip trembled.

"We will get her." Gabriel said with determination. "We *will,*" he said this lowly, in my ear. I tried to nod but the skeptic in me was rearing its head. It all seemed so impossible.

"So, what do we do?" Daniel finally asked, after a few beats of silence.

Finnian appeared distracted; you could almost see his mind moving a mile a minute. He turned to us with a smile. "For now, just be patient. I know it's a tall order, but I need to get some things together before we can even attempt this. It will be a *massive* undertaking."

"Well, when can we try?" I asked.

"Tonight, at sunset will be the best time. The time between morning and afternoon, the area between the two isn't strong enough. Dusk will be our best time," Finnian said. "Until then…relax. Rest— or try to, anyways. This will be an exhausting endeavor."

I sighed. "Wonderful."

"Are they anything but exhausting?" Gabriel groaned in exasperation.

"No. Apparently." I retorted dryly.

Finnian sent us on our way; we tried to relax but it was nearly impossible for me. He instructed us to try to get some sleep, and see if Daniel could dreamwalk into my head again but seeing as how he didn't even know he could do it until last night, it was pretty impossible to assume he would be able to. Finnian did call on a dreamwalker person and had him meet with Daniel. As of later in the afternoon, I had no idea yet what became of that.

Of course I had no idea what a dreamwalker actually was: a witch or sorcerer who has magic over the subconscious. Chances are they can compel people and change perspectives. A bt more complicated than that but I was assured that was the gist. It sounded creepy as hell to me.

Finnian surmised that since my main element was "spirit", that that is how Daniel was able to access my dreams so easily; and somewhere along the lines Daniel quite possibly had some spirit powers as well, possibly lying dormant for years, like mine.

It was all quite confusing, actually.

I tried to lie down and sleep back in the room but I just could not no matter what I did. I just sat on the barstool in the kitchen, leaning over the counter, rapidly shaking my leg up and down and drumming my fingers on the countertop. Gabriel was more relaxed, managing to do some work on his computer. I must have gotten to him after a while because eventually he set down the computer with a sigh and joined me at the counter.

He snaked his arms around my waist and leaned his cheek into the back of my neck, placing gentle kisses on the top of my spine, around and to the spot under my ear. Normally it'd be enough to drive me *mad* but right now, I was just pissed.

"Really? *Really*? My best friend is dying, and you're trying to get in my pants?" I attempted to pull out of his grasp, scowling.

He pulled away. "I'm sorry, that's not what I was trying to do: I wanted you do relax."

I snorted. "Right. Nothing in it for you, eh?"

He sighed, folding himself into the stool next to me. "I won't lie; I would enjoy it immensely. *Immensely*," he added, with a faraway grin.

I furrowed my forehead. "But?"

"Well, Finnian said you need to *relax* to get this to work. So...let's go relax," he elbowed me playfully, a flirty lilt in his tone.

I rolled my eyes. "Really?"

"Seriously, I'm just thinking about watching TV, sheesh!" he retorted, with a grin. He scoffed. "Honestly, get your mind out of the gutter...I wasn't talking about *that*."

I groaned. "*Riiiight.*"

He shrugged lightly. "Okay, I wouldn't object to making out a little bit, at least."

I narrowed my eyes at him, but couldn't help laughing at the mirthful expression on his face. "Well...maybe." I allowed him to take my hand and lead me to the bedroom where we exchanged a few giggles and flirty kisses while we watched old episodes of *Vampire Diaries* on the computer before there was a knock at the door. I practically flew out of bed to answer it.

Finnian stood on the other side, looking distracted and serious. He held up his wristwatch and pointed. "It's about that time. Are you ready?"

I nodded feverishly, and called for Gabriel. The rest of the group—Kiarra, Daniel and Maxxus—joined after a few moments.

"Won't this be dangerous? Should they be here?" I asked, pointing at Maxxus and Kiarra.

"I—we—wouldn't miss it for anything." Maxxus spoke factually and that was that. Kiarra nodded fervently.

"Okay, then." I agreed amicably. This wasn't the time to get into an argument with anyone.

"This way." Finnian gestured for us to follow, and we trudged through the town, shielding our eyes with our hands against the setting sun as it pierced our vision with its bright oranges and pinks. Along the way we were joined by two unfamiliar people—one male, one female. The female had small, spritely wings so I assumed she must be a fairy, or pixie. The male was on the shorter side with plain features, long sandy blonde hair and pale blue eyes; he appeared entirely human. Daniel nudged me as he joined us and grinned, while I rolled my eyes at him.

"He's cute," he whispered. I took another glance at him; I suppose he was, in a way. He walked with confidence, didn't seem to be putting on any airs with his jeans and plaid campshirt and had a friendly smile. His long, thick, straight hair was tied in a ponytail at the base of his neck and it trailed down the middle of his back.

I raised my eyebrow. "He shouldn't have nicer hair than me, that's just not fair."

Daniel chuckled. Gabriel, who'd been walking cautiously a few steps behind us, deep in some sort of private thought caught up to us and questioned, "Okay, what are you hens cackling about?"

I made an odd face at him, but it was Daniel who replied. "Oh…just admiring the single boys. For me," he quickly added.

Gabriel shook his head at him. "You never stop, do you?" He grasped my hand and pulled it into his chest as we walked through the border of the forest and a few paces inwards. "You ready for this?"

I shrugged. It was a moot point; it didn't matter if I was or not. It was something I had to do. "I'll be fine."

"I hope so," he said nervously, bringing my palm to his lips and placing a soft kiss on my knuckles, sending an electric shiver down my spine.

We stopped a few moments later, at a clearing in the middle of the woods. Sure enough, there was the log remains of a burnt-out campfire and a handful of spots worn in the dirt where sleeping bags had sat. I didn't recognize it from any "dream" but Daniel spoke up, reassuring me.

"Oh...this *is* it!" I breathed out a breath I didn't even know I was holding at his confident words.

There was rustling in the woods, and Esmè appeared in the clearing seconds later, carrying her woven shoulder bag. "I'm sorry, I got here as soon as I could. After everything that happened, Becka insisted on smudging the entire house." She set her bag down on the ground, and nodded a friendly greeting me. "You are looking well, Leorah."

I offered a friendly smile, but was much too distracted to put up a conversation. I was however curious why she was here. I didn't even have to ask to question it; somehow she knew.

"I'm here when you're successful. Your friend will need much spiritual healing, right away if we want to save her," she explained. I nodded, giving her a grateful smile.

"Okay." Finnian clapped his hands together, removing himself from the group and standing opposite us, facing all of us, clearly indicating he was a leader. "Brief introductions: this is Nomi," he said, pointing at the winged girl. "She is fae, and a dreamwalker. One of few fae to be gifted this ability. You know Daniel already," Finnian said to her, and she nodded, with a pleasant smile.

"He came really far, very fast. He will be a very talented dreamwalker," she said, in a loud but very young, almost melodic sounding voice. Daniel blushed under her praise.

"This," he said, pointing to the friendly, long haired gentleman, "is Connor Styles, mage extraordinaire."

"Wait, what now?" I blurted quickly, in surprise. "Mage?" I couldn't get the image of a video-game mage out of my head, wielding purple balls of magic and wearing long robes, carrying tall, glowing staves.

Connor snickered momentarily, and I immediately recoiled, feeling like an ass. "It's okay, really," he said. "I get that all the time."

"A mage is technically a sorcerer who has been gifted with the powers of bending time and space," Finnian described. "Much like Gabriel with his control over the elements, Connor here has been gifted with extraordinary powers of the arcane, and mages—very rare—can make portals into other dimensions and have some control over time. This will be most helpful for us if we want to get to Kit." I nodded to him slightly, recognizing that it was somewhat like the skills of the portal bending and such of the black and violet dragons back home.

"And this is Daniel, the Seer and novice Dreamwalker; Maxxus, green dragon and friend of Leorah, the last living pink dragon," he said, nodding at each of us in turn, "and Gabriel, elemental sorcerer and knight of The Ancient Order of Dragons, or *Ord na Draconica Dianthus*. Kiarra you already know."

We all murmured shy greetings at one another as Finnian checked his wristwatch and glanced backwards over his shoulder at the sun just beginning to set over the treeline. "Only a couple of minutes until sunset. Positions!"

Esmè draped soft blankets on the ground next to each other. She pulled a handful of small candles from the mysterious depths of her bag and started placing them in a circle around the blankets. "You, and you…sit," she pointed at Daniel and me.

Gabriel grabbed each of one our hands and squeezed. *Good luck*, he mouthed to us. I offered him a wry but hopeful smile. Daniel took my hand from his brother and held it close to his heart, giving me a nervous look.

"We can do this," he said, biting his lip. It was more a question than a statement, seeking confidence he didn't have.

I nodded. "We *can*." Daniel led me to the blankets in the center of the circle and we sat down in the center, one for each of us. We glanced at each other and exchanged nervous expressions.

"You." Esmè pointed at Gabriel and instructed him to sit in between his brother and I. "Once the portal is open from the outside of it, we need you to summon all the light you can. Fire if you have to—just give it everything you have and shoot it in the darkness. Leorah won't be able to extract her friend if the Shadows won't release her and her powers are useless in the shadow realm." Gabriel nodded, and came to sit on the ground in between us.

Esmè and Finnian arranged the rest of us; Finnian at Daniel's side, ready to describe the scene to everyone via his mind "melding," Nomi nearby to help Finnian tell Daniel what he was to do, if necessary, and Connor just outside the circle, hands at the ready to summon the portal or whatever it was exactly that mages did.

Kiarra and Maxxus hung back, just there for moral support I guessed. Kiarra appeared neutral as she spoke in hushed tones that I couldn't hear to Maxxus who kept shifting his human feet around fretfully.

Esmè entered the circle and offered Daniel and me both small vials of thick, gray liquid. We took them as she explained, "For sleep. They will put you in that state just before REM sleep where dreaming is possible, and will only last thirty minutes at most before you awaken so this will have to go quickly." Daniel and I twisted off the plastic tops and tossed them on the ground.

"Bottoms up," he said, with a quick, tense laugh as he raised the potion in a sign of *Cheers*!

I raised mine as well and we both swallowed our vials in one forced swallow; it was bitter and chalky tasting and surprisingly thick. Daniel even gagged a little as he choked it down. "Damn, that's nasty," he mumbled with a grimace on his face.

Esmè turned to Gabriel, as she stepped backwards. "Would you light the candles, please?

Gabriel nodded and effortlessly conjured a small flicker of fire in between his palms. He shot it with a flick of the wrist at the nearest candle to him and urged it to bounce from wick to wick around the circle until all the candles were lit.

I grinned at him proudly, still awed at his natural use of magic. It was like breathing to him, he didn't even have to think about it. Gabriel smirked, and winked back.

"Ugh..." Daniel groaned from next to me, his eyes appearing heavy as he slowly lay back on the blanket.

I felt his fatigue as the potion started to take effect in me too; it felt like a giant yawn was waiting to escape but couldn't. I too lay back, not before turning my head towards Daniel and reaching for his hand. He grabbed it and squeezed lightly, relieved for the anchor my grasp provided before I watched his eyes roll back into his head and he was out. I was asleep moments later.

Everything around me was gray. Gray and silent; there was nothing around. It was a few moments before I heard a nervous voice. "Leo?"

I turned, and Daniel was right there behind me, looking nervous.

"You're okay?" I asked, as he nodded. "How are you doing this?"

He shrugged. "I'm just supposed to fall asleep with an image of my mind, of a place. This was the best I could come up with," he added with a chuckle. "Not too creative yet."

I smiled, and patted his shoulder. "It's better than the shadow realm. It'll be fine."

He beamed, thankfully. "The rest is rather involuntarily, actually. Finding you here, talking to you...it just kind of happens."

"Huh. Weird," I said thoughtfully.

He nodded in agreement.

"Okay, Connor is going to open the portal now," Finnian's voice rang out from above, kind of like "God" and we looked up and around to find the source of the voice. Of course he wouldn't be here but he sounded as if he should be right next to us. "Once he does, Daniel, you'll need to lead Leo in. Just focus on her, nothing else. We'll do the rest, because once you lose your focus, that's it, this is done. So...no pressure," Finnian added with a wry chuckle.

"*Fuck.* No pressure at all," Daniel mumbled with a scowl.

We heard the sound then of...well it almost sounded like a hundred papers ripping, following by anguished low squeals and before us a hole opened up in the gray expanse, and exposing the darkness of the shadow realm that was nearby.

Daniel held out his hand and I grabbed it without looking. "Here we go..." he said, and we stepped through the veil and safety of Daniel's gray, neutral dreamscape into the anguish of the shadow realm.

Immediately it felt stifled, choking, like all the will to live was escaping my body out of every pore. Daniel obviously felt it too, he swallowed nervously and his eyes widened in terror.

Kit. Must get Kit. I told myself, with conviction. I tried to push the terror of the Shadows out of my mind, and focused on my friend. With a newfound confidence, I urged Daniel and I further into the shadow realm.

I nearly tripped over a large object, much like last night. Daniel struggled to keep me upright, as a handful of needy tendrils taunted my feet.

A blast of light came from behind me—out of nowhere—and I knew it must have been Gabriel shooting his light magic at them. The tendrils shrieked and recoiled back into the ground below.

Relieved, I finally looked down. All I saw was a large, black mound below that shook and let out a whimper.

I gasped. That couldn't be...Kit? I fought back the stinging tears in my eyes that would surely be falling if this wasn't a "dream", feeling the emptiness emanate from Kit in waves.

"More light!" I commanded, hoping that Gabriel or Finnian could hear me.

More beams of light came shooting through the portal hole, attacking the blackness at my feet. They didn't appear to be having an effect at first and then finally they began screaming and dispersing back into the ground.

When most of them had been burned by the bright light Gabriel had flung at them, I knelt down at Kit's side, who was now exposed, shaking violently and mumbling incoherently.

Gingerly, I reached out and touched her shoulder. No reaction at all.

"Kit? Kit it's me, Leo. I've come to take you away; some place safe," I said, trying to sound as comforting as possible.

A small noise—perhaps one of recognition—squeaked from her mouth.

"Kit?" I tried to shake her lightly and she just whimpered.

I looked over her listless body at Daniel who appeared extremely concerned. He sat down beside her and reached out, stroking the side of her arm. "Kit? My name is Daniel. I'm a...friend. We're here to get you out. All you have to do is stand up, and we can get you out of here to someplace nice."

I flashed Daniel a thankful smile. He caught my face and replied back with a silent nod.

"Leorah, talk to her like normal, just like any other day. Remind her of what she likes, or what makes her feel good, just like you were talking normally," Finnian instructed from above.

I nodded at no one in particular and summoned up all my assurance in an attempt to urge my friend out of the void that she was in.

"Gabriel and I went to your house. We fed your cats," I blurted, it was the first thing I could think of. "So, they're fine but they miss you." I didn't know if they did or not really but I was willing to try anything, knowing how much she loved them.

"Cats?" she mumbled faintly. If I hadn't been a dragon with keen hearing, I probably wouldn't have heard anything.

"Yep. They're good," I said, trying to sound chipper but struggling, feeling the weight of the darkness pushing down on me. More flashes of light and I forced myself to continue. "Yeah. They actually like Gabriel. Funny huh?" I chuckled lightly. There were no words from Kit, but she did stop whimpering.

"Something more, Leo!" Finnian's voice boomed and I cried out in frustration.

"I'm *trying*! But it's hard! It feels so— "

Daniel shushed me, with a finger to his lips. "Don't say it. Positive thoughts."

I fought the urge to growl because I knew he was right.

"Do you know any gossip?" Finnian suggested. Someone must have given him grief because he continued, "What? Girls like that stuff, don't they?"

I snickered shaking my head.

"Kit? Please just come out of...whatever that is. Wherever you are. I miss you. I need some girl advice...I actually went out on a date a little bit ago, and who knows? I might have an actual boyfriend soon, and I need your help. You know how stupidly clueless I am," I said, trying to sound light but I knew the desperation was leaking into my voice.

A small chuckle escaped Kit's mouth. "That...coffee...guy," she stammered, trying to find the words.

"Yeah. Gabriel. You need to come back, I need you to go shopping with me. I need new underwear," I said, before realizing what I said. I covered my mouth with my hand as Daniel smirked at me.

"It gets even worse, because there's another dra—errr, man that wants her too!" Daniel blurted out.

"What are you talking about?" I squeaked in reply

Kit's head lifted slightly. "Oh?" She couldn't hold it up and she promptly allowed it to drop back to the ground, and I sighed.

Daniel shrugged. "What? It's gossip, isn't it?"

I fought the urge to shoot Daniel a dirty look and continued. "Yeah I just know I'll do something dumb so I need your help. You have to come back."

"Not...sure...can..." she stammered, in a small voice.

"But...you have to. We need to fix up the shop and get it open again." I didn't know if that would actually ever happen—at least not with me—but I hoped it'd get a rise out of her. "Now everyone's forced to go to Starbucks in the town over." Mentioning the huge coffee-giant generally got a rise out of her, sending her on an anti-corporate tirade.

"Damn..." she started to say. She laughed weakly, and I watched her struggle to lift her head. She cried out in pain as a tendril attempting to pull her head back down. Another flash of light and it recoiled but not before another handful of them began emerging from the ground.

She let out a shriek as they began closing over her appendages. She struggled for a moment before going listless again. "Can't...do..."

I gave Daniel a panicked look. He just shrugged.

"What's her favorite things to do? Talk about? *Anything*, Leo!" Finnian called out.

I sighed, trying to recall things that were important to her. Her cats. The shop. Neither had evoked the kind of response in her I wanted.

I snapped my fingers then as a lightbulb went off in my head. "Unicorns!" I cried out.

Daniel looked at me as if I were daft. "Huh?"

"She loves them! I bet she'd like to meet one, for real. Before the storm the entire shop was filled with unicorn knickknacks."

Daniel grinned at me knowingly. "Really? It's too bad they weren't real."

"Oh, but they are!" I corrected him cheerfully. "They're here!"

Kit ever so slowly lifted her head upward. Her eyes flew open and she peered around. "Where?"

"Here! Well...not *here* here. Not in this place. But they're close! And you can see one—a *real* one—if you just get out of here. I'll show you one!" I reached out and stroked her dirty hair across her shoulders.

"Where...here?" she stammered.

"This is an icky place. You don't want to be here. Bad magic. Bad juju. We need to leave," I said.

She nodded, small. "Yes. Want to but...not sure how."

I gave Daniel a hopeful look.

"Just...take my hand." I held out my hand in front of her. "I can show you how. Just come..."

Slowly, gingerly, Kit reached out a weak hand and tried to put it in my grasp. "Not sure...if...can...so tired. Just wanna...sleep."

"You can, though! Just not here. I know of a nice place, you'll love it. I will show you...just come. You have to want to, though." I insisted. "And once you feel better I'll show you a unicorn. For real. They *really* exist. You just have to want to leave."

"I...I do..." Slowly—ever so slowly—she peeled her upper body off the ground. Slowly, she turned to me and even though her expression was blank and grim, she gave a small smile. "Leo? It really is you," she said, much more intelligibly this time.

I nodded, with a grin. "Yeah. It's me."

Her lower lip trembled. "I want...to leave."

I nodded vigorously. "Then just...give me your hand. Stand up. I'll get you out. All you have to do is...take it." I outstretched my hand and she looked at it, like it was a foreign object. Reluctantly, she lifted her own heavy hand off the ground and slowly placed it in mine.

Daniel and I helped her to stand. She cried out as more tendrils, suddenly realizing they were losing their grasp on her, started furiously nipping at her bare feet.

Flashes of light shot through the opening in the portal at her feet. She yelped, but realized after a moment they were fighting off the tendrils she calmed. I wrapped an arm around her shoulders.

"Let's go, okay?" And she nodded, leaning her weak body directly into mine, and she allowed me to slowly walk her to the portal, ignoring the flashes of light that kept shooting through.

"Okay." She dragged her feet but I held her weight against me. It felt like eons before we finally reached the portal opening, but we did. I felt a shove as Daniel pushed us. We crashed through, feeling a temporary disorienting sensation as we fell a short but unexpected distance to the ground. But only Kit actually fell, of course. Daniel and I sort of...*dissipated*.

I awoke with a choked gasp, starting violently. From next to me, Daniel sat up, abrupt, making appalled choking noises.

I felt a weight over the lower half of my body and cried out in relief, seeing Kit draped over my legs, listless but her chest was steadily moving up and down.

Esmè was at our side in an instant, Gabriel waving out the candles with his air magic so as to not burn her. She hovered her hands all over Kit's non-reactive body and looked up at me.

"She's alive...but only just. Her mind is in a bad place. I need to get her to my place. Fast!" Esmè pulled an arsenal of vials, herbs and trinkets out of her bag and started draping things over Kit's body, sprinkling things on her or waving twigs over her, chanting rhythmically.

Maxxus rushed to her side—the largest and the strongest of us right now and heaved her off the ground in both of his arms. Her neck went slack and her head was heavy, limbs languid as he clutched her close to himself.

Her eyes fluttered momentarily, as Esmè put a vial to her lips, pouring some green liquid over them. Kit slowly and involuntarily pressed her lips together, and some of the substance seeped in. "You'll be okay, dear," Esmè said, putting a comforting hand to her forehead. She looked up at Maxxus and nodded. "Let's go. It's not far." Maxxus grunted in acknowledgment and they began walking off, as a small noise came from Kit.

"Leo?"

I leaped up and was by her side in a flash. "Yeah?" I said, Maxxus lowering her slightly so we could properly look at each other.

There was recognition in her eyes, a spark in her eyes when she saw me. She tried to lift her hand to grab mine but was unsuccessful, too weak. I brought my palm to her cheek and held it there.

"Do I really get to see unicorns?" she asked, hopefully.

I chuckled lightly. "I promise...as soon as you feel better."

She flashed a small smile before allowing her eyes to shut again, too weak to keep them open. She leaned her head against Maxxus' chest. I gave him a look of *thank you* before Esmè urged him to hurry.

I began to follow, but Finnian grabbed my shoulders. I tried to pull away but he only grasped more firmly, spinning me around on my heels to look into his face. His expression was stern and commanded compliance, his eyes flashing to a bright, bright grass green. "Esmè will do what she can, but no distractions. Let them be. For now, you need to recover. You may not feel it now, but you will be drained in a while. And...uhh..." he looked slightly past me, and nodded.

"What?" I asked, confused. I tried to glance over my shoulder and when I saw it, I groaned. The wings I had just gotten rid of were jutting out my back and draped down towards the ground again. They had ripped plum through my t-shirt and sweatshirt (but I was thankful the front of my shirts remained intact!). "*Why?*"

Finnian shook his head. "Don't know. But—"

Suddenly, I was overcome with a wash of fatigue. My vision became cloudy and my knees unexpectedly weak. They began to give out from under me before Finnian caught me, before I could fall to the ground.

"Get her to bed," Finnian instructed to someone. I couldn't distinguish to in my fatigued haze. A pair of arms wrapped around me and for the second time in such a short time frame, I blacked out.

Chapter 21

Slowly, I opened my eyes, blinking the blurriness out of them, revealing myself to be in unfamiliar surroundings; almost a hospital type setting.

"You're in the infirmary." Evie peered over me, obviously seeing the quizzical expression on my face. "All of you are, actually."

I tried to sit up and felt something crash into my head like a ton of bricks: a surge of pain. I groaned and quickly lay back down against the pillow. "Uggh...."

"Headache?" Evie questioned, and I nodded. "Good. Believe it or not pain is a good sign that you're recovering."

"Recovering?" I asked, rubbing my forehead with the tips of my fingers.

She nodded. "Apparently, when you pulled out your friend, some of the Shadows had spilled out of the portal and started attacking your friends."

I gasped. "Oh, no!"

"Everyone's fine," she said, quickly. "The sorcerer—err, Gabriel managed to summon down an incredible amount of light magic from seemingly out of nowhere. I've never *heard* of a sorcerer able to wield that much magic."

The vampire continued: "The light was enough to burn all of the Shadows into oblivion but not before they grabbed on to a few of you, leaving a dark imprint. So...you all were sent here and having been receiving light infusions and healing pots for the past four hours."

I groaned, trying to shake the confusion out of my brain. Sluggishly, I was able to pull myself to a sitting position and fully take in my surroundings. I was on top of a white-sheeted gurney, much like you'd see in a normal hospital. Daniel was asleep soundly to the one on my left.

"Is he—" I began to ask, pointing at him.

"Fine, fine. Just a bit tired." Evie explained.

On the other side of Daniel sat Connor—the mage—who was upright with his legs slung over the gurney, slumped down with his head in his hands, mumbling something about a headache.

"How about him?" I asked.

Evie began to speak, but Connor cut her off. "Oh, I'm fine. But your sorcerer blasted me with a bit of that light magic accidentally." He let out an unexpected peal of giggles. "Now I just feel…weird." He wobbled and slumped back down on the pillow, legs still draped over the side.

Evie chuckled. "Too much light magic directly taken makes you feel…tipsy."

"Wheee!" Connor blurted, with a giggle, sitting up again and allowing himself to fall to the pillow once more, followed by a hearty laugh.

I snorted and grinned. "That's funny." Evie nodded in agreement.

I glanced on the other side of me, Maxxus was curled up under a blanket, sleeping peacefully with a small smile on his face. I felt crushed seeing him sleeping, seeming all vulnerable. I fought an urge to reach out for him and touch a small scrape over his eyebrow but resisted because it didn't feel appropriate.

"Him too?" I sighed, regrettably. "He shouldn't have even have to be here."

"Since he was the one carrying your friend, he got a good dose of the Shadows too. But, he'll be fine. He is *strong*, that's for sure." Evie glanced over at him, smiling in admiration.

I raised a brow. "Oh?" was all I said.

She nodded, still smiling at Maxxus' sleeping form before shaking herself out of a daydream. "Cute, that one is. But…his mind is clearly elsewhere."

"What do you mean?"

"Oh...nothing." She shrugged, dismissing the topic. I groaned under my breath; more cryptic words about the green dragon. *Goody.*

I noticed that Kit wasn't in the room. "Where is Kit? She's not here?" I asked, my eyes darting around the room in a panic.

"Esmè is keeping your friend at her house. She requires regular, round the clock treatment," Evie explained.

I bit my lip, sorrowfully. "Is…she going to be okay?"

Evie was hesitant. "I…won't lie. It's pretty bad. But Esmè is a great alchemist. She is in good hands."

"Hands…" I looked down at mine in my lap. "Could I…maybe…??"

Another voice interrupted then, from one of the far beds. "No, Leorah. It's too dangerous." It was Finnian, sitting himself up on one of the gurneys, a rag to his head. He winced as he pulled it away, revealing a black and blue goose egg on his forehead. "Your healing powers are...great. But the Shadows were clearly after you. *Clearly.* You may see her but I'm afraid using your powers on her is out of the question. We can't risk having you turn Shadowtouched too."

I frowned, crestfallen.

"Your wings detracted again, I see," Finnian said. I hadn't noticed, craning my head around to see the holes that remained in my clothing where the wings had jut out from.

"Huh...that's weird. Seems to happen when I sleep?" I hypothesized, with a shrug.

"I wonder if you can call them out on command?" Finnian mused.

I shrugged. "Why would I want to?"

"I do believe they act as a protectant for you. A shield, basically," Finnian said, gingerly poking the bump with his fingertips and replacing the cloth over the injured area. "I also believe that they might make your magic stronger."

"I guess...maybe? It's worth a shot." I closed my eyes and pictured the wings on my back. I held my breath and I felt a pulling and tingling on my back.

"I'll be damned." Finnian said.

I opened my eyes and turned to look behind me. The wings had morphed out of my back and were forming down my body as I watched. I raised a brow. Even I thought that was kind of neat. "Huh." I closed my eyes again, and imagined them retracting back into my body...nothing.

I sighed. "Well...I got it half right."

Finnian chuckled. "It'll come to you."

I scooted backwards so the wings were hanging down the other side of the gurney. "So, can I at least see her?"

Finnian and Evie exchanged a glance; Finnian nodded. "I suppose that would be okay. Just...no magic. Promise?"

I held up my palm like I was giving a vow. "Yes, yes...no magic. I don't know what I'm doing anyway."

"And...you should probably wait for those wings to go away," Evie said, with a chuckle. "Does she have any idea what you are?"

I shook my head. "No. At least...I don't think so."

"It'll be a surprising day all around," Evie muttered. "But if you think it's okay, Finn, then after I finish these rounds I'll walk her over. I should check on her myself; take her vitals."

Finnian nodded in agreement. "That works."

I glanced around at my friends laying or sitting up on their beds. "Are...are they all going to be okay?"

"Oh yeah," Evie replied confidently. "Kiarra and Nomi were already released. Maxxus is fine, but he's asleep so I didn't want to wake him. The brothers are the only ones we're still worried about—and you—but they're responding nicely. All human vitals are good."

"How about him?" I gestured my head towards Finnian.

He grumbled. "I'm right here, you know."

I scoffed. "I know, I know. How did that happen?" I asked, pointing to his forehead.

"Eh, just collateral damage. When Kit came flying out of the portal, she was pushed towards me and kicked me *accidentally* in the forehead." He smirked. "Looks worse than it is, but I do have a nasty headache."

I chuckled. "Well...sorry about that," I said, not sounding very sorry at all. Served him right.

Finnian shook his head, with a grin. "I'm sure that's the only apology I would ever get from you, so snide as it is, I'll take it."

"It probably is," I replied, with a small laugh. Evie scooted over to me and grasped her fingers around my wrist, peeking at a pocketwatch she had pulled out of the pocket on the front of her white lab coat. She dropped my wrist after a moment, and put a hand to my chest. I gave her an odd look.

"Vampire thing. I can actually hear your heart beating across the room," she explained. "No need for a stethoscope."

"Odd," I said with a laugh.

"Freaks most people out," she replied. She produced a small pen light from her other pocket and clicked it, turning on a light at the end and shined it briefly in each of my eyes. "Looks good. I'd say you are clear to get out of here."

"Good." I slid off the gurney, trying to be careful not to snag one of my wings—not that it would do anything but feel weird—and glanced back and forth at Daniel and Gabriel still resting. I felt a momentary pang of guilt just leaving them behind. Evie must have sensed my hesitation because she said:

"Oh, they will be fine. But you can come back after seeing your friend if you like and stay with them. If that will help you feel better." She flashed me a friendly smile, trying to conceal her fangs with her top lip.

"Thanks," I said, nodding thankfully.

"Well…I'm set to go if you are," she said. I started to follow her out of the infirmary before I paused momentarily at Maxxus' bedside. I started to reach out to brush a strand of his ginger hair out of his forehead in a pang of momentary guilt. The strong earth dragon looked so vulnerable and peaceful sound asleep; breathing soundly. A lone tear stung at my eye before falling slowly down my cheek. "I'm so sorry…" I said, with a sniffle.

Evie let out a noise, to remind me that she was still here. "Are you okay? He'll be fine, I promise."

I nodded slowly. "I know, it's just…" I felt choked. Yes, I felt guilty as to his being here but there was…something else. I couldn't find the right words so I just shrugged. Feeling exposed, I pulled my hand away. "Let's go." I had to practically force myself not to turn back and take one last glance at him. I followed Evie out the set of metal doors out of the brick building that sat on the west edge of town. She led me through the town square and down several rows of family homes and huts, all of a different construction than the other before we arrived at a terra cotta cottage, complete with scalloped red roof and rounded, wooden door. She didn't bother knocking before going in, and I assumed we had reached Esmè's home.

I honestly didn't pay much attention to the décor as we traipsed through a front room with couches, down a hallway and we paused briefly before entering the small bedroom.

She did pause to ask me, "You think it's wise to let her see those wings?"

I shrugged. "She'll have to know sooner or later."

"You're the boss," she said with a chuckle and we entered. I gasped, when I saw her.

Kit lay on her back on a twin size bed, covered with handmade quilts her head rolled to the side, still pallor and fairly lifeless.

I tried not to cry out in despair at the state of my friend. I did notice that someone had taken off her rags and replaced them with a set of sunny yellow robes (her favorite color—I wondered if they somehow knew) and her face had been washed of the dirt marks, her long hair had been thoroughly brushed and braided off to the side, and trailed down her chest.

Esmè had been sitting at her bedside, swinging a blue crystal from a silver chain over her and whispering something rhythmically that I couldn't quite make out: I wasn't sure if it was another language or if I was too panicked to care.

"How is she?" Evie spoke for me, as I was too dumbfounded to open my mouth.

Esmè startled and gasped. She turned to see us there and laughed. "Oh my...sorry! I was in concentration; I didn't hear you come in."

"How is she?" I repeated nervously. Esmè reached for a small vial and dropper from the table next to the bed and dipped the dropper inside, squeezed the rubber top and hovered it over Kit's lips a short distance. She dropped a couple drops of grayish liquid from the dropper and they landed on Kit's lips. Instinctively, she pressed them together, swallowing whatever it was that had been in the dropper. "Healing potion," Esmè explained, setting the vial back down. She stood up and motioned for me to sit in the stool that she had been sitting on.

"I believe your friend will be fine, but she will probably feel better hearing from a familiar voice," Esmè said.

I nodded, sitting down gingerly next to Kit in the stool, tossing my wings behind me like they were hair. "She can hear?"

"Oh yes. She's awoken a handful of times, but only for a few moments before she drifts out again," Esmè said. "She would appear to be in a state of shock." Esmè putzed about the room, rearranging dried flowers in vases, moving crystals around. Briefly I noticed that the room—adorned with rose-floral wallpaper—looked like it should belong in what I assumed rooms in the New Orleans French Quarter would look like, complete with voodoo ware and other mystical objects—glass orbs, crystals and bones hung from strings in various spots, beads instead of curtains over the windows. The wallpaper appeared severely out of place. She smiled at me briefly, gesturing to Evie with a nod of the head. "We'll give you some privacy, but not for long, she needs rest."

I nodded, and Evie followed Esmè out of the room.

I turned back to Kit and reached for her hand that had been placed over her heart; it was cold but not clammy. Just cold, like she'd just been outside in the winter. I noticed a rune-like object had been drawn in her palm and wondered what it meant. I didn't know so I just placed her hand between mine and gave a light squeeze.

"Kit? Can you hear me? It's...it's Leo," I said softly, gazing at her with concern. I peered at her face, looking for any sign of recognition. I didn't notice anything, not even a flutter of the eyes. I sighed. "Kit, I'm so sorry...this whole thing..." I sniffled, feeling the sting of hot tears brimming in my eyes. I didn't fight them and allowed them to trail down my cheek and fall to the bed. "I'm so sorry..." I murmured over and over again, as I cried quietly. Feeling weak with despair, I rested my head on her shoulder and just let the tears fall in silence.

"L-Leo?" Kit's voice was quiet and raspy, but she spoke.

I sat up immediately. I quickly wiped the tears from my eyes with the sleeve of my sweatshirt and sniffled. "Kit?" I looked her over; her head had turned towards me slightly and she struggled to open her eyes.

"Leo..." it was a statement, not a question. I clenched her hand between mine, feeling a surge of hopefulness, and watched as her eyes finally opened.

"Kit!" I gave her a relieved smile. "Oh my god—you're awake!"

She blinked a couple of times and a smile struggled on her lips. "Leo. I'm...I'm glad to see you," she stammered. She glanced around briefly and groaned. "Where the hell am I?" Her voice was labored and hoarse but I smiled at her sarcastic tone that was fairly typical of her.

I let out a low whistle. "Well, that's kind of a long story."

Kit allowed her head to fall to the side, and she struggled to smile as she looked at me. "I'm so glad you're—" she stopped mid-sentence, obviously noticing my tell-tale mythological feature. "What the..." she snorted. "I knew it," she giggled.

I cocked a brow. "Knew what?"

She wiggled a weak finger at me. "I knew there was something different about you. I was right."

I smiled sheepishly. I stretched out the wings on either side of me slightly. "Yeah...you were right."

"So, what are you? Fairy?" she questioned

"Um...no. Dragon, actually," I replied, with a hesitant bite of my lip, awaiting her reaction.

"Dragon? Huh..." She was thoughtful. "How does that work?"

I explained to her the human-to-dragon form thing, the shifting and her eyes widened, briefly touching on the fact that the wings in my human form were unexplainable.

"That is so cool!" she said, awed. I grinned.

"Not really the reaction I was expecting," I replied, with a laugh.

She gave a small, weak shrug. "Eh. I always knew there was something more to the world than just humans. There has to be. I'm just glad to know I was right."

"There's bad things too…" I added.

She sighed. "Yeah. The bad things." She looked away momentarily, appearing hesitant. "Leo, I'm sorry. This is all my fault. All of this."

I scoffed. "*Your* fault? If I hadn't been in your world; if I'd stayed home—"

She shook her head. "No, no Leo. I did something very bad." She exhaled slowly.

"What did you do that was so bad?" I inquired, doubtful.

She breathed through her mouth, her eyes avoiding my gaze shamefully. "I…well I was messing with things I shouldn't have been. I did some…spells. I didn't know *this* would happen, but umm…yeah."

"Kit, what do you mean? What could you possibly— "

She interrupted me. "I was…feeling frustrated. Lost. I can't really explain why but…I felt so depressed."

"You mean, after the storm? After everything that happened, Kit, I think you're entitled," I said.

She shook her head. "No…no this was before the storm. I was just…down. Besides you, Leo, I have no one. I barely speak to my family; you know they aren't okay with this…*witch* stuff. And, I haven't been on a date in years. *Years*. I'm in my thirties, for shit's sake!" She paused, summoning up her courage. "I…cast a love spell. But only…it wasn't actually a love spell, I found out."

I narrowed my eyes, confused. "I don't understand."

"This…this *spell* just fell out of one of my books. It was to call someone who could help me with my love life." She slapped her palms against her forehead and groaned. "Ack! How could I have been so stupid?"

"Still not following," I replied.

She sighed. "It wasn't really a spell for love. It was…a spell to invite a demon to assist me. Only I didn't know that at the time." Kit fidgeted with her hands over her chest. "I don't even know why I did it; it's just been so frustrating…

"Well I'd had a couple successes with writing my own 'love spells'," she continued, making quotations with her fingers. "A couple of men had come into the shop before that I hadn't recognized, one flirted with me and seemed really cute. The other didn't, but later left his number behind for me. No one is *ever* interested in me!"

"I'm sure that's not—" I began but she didn't let me finish.

"No, it is. I've been so consumed with...well the shop and everything I haven't given it much thought until recently. So, when I picked up that book and saw that spell fall out—I don't even know how it got there, probably from its previous owner. It's a used book. I decided to give it a try. I should have known better...I..." She buried her face in her palms and started sobbing. "The storms—they're my fault! I realize now that *I did them!*"

I reached out to pat her shoulder, allowing her to cry. She continued on, explaining that in a fit of despair, she cast the circle with one extra candle as it asked for—black candles—and spoke the incantation. The instructions said to cast it at either sunrise or sunset when the world was most open to magic (I snickered at that point) and she did. Next thing she knew, she felt a dark presence and she blacked out for a while. I held my breath, as she proceeded to tell me she would black out for moments at a time, and find herself in strange places, like in the woods after the storms. She'd find herself in the woods because she *conjured* the storms, with the help of the presence that escaped from the spell she released. She had no idea how but somehow she just simply knew she did it.

Finally, a couple days ago, a handful of unfamiliar people took her while she was on her way out the door and forced her to drive to the clearing in the woods and they pushed her somewhere where she felt like she was being sucked into a vacuum. They blindfolded her and she ended up in a dungeon-like room somewhere, where some angry people started asking about me. After a while, she was locked up and things got dark and she found herself in the shadow realm—although she didn't call it that, she just referred to it as "the dark place" and shivered a lot when she thought about it. She didn't know exactly what she was talking about, or what she was doing most of the time, but at a handful of moments she felt urges to injure me, and it was the same presence she felt when she originally cast the spell.

"I think..." she continued, in a small, shamed voice. "Somehow I cast the spells to make those storms. I...felt compelled for them to hurt you. I..." she trailed off, avoiding my gaze.

I frowned. I reached out for her hand and grabbed it. "Kit. It wasn't your fault."

"How can you say that? If I hadn't cast that spell none of this would have happened!" she exclaimed.

I shook my head. "Then they would have found another way." I began telling her about the Shadow realm: how somehow a rift had been opened in between our worlds and how we assumed they were trying to seek me out and either recruit me or kill me. Why, we didn't know other than they craved power and I apparently had it. They needed it, or needed me to be eliminated to tip the scales in their favor.

Kit was wide-eyed at this point, and I continued to try to explain everything to her as best as I could from the dragon realm, to some of my life as an outcast, Gabriel's coincidental arrival and finally bringing us around to the supposed safe-haven of Castle Danger, where we were now.

Esmè entered after a while, carrying a tray with a bowl and glass on it. "You need to eat, now that you're awake. Start building up that strength." She set it down over Kit's lap, and both she and I assisted Kit in sitting up.

"What is this? Super-secret potion?" she inquired.

Esmè chuckled. "Very powerful potion. Chicken broth and orange juice. After you're feeling better, we'll add the veggies and what not. I know you're a vegetarian, but I must insist. But for now...we need to see if you can keep this down." Esmè reached for a spoon on the tray and handed it to Kit. "Eat."

"Yes, Ma'am." Kit gave a small smile at Esmè.

Esmè looked at me and smiled. "She is strong. She will be okay, I am confident. There is a...a power in her."

"Power?" Kit echoed.

Esmè nodded. "Yes. Leorah told us you were a witch, but she didn't think you had powers," she explained. "For the Shadows to be able to use you as it did, you obviously do. Untapped, yes. But they're there...somewhere."

I exchanged a look with Kit.

"Sometimes witches can learn powers, at least that's what Gabriel told me," I offered.

"He's a witch?" Kit asked, taking a small sip of orange juice.

I shook my head. "Sorcerer. He was born with his powers. Witches learn them."

Kit considered this.

Esmè crossed her arms over her chest, a smug look on her face. "You don't seem all that surprised."

Kit shook her head. "No...I just always thought there was something...more."

"Interesting..."

Kit smiled weakly. "Oh but...Leo. You need to know something."

"What's that?"

"When I was held captive—wherever I was. Over in your realm, or whatever. I didn't know they were dragons at the time but...the Shadows...they were there. The same...*thing* that was summoned when I cast the spell was there too. It was hard to see; they were dark and sort of formless. It looked like some sort of dungeon; it was cold and hard and sort of foggy." Kit shuddered violently.

"What? Are you sure?" I questioned.

Kit nodded vigorously. "Yes. I'm sure of it. One of them..." Kit's expression soured, like she was going to vomit. "One of them was just...dark. I can't explain it. I felt the same things there as I did when I was in the shadow realm. Dark. Hopeless."

"Shit." I yanked my phone out of my jeans pocket and started texting furiously. "This is bad. Real bad."

"I...don't remember much. There were two people there; both of them just...surrounded by dark," Kit stammered, struggling to find the right words.

"Like an aura?" Esmè offered helpfully.

Kit snapped her fingers. "*Yes.* An aura. Entirely black, a little gray. My skin just crawled being in the same room with them."

"You're sure these were dragons?" I asked, hesitantly. "You were over in the dragon realm. You know this for sure?" She had to be. That portal didn't go anywhere else to my knowledge. But who would be working with Shadows from the dragon realm.

She nodded. "I am now. Oh..." she said, suddenly realizing something. "One of them said the other's name...a big guy. It was...Nicholas? Nicky?"

My eyes widened; I nearly dropped my phone on the floor but I caught it before it hit. "Nicodemus?"

"Yes! How could I forget that? Such an odd name..."

I let out a low whistle, slumping in the stool. I continued sending out text messages to everyone that remained on my contact list: *Big news. Need to meet ASAP. 911 911 911.* I ran my free hand through my hair and grasped, trying to handle the realization of what this meant.

"Leo? Is everything okay?" Kit asked, reaching out to me.

I looked at her, a stone-cold expression on my face. "No, actually. Everything just got much worse. Nicodemus—he was a portal guard. A guard for the Court."

Esmè let out a low whistle behind me, surely realizing what that meant.

"I don't get it," Kit said, looking confused.

"Court is our form of government, basically. If Nicodemus is working with the Shadows, it means that the Shadows have infiltrated our Court."

Kit's eyes widened as I jumped out of the stool to my feet. I got a handful of texts in reply. Uncharacteristically of me, I leaned over and placed a sisterly kiss on Kit's forehead. "I need to go like…now. I will be back." Kit seemed only briefly surprised but smiled weakly.

"Stay safe, Leo!" she called after me, as I tore through the house, causing both Evie and another—I assumed Becka—whiplash as they watched me dart out of the house.

Stay safe…Kit's words echoed in my mind, haunting.

But…perhaps it wasn't that far gone yet. Perhaps it *was* only Nicodemus and we could easily take him out and down before he caused anymore mayhem. Right? Right. I kept coaxing myself with this thought as I stalked mindlessly towards the guest quarters.

"*Leo*? Leo!"

The voice didn't register in my mind as I kept on running. If I distracted myself for even a moment more, I wasn't sure how I was going to deliver the news to everyone because I felt ill myself thinking of the possibility. I couldn't even think of it…my grandfather, my brother, succumbing to the Shadows. The mere thought brought painful tears stinging to my eyes.

"Leo? What the hell?" She grasped my shoulders to prevent me from running off, forcing me to look directly in her face. My expression must have been dire and frantic to hold me there, seemingly nailed to the ground as she did.

"*Shadows*." I said, breathlessly. "Shadows at Court."

Kiarra's eyes narrowed. "How do you know?"

"Kit…" I had to pause momentarily, gasping for air both strangled out of me due to panic and over-exertion from running; my wings were breaking the wind as I dashed. They wanted to fly; but I had no time to deal with that. It would have been faster if I'd been in my right mind but I wasn't thinking clearly. I gazed around me momentarily; I was well past the square and down the rocky, well-worn path and essentially was only about a block away from the guest quarters. I'd covered about five minutes' worth of ground in about thirty seconds, I realized. Perhaps they had helped me after all.

I doubled over, clutching my chest as sharp pains stabbed under my rib cage. "Oh shit," I mumbled, feeling my stomach protest and rumble. I fought the urge to dry heave and took a few deep, calming breaths.

"Kit *what*?" Kiarra prompted, her expression confused with a hint of terror in her eyes.

"Kit… she said… one of her captors… Nicodemus." I managed to finally get out, after another cleansing breath.

Kiarra's eyes doubled like saucers. "Oh…gods…" She clutched my hand and began yanking me down the rest of the path towards the guest quarters and the room that Gabriel's and I had been sharing so far. I waved my hand quickly over the doorknob for my magic to register and we practically barreled in, causing the befuddled expressions of the guys who had gathered, talking uncomfortably from various spots in the room who'd apparently been well enough to be released in the time I was visiting with Kit. Thank the gods for that, I thought.

Gabriel was the first to stand. He came up to me, as Kiarra, appearing in shock slumped into the sofa.

"Geez, Leo…what's going—"

"We think the Shadows are working with someone in the Court!" I declared.

Gabriel and Daniel exchanged confused looks, as I fell to the ground, weak in my knees from panic. My wings prevented me from falling all the way and I cursed, trying to shove them aside so I could panic properly. "Dammit… go away!" I yelled behind my back, not really expecting anything to happen.

I watched as the wings retracted into my back, causing a momentary sensation of dizziness. Gabriel attempted to catch me but I fell to my knees. Maxxus was by my side on the ground in a split second. "Thank god." I muttered, shrugging my shoulders and shaking my arms out at my sides to re-adjust to the feeling of suddenly being lighter. Gabriel smiled, assumedly about to praise my sudden control over something I hadn't been before, when Maxxus spoke:

"Shadows? In the Court? How do you know?" he asked, his mouth set in a firm line, worry lines imprinted on his forehead as he expected an answer.

"When Kit was kidnapped, they took her through the portal," I explained. "She didn't know what it was but the way she described it—"

Maxxus gestured with his hand to go on, impatiently.

"She was in a dungeon. She said she could…feel them. She described it exactly the way I felt it when I experienced it in my dream and then…then when we actually went over there. Dark. Hopeless. She could *see* them there, surrounding the captors."

Maxxus shook his head. "I don't see how that proves—"

"—Nicodemus was one of her captors. He was Shadowtouched."

Maxxus' confusion was quickly replaced with one of rage. "Nicodemus?" He raised to his feet, clutching his fists at his sides. "Nico… that explains why he was such a raging bastard the past couple times I spoke with him." Maxxus briefly told us about a couple of uncharacteristic arguments he had with him. One time, Maxxus said he just blew up, accusing him of treason and cursing him for having any sort of friendship with me whatsoever. It hadn't ordinarily been cause for concern; dragons had nasty tempers no matter the dragon and could be volatile. But Maxxus claimed he'd been worse than normal; they'd feuded after I left the portal that day after Nicodemus claimed I shouldn't be allowed to go back and forth because pink dragons of course are "unpredictable" and then of course, the time he tried warning me that day in the portal. Of course Maxxus had been up to something, but he didn't know that and got in Maxxus' face. More so then usual.

"I thought it was strange; he was suddenly always in his human form during shift changes. He never does that, he thinks humans are below him!" Maxxus growled.

A sudden realization hit me. "So it was *his* boot prints I saw outside the portal that day! It has to be!"

Maxxus nodded vigorously. "He's always been an ass, but, at least he was honorable. Not… not this confrontational." His face heated, cheeks red with anger. He began pacing around the room, muttering under his breath. He paused in the kitchen, threw his head back and let out an angry snarl, so loud it reverberated off the walls. "I'll *kill* him! I'll rip his head off, and—"

"First things first," Kiarra piped up, the voice of reason. "We have to find proof. And…who exactly is he working under. Is it just him, and a handful of others? Or does it go further up the chain?"

"What more proof do you need?" Maxxus roared. "We have a witness!"

It was my turn to speak up. "Yes but…she's not magical. Not entirely. Esmè thinks she might be but…" I shrugged. "She's been through a terrible ordeal, and putting her through anymore…" I shook my head. "No. Out of the question."

"But—" Maxxus began to protest.

"*No*." I stood, narrowing my eyes, my tone commanding.

Maxxus backed down, releasing his clenched jaw and allowing himself to relax. "I'm sorry, Leo…of course. I just can't imagine…"

"No worries," I said, dismissing his apology.

"But, if he is working with the Shadows…for how long? How long have you been at risk and how long have I been oblivious to it?" He turned away, suddenly feeling shameful.

I crossed the room and offered Maxxus a friendly hug, wrapping my arms around his waist and resting my head against his upper arm. "Whatever happened, it wasn't on purpose. You'd never let me be hurt. I know that."

Maxxus glanced briefly at my hand on his arm, his expression softening. I offered him a reassuring smile that he returned. I felt a shiver clutch my body briefly; he must have sensed it by the look of surprise on his face. I pulled away quickly and he grunted a growl of approval when the door to the room clicked open on the outside and in poured in Finnian, looking somewhat frantic.

"Shadows you say?" his eyes flashing between an ocean blue to a muddy yellow; indicating he felt panicked about something. "In the *Court*? You know this for sure?"

I nodded vigorously. I recanted what Kit had told me and as I did his eyes widened in horror.

"This is not good. That means they're growing in power, somehow," Finnian said, heaving a heavy sigh and plopping down on one of the couches. He ran his fingers through his curly, messy hair before pulling them out and staring us each down earnestly.

"Leo, tomorrow we start compulsion training. You need to practice disguising us with your magic in case we need to infiltrate the Court. Meet at my office tomorrow, 9AM sharp," he commanded as he stood. "Go. Rest up. Eat. You'll all need your energy. Except Maxxus and Leo. I need to speak with *both* of you," he instructed, "the rest may leave." He gestured dismissively to everyone else. Maxxus and I exchanged looks of bewilderment.

The brothers exchanged looks but nodded in agreement. Daniel yanked me away from Maxxus briefly and offered me a strong-armed hug. Gabriel started to reach for me but, he stopped in his tracks, recalling our precarious relationship and patted the side of my arm.

I offered him a wink and they disappeared out the door to the hallway.

Kiarra paused momentarily, crossing her arms over her chest and pouted lightly. "I'm left out?"

Finnian glared at her sternly. "I will clue you in when the time is right."

She heaved a sigh. "Fine." She said no more and spun on her heels in a huff, heading towards the door. "But you all owe me!" she said over her shoulder before exiting.

I raised a brow at Finnian when it was just us three remaining. "What is going on?"

Finnian urged us to sit down, and we did. "You need to infiltrate the Court and get at this Nicodemus fellow before it's too late and the Shadows spread. Are you up to it?"

I let out a little yelp. "But—why us? Why not the whole group?"

"Because, it's too risky. We need your magic to conceal you, and Maxxus' knowledge of Nicodemus' habits to find him. Kiarra is a liability even though she's a dragon because she is not a fighter, and Gabriel's competitive nature with Maxxus might derail the mission. Daniel is merely human—need I say more about that?" Finnian drummed his fingers on his thighs rapidly, his leg twitching up and down nervously.

"This is bad, isn't it?" I questioned, noticing his anxiety. The Loremaster *never* became nervous about anything so, the fact that he was this worried was cause for concern indeed.

Finnian looked up at me sternly. "The last time the Shadows infiltrated anywhere, the region erupted in a war. I don't need to tell you how grim that would be for Anarach."

I gulped and looked at Maxxus who sat silent, grim faced staring at the floor. His head snapped up defiantly and said with determination, "I'm in."

"Are you sure? I mean, Gabriel's magic is complimentary to mine, and—" I began, my voice squeaking with nervousness.

"I must insist. It's the only way." He clearly wasn't offering any more information. I heaved a sigh, leaning back into the sofa. "We'll discuss it more shortly with everyone else. They won't like it but that's why I'm asking you this now so you aren't blindsided. We'll work on getting your magic up to par before then, whatever it takes."

"All right, then."

He was right. We were the best dragons for the job. We had to get to him before it was too late.

"Good. We'll start preparations and hopefully, we'll send you along in a few days but the sooner, the better."

I exchanged a look with Maxxus and he grasped my hand in his and offered me a light smile.

"You and me I guess, to save the Court. Ironic, isn't it?" he said with a short laugh.

I snorted. It was. It was indeed. The safety of the Court may possible rest in the hands of the two outcast dragons they were after. If we were caught and they tortured us or kill us—they were probably toast. We were their saviors, and they had *no* idea.

I didn't need to even think about how dangerous it was for us...but even more dangerous if not. For everyone.

...to be continued...

Acknowledgments

Fated Souls began years ago in a sleepy haze while I was mindlessly at work like a zombie, stocking shelves and trying to stay awake. I had this funny idea of dragons who could turn into people and vice-versa and other such magical things to occupy my mind as I worked so that I didn't pass out. Years later, two computers and a billion edits later, here it is and I'm so thrilled that you've allowed me to share it with you. But, these books do not come about without so much help and support so bear with me while I acknowledge a few of you.

First, my grandmother and my mother. *None* of this exists without you. From my grandmother who told me, "Go write it yourself!" when I was five and ticked off that I couldn't find a book on a particular subject I wanted to read about to my mother reading to me every night—thank-you. Thanks for believing in me. I'm only sorry that Gramma wasn't able to see this happen in her lifetime. I love you so much wherever you are, and thanks for everything. You're missed so much every day. Mom…sorry for the kissing and stuff. Not about the swear words. You know I'm never sorry for those. (*winks*) Thanks for being there…always. I love you!

Next, my husband, Ricky and two kids: Ryan and Mattie. Thank you so much for allowing my crazy behavior, the nights where I never quite got dinner on the table, all the times I stayed up too late (okay so…every night), the times I got cranky (okay so…all the time) and just allowing me to dissolve into my own little word and get this out. I love you all to Pluto and back (YES IT STILL COUNTS!) and thank you for your support and mostly…your patience.

For my grandparents in Mississippi—Lynda "Mimi" and Pawtom. Thanks for saving me when I needed it most. Thanks for encouraging and understanding and never letting me give up and for being proud. It means so much; I miss you every day and love you very much!

For my sixth grade English teacher, Mrs. Thomas—formerly of Richfield Intermediate School circa 1993. Thank you for challenging me and pushing me to give more and appreciating my crazy antics in class. I have such high standards in books and such now, because of the values you imparted on me. It mattered. So much. If teachers ever don't think what they do matters; I'm here to say it does. I know you'll probably never see this but, I'm putting it out there anyways: thank you so much. I keep my blinds crooked still to this day to watch that darn roof.

For Amy. Probably my first fan, ever. You believed in me when no one else did—not even myself—and never gave up on me. Thank you for your endless love, support and cheers. I love you forever, Miss Kira!

To Jaymin Eve…without your encouragement and advice I never would have had the guts to try this. No matter what happens, your kindness, humor and skill was massively helpful. Hopefully I can pay it forward and help others as you did me. You are simply the greatest; thank you so much! I'll always be one of your biggest fans!

My alpha reader—Olga—and betas: Myra, Gilda, Dee, Lela and Brittaini and Steven. What y'all did for me is so endlessly important. Thanks for helping me catch the errors, the typos, for accepting my crazy story and characters into your hearts and minds and loving them as much as I do. Thank you for allowing me to message you all hours of the night and talk to your walls (Facebook walls—I'm not *that* crazy!), or respond and talk me down from chucking my computer against a window, for your support, and your encouragement and just—*everything.* Can't thank all of you enough!

Super mega thanks to author L.C. Hibbett for your help with the doggoned blurb! YOU ROCK! I'll never try to write another blurb at 5am ever again. Promise. Well…maybe not.

To the Nerd Herd (Jaymin's) and the Blind Date with a Book group. You all came into my life at a time when I didn't have much hope for things. I was down on humanity, sad with loss and here you all come and make me laugh, cheer me on and just share your love of books with me and each other. You reaffirmed my faith in humanity, once again. Thank you for the reminder that book lovers and geeks are the *best* people ever—I truly believe that books can bring people together, from all walks of life! Thanks for listening to my rants, raves and supporting my writing venture! I wish I could name each and every one of you individually but we all know I'm long winded enough. Ha ha! But just know I notice and appreciate all of you. *All of you!*

Lastly but certainly not least, the readers. The reason I write is to provide an escape; bring a smile or a laugh to someone. I hope you enjoy it as much as I enjoyed writing it. Thank you so much for giving me a chance to share this world with you. You all rock so much! I appreciate you because without you—we don't exist. So an endless bounty of "thank yous" to you all!

If you read and liked this book, please—pretty please—go to Amazon and or Goodreads or wherever you got this from and leave a review. Indie authors depend so much on your reviews so if you could take a moment and help get the word out I would greatly appreciate it. Thank you!

About the Author:

Sariah Skye lives physically in southern Minnesota with her husband, two kids and dog but mentally her head is in the clouds dreaming of anything *not* requiring being an adult. When not writing she's probably watching another *Star Trek* marathon, playing *World of Warcraft*, reading more fantasy books or staying up way too late. She'd love if you'd drop her a line at:

Facebook: www.facebook.com/SariahSkyeauthor
    Twitter: @realSariahSkye
    Instagram: sariahskyeauthor
    Email: sariahskyeauthor@gmail.com

Printed in Poland
by Amazon Fulfillment
Poland Sp. z o.o., Wrocław